Watch over me

Drifters, Book Twelve

SUSAN RODGERS

Edited by Kathy Gillis and Stephen Reaman.
Book design and formatting by Valerie Bellamy, Dog-ear Book Design.

ISBN: 978-1-987966-14-5

It's easier to believe in this sweet madness,
in this glorious sadness
that brings me to my knees…
(*Angel* – Sarah McLachlan)

For the rest of you who see the beauty and sadness in life's deeper layers.

Contents

Prologue

She is fifteen.

When life gets to her, she finds a good place to hide. Usually it's inside music, where she can curl up and disappear. Sometimes she stays in her room but this afternoon she needs space so she can breathe. Fishing her iPhone out of the dirty school knapsack she's dumped on her twin bed, she fires up a Jessie Wheeler playlist, her favorite. Positioning old earbuds in her ears, she adjusts the volume to as loud as she can stand, and she jogs down the cement steps of her mother's two-story townhouse and starts for the sidewalk.

A hand grabs her shoulder. Twisting, she pulls out one earbud and faces the woman who gave birth to her, who loves her despite what the kids at school say about her, 'that she is green, that she likes dolls, that she still takes her teddy bear places. That she is naïve and stupid, too stupid to see what *he* was doing,' even though the whole school knew.

He being her father.

She's learned to leave ragged, weather-beaten Alfie the bear in the car when she goes somewhere these days, like to Wendy's for lunch.

"Mom, I'm just going for a run," she mumbles now, looking at her feet. She leans on one foot as she says it, her 'haughty posture,' her mother calls it.

Her mom reaches out to affectionately stroke her daughter's silky blonde ponytail.

"Where to?" This is asked carefully, because her mom knows Carly will be annoyed if she, Catherine, is too pushy. Catherine has just arrived home from her job as a high school English teacher. Her dark shoulder length hair is frizzy from the early February ice pellets that fell from the sky all day and which have just abated. "It's slippery out. Why don't you go to the indoor walking track?"

"Mom!"

It takes nothing to set Carly off these days. Her unhappiness comes through like the frozen rain today, icy and in abundance. It glistens in razor sharp edges on the words she barely speaks and in the way she moves through her days, head down and shoulders hunched.

Carly's only relief is music. It carries her away, it transports her, but she doubts her mother would understand this. Jessie Wheeler's songs are sometimes sad but they almost always offer hope. When Jessie sings with Jacob Ryan, their vocals wrap around each other and lift each other up; they do this for Carly too. She closes her eyes when the highest notes reach sublime perfection; she raises her arms and feels an inward smile whisper against her outside skin. When Carly hears Jessie sing, every nerve opens and stands on edge; every pore is briefly cleansed of its pain.

She goes now. Heads down the sidewalk in the slush. The day is warming; the ice pellets had turned to rain before the clouds decided to stop their leaking.

Watching her daughter jog away, Catherine notices that Carly is wearing jeans for this run. This tells her that today was a particularly bad day for her lonely teenager, since Carly didn't even bother changing into running clothes when she got home from school.

What happened today? Catherine asks the girl's back. *What did that high school do to hurt you today?*

Catherine is in her early forties. She is a planner. With the exception of long walks around her middle class London, Ontario neighborhood, she doesn't exercise much. Salty, buttery popcorn at movies is her favorite indulgence. Not wine, like her few friends. Or even chocolate. The movies are her escape. Music is her daughter's.

She goes inside now, because Carly has disappeared around the corner. Catherine will start dinner—a Mediterranean pasta she knows Carly likes, because Carly loves feta cheese and kalamata olives. At least she used to. Although Carly never says much, she still eats the tasty pasta dish when her mother prepares it, right down to the last olive, and today Catherine wants to ease her daughter's hurts the best way she can.

She's just taking the boiled pasta off the stove and dumping it into a plastic colander in the sink when she hears sirens.

Carly doesn't come home, but police approach the townhouse's front door after a neighbor recognizes the girl's body. A man and a woman in uniform knock quietly. Catherine saw their cruiser amble slowly up her short driveway and creep to a halt behind her rusty SUV. She took note of how slowly they walked up her concrete block path, how drawn and pale their faces are, and she knows.

She intuited it the second she heard the sirens. She felt a wave of grief shudder through her soul.

The policeman has Carly's iPhone in his hand. Catherine holds out a shaking palm, right side up, and he drops it into her grasp. The cops want to call a friend to be with her but there is nobody Catherine wants by her side. Her friends are more like surface-level acquaintances than the kind of friends she would want to walk her through a tragedy as personal as this. Catherine is as disconnected as her daughter; she hasn't felt real connection to anyone for a very long time.

The police stay for a bit. The young woman brews some old, stale tea she digs out of a cupboard. The whole time they are in her home, Catherine knows they want to go. They want to vault as quickly as they can out of the life of a grieving mother who just lost her teenage daughter to a fast-moving car on a slippery corner.

When the police finally go, Catherine lets the warmth of a fingertip poke the 'home' button on Carly's iPhone. The screen lights up. The last song Catherine's daughter was listening to was part of a Jessie Wheeler playlist.

Carly was a quiet, lonely teenager who still slept with the teddy bear her father gave her when she was seven. She was a girl who needed Jessie Wheeler, who craved the Vancouver-based singer's sad, hopeful music.

Because Carly needed a safe place to hide.

Carly was fifteen.

And fifteen she would remain—forever.

Chapter One

Matt was no longer driving his Audi. Today, as he reclined in the driver's seat of a small red Toyota Tacoma and chewed on a tasty cheeseburger from the Frosty Treat in the small town of Kensington, Prince Edward Island, he reflected on the weird fact that he was now the driver of a pickup truck. This one was new, purchased at a dealership in Charlottetown the day after his arrival on the pastoral island. The salesman had been happy to take the pristine Audi as a trade-in, and Charles Keating had given Matt his blessing.

Matt was still on the Keating payroll, coordinating Keating-Sawyer security from a distance. But Matt didn't need to drive a spoiled princess superstar or her children anywhere anymore. Matt no longer needed to drive anyone around. He was almost his own boss. He could drive whatever the hell kind of vehicle he wanted.

The Internet had made it real easy to run away and still collect a paycheck.

Scanning the Frosty Treat's narrow parking lot with its single row of vehicle spaces, Matt shoved the last bit of the scrumptious, moist cheeseburger into his mouth. Opening a package of white vinegar, he dumped it in full on his fries before he ripped open a small packet of salt and dumped that all over them too. Pepper was next. The greasy supper was summer food on P.E.I., and Matt was taking full advantage of his freedom and his irascible mood of late.

Quite simply, he didn't give a shit—about anything, about anybody, or about what he put into his body. His eighteen-year-old daughter was living her own life, his ex-wife was supposedly happily settled into Matt's former house with her newish man, and Jessie... Well, what was there to say about Jessie? Matt's heart hurt to even think about her.

Grabbing the rearview mirror, he angled it down so he could see the scruff on his cheeks. The new whiskers were scratchy, but Matt was getting used to the feeling. His eyes were stones, polished and hard yet cloudy on the inside like worn playground marbles. Unbreakable. His cheeks were red from the sun, but pale underneath from all the drinking he'd indulged in of late.

Matt touched the top of his head and ducked his chin so he could see his hair. *Spike.* Jessie used to call him that when she was in a teasing kind of mood. Not today, no. Now she didn't call him anything, and these days the name Spike wouldn't suit anyway. Matt had stopped gelling his hair when he hit about, well, Montreal, he thought, trying to remember past the fog of pain his leaving had laid over him like a sticky web he was powerless to crawl out of. He'd left his Vancouver condo a few nights after he last saw Jessie outside Josh's hospital room in Calgary, and he had drifted at loose ends around Canada. Now, in P.E.I., Matt still wanted to float away but there was something mystical and magical about this patchwork island that was rooting him to its robust red earth.

Jessie. Her essence, her spirit. That's what was keeping him here. The island was once her home, and after almost two decades of watching over the obstinate, often childlike singer, Matt needed to keep her close in any way he could.

The Frosty Treat was a part of that. A small guffaw left his lips when he looked around and saw that the place was packed. It was August 1st, and today had been what the local yokels called a perfect beach day. An indigo blue sky and not a cloud in sight. Temperatures warm enough for bikinis and beers on the beach. No breeze to speak of, although Matt felt he could use one. A breath of fresh or even humid air could never be a bad thing on a day this hot; on a day when tiny rivulets of sweat trickled constantly down his back, tickling his toned, muscled body.

Not that it mattered if he got stinky. Matt had no illusions about getting close enough to anyone for him or her to smell him anytime soon.

Wolfing down the last few French fries, and starting on the coleslaw side with a white plastic fork, he froze, suspending the fork above his take-out dinner's cardboard dish. Extending his left hand, Matt turned the volume up on the radio.

Jessie and Jacob's first *Sacred Peace* release was playing in regular rotation these days, and the announcers were all over it. Jacob and Jessie together again, at least in music, was news. Playing a song they wrote to support Josh Sawyer's new series? Weird but cool, some kind of healing press spin, they told their captivated audiences. The song itself? Heavier than most of Jacob and Jessie's tunes, with driving bass, serious percussion and sweet, perfect guitar that hit just the right notes at just the right times. The song was skyrocketing up the charts, and Matt was humbled to know he'd heard it first.

"I can't get used to it, though," he mumbled to himself now. "Popping up on the radio like that."

Someone else down the row of cars and pickups was listening to the same station. The driver cranked up the tune, which careened out of an open window and reverberated in the ears of everyone close by. Matt hung his head, and closed the lid of the takeout dish without finishing his coleslaw.

Ten minutes later, he turned the pickup right (an homage to his brother Michael's old red Ford pickup, he told himself) onto a two lane country road that, a quarter mile down, would open up into one of the most beautiful places he felt existed on the entire planet. The turnoff was in a tiny village called Malpeque, historically one of Prince Edward Island's oldest populated areas, famous now for its Malpeque oysters, which were sold in fine dining restaurants the world over. A quaint white church stood at the north corner; down from it on the right was a butter yellow historic building, another old church, Matt supposed. Utilized as a museum these days to interpret the area's compelling history, its lush green lawn was peppered with a motley collection of rusting century-old farm implements.

Just down the road was a new bridge, a replacement for the charming wooden one that watched over the tides for years until the provincial government determined it unsafe and had it replaced. By the time Matt got to the bridge today, though, he didn't care what it was made of. His searching eyes were locked on the simple, peaceful beauty of the tranquil landscape. The bridge crossed what was known locally as the Darnley Basin, which looked the way it sounded, like a rounded basin of water. Populated with isolated as well as rows of colorful buoys that Matt was told fishermen planted to mark their mussel farms, it was perfect for relaxing, restorative kayak rides, and was a conduit for more adventurous jaunts if paddlers wanted to challenge the waves in the Gulf just beyond a sand-duned point.

As he crossed the bridge, Matt noticeably felt his blood pressure deflate. Usually he only went into town when he had nothing left in his fridge but moldy leftovers. Today there had been a bigger crisis to motivate his short trip—the need for alcohol and cigarettes, the former obtained from a low square building just past an old stone train station that was popular as a pub and restaurant these days.

Groceries he could do without, although he had picked up a few today since he was in town. The painkillers were needed.

Glancing now to the left, Matt spied a cluster of distant cozy buildings spread out just past the eastern coastline of the Darnley Basin, which featured one of the island's characteristic low red sandstone cliffs about midway. Right above that, almost in the center, was Matt's temporary home. He could make it out if he squinted, but he couldn't get to it by land without driving a few more miles up the slightly curvy road, up a low hill, and then left onto the Lower Darnley Road after passing an abandoned grey cedar-shingled building that he surmised must once have been a schoolhouse.

The building was kind of an enigma to Matt. On its left, on the front facing, was a broken window, a large one. The broken panes meshing with the unbroken panes left the impression of what could be interpreted as a six-foot tall angel. It gave Matt the creeps yet somehow made him feel as if he was being watched over by some unseen angelic power of the universe. Depending on the day and how he was feeling as he jogged or drove by, his interpretation of the jagged angel changed. Today, as he flicked on the Tacoma's left blinker in preparation for turning left, which he would do just after he passed the deserted schoolhouse, he felt safe.

A ways down the road, he turned left again, and cruised slowly down a gravel lane to his rented cottage. He'd found it on the Internet after getting the email from Josh the night of the Alberta Children's Hospital fundraiser, when Matt was kind of stuck in Montreal feeling lost and not sure which way to go. Josh's note that Jessie was feeling 'out of sorts' and missing her old security friend made Matt miss her all the more. Then, it was like Atlantic Canada called his name. It felt as if Jessie's idyllic green and red Prince Edward Island landscape was pulling him towards it; as if a fisherman near the shore was hauling in a net with Matt curled up in a fetal position inside.

Matt's rental was in a little cluster of small bungalows and one-and-a-half story loft style summer residences. When he first pulled up a week earlier, he was pleasantly surprised to find his on the lane closest to the water. Only one neighbor was near enough to throw stones at. So far that bungalow—a pleasant, modern grey one-level with white rails and Victorian trim around a narrow front deck—was vacant, although Matt had been told by his landlord, who rented both cottages, that it would be occupied by a woman from Ontario for much of August and September.

Drifting to a stop in front of his own temporary home, Matt slipped out of the driver's seat and stretched catlike. The stretch was accompanied by a wide yawn. Twisting around to face the water, he watched a white fishing boat chug its way through the channel opposite, on its way back to Malpeque Harbor across the Darnley Basin from the cottage property. The boats went out at five a.m. most days. Matt heard them every morning, a complete departure from the traffic sounds of Vancouver that he was used to. At first, the chugging annoyed him. It woke him earlier than he wanted to be awake, but he was adjusting. Now, hearing the boats venture out on the water with their crews of two or three hardy folks, it was a comfort to know there were 'normal' people in the world who worked hard to make a living, at careers completely unlike those of Jessie and Josh's superstar circus.

Scanning the horizon, Matt saw another boat head into the narrow channel. The boats would be coming in regularly now, navigating the man-dredged channel between the point bordering the campground north of Matt's cottage, and a second campground on the Malpeque point where, Matt was surprised to hear, a television show based on Lucy Maud Montgomery's *Emily of New Moon* book series had been filmed for four consecutive years in the nineties.

"Can't get away from it," he had muttered although, inside, that knowledge somehow seemed to bring him closer to Jessie, and to the much-missed Sawyer children.

Pivoting on a dirty flip-flop, Matt opened the truck door wider and reached in the back half-seat for his booze and groceries. The burger and fries weren't sitting well. They were heavier, greasier fare than he was accustomed to. A chocolate milkshake had come with them. He grasped that in his left hand, maneuvering his bags and the beer on his hip to grab everything all at once as opposed to taking a second trip.

Matt's cottage was one of the small loft style buildings. Shingled in grey cedar shakes faded by the sun and salt, it was cozy and welcoming. Still, considering his usual digs, which were modern and sterile, it was a far cry from homey feeling, to him. Sighing now, shoulders sinking, he made his way up a lonely dirt path lined with pink petunias, and jogged up six steps. Crossing a small wooden deck, he unlocked the door.

Inside, to the right was a serviceable kitchen with new enough appliances, including a microwave and an old-fashioned drip coffee machine. Opposite was a propane fireplace (he had a fire pit outdoors for when he craved the smell of flaming wood), comfortable wing chairs and a sofa, and multiple large windows for an unequalled view of Malpeque's sand dunes and meadows across the Darnley Basin, and of the crystalline water itself, which twinkled too merrily for Matt's low spirit on this blissful midsummer late afternoon. Between and behind the open concept space was a small storage and laundry room with a stackable washer and dryer; there was a bedroom there too, unused.

Matt preferred the large upstairs King-sized bed. He could lie on it at night, covered in a light blue and white duvet, and watch the stars and try to guess the constellations and planets. In the early mornings, there was usually blue sky (sometimes it was grey, but not often, so far) and airplanes to contemplate. One arm folded behind his head, he would lie there until his stomach churned with anxiety and his body ached with remembered desire. The only way to fight both was to get up and get moving; later in the day he would drink the pain away, but in the mornings he found things to do.

Puttering around the cottage on those lonely mornings, Matt weeded and watered, fixed a few loose boards on the deck, messed with the appliances, and mowed the lawn every couple of days even though it didn't need to be mowed that often. Afterwards, he usually took one of the bicycles that came with the cottage rental, and rode to the main road, turned right, then left, and spent the afternoon lying on the beach at a rugged place called Thunder Cove, on the roiling Gulf side of Darnley. He'd lay a blanket down far past clumps of other cottage owners and local beach-goers. He learned to bring potato chips and a book to help pass the long hours, and always there was a cooler of beer to drain before Matt cycled home. Swimming in the Gulf was a must after all the beer—he had to piss somewhere—but it was damn cold compared to the temperate Keating and Sawyer swimming pools. Matt rarely stayed in the cool ocean for long.

Matt craved physical activity. Runs along the lanes and sometimes down through the tents and expensive motorhomes of nearby Twin Shores Campground were usually part of his early mornings. He often ran up to the old schoolhouse miles up the road, too, and sometimes as far as the bridge. Kayaking was a must. There was a kayak at the cottage for his use—two, in fact. Matt occasionally dragged one to the Basin and hoisted it down over the small cliff by lifting it overhead. The fishermen's markers were perfect for setting a course which inevitably took him to the bridge to his left or across the water to the fishing harbor, where Matt paddled around the boats docked there, and watched the fishing crews at work. They'd be moving crates off their boats, some by late morning when Matt was often on the water, although on average it was still fairly quiet around the docks at that time.

The first day he went out on the water, Matt had also gone exploring over to the opposite campground, which he'd found out was called Cabot Park, or Cabot Beach by the locals. This was where the Lucy Maud Montgomery television show had been filmed years ago. Pulling his yellow kayak up on the beach, Matt had wandered past the locals and tourists sun tanning on the white sand, and made his way up into the campground. There was an old white schoolhouse there, too, but this one was used for programming. Matt bought an ice cream to enjoy as he wandered around, Puppy Paws flavor, which reminded him of Emily-Grace and her peanut butter-chocolate loving momma. A dense trail in the woods beckoned him, and he sauntered around wondering where the cameras had been placed back in the day, where the sets were built (he was told they had been dismantled for safety reasons), where the cast trailers and gear trucks were based. The exercise occupied some time and settled his anxiety as he remembered years of hanging out on sets with Jessie and Josh, but the walk did nothing for Matt's loneliness. It got worse when he got back out on the water on the kayak.

Not far from the shore in the Basin near Matt's rented cottage was a small white sailboat. Anchored at all times unless it was out for a sail, it was maybe eighteen feet in length, of some modern fiberglass composite. While unused, its sail was wrapped for storage around its boom, which was lashed to the open cockpit. Matt's first evening on the deck of his cottage was spent just looking around, and the little sailboat intrigued him. From his perspective, it was a small white bob in the distance, a pleasant toy for cheerful sojourns skipping over the diminutive crests of the Darnley Basin's sparkling waves. Matt was curious about the little boat; after sailing in the Caribbean with Jacob, he felt a pull towards vessels powered only by the magic of a rushing wind, and he absently wondered if he could get his hands on this one, or perhaps purchase some other kind of small one-hander day-sailing vessel.

So after his tour of Cabot Park, Matt had steered his kayak across the narrow channel towards the point on the Twin Shores / Darnley side. He powered past two fast-moving keen kite boarders and navigated growing waves until he reached the small white sailboat. Circling the bow, he studied its frame and the puddle of stale water rolling around inside the cockpit. The mast seemed to be in good shape. There were marks on the hull, but nothing major. The craft was definitely seaworthy, just the right size for one man who wanted to crest the waves and go flying on a good salty sea breeze.

Paddling around the stern, though, Matt was in for a shock. There were two letters painted on the boat—its name, obviously. *J & J.*

"I don't fucking believe this. Unreal." Buffeted by the waves, the warm Darnley Basin water crashing over his lap, Matt sat with his paddle resting across the kayak and stared. "Is this some kind of joke?" With a low growl and his lips pressed into a thin line, he mobilized his paddle and started for a landing spot up the shore a ways. And decided against trying to buy the boat or another one like it.

Evenings were for a late dinner, some kind of burned flesh, usually; steak or chicken, and zucchinis or peppers or potatoes or whatever he could grill. Matt liked to cook but his first week at the cottage was more about just getting by. Maybe later he could muster up some energy to pull his old self up from the gutter. For now, he wore baggy shorts and T-shirts or hoodies, didn't bother shaving more than once a week, and ignored his hair altogether.

Nor did he go anywhere but to town. Eventually he would explore the island, but he wasn't up to it yet. A niggling feeling inside made him curious about Jessie's mother, and Jessie's childhood home in the south shore village of Bedeque, though. Some day he would take a drive farther then Kensington, which was fifteen minutes away. Just not yet.

Matt had spent today on the beach. For the life of him he couldn't understand why someone would want to spend days and days lying on a beach. Only a week and he was getting bored of napping uselessly. Often the heat on his body and a sun-drunk feeling led to careless memories, thoughts of Jessie being Jessie, which inevitably led to a redo of their twenty-four hours fighting loneliness in each other's arms. And that always led to a hopeless sadness and a sizzling lust that Matt was helpless to eradicate without a dip in the cool Atlantic.

Now, supper via the Frosty Treat done, and another day coming to an end, Matt fixed himself an après dinner drink and pulled on a baggy blue zip-up hoodie. Meandering out onto the deck, he eased back into a low yellow Adirondack chair and put his feet up on the rail. Before him lay one of the most serene, beautiful, restful sights on the planet—sparkling water bordered by a lazy country bridge in the distance, magnificent green meadows and red cliffs on the western Malpeque side of the Basin, sand dunes to the north, and not one living soul to impede Matt's view.

Not one living soul to notice if he lived or died, drank himself into a stupor, or tipped a kayak and drowned himself in the Basin.

"Get over yourself, Matt Kelly," he scolded himself as he hunkered lower into the big wooden chair. "Katy cares. Michael cares. Charles and Dee care. Jessie? Hell, yeah. She cares. She just isn't accessible."

Would she be a part of his life again some dreamlike day? Even if not to love in a physical way?

Just to be around her again, to watch over her, to keep her safe, to watch her sleep on the jet, to laugh with her or growl at her or...to walk her to the stage... to stand in the wings and watch her sing...

Just to have her near again would be enough for me, he told himself. *To hear that voice once more in conversation with me, to see the sparkle in her eyes, to see joy in her face once more, would be enough for me.*

Maybe.

A final sip of his drink and Matt felt ready for an après dinner nap. As the first star of the evening popped out over the Basin, he let his heavy lids close, and let the sweet abyss of sleep carry him off to some far-off dimension that no longer hurt.

Chapter Two

Jessie was home at the ranch nursing a summer cold and a sick son when Charlie called her from the set of *Sacred Peace*. YouTube surfing on the couch with a feverish David asleep next to her, she almost panicked when she saw Charlie's name light up her iPhone screen. Jane had graciously offered to take Dylan and Emily-Grace for the day to let Jessie and David rest. Taking the call, Jessie whispered so as not to wake her son, but even so her voice was high-pitched and nervous.

"Charlie? Is everything okay with the kids?"

On his end, Charlie rotated his office chair around with one foot and stared out of the large window in his production office. It sickened him that any out-of-the-ordinary call frightened Jessie—and Josh—so much. Unfortunately, this call was likely to trouble Jessie too, but not for the reason she thought.

"The kids are fine. Jane's baking cookies with them as we speak."

"Jane's amazing." Exhaling slowly, Jessie closed her eyes and said a silent prayer. Something terse was cutting through Charlie's voice, though. Her eyes snapped open at his next sentence.

"Look, Jessie, there's been an incident on set. I don't want you to worry, though, everything's under control."

"What? Charlie, what's going on? Is Josh okay?" Quickly sitting up, Jessie dislodged David's comfortable position.

Over the phone, Charlie heard the little boy groan. Jessie was speaking in a raspy tone, and now she coughed. Wincing, Charlie felt awful for having to give her awkward and distressing news when she was feeling so low and likely could use Josh's help with David tonight.

He sighed and dove in. "Something at catering made a lot of people sick today, that's all. We wrapped production early and had to call in EMTs to transport a few cast and crew to the hospital."

"What? How sick? How many cast and crew?"

"Too many. A lot. Like…fifty. Look, Jessie, keep this quiet, okay? It looks like someone was trying to have some fun and things got carried away. Something at lunch must have been laced with some nefarious drug. A chowder, we think, got laced. We're working on finding out who did it, but so far we're at a loss."

"A drug?" Confused, Jessie tried to digest this weird news.

"Hallucinations, weird laughing and crying jags, people throwing up… Yes, a drug. We think. Not sure what exactly, at this point." Charlie bent his head onto his hand and repeatedly squeezed the already furrowed worry lines in his forehead with a thumb and forefinger.

"And Josh?"

"Technically, Jessie, your husband is stoned. He needs a night at emerge to sleep it off."

"Stoned? Josh?" A sick feeling slid down Jessie's already sore throat.

"He'll be okay. This wasn't his doing."

"Duh, my husband doesn't do well with drugs, Charlie."

"He's fine these days, kid. He's happy, he's going to meetings. This won't derail him."

"Didn't this kind of thing happen on the set of *Titanic* years ago? In Halifax?"

"Yep. I expect this is a copycat crime."

"Was it drugs then or was it food poisoning? I don't remember."

"PCP. Phencyclidine. Also known as angel dust. A breeze to sprinkle into food."

"How sick is Josh, Charlie? Did he—did he do anything? Should I go?"

Charlie cringed. "No, kiddo. Stay put. He's under supervision, he didn't do anything stupid, but he was definitely affected." Lowering his voice, he added, "Josh didn't lose his temper or anything weird like that. He's all right. I'm heading over to the hospital now but I wanted to let you know before you hear this in the media. It's bound to get out. In fact, it's likely already made the rounds on Twitter. I can't say that I've felt much like looking."

"Jesus Christ, Charlie." Swinging her legs over the end of the couch, Jessie shuddered and hung her splitting head in her hands.

"I know, sweetheart. It could have been worse but it's not. Everyone's okay. Look, Jane will keep the kids overnight. I'm staying in the city. Shanda's actually offered to go keep Jane company. Shanda's okay, she didn't eat whatever it was that got laced. Will you be okay? You have Dan there, right?"

"Yeah, he's hanging around somewhere. Him and a couple other local regulars. It's like we're under freaking house arrest or something."

"Stop exaggerating." Charlie sighed. "You can come and go as you please."

"Yes, as long as we have guards alongside."

"What's really changed, Jessie? You had Matt with you for years."

"That's what's changed, Charlie." Thick emotion was clouding Jessie's voice. Being sick and worrying about David's little chest hurting him too was a worry. Being holed up was frustrating, being alone sucked, and having Matt's friendship and guardianship replaced by formal 'guards' was demoralizing and lonely. "I miss Matt. If he were here right now—"

"He's not, Jessie, and right now there are people with bigger problems bouncing around my brain, so if you don't mind I'm just going to say suck it up and hang up, okay?"

Her sudden silence erased Charlie's hostility as quickly and efficiently as his computer's 'delete' button could.

"Oh, Jesus, Jessie. I'm sorry. This whole thing put me over the edge today. It hasn't been a great day in the annals of *Sacred Peace* history."

Jessie was subdued. "It's okay, Charlie. I get it. I'm the one who is sorry. I was being selfish."

"On that note, rest up. I'm going to the hospital to see my cast and crew." Charlie's chair squeaked as he stood, protesting the heavy weight of the day and echoing Charlie's concern. "I'll call again after I see your husband. Do you want me to get Shanda to check in on you on her way by?"

"No." Jessie's grump sliced through the line to Calgary. "On top of today's nefarious events, you don't need your cast getting sick with this bug. Trust me."

"You got some meds?"

"Yep. Over the counter stuff. Josh got us a whole pharmacy on his way home last night." She wanted to add *but I'm worried about David. He had pneumonia, remember? It started at the Langley House?* But Jessie, in reading Charlie's fear, held back. This was not the time. And now Josh was not accessible, either. She glanced towards the main door to the ranch house. Feeling woozy and feverish, Jessie said her goodbyes to Charlie and considered asking Dan to drive them to the hospital in Canmore, twenty minutes away.

"What do you think, little guy?" she asked David, who was moaning in his sleep. His chest was rattling. Fear bad enough to cause a rising nausea gripped Jessie. The memory of those horrible, hopeless days in the Langley basement assaulted her, a time when she could do nothing to help her son. David was definitely worse today than yesterday. Tylenol was barely controlling his fever, and he was listless. This new thing with Josh and the cast and crew of *Sacred Peace* sickened Jessie. It mobilized her into action.

Standing, she laid David further into the couch so he wouldn't roll off, and she tucked a light blanket around his legs. It was a grey, bleak mid-summer day. The light rain misting down outside would have made the ranch seem cool if both she and David weren't fighting fevers.

Shaky but upright, Jessie tiptoed towards the front door. Dan was down by the barn shooting baskets.

"Hey, you," she called, leaning against the doorframe and crossing her arms and ankles.

"How you doing, Jessie?" the big Scandinavian asked, catching the ball and starting across the clearing towards her. "Anything I can get for you?"

"Yep. Fire up my car, will you? The SUV." The Mustang was finally parked at the ranch, inside a garage at the far end of the property at the moment, snuggled up next to Josh's Harley. They'd had them sent down two weeks ago. "We need to take a drive."

"You got it. Hospital?"

"Yep."

"I think that's wise, Jessie. Never hurts to get things checked out. You and the little guy could likely both use a shot of antibiotics. Calgary or Canmore?"

"Canmore. I hear Calgary's overwhelmed by the cast and crew of a certain television production at the present time."

Dan froze. "What?"

"I'll explain in the car. Let's go, Dan."

She ducked back inside to gather her purse and her son. David protested vociferously but wrapped his small arms and legs around her body, and laid his hot cheek on his mother's shoulder. Fighting back tears, worrying about him and now Josh, too, Jessie made her way to the SUV, which Dan pulled up to the front door.

Taking David out of her arms, Dan led his boss by the elbow to the passenger side. "Did you take Tylenol, Jessie?" he asked, a note of concern coloring his usual steady voice. "You're burning up."

"I'll be fine," she murmured, easing back against the seat and gratefully allowing her eyelids to flit shut. "Can you stay tonight, Dan? In the guest room? Josh won't be home."

"You got it." Dan secured David, rested the back of his hand against the child's forehead and, with a furrowed brow, slid behind the wheel of the SUV. As he pointed the nose of the car down the lane, he speed-dialed the hospital and prepped them for Jessie's arrival with her son. Protocols already worked out with the hospital ensured an immediate private room, although Jessie was stubbornly insistent that she wait as long as everyone else to see the doctor. Still, she was grateful not to have prying eyes and cellphone cameras catching her sneaky tears as frustration and sickness got the better of her.

That night, armed with antibiotics and Charlie's assurances that Josh and the others from the production were recovering, and after having spoken with Jane, Emily-Grace and Dylan, Jessie took David to her bedroom's ensuite bathroom and gave him a cool soak to help bring his fever down. Dan was settled in the big spacious living room, on the computer likely conferring with Charles, she figured.

"We'll sleep well tonight, baby," she told David, who sat hunched over in the tub with tears streaming down his face. "You and Momma have meds now, and Daddy is fine. We'll see him tomorrow. We'll all be feeling better by then, I'm sure."

Soon, David was asleep on Josh and Jessie's big bed, and Jessie curled her body around him, leaving a little room so she wouldn't make him hotter than he already was. Her phone rang around midnight, waking her from a murky nightmare that left her toes curled in fright.

"Josh?" she asked when she answered, her voice slurred with meds and the need to sleep.

"It's Charles, Jessie. Sorry I didn't call earlier."

"It's okay," she managed as her brain tried to focus. "Charlie called a few times. How are you doing?"

"Well, we might get sued but thankfully everyone's fine. Dan said you took a little trip to the hospital in Canmore?"

"We're both on drugs now. Lots of 'em."

"David's doing better?"

"His fever's under control. He's sleeping."

"All right then. Don't worry about Josh. He, too, is off in dreamland. He'll be released in the morning. I'll get Arnie to drive him home. We cancelled shooting tomorrow."

"Ouch. That'll cost ya."

"The police are trying to sort this out. We're a little afraid to go ahead until we have some answers."

"Okay. Good." Jessie's nerves went into overdrive. "Charles, do you think this was a deliberate threat against the production?"

In one hand, Charles was holding a white envelope. In the other, he held a typed note. He studied the note as he lied to Jessie. "I think it was just a nasty prank, Jessie. Someone wanted to have a little fun with the crew. They went a little heavy on the PCP, that's all. If that's what it was. We're still waiting on the results."

"God, I hope so."

"Me too, honey." Charles was physically sick, lying to Jessie this way. But he couldn't afford to scare her any more than he knew she was already scared.

"I want to see him," she whispered. "I need to see Josh to know he's okay, Charles."

"You'll have to take my word on it this time, honey. I just saw him. He's sleeping off a good bender."

"Not funny, Charles."

"Not meant to be. Look, I'm sorry I woke you. Go back to sleep. I'm glad you invited Dan to stay overnight."

"Yeah, me too. The local regulars are fine, but I…I just needed someone around I knew, you know?"

"I know. Good night, Jessie. I'll call in the morning."

"Not too early. Us Sawyers need our beauty sleep."

"You call me, then. When you get up."

"I will. 'Nite, Charles."

After they disconnected, Jessie kissed the back of her son's head, and smiled wistfully at the blonde hair that fell over his cheek. "So much like your daddy," she murmured. "So handsome." Settling in behind him again, she closed her eyes and almost immediately fell back to sleep.

In Calgary, in his rented condo, Charles studied the note in his right hand. His fingers were shaking, the quaking not at all eased by his third Crown Royal of the night. His lips formed the words on the page and let them escape into the cool grey air. "Just thought Josh Sawyer might enjoy a good binge," he read. "And some company along the way. Signed, A Jacob Ryan Fan. P.S. I'll be around again. Someone's got to teach your tough guy actor a lesson."

The note was voiced to the man sitting across from him.

Jonathon, Josh's biological father, was sitting on a low-slung black leather chair in Charles' away-from-home study. Gritting his teeth, the man's face was a deathly shade of pale.

"This better not be for real, it better be a one-shot deal, Jon," Charles was saying. "We don't need Josh going down another dark path fueled by some sadistic asshole. We just got him sorted again."

"This sadistic asshole will find himself at the end of my fist when we find him," Jon replied, his knuckles white on the arms of the chair. He raised a pointed finger at Charles just as the producer was about to speak. "Don't say it. We will find out who did this. Call the police. Let's get them that note."

A few minutes later, as Jon stood at the floor-to-ceiling window and stared without seeing at the Calgary city lights below, he heard Charles say, "I wish to hell we still had Matt with us. In person, I mean. Phone calls, emails and Skype calls just aren't the same. We could use him tonight."

Secretly he was thinking *Jessie could have used him today.*

Earlier that day, in Prince Edward Island, when Matt got the call from Charles that told him what was happening in Alberta, he felt the very same way.

Chapter Three

Disgusted, Matt hit the 'end' button on his phone. Would Josh ever live a life unaffected by the endless bad wishes of others? Discussing with Charles the bad intentions of some nut job had left Matt drained. Always there was fear associated with the Sawyer family. Always there was pain.

Jessie. Storming out to the rope strewn across his yard from the deck railing to a half grown tree, the only one in his yard (*must have been strategically placed to grow into a clothesline,* Matt thought), Matt started hauling towels, shorts, jeans and shirts from it, draping them over his arm and cursing because he forgot to bring out a basket. His mood didn't improve after he dropped a white T-shirt onto the red dirt of Prince Edward Island.

"Goddamnit!"

Bending beneath the duvet he also had on the line today, he stilled. Staring at him were a pair of wide eyes—his new neighbor, whose hazel eyes, fringed with long, wet lashes that lent them an air of guarded grief, was just moving in. Just now she was standing beside the raised back door of her SUV, an older clunker, a Mazda Tribute which must have been manufactured in a particular year, Matt surmised, because Julie once had one, and the paint above the wheel wells was rusted all to hell, as they were on every Tribute and its twin Ford Escape from that year.

Standing, Matt sent her a half-wave, and spun around on the dirt to take his laundry inside. The last thing he needed or wanted was some judgmental woman on his case, reporting him to the landlord for swearing, or just being a general pain in the ass.

A low shuffling sound accompanied by panting coming from the general direction of his ankles caught Matt's attention just as he reached the wooden steps to his cottage. He almost tripped over its source—a puppy, maybe six months old at best. Big heavy paws too big for its grey body, perky ears, and eyes conveying a moist innocence made up the creature, which Matt idly thought had to be some kind of pit bull-cross mutt. The annoying thing was rather unidentifiable.

The woman was parting Matt's duvet and sheets now, walking between them, striding quickly, wringing her hands. "I'm sorry," she mumbled, bending and reaching for the puppy, which wholeheartedly averted her probing hands. "He's just a baby. Everybody's his friend." To the dog, she called, "Drifter. Here! Come. Now!"

Matt shifted his laundry to his other arm, and adjusted a pillowcase to keep it from dragging on the ground. He stared at his new neighbor in disbelief. "Your dog's name is Drifter?"

Catherine cocked an eye at him. "Benji and Max just seemed too, you know, overused. My daughter was a fan of the TV show. I took off the s. 'Here, Drifters,' just didn't quite work."

"I see. Top of his class, huh?" Matt's raised eyebrows highlighted his eyes, which appeared pale and tired on this cloudy day.

"What?" The woman stopped trying to catch the mutt, and tried to source out what her neighbor was trying to say.

With his armful of laundry, Matt gestured to the dog. "Puppy school. He listens well."

The woman drew her shoulders back and fixed an angry glare at her neighbor. "I just got him. I haven't had a chance to train him yet. And he just spent the last two days penned up in a car, so if you don't mind, keep your opinions to yourself."

Finally, she managed to grip the puppy's collar, haul him towards her, and scoop him up. "I'll keep him off your property," she announced, and thought about storming away from this disheveled looking man, but the teacher in her won out. "Catherine," she said. "That's my name. I, too, will make a point of avoiding your space." At that, she wheeled around and headed for her cottage, the grey bungalow with the pretty white trim to the right of Matt's place, facing the water.

"Suit yourself." Watching her go, Matt couldn't help but notice the way her butt moved from side to side as she walked. Her jeans seemed a mite tight, and he wondered how she managed to get them on in the mornings. *Painted them on, I guess,* he thought sarcastically as he jogged up to the front door and went inside to deposit his armload of clothes and towels, and to grab the basket so he could retrieve the rest of his laundry.

Later, after a delicious grilled steak loaded with steak spice, asparagus that had cozied up next to it on the barbecue, and a sliced, buttered potato that had steamed perfectly alongside both, Matt settled into a porch swing on the south side of his deck for a nap. He was still running thoughts and ideas around his brain re: the incident in Calgary. Mostly, though, he ached to call Jessie to see how she was doing. Charles had reported that both she and David were sick and had taken a trip to the hospital in Canmore, where they were issued antibiotics for chest infections. It was worrisome, to say the least, to know things weren't all perfection and roses in the Sawyer camp, as Matt felt both Josh and Jessie deserved.

Forty-five minutes later, a wet tongue on his cheek startled him out of his nap. "What the hell?" he cried, and vaulted upright, swatting at his cheek.

Drifter. The puppy. The mutt's sappy eyes were fixed on Matt, and the little body was vibrating from side to side, its tail was wagging so hard. Drifter seemed to want to jump up onto the porch swing, but the puppy was just too small to make it on its own. Frowning, Matt reached down and picked up the active body, and deposited the puppy on a pink floral cushion next to him.

"I know some kids that'd love you," Matt muttered. He and Jessie had once had a serious conversation about the kids having pets.

"Emily-Grace wants a dog and David wants a kitten," Jessie had told him during one of the seemingly endless flights on the Keating jet. They were sitting next to each other, just the two of them on the jet, long before the incident in Brussels, when things were more normal between them after Jessie and Josh had gotten back together, when Dylan was about a year old. The trip was a quick diversion from Jessie's longer tour to a one-off summer concert venue that was featuring a number of female singers. Deirdre had sent her assistant Pam to meet them at the concert to help out, while she travelled to the next city on the regular tour with the children. Josh was shooting in Kansas at the time.

"Josh and I are like, nope. No pets." Jessie had knife-sliced her hand through the air to illustrate her point.

"Pets are good for kids. They teach them responsibility."

"I'm lucky to remember the kids when I travel. Imagine us trying to corral a dog and a cat."

"You've got assistants up the yin-yang when you travel, Jessie. Assign some of them to the animals." Matt wasn't joking. Deirdre always made sure they had a number of assistants to help them on tour, but Jessie got to know none of them, with the exception of the mainstay, Pam. She was very careful about who she let into her life, and with the children around, doubly so.

"Nope," she had said, ending the conversation and casually taking Matt's hand for the rest of the flight.

Thinking about that conversation now, Matt considered all the times Jessie had so casually taken his hand and absently played with his fingers, or rested her own hand on his thigh. To both of them back then, the behavior was never really an issue. She did it in the Jacob days, she did it in the Josh days. It started after the whole Deuce McCall thing, as a crutch, to begin with, and it just continued even as things in Jessie's overall life improved. The casual movements were never sexual, and they never came with twinges of lust or desire. But they did come with love.

Remembering, Matt felt his gut twist now. He clearly recalled his heart swelling with love for Jessie during some of those moments when her fingers were wrapped around his; while they were watching a movie during one of the flights, or with Jessie leaning against his shoulder as she listened to music. While she was working out songs, sometimes, humming in his ear, occasionally with both of her hands wrapped around his.

I was her anchor, he thought inwardly now. *Hanging onto me kept her grounded.*

Footsteps sounded across the lawn, swishing through the low grass nearer the walkway. Looking up, Matt spied Catherine making her way towards him. He put her in her forties, but there was something tired and worn out about her. She was slim enough, not fit in an athletic way like Jessie was, but she certainly hadn't let herself go, either, although Matt discerned a few grey roots peeking out of her dark hair, which was swept up in some kind of small plastic clip at the moment.

Wiping any signs of suspected nap drool off his chin, he rose as she positioned herself at the bottom of his steps, leaned on one leg, and put her hands on her hips. A wide frown made its way up to him.

Matt sent one of equal measure back, but he held onto the dog's collar. Drifter was happily chewing on one of Matt's flip-flops now, with Matt's permission, since he had handed the animal the 'chew toy' to begin with.

Catherine started. Her hand came up with a flourish as she spoke. "Look, whatever your name is—"

"Matt," he interjected, not unkindly.

"Matt. Fine. Once again, I apologize. I'm not used to having a dog around. Open the door, and vroom, he races through it like he's on the bloody Nascar circuit."

"So keep the door closed." Matt's eyes started to twinkle, not much, just ever so slightly.

"Oh, yes, and then I...Oh. You're joking. Whatever." Catherine's tense shoulders shrunk, just a little bit. "I've had a long couple of days. I'm trying to get things unpacked. This little monster is driving me a bit nuts. It's like having a baby in the house."

Tiny curves turned up the corners of Matt's lips. Many times he'd heard Jessie say the same thing, the monster bit at least, only it had been in reference to Dylan.

"You're amused. Lovely." Switching her weight to the other foot, Catherine crossed her arms. Her eyes flickered over to Drifter, and immediately switched from general consternation to sheer alarm. "Oh, Jesus. He's chewing your shoe with those sharp little puppy fangs of his..." Her words faded into embarrassed oblivion.

"From what I hear, puppies like to chew," Matt said with a chuckle. "I have another pair. It's fine."

"You're not gaining any points by giving him your shoe to chew, mister."

"Matt. It was either that or my fingers."

"Hand him over. I'll get him out of your hair." Catherine moved up a couple of steps and stretched out her arms. Drifter stayed put, Matt's hand comfortably resting on the back of his neck.

"Why don't I keep him with me for a bit? You can finish whatever you're doing. Drifter can help me get a fire going when he gets bored of the taste of my dirty flip-flop." Eyeing Catherine carefully, Matt almost held his breath. It had been so long since he had the company of anyone…since he touched anyone…

The puppy was perfect. Safe and loving, in an unconditional kind of way. Not to mention soft. Its liquid eyes were filled with love for Matt, and Drifter didn't know him from a hole in the ground.

"Oh, I don't know. That might not be setting a good precedent." Catherine just wasn't sure. This man was…well, he was very good-looking in a sad, mixed up kind of way. The guy's eyes were pale and lined with worry, and he seemed so…lonely. Her mirror. Shaking the thought off, she backed off from trying to grab the very unconcerned Drifter from her neighbor's porch swing.

"I could use the company." *I'm not exactly begging,* Matt told himself. *But there's something about this dog…* Refusing to admit there was also something about the woman who stood near him now, he swallowed and shifted his gaze to her toes, which were half-polished with some tacky green nail color. Matt grinned. She was so unlike Jessie, who would prefer to be this kind of woman, but whose life had catapulted her into a kind of stardom and fame that generally meant needing to keep up appearances.

Am I going to start comparing every woman to Jessie? he asked himself as he dared a peek back up at Catherine.

Oh God, he has the sweetest dimples, Catherine thought in return as she took a closer look at her neighbor. Her brow creased. The man looked slightly familiar.

"All right," she said. "Keep him for a bit if you don't mind. But bring him over if he bugs you." Catherine started back down the stairs, tossing one more line over her shoulder. "And don't get any ideas about roasted puppy for a midnight snack. On your fire pit." She threw a hand up in the air. "Don't even think about making hot dog jokes. I'm so over those."

Laughing, Matt felt lighter than he had in days. This woman was rather entertaining, and not too hard on his tired eyes, either. "Listen, drop back over when you're done getting organized. The clouds are clearing, there's going to be an amazing sunset tonight, and I'll be sitting by my fire watching it."

"Do you have beer?" Catherine's heart started racing.

"Tons. Too much."

Twisting around to see if he was serious, Catherine paused. One foot turned over on its ankle, and Matt caught his breath. *Jessie does that.* Catherine saw the look, and hesitated. Walking backwards, she decided this man was an open book. He quite obviously was suffering from a broken heart. But she was intrigued enough to find out more. And there was the fact that he seemed so damned familiar...

"See you in a bit, then," she said, cursing inwardly at herself for even considering his offer. But he had her dog...

Dropping back down to the swing, Matt adjusted the puppy's position so he could lean back and let Drifter half lie on his legs. His flip-flop was well chewed already, which brought forth another chuckle.

"You think you're putting this innocent thing by me, you're so wrong. I'm on to you, you little mutt." Teasing the dog, Matt rubbed him at the scruff of his neck. Drifter locked adoring eyes on his new friend and kept chewing away.

Soon, over the Gulf, the skies turned a stunning orange with zigzags of purple betwixt and between. Backlighting the dappled clouds overhead, the effect was otherworldly, Halloween-like in intensity and shape, lining the sky with a humbling, grandiose gesture, promising light before darkness. Matt was almost too knocked out by the simple beauty and universal appeal of this incredible place Jessie knew as home to get up and start the fire. Drifter had dozed off, dreaming his puppy dreams with Matt's shoe solidly locked in between his paws. Gently pushing him aside, Matt finally found the will to leave his comfy spot with the dog resting comfortably on his legs to get some kind of flame going.

Catherine joined Matt for the first of many such gorgeous going-downs of the sun. By the end of the night, with Drifter on a leash between their portable lawn chairs to keep him from burning his nose on the fire-blackened metal surround of the pit, they were amenable neighbors, although their stories remained surface level and, apart from general 'I have a brother in the states' type stuff, they also remained secret. Relationship statuses were not discussed; hometowns remained private.

When Catherine asked what kind of work Matt did, he told her he was working via computer, coordinating some boring logistical stuff for a boss in Vancouver. "Travel, that kind of thing," he said in an offhand kind of way. "Internet's really something, isn't it?"

She admitted she was a high school English teacher, and wondered why he ducked his head and blushed when she said it.

After hearing that, Matt was desperate to text Jessie and tell her he had met a woman who was a teacher, which was what Jessie always said she wanted to be when she got on her 'wanna be normal' kick. To Matt, it was a great joke.

After he doused the fire and Catherine waved and took Drifter home, Matt found himself standing on the deck staring out at the moonlit water of the peaceful Darnley Basin. He caught the silhouette of the little white sailboat, and managed a small grin. Catherine was fine company, and if he played his cards right, Matt might manage a few bedtime rendezvous with her. As long as he was careful to not get emotionally involved, he was good to go. He was good at keeping his heart buried, and at a distance. After all, he'd operated that way for years with Julie and Katy.

Jessie had his heart. She would always have his heart. Matt didn't see anyone ever replacing feelings that strong. He figured it would be impossible. Too many years had flowed through that riverbed…they'd been through so much together.

As he wandered up the stairs to his palatial loft bed with the eternal view of glistening stars, Matt thought about Charles' earlier call which, with Catherine's company, he'd almost forgotten about. Was there anything Matt could do from here to police the situation, to help? No, unless he counted stepping up Arnie's duties and having him accompany Josh more and more, which he knew Josh would absolutely hate. Had Charles even told Josh he was apparently the target of the chowder PCP fiasco? No. Nor would he, at least not right away, not unless something else happened to reveal Josh as someone's pet sabotage project.

God, don't let it happen again. Let this be a one time thing, Matt thought as he slowly drew his toothbrush back and forth across his teeth.

As always, as he drifted off to sleep Matt turned his face into his pillow's fresh white cottony softness, and dreamed of the night he brushed his lips against the scars on the side of Jessie's breast, and went to sleep with her in his arms, safe from everyone and everything but her own long-felt hurts.

Only tonight, the pain was a little less acute, and the memory a little more faded.

Chapter Four

Jessie had to go back to Vancouver for five days to start preliminary rehearsals for the post-Thanksgiving *Sacred Peace* album and press tour. Both she and Jacob had just signed on to film shoots for most of the month of September, so the tour, which would start a few weeks after the *Sacred Peace* premiere, had to be scheduled afterwards. It was mid-August now, so the production team was starting early. They would miss much of September, and would pull together again in early October to put the finishing touches on the tour.

As she prepared to leave the ranch, Jessie fired off instructions to Carlotta and Deirdre, who flew in to care for the children since Josh was still working long days on the *Sacred Peace* set.

Her voice echoed her mood—tense, cranky and concerned. "Dee, don't forget David's meds. He's got another few days and he needs to take them like clockwork."

"Don't you forget yours, Jessie." Deirdre, uncharacteristically in jeans and a light summer top today, took Jessie by the shoulders and turned her so Jessie was facing her. She couldn't avoid a glimmer of a smile at the deep frown on the singer's lips. "And rest as much as you can. You're still getting over this chest bug too, you know."

"I'll be fine." Shaking her off, Jessie stole a look at David. The little boy was playing happily with his two siblings, a rare enough thing for the three kids. Right now, with Emily-Grace's air of superiority and skill due to her 'advanced age,' they were learning to piece together a Lego Ninjago set Deirdre had brought for them. Heads down, all three were squatting on the floor, deeply focused on their tasks, much to Jessie's relief since she had some last minute packing to do before joining Josh for the ride into Calgary. Josh would drop her off at the jet. Dan, who was coming off a few nights of 'r and r,' would meet her there. Sam and Ulysses were both at the ranch, and Arnie would tail Josh and Jessie, and then follow Josh to work.

Now, Jessie turned to the fridge to triple-show Deirdre where David's meds were. As she moved to open the door, she glanced over to a computer monitor newly mounted on the wall nearby. It was sectioned off in eight parts, all showing individual areas of the ranch house and its adjacent buildings. Cameras mounted in those key locations fed into this monitor as well as into the Calgary security firm that was now providing reinforcement patrollers around the Sawyer ranch.

Jessie blinked and paused when she caught sight of uniforms she didn't expect to see at the base of the lane that led up to the ranch. "Josh," she called, and twisted around to give him a curious stare as he made his way towards her, his arms full of laundry he'd just pulled from the washing machine. Carlotta took the wet clothes from him and headed to the clothesline out back.

Wiping sweat off her forehead, Jessie groaned as Josh approached her. "When are we getting a pool put in?"

"Next summer," Josh replied casually, wrapping one arm around his wife's waist and following her gaze to the security monitor. "You whiny Prince Edward Island girls and your constant need for water to soak in. You're not near as hardy as us west coasters."

"No, you just *think* you're tough. I've caught you having cold showers when you thought I wasn't looking."

Grinning, Josh put his second arm around his wife and pressed her body close to him. "I prefer to deal with my needs appropriately as opposed to succumbing to cold showers."

"Ha ha. Appropriately? FYI, sexy man, we were talking about swimming." Eyes alight, Jessie wrapped her arms around her husband's shoulders and buried her face in his neck. "Mmm," she moaned. "I already miss this. I already miss you."

"Five days," Josh consoled. "We'll be okay." But his voice was gruff. This leaving thing was still excruciating. Neither Josh nor Jessie ever felt safe. Leaving the children behind was terrifying for Josh during the workday, and for Jessie on her numerous trips, which she'd cut down as much as she felt she could. The thing is...whenever the family was apart, they couldn't help but wonder when they would ever be together again. They'd had far too many unplanned partings over the years. "Now," Josh said, breathing in and gathering his courage, "what did you call me over here for? Just another cuddle?"

Swatting him, Jessie giggled. "As if you'd ever turn down the opportunity for a 'cuddle.'" Raising her fingers as quotes, she winked, then rotated back around to the monitor and spoke in a more serious tone. "We have visitors," she told him, pointing to the out-of-the-ordinary uniforms.

"Cops?" Wrinkling his nose, Josh bit his lip and considered why uniformed police would be at their house. "I'll deal with this, Jessie. Keep getting ready. We're hitting the road in ten. I hope." Leaning forward to brush his lips against her forehead, he paused before leaving Jessie's side. "Stop," he demanded, referencing the worried countenance that had Jessie crossing her arms and frowning at him. "I'm sure it's nothing. They're probably just looking for autographs and using their uniforms as leverage to get inside the gate. Go. Brush your teeth. Curl your hair. Kiss your babies."

Forcing a smile, Josh kissed her again, sighed, and wandered over to the front door where Deirdre was standing. Together, they stared curiously at the police car cruising to a stop out front.

"What's this about, Josh?" she asked him.

"I'm about to find out," Josh responded darkly, pushing open the squeaky screen door and stepping outside. Watched by Jessie and Dee, he was joined by Arnie, who crossed the clearing to meet the cops as well.

"Good morning," Josh said amicably to the police while, inside, Jessie curled up into herself. Something about this visit just didn't feel right.

Deirdre pushed her own curiosity away and turned to Jessie. "Come on," she said. "Let the menfolk handle this, whatever it is. Let's get you ready. You know your husband, he has less patience than a mosquito. He'll be raring to go the second the police get back in their car."

"That's because your husband is a dictator, Dee. Josh is terrified of being late for call."

Easing the pressure with a few light laughs, Deirdre helped Jessie sort the last of her things, and by the time Jessie had everything gathered and was moving towards the front door with her suitcase, the police were trundling off towards the barn with Arnie. Josh didn't look happy, though.

Jessie held the screen door open for him as he came back inside. "What?" she asked. "Is everything okay?"

"They want to do a check around the ranch. Just precautionary stuff, they said. Because of what happened on set, I guess."

"So, what, they're scouting the homes of all the cast and crew?"

"Just some of the cast, apparently." Josh watched Jessie to see how she would take that news. As he figured, she didn't take it well. He braced himself for the onslaught he knew was coming.

"What? What the hell, Josh? Do they have some reason to think you're a target?"

"Not that I'm aware of, Jessie. Just relax." Looking over her shoulder, he saw Emily-Grace fix a nervous gaze on them. "Look." Lowering his voice, Josh lifted his wife's chin and tried to smile at her but he, too, was succumbing to an icy new fear as it crawled up the backs of his legs and settled into his stomach. "They said it is just a precaution. Arnie's gone to talk to Ulysses, he's in the barn shooting the shit with Gary. Let's not blow this up into anything bigger than it is."

"Growl."

"Did you literally just say growl to me?" Unable to help himself, Josh's eyes lit up and he cracked a smile.

"I did. Growl. I'm not impressed."

Turning away from him, sauntering over to the kids, Jessie bent and wrapped her arms around her daughter. "Show me what you're making," she said, trying to keep quickly rising emotion from leaking into her voice.

Deirdre sat back on one of the kitchen island chairs and watched her, as Carlotta came in from the clothesline and broke the new silence with a vociferous complaint that everything would dry stiff as a board today because there was no visible breeze to even stir the leaves in the trees. She took up a perch next to Deirdre as Josh, too, watched Jessie with the kids. They were like a mirage to him, to all of them sometimes, as if they were just a gift on loan for a while.

As if the moments when Jessie and the children were present weren't, in fact, real.

Sessions with Trudy had helped Josh figure out that he thought about his wife and kids that way for a reason. It wasn't a big stretch to figure out why. The hard part was drawing himself back into the present and reminding himself to cherish what he had, and to not worry about the future. Having uniformed RCMP show up at Josh's door the morning his wife was heading back to Vancouver for five days didn't settle today's already increased anxiety. Not one bit.

Looking away, Josh made a small *pfffttt* sound and fought a rising panic. Jessie was hugging all three children at once now. No way was Josh getting her away from the ranch without a full-blown mess of tears, which was only going to upset the kids, and Dee and Carlotta along with them.

"Come on, Jess," he said quietly, walking towards her and scooping up Dylan to give him some belly raspberries to lighten the mood. "Time to go. Leave these little ones to be spoiled righteously by Grammie Dee and Carlotta." To Dee, who, to Josh's chagrin, was already wiping at tears, Josh frowned and said, "Go easy on the sugar today unless you want these three wired and driving you nuts. I'll see you tonight."

Dylan was wriggling around in Josh's arms, squealing and offering his own slice of happiness to the small family. Setting him down, Josh grabbed for David, who fought him with unrestrained glee. Turning him upside down, Josh held him up by his ankles as David clawed for the floor. Flipping him over the right way, Josh held him close before planting a few raspberries on his belly as well.

Jessie was standing now, swiping at trails of tears but laughing at her husband and kids. Emily-Grace leaned into her side, eyes big and wide.

"Don't go, Momma," she begged. "Stay home."

"I'll bring you something from Vancouver," Jessie offered. "What would you like? A new stuffie?"

"A Justin Bieber poster for my room," was the immediate answer, which did a better job erasing the tension of the imminent parting than Josh's horsing around with the boys managed.

"Oh, Lord. Justin Bieber? Really? You do realize he's my competition." Aghast, Jessie was finally laughing.

"What do you mean, Momma? Why, because he sings?"

"Uh, yeah. Because he sings. But I have more Grammys than he does. C'mere, baby girl." Drawing her firstborn close, Jessie held her tight.

Josh brushed a hand over his daughter's head. That was his only goodbye to her, which the grown women in the room noticed and pushed aside. Emily-Grace only came around to her father in moments when she felt super safe and secure. Now, knowing that her mother was leaving, and the main parent in the evenings would be Josh, was disconcerting. All the bonding Emily-Grace and her father managed to do while Jessie was shooting in Brussels had been almost entirely undone when Josh moved to the ranch without his wife and kids back in March. He was inaccessible then, for the most part, and to a little girl who knew another seemingly more dependable man, Josh was a shot in the dark.

She did manage a small, "Bye, Daddy," though, accessorizing it with small pink downturned lips and pale, almost vacant eyes.

Ten minutes later, on the highway heading towards the airport, Josh exhaled in frustration and ran his fingers through his layered hair. Jessie was silent. They didn't even have the radio on, they were so lost in their own dark thoughts.

"Jessie, you can't be getting all emotional every time you leave," Josh finally decided. "Kids pick up on those vibes."

"Emily-Grace is getting old enough to understand what happened to us, Josh. She's already hearing things from other kids."

"She's not around other kids. Just Stella. Who is also not around other kids these days."

"Well, they will be. Someday. And for now they've likely stumbled on crap on the Internet." Jessie stared out of the window as the sweltering Alberta landscape flew by. In a nearby meadow abundant with pretty wildflowers, a half-dozen horses were frolicking gladly. Two were running parallel to Josh's truck as it sailed by; their manes and tails were held proudly high as they galloped over the wild grass. Idly, Jessie wondered if they knew their freedom ended abruptly at an electric fence.

"We need to sort that out," Josh was saying, his knuckles tight on the steering wheel. "Keeping the kids alone so much, away from other kids, I mean. We can't keep them in a protective bubble forever."

"Emily-Grace went to school. David went to school. Lots of kids are in bubbles over the summer."

"You're scared to hook them up with other kids because Matt's no longer around. You don't trust anyone else. Admit it."

"You seriously always want to fight with me when I'm about to get on a plane. Really, Josh? Is that the only way you know how to deal with how you feel? You're the one who's scared." Locking her gaze on the window and more farmland rushing by outside, one with prolific hopeful white and yellow crocuses lining the fence, Jessie puffed up her cheeks and blew out.

"Jesus," Josh grumbled, his blood pressure rising. "I'm not trying to start a fight, Jessie. It's just that I know how this next year is going to go. The kids will be tutored because you're on a film in September while I wrap *Sacred Peace,* and then we'll all travel for the press tour, which wraps the first of December. Putting the kids in school for just a few months is going to be painful for them. Especially Emily-Grace. *Sacred Peace* will be starting up again by March."

"My thoughts exactly." Jessie finally looked back over at him. Extending an arm, she laid a hand on his thigh.

Josh dropped his fingers to his lap and enclosed hers tightly as he spoke again. "Emily-Grace and David need some stability, Jessie. Next year for season two we need to put them in school in either Canmore or Calgary. Canmore might be best, it's smaller, easier to keep secure. They'll get four months. As much as it sucks, they'll just have to do Point Grey from December to March."

"That's a helluva lotta changes."

"Ulysses can handle it."

"I'm thinking about the kids." She turned back to the window.

Josh paused. "No. You aren't." He lifted his hand back to the steering wheel. His grip tightened.

"I don't want to talk about Matt. Because that will just lead into what I did to fuck things up for all of us, for us to end up losing him." Letting her gaze drift back over to her husband, Jessie pleaded with him to understand. "And now we have this new threat hanging over our heads, whatever the hell it is. And we don't even know yet...what...how bad...Oh, Jesus." Sinking back into her seat, Jessie pressed the heels of her palms into her eyes.

Josh grabbed one of her hands and pulled it away from her eye. "I accept as much responsibility for what happened with Matt as you do, Jessie. If I was available to you then, you wouldn't have turned to him. We've established that. But the point is, he's gone, and we need to trust Charles and Ulysses to do what they think is right for us, for our kids. But we also have to consider getting the kids back out into the public, back out to birthday parties, to activities and playgroups, to school."

Jessie wasn't handling this conversation well. The color had drained from her face, and the hand Josh was holding was sweaty and trembling despite the cool air conditioning in the King Ranch.

Josh noticed. He backed off. "You know something though, little one?" he asked her. "We'll have them with us until at least December. And we have a lot to look forward to. We'll be together for the whole *Sacred Peace* tour. We'll teach them ourselves."

"We'll have to have a tutor, Josh."

"For part of the day. And Sam or Dan will always be nearby. The other part of the day, we'll take them to museums and out swimming or skating or whatever. We'll just have some good family time. Jacob can hang out too, okay?"

Finally, a warm smile flitted over to him. Jessie twined her fingers around her husband's again. "Speaking of Jacob…"

"Kayla says next spring." Josh grinned. "My baby sister's marrying Jacob. I might just lose my mind."

"Deal with it. I've never seen him this happy." At Josh's raised eyebrows, Jessie added, "I mean it. When he was with me there was always an undercurrent of loss screaming your name. With Kayla, Jacob is truly happy. And that makes me happy."

"Me too, then." Josh smiled and squeezed her hand. "Now," he winked, "where can I pull over for a quickie before we get to the airport?"

A quick laugh from Jessie prefaced a question. "I'd say the condo, but won't Charles be pissed if you're late for call?"

"Charles can be pissed for once. We haven't broken in this new King Ranch yet, baby girl." Josh winked.

"Then find us a deserted country lane, husband. And while you're looking, how about I just get started? I can warm you up. After I text Arnie and tell him to get lost, that is."

Her text to Arnie read *pull over give us ten we need some privacy*

After gliding to a stop to wait, Arnie texted back *is that all it takes? Ten?*

Laughing, Jessie typed back *I'll text u in a half hour, then.* She added a smiley face emoji with an embarrassed red blush and a second one with a mischievous wink on its yellow face.

Leaning towards her husband, Jessie unfastened his wide belt, practically purring as he relaxed enough to help her get his zipper down, but they were both laughing too hard to accomplish much until Josh pulled to a crooked stop on a side road and loved his wife properly.

Afterwards, they spent a few extra minutes just quietly cuddling, enjoying the sweet bliss of being alone together without a household full of security, children, and extra people.

"I love you, Josh," Jessie told him, holding his cheeks between her palms. She was on top, straddling him, to spare him extra pain from his still sore shoulder and slightly tender ribs and leg. "I'll see you in five days, okay? Take care of yourself. Stay safe."

"No more tears," he replied in a soft murmur, laying a hand over hers and closing his eyes to better soak up her energy. "Happy leavings are easier."

"Okay." Laying her cheek against his good shoulder, Jessie breathed him in. "Happy leavings. All right."

Later, when the jet crested off into the clouds, Jessie tucked her legs up onto the seat, wrapped her arms around her knees, and stared idly at the white cotton outside the window that she'd become quite accustomed to over the years as it swallowed her up and spit her out in strange locations. At least this time she would end up in Vancouver amongst people she loved. Even Steve and Sophie were back home, and she couldn't wait to see them.

Josh would be okay too, she knew. Carter was around the set now, and word from Charlie was that Josh and he were spending more time together than Josh and Shanda, which was a huge relief. As far as today's police? And last week's PCP incident? Jessie tried not to think about them, but she sent a silent prayer up to God, as she'd gotten in the habit of late, and she sent a telepathic message to Matt, her gut twisting with the pain of missing him—her guardian angel, her watcher.

Back in Calgary, Josh leaned against the King Ranch's grill in solemn silence, ankles crossed and mouth pressed into a serious thin frown, as the jet took off and disappeared amongst the fluffy cotton of the day's soft clouds. He knew what he needed to do, though, and the second he could no longer see the jet's wings reflected in sunshine, he hauled himself up into the big cab and pointed the truck towards the rugged area just outside Calgary where *Sacred Peace* was shooting exteriors today. Josh had a later call time because Charlie and Charles had wrangled a schedule change to accommodate Jessie's trip. There were some advantages to being so closely connected to the show's producers. Even so, Josh was late, but it didn't matter. The shoot day was running behind. He went off in search of Charlie.

It was eleven by the time he found his buddy. Charlie was lounging in a travel lawn chair outside his trailer with a messy pile of papers on his lap and confusion crisscrossing his face.

When Charlie spotted Josh, he tossed the papers on the ground and said with an air of disdain, "Tell me again why I wanted to produce this show? Next time I'm sticking to acting. You don't know how easy you have it, man. Tax credits and financing and. . . Jesus. I hate all that stuff. I despise it, in fact."

Easing into a chair next to him, Josh counseled, "Let Jon and Charles do that shit. That's what they're both good at."

Charlie reached into a cooler at his side and tossed Josh a plastic bottle of orange juice. "I try, and they'd be happy to let me, but I feel like a goddamned idiot." Charlie scratched at his chin with a thumb and forefinger. His hair was longer now, too, falling in waves over his eye, which Josh could tell annoyed the hell out of him, since he was always shoving it back over his head, only to have it fall forward again the second he bent his head back over his phone or papers or whatever. "I need to at least pretend I understand where all the money's coming from. And where we're at, that kind of thing."

"Fake it til you make it, Deacon." Josh allowed a small smile to widen over his face as he raised his boots up on a picnic table and twisted the cap off the juice. "What's that old saying? Never let them see you sweat?"

"Jonathon's onto me. He's only here once in a while but your poppa has a knack for numbers. And a rather frightening stare in meetings, I might add."

"I wouldn't know," Josh muttered. "He's been pretty cool to me since the whole *Wyatt Boys* disaster."

"He's just scared, Josh."

"Yep, I know. Everyone's scared good old Josh Sawyer is going to go back down the rabbit hole one of these days. I already pissed him off getting spun and tossed off poor old Blue."

"Woulda been worse if that cougar'd et ya."

"Et me? I woulda strangled her with my bare hands if I coulda after what she did to my horse. Then I woulda roasted and et *her.*"

Charlie tried to laugh but the sound came out choked. He countered right. "Speaking of feisty women..."

"Jessie's on the jet on her way back to Vancouver for rehearsal. Steve and Kayla both promised to keep an eye on her."

"If I know Jessie, she'll just work herself raw to avoid feeling anything. Then she'll come back and crash until it's time to fly off again. Where's her new film shooting?"

"New York. She'll be staying in her condo there."

"Oh, that'll help her. No memories there." The sarcastic jibe was followed with a quiet afterthought. "She ought to sell that big mausoleum."

"I think Jessie wants to hold onto this one. And its memories."

"Ah. I see." Charlie reached back into the cooler and grabbed another oj. "Want another one of these for the set?"

"No, thanks." Biting his fingernail for a minute, Josh waited until Charlie opened the drink and took a healthy swig before he broached a new topic. "Charlie, I've just got a few minutes before blocking unless...well, how far are we running behind?"

"We're a good hour behind the eight ball today, Josh. Relax. What's up?"

"I just...Look, we had RCMP nosing around our place this morning. Said they were just checking things out. Like...checking out the homes of cast, I mean. Not just ours. Is there something I need to know?"

He knew the answer before Charlie said a word, because Charlie suddenly suspended his juice in the air, then lowered it without taking another drink.

"They weren't supposed to show up until after you and Jessie left." Charlie's voice was quiet but serious. He stared straight ahead, then looked down and fidgeted with his drink. Starting to peel at the label, he swallowed bitterly, and then cursed as his longer hair fell over his eye again. Charlie brushed it back with a furious swipe.

Josh tried to appear relaxed. He tipped his oj up and drained it before querying his boss and friend further. "So what's up, Charlie? Is there a real threat against the production? What don't I know?"

Charlie hesitated before speaking. Then he jumped in with both feet. "What you don't know, Josh, is that it's probably all just a bunch of bullshit meant to scare us. But yes, there was a threat made. It's in the hands of the police." He was staring straight ahead again, trying not to feel like puking. As much as he would have hated to admit its possibility years ago, Charlie now loved Josh like a brother. And Jessie and the kids…

The idea of anyone ever coming after any of them again plain sickened him.

"What kind of threat?" Josh's voice was low and contained but he was starting to tremble. He squeezed the plastic orange juice bottle until it crumpled under his nervous fingers.

"You got Hilary coming out here anytime soon, Josh? And maybe Zach?" Finally, Charlie got up the guts to look into the liquid brown eyes of his friend. Eyes that were regarding him carefully, starting to sink back into the old fear.

"They're both coming out later in the week, to make sure you're treating their actor okay."

"We're spoiling you rotten." Charlie's unsuccessful attempt at lightening the mood fell on deaf ears.

"Why? Why do they need to come here?"

Shrugging, Charlie tossed a bit of the torn label onto the grass at his feet, making a mental note to deliver it to the proper garbage bin later. "We may need to do some scheduling changes, that's all. It would be good to have Hilary around while we go over things, since she takes care of your career."

"Scheduling changes?" Josh's body went rigid. "Is that code for adding security? You're not fooling me, Charlie. What the hell kind of threat is there to the production?"

Charlie's silence may as well have been an anvil dropped in Josh's lap. Once Josh clued in to what Charlie wasn't telling him, fear sucked the breath out of his lungs. One at a time, he lowered his feet from the picnic table and had to bend his head forward and focus on a blade of grass while he recovered his senses and the ability to speak.

"You've got to be fucking kidding me." Glancing over at Charlie, he saw by his friend's anxious movements and the cloud of fear crossing his face that Charlie was not, in any way, pulling a fast one.

Steeling his nerve, Charlie looked up and met Josh's eyes. "Like I said, it's probably nothing."

Leveraging himself fully upright, Josh paced, ending up with his hands on his hips directly in front of Charlie. Glaring down at him, he spat, "So the threat is not against *Sacred Peace*. It's against me. Hence the drugs in the chowder. How do you know that?"

Muttering almost incoherently as he stared at the juice in his hands, Charlie managed, "A note. It was a goddamned note."

"Against...just me, Charlie? Or...or Jessie, or my family?"

"Just you. Someone who said they were, of all things, a fan of Jacob's."

A weird high-pitched laugh escaped Josh's throat. Staring off into the distance, he spotted the Third A.D. walking towards him, likely needing to beckon him to the hair and makeup trailer. "It doesn't matter how hard I try to befriend that guy, or put up with him around Jessie and Dylan, and now my sister. He is, and always will be, a sword in my side."

Rising, Charlie faced Josh, aware that the A.D. was drawing closer. He spoke in a low tone couched with warning. "Josh, I'm sure you'll agree that Jessie does not need to know about this. I'm sure you'll also agree that it's likely just some sick fan who will be happy as a clam once he or she realizes Jacob and Jessie are singing together again."

A new thought struck Josh. "It's someone on the crew, Charlie. It has to be. Exactly what kind of threat did they make?"

"Nothing specific. Look Josh, you'll see Arnie sticking close to you in the days to come, and the firm from Calgary will be around more as well. There's no reason to think your family is at risk, but just in case..." He shrugged.

"The cops this morning. Yeah, all right. Jesus Christ." Averting his eyes, Josh waved at the Third A.D. who did, indeed, tell him to go to the hair and makeup trailer. After the A.D. wandered away again, Josh's shoulders sank. "My fucking life. Seriously."

Watching him, Charlie sensed that Josh was fighting some heady emotions, that he might in fact be ready to break down. And why not? His life seemed to be in constant turmoil. The guy deserved some real peace.

"Go inside if you need a minute, Josh," Charlie suggested. "Hair and makeup can wait."

"Hair and makeup might have a knife ready to slash my throat. Or a fucking razor, maybe, hidden in one of their drawers buried under those things the women use. Bobby pins or clips or whatever."

"I have no answer for that, Josh. Just watch your back. We're doing the best we can here."

Nodding, Josh's wide eyes agreed, but telegraphed clearly that this new threat was very, very unwelcome. Storming away from Charlie, he thought about Jessie and how frightened she would be if she knew. Vowing not to tell her, he decided he should likely check in with Charles at some point, to assess the risk and see what he himself could do to help alleviate the stress on the production.

Heading towards hair and makeup, his head down, Josh avoided all crew he passed. His mouth was twisted in fear, and his stomach was threatening to erupt. *No more,* he begged the universe. *No more.*

Behind him, Charlie's heart ached. Simply safeguarding an actor was one thing. Loving him like a brother was quite another, especially when Jessie's often frightened sea-pearl eyes crossed his mind.

Bending forward and grabbing his pile of earlier tossed papers, Charlie was about to turn and head up the metal steps into his trailer when he saw Josh stop and shove his hands in the pockets of his jeans. He was about a hundred feet away now, lit by the sun so his white T-shirt and faded jeans looked brighter than normal. Charlie's breath caught at the otherworldly, almost spiritual effect.

Josh turned towards him then, just pivoting from his waist, keeping his feet planted. There was no way Charlie could read his expression, but he knew exactly what Josh was telling him.

If something happens to me...keep my family safe. Take care of my girl.

"Jesus Christ." Charlie echoed Josh's earlier thought. When he stepped into the trailer after Josh turned back and continued walking towards hair and makeup, it was Charlie who needed a few minutes to compose himself. Because it was Charlie who sensed intuitively that this new fear was real, and that it was not going away anytime soon, and that the television show he loved and had been developing over a number of years was at risk, and so was his friend.

They were now, officially, at war with an enemy they couldn't yet hope to identify.

They were under siege, likely by an insider, with no clue just how, or when, this new threat could be quashed.

It was daunting to consider, but Charlie knew one thing for certain. Josh Sawyer was someone he cared about, for all kinds of reasons, and if it came to having to choose between the production and his good friend, Josh would come out on top.

Friendships like theirs were rare. Friendships like theirs were worth hanging on to.

Friendships like theirs had the power to tear a person apart.

Chapter Five

A nimble landing followed an uneventful flight to Vancouver, although a heavy bank of grey clouds filled with moisture was a disconcerting welcome to the often moist west coast. The jet sliced through the disparaging bleakness like a knife through a ripe avocado. On the ground, Jessie didn't bother grabbing an umbrella. She ran for the car with all guns blazing, relishing the fresh summer mist on her skin and laughing despite an overhanging sadness for the family she'd left behind in Alberta.

Big Dan took her straight to the Deacon space on the Downtown Eastside. Kayla and Jacob were waiting. The rest of the gang was expected within the hour, but Jessie had arranged to meet Kayla and Jacob first, partly to say hi and to share news, and partly because she and Jacob needed to settle something first.

"Come, sit," she ordered Jacob after initial pleasantries had been exchanged. Patting the edge of the stage, Jessie levered herself up, made herself comfortable, and waited for Jacob to do the same. Swinging her legs, she had to force herself not to lay a hand on his thigh as they talked; the impulse wasn't desire based, instead it was just one of their old, casual intimacies. But out of respect for Kayla, and also because Jacob had tuned Jessie in pretty good back at the Robson studio months ago, Jessie resisted.

Jacob seemed blissfully unaware. His eyes were following his pretty blonde dancer as Kayla moved towards Priya, Jessie's usual choreographer, so they could start mapping out ideas.

"What's up, Jessie?" he asked, as Jessie rather dramatically cleared her throat in order to get his attention.

"Eyes here, loverboy," she teased. "We've got to come to some agreement about your little friend Casey."

"I'm curious as hell what you think. I know you're not a fan."

Tossing her curls, Jessie said, "You're wrong. It's the other way around. Which will work against her unless she gives me a reason to trust her today."

"I've been picking away at her ambivalence towards you. She's warming up to you. The two of you have a lot in common, anyway. I think you'd be good for her if she'd open up a bit."

"I'm only willing to take her on if you think she'll be a team player, Jacob."

"So…you're seriously thinking of letting Casey come on tour with us?"

"What I'm willing to do is let her come on the tour as a student, basically. She can work with Phil on drums and soak up whatever he's willing to teach her, and if he thinks she's good enough she can play a tune or two during a few of the shows."

"Jessie, that's a very generous offer." Humbled, Jacob nonchalantly waved to one of the band members who blew through the entry with two trays of coffee, one tray piled on top of the other. The guy had used his foot to hold the door open, and Kayla dashed forward with effusive thanks for the caffeine jolt. This initial rehearsal would make for a long, tedious day. Revolver, not far away, would do well by the hardworking musicians and dancers in the Jessie-Jacob camp today.

"She'll get paid whatever Charles deems is appropriate for an intern. And if she takes this opportunity seriously, Casey will have no shortage of work for the near future. She's clean, right Jacob?"

"Yeah, she's got a few walls but she's pretty naïve overall, Jess. No drugs except nicotine. And she wants this. I know she does."

"Maybe just not with me."

"Benjie, Kayla and myself will keep her in line. She was a real gem on the workshop tour, always helping out with luggage or props or whatever, and she's pretty even-tempered overall."

Hopping off the stage as she saw Casey come in with Benjie, Jessie turned her back so Casey couldn't see her speak. "I'm not kidding, Jacob. I'm happy to do you this favor and try to help the kid out, but I've got enough stress on my plate right now. I don't need some moody youngster making me feel like shit. I do that well enough on my own."

Sobering, Jacob remained seated on the stage. Studying Jessie, he asked, "What's going on? I thought things were good with you guys."

"They are. Really, Jacob," she added when his raised eyebrows became question marks. "There just always seems to be a dark cloud trying to do us in, that's all."

"I heard about the PCP thing. Josh handle that okay?"

"He didn't bury himself in drugs or booze after that, if that's what you're asking." Peering backwards over her shoulder, Jessie caught Casey's eye. The girl seemed hesitant, and looked at Benjie for guidance. Jessie saw him give her a little push, and Casey moved towards her and Jacob. She turned back to Jacob and continued. "We had police around our home this morning and Charles has stepped up security. I left the kids home with Carlotta and Deirdre, which makes me sick with worry, and I could tell it freaked Josh out too, leaving them while the police were going over the place. Casey might want to reconsider getting into this crazy business."

"What about Matt?"

"What about him?" *Ouch. Even hearing his name hurts.* Jessie slouched and buried her hands in her pockets.

"You in touch with him at all?"

"Nope. Josh is, once in a while."

"Maybe you should give him a call, Jessie. Talk through some of the security stuff. It might put your mind at ease to get his opinion on things."

Pausing, Jessie searched Jacob's eyes. It had been a while since he and she spoke alone, much less brought up any of the old feelings. Now, the tenderness in the way he was looking at her transmitted that he understood exactly what she was feeling. The realization made her both grateful that somebody 'got' her fear, and made her want to collapse in tears at the same time.

"I can't." The simple statement was made with a hunch of the shoulders and a trembling lower lip. "I know you get that, Jacob."

"Yeah. I do, Jessie. I'm sorry." Jacob hopped down from the stage and sent Casey a one-minute signal with a raised finger.

"What about you?" The question caught Jacob by surprise.

"What about me?"

"Are you in touch with Matt at all?" Suddenly Jessie's eyes were hopeful.

"We've swapped a few emails."

"So? Tell me."

"He's in P.E.I."

"I know that. I know where he is. What I need to know is how he's doing."

Cornering right, Jacob grinned. "First, tell me what he was like in the sack. An old guy who was married to the same woman for years..." A diabolical light danced its way across Jacob's puppy dog eyes, which gave him the appearance of a mischievous child.

"I've never felt the age difference between me and Spike. He's adorable, and I miss him like crazy." In a smaller voice Jessie finished with, "It's not really something I can share with Josh, this whole talking about Matt thing, even though he's been pretty good about understanding why we went there."

"And? The sack?"

"Jacob! You frustrate the hell out of me. You think this was some kind of contest?" Jessie was laughing, though, lightly, enjoying this repartee with her ex-lover.

"Hell, yeah! My ego's at risk. I can't lose to an old guy."

The volume in the space was increasing as more and more musicians and dancers arrived. The tour manager, a thirty-something artsy white guy with a plaid scarf wrapped around his neck, had moseyed to the middle of the space after grabbing one of the available coffees. Jessie could tell he was anxious to chat but he, like Casey, was respecting Jessie and Jacob's space until they were ready for him.

Jessie leaned over to Jacob and smirked. "You remember New York? The Eva Cassidy tune at the fundraiser? Going back to my place the night Josh showed up drunk?"

"Hell, yeah." The memory softened Jacob's playful banter into a more serious recall that sparked of true love and desire. "Not like I would ever forget that night, Jessie."

The way Jacob was looking at her now almost rendered Jessie speechless. Soft blue eyes with a hint of dampness. She melted. "Babe, that's all I want to say on the subject. Forever."

"So. Lust and love. Musta been some night."

"It was. They both were. Now stop. It's hurting again."

"The memories, huh?"

"My heart." At that, Jessie reached out and squeezed Jacob's fingers. She bent forward and brushed her lips against his cheek. "I love you," she whispered softly. "Always. Now go get Casey and let's choose to honor the past instead of always diving back into the stuff that makes my heart ache. And tell me if Matt is doing okay."

"Matt's doing about as well as I was before I met Talia. He's lonely as hell."

Slumping, Jessie frowned. "Seriously, Jacob? You couldn't couch that in some kind of fake reality to make me feel a little less like some kind of louse?"

Solemn now, Jacob sighed and signaled to Casey. "You want me to lie?"

"Hell, yeah." After a moment to regain her equilibrium, Jessie twisted around at the waist to watch Casey pad towards them on old blue high-top Converse Chucks, which struck Jessie as somehow more painful to consider than the memories Jacob had inadvertently raised. Something about the Chucks just screamed innocence, but Jessie knew from her own experiences that their wearer, Casey, would be leaving a good chunk of naiveté behind her, should she choose to take the step Jessie was prepared to offer today.

Jessie almost turned away. For her, being a star had its rewards, but the loss of privacy and becoming a seemingly constant target hurt like hell. *Careful what you pray for, Casey,* she thought, running a forefinger over her top and then her bottom lip.

"Hey," the girl managed as she sidled nervously closer.

Jacob summoned up a grin. Casey was her old self today in terms of clothing choices. Baggy hoodie, messy hair, no makeup. "Hey, kid," he said, drawing her into his arms for a hug that for some reason bothered Jessie, who cringed slightly.

Casey, one arm still clinging to Jacob's waist, revolved around to face the woman she felt betrayed him. The guard she carried back in the early days of the workshop was gone, though. In its place was a careful scrutiny and an almost apologetic lowered chin. Casey was not exactly portraying confidence or affability, but Jessie exhaled slowly and dove in anyway.

"Jacob's asked me for a favor, Casey," she started. "And I have to tell you,

I would have said no outright except that someone once believed in me, and I want to believe in you. Plus I love Benjie to pieces and I think he'll be a miserable travelling partner if you don't come on this tour with us. All mopey and sad, you know. Like Eeyore."

Casey straightened and her face went blank. "Am I hearing what I think I'm hearing?" Afraid to look away in case Jessie changed her mind before she looked back, she focused on the pale eyes and the guarded kindness aimed in her direction.

"You come as a student. You study with Phil—a private tutor. You know him from the workshops."

"Uh, yeah. He's amazing!" Casey couldn't breathe.

"Honey," Jessie told her in a subdued voice. "This will change your life. You have the potential to do well. But you still have a lot to learn, and your attitude is going to determine your altitude. And I gotta tell you. The first attitude adjustment has to start with me."

Crestfallen, Casey tried to hide her fear of being left behind by raising her chin and fixing a solemn stare on Jessie. "I can't lie to you," she said. "I'm never going to be a fan of yours."

A groan from Jacob alerted Benjie, across the room, to the fact that Casey had just royally fucked up. But to his, Jacob's, and Casey's surprise, Jessie whooped loudly.

"Finally," she laughed, extending an arm to the young girl whose natural ability on the drums constantly wowed everyone who saw her play, "some honesty. I get so damn tired of everyone kowtowing to me and lying! Charles will sort out the details with you. Welcome aboard, Casey."

"So...." Casey paused, a little confused. "I tell you I don't like you and you still want me to come on tour with you?"

Softening, Jessie spoke quietly, but there was a serious undertone to what she had to say, which Casey picked up on, and which made her listen carefully. "You won't last on the tour unless you can put your prejudices aside, Casey. But I know why you dislike me, and I accept your reasons as honest and true. You're probably the most truthful person I've met in years. Being where I am, where Jacob is now..." She sighed. "You can no longer trust a lot of folks. These people around you now are your friends. They're the ones who you will start this journey with, who know you as you. The ones who join up later will often be tough to figure out." Tilting her head as Casey grasped her hand and shook it, Jessie added, "Do you know what I'm trying to say?"

"Sure. You're telling me all those people who say they like your music really don't." Casey grinned.

"Ha. Good. You get it." Jessie couldn't help herself. She laughed outright.

Jacob cut in. "Casey, what Jessie is saying is that she understands where you're coming from, why you claim to dislike her. But I know you. You like her just fine. You like her music, or you wouldn't be here hoping for an opportunity like this. You have a strong enough backbone that I know you would have no interest in touring with us if you hated the music. But make no mistake—you are being invited on this tour as a favor to me, and to Benjie, too. It's because of your skill, yes. And your potential. But it'll be up to you not to fuck it up by treating Jessie with disrespect. We need your word. You have to let the past go. We have."

"Why do I feel like this is some kind of test?" Casey let go of Jessie's hand, but stayed locked in her gaze.

Jessie met her straight on. "Touring is intense, Casey. You know that, you've done it now. But you got along with everyone you were on tour with. If you hate my guts, my tour will throw you. It won't be the place for you to hone your skills on the skins. Tight quarters, you know the drill. Everyone living out of everyone else's back pocket."

Taking in Jessie's slight frown, Casey hesitated before saying, "I accept your offer, Jessie. I will treat you with the respect I know you deserve. But I will not apologize for believing that you picked the wrong man when you went back to a man who beat you, who has addictions issues and a problem with his temper. And I will not forgive you for letting a man like that raise Jacob's son."

Oh, shit. Jessie's eyes darted over to Jacob, and the blood drained from her face. In a nervous gesture, she tossed her curls again and swallowed.

Jacob jumped in. "I told you, Casey. Jessie and I are good. We've made our peace with who she chooses to spend her life with, despite my reservations about Josh as well." The words he spoke were ringed with warning as he went on. "You can't go there again, kid. You can't bring this up. I'm sorry about your past, but what happened to you and your mother is not our reality—mine and Jessie's, I mean. It's different. And there is a line between business stuff and personal stuff that you can't cross unless you are invited over. Get it?"

"Okay." Casey fixed a solemn gaze on Jessie and waited to see how her new 'sponsor' would respond.

Jessie took the high road. She blinked back tears as she spoke, while at the same time making a mental note to ask Jacob about Casey's past. "When you love someone who eventually knows you as well as Josh and I know each other, on a soul level, and who needs you the way Josh and I need each other, on a soul level, you'll understand, Casey. Although," she murmured, the light fading a little from her eyes, "let me add that I hope you never need anyone as desperately, on any level, as Josh and I need each other."

That shut Casey's high-horse attitude right up. Blinking, the girl simply took that in and nodded, before Jacob sent her back to the crowd with a, "We'll talk later to sort out the details." She strode over to Benjie and accepted his hug with a confused, grateful expression.

Jacob stared at Jessie, and raised a hand to scratch the usual fuzz on his jaw. "Huh," was all he could manage.

"You want the truth?" Jessie asked him, and waited for his half-shrug before she continued. "I wish I was in Calgary with him right now. I always look forward to singing with you, Jacob, but I know you have Kayla now. I know the two of you are watching out for each other, that you've got each other figured out. That you need each other and are there for each other in a way that I couldn't be for you."

"Because of him." There was still hurt in the sad eyes, in the subdued Jacob-duskiness Jessie knew well.

"I'm worried about him, Jacob. He's so deeply imbued in me now that I'm not whole when we're not together."

"Well," Jacob said quietly, studying her to see just how worried she was, "good thing we've got a lot of work ahead of us, then. To take your mind off him."

Jessie's light laughter took him by surprise.

"What?" he asked.

"You think music takes my mind off Josh? My music is all about Josh,

Jacob." Winking, Jessie took his hand, and led him towards the center of the space where everyone was starting to gather so they could get their first rehearsal underway. "Except for the bits that are about you."

It was Jacob's turn to laugh. Drawing up alongside Kayla, he wrapped his left arm loosely around her, and planted a kiss behind one pretty ear. Then he leaned back over to Jessie and whispered in her ear. "And the bit that's about Matt."

At the wistful sadness that crossed her face, Jacob was almost sorry he said it. But Jessie squeezed his hand and said simply, "It's complicated, isn't it? Love?"

"You don't have to tell me twice." Jacob let go of Kayla and treated Jessie to a big, loving hug, which Jessie melted into with closed eyes and a deep inhalation of the green apple scent that seemed soaked into Jacob's being.

Curious, Kayla watched the two embrace, but she knew this was okay. They were all okay now. She understood that some memories were just damn hard to let go of, and that love was eternal when it came to Jessie Wheeler-Sawyer and the men who passed through her often lonely life.

Casey watched them too, with a sense of longing she couldn't begin to understand, until Benjie draped an arm over her and snuggled his lips into her neck. As she turned her small pink lips up to her dancer boyfriend, and lost herself in his gentle warm brown eyes, a sense of belonging passed through Casey. It was accompanied by a sweet feeling of safety that almost, but not quite, erased the hurts she'd carried for most of her life.

"You okay?" Benjie was alight. Casey was coming on the fall tour. As far as he was concerned, her future was assured.

"I thought I was," she told him. "But now I'm not so sure."

Puzzled, Benjie frowned, but the powers-that-be were wrangling the stragglers at the craft table, and the session was starting with a general dissemination of tour information. He would have to ask her later what she meant by that cryptic statement.

Casey, on the other hand, had no intention of explaining. She barely understood it herself, that letting yourself love someone deeply was like exposing the most vulnerable raw nerve endings of your soul; it was like carving their name in the innermost layers of your skin.

Watching her, Jessie had a sense of what the girl was feeling. *I wish you well,* she murmured on unseen fairy wings she sent on rainbow colored light-beams in the girl's direction. *I wish you love without pain. That's what I wish for you.*

Feeling eyes on her again, Casey glanced over at Jessie, leaned her head on Benjie's shoulder, sighed deeply, and nodded. A small smile lit the corners of her lips, and she mouthed, "Thank you."

Biting her lip as a watery depth that she was powerless to hide filled her eyes, Jessie raised her right hand and gave Casey a thumbs-up. "S'okay," she murmured.

A final forced smile, and Jessie turned her face towards Priya, who was laying down the law for her dancers. Jessie crossed her arms, tilted one foot over on its side, and inhaled deeply. Her body was in Vancouver, her heart was in Calgary with Josh and on the ranch with her children, and her spirit was floating somewhere above those cities and above the little province of Prince Edward Island as well, touching and caressing and caring.

And, like God, simply sending out vibes of hope, peace and love.

Chapter Six

A hard knock came at Matt's door just after he got out of the shower one morning, after he'd washed off the sweat from his morning run. Also down the drain that morning had gone a chunk of the loneliness he woke with, that clung to his soul like a ghost. The knock interrupted his weekly shave, which Matt was carrying out in the nude as he drip-dried. He cursed at a drop of blood forming on his jawline, which was a direct result of being startled from the knock. Nobody ever knocked at Matt's cottage door.

"Coming, coming, hold your horses," he called to his visitor as he grabbed a well-worn pair of dark plaid shorts and stepped quickly into them. Zipping and buttoning them up as he moved to the screen door he saw, from his side, that his visitor appeared to be a hefty middle-aged man who was quite distraught. The guy was carrying something, something not too heavy, but something...limp and grey.

"Oh, Jesus!" Launching himself quickly forward over the last few feet, Matt swung open the screen door and stared at Drifter, who was quiet and still in the man's arms, but whose doe-y eyes searched Matt. Matt reached out a trembling hand and grazed it gently over the puppy's head. "What... how bad?"

The visitor was beside himself. "I was watching the kite boarders in the Basin. It's my fault. I didn't see the little guy. I think his front leg might be broken."

Upon closer scrutiny, Matt had to agree. As if he, too, thought the man holding him was correct, Drifter managed a tiny whimper and closed his eyes, but he shifted his body as if he wanted to be in Matt's arms.

"Can I?" Matt reached for the puppy.

"Look, do you want to get a blanket or something? We can lay him on that. It might make it easier for you to move him in order to get him to the vet." Stricken, the tourist stayed still.

"Oh. Yes, that's a…uh…the dog's not actually my dog. Drifter belongs to the woman next door. Catherine. But I'll get a blanket. C'mon in." Vaulting into the small sun porch, Matt grabbed a country quilt and laid it on the sofa. "Let's put him down here."

The movement hurt the dog, and Matt winced. The tourist extended a hand. "Name's Mac. My family and I are camping for the week at Twin Shores, down the road." Hesitating, he pointed a big finger next door. "Should I go get your neighbor?"

"I'll go. Look, Mac, this puppy is impulsive and stubborn. Has a mind of its own." *Like someone else I know.* Matt guffawed quietly as Jessie crossed his mind. "This wasn't your fault."

Mac reached in his back pocket and removed his wallet. "Here's my card. I'll cover the vet bill."

Looking past him, Matt scanned the man's vehicle. An older model Dodge Caravan, licensed from Ontario, was parked there. A young blonde woman in the passenger seat was focused on the cottage, and a small child, a red-haired girl, stared out of the open back window, her face tear-streaked. Behind her, Matt could see a younger child, a boy, in a booster seat. This husband and father struck Matt as someone who likely scraped his dollars together to make this dream trip to Prince Edward Island happen.

Glancing at the card, he noted that the man lived in the Ontario city of Kitchener and worked as a sales associate at a plumbing store. Matt made a mental note to ask Charles to coordinate some concert tickets for this family, for Jessie and Jacob's Toronto *Sacred Peace* concert. Accepting the card, he shook his head. "Consider it already covered. What's your site number? I'll drop by later and let you know how Drifter's doing. If you're down at the beach, I'll leave a note on your windshield."

"We're always to the right of the boardwalk on the beach. Just come down. I'll have a few brewskies on hand." Extending a hand, Mac said a quiet, "Thank you, uh…You sure, man?"

"Matt. No worries. Tell your wife and kids this puppy will be just fine."

Mac stood for an extra second at the screen door, holding it open with his foot. "You strike me as a good man, sir. Drop down to the beach later. I'll see you."

Salt of the earth, Matt thought as he watched the big guy move hurriedly towards his family. *Good guy living a good life, trying to do the best for his family.*

The more Matt was away from the circus of the Keating-Sawyer world, the more he was becoming aware that there was a whole world out there of good people just trying to do the best they could with what they had to work with. Twin Shores, the nearby campground, was full of such people—middle-class families, some in tents and some in old trailers, some staying there seasonally and some, mostly retirees, travelling North America in large, expensive motor homes. They all had a few basic things in common, starting with a love for nature and for a simple life by the water that delivered glorious sunsets. They had sincere gratitude for what P.E.I. and the cozy campground had to offer them—white sand dunes, red cliffs, après beach ice cream, an active and involved programming staff, and a relaxed community that loved to welcome newbies at their evening campfires. Regardless of the campers' circumstances in life—how much financial security they had; how much tragedy or loss they experienced; whether their families were large or small; whether they spoke French, English; whatever culture they hailed from—visitors to Twin Shores went home with healing memories of a peaceful place.

This man, Mac? Well, obviously hitting someone's puppy wasn't on the agenda of his family's trip. But Matt felt certain Drifter would recover, unless there were internal injuries… Leaping back into the sun porch, he knelt by the puppy and touched his head. With a gentle scratch on the soft grey fur, he said, "Let me go get your mother, Drifter, and we'll take a little drive. Give me five."

He didn't have far to go to look for Catherine. Matt's neighbor was in a panic, hurrying over the lush grass leading up from the cliff bordering their section of the Darnley Basin. A leash was dangling from her right hand.

Spotting Matt, she called out to him. "Have you seen my little mongrel? Drifter took off on me, and I…" Spying Matt's drawn, serious eyes, she froze. Catherine had seen eyes like those before.

"Come with me," Matt said. "Let's take a drive." He was already fingering through his iPhone to find the nearest vet. "Drifter got in the way of a family from Ontario. He won't go near cars again."

Catherine went pale, and remained as silent and still as a statue.

Matt, who was already walking back up the gravel road, spun back around and studied her. "He'll be fine, Catherine. He'll get a little extra attention on the beach, that's all, lots of hugs from kids. Drifter's just ramping up the cuteness factor by likely getting a cast put on one leg."

"I can't…he got hit by a car?"

Dropping his cell phone to his thigh, Matt tried to wrap his mind around what was immobilizing his neighbor. Yes, it was scary, hearing that her dog had been hurt, but why wasn't she running to Drifter's side? Why did she look like she was about to go into shock? *Or maybe she is in shock,* Matt thought, wondering at pet owners and their capacity to love their animals as humans. Although…yeah, he was kind of in love with Drifter already too. Drifter who was, at that moment, likely lonely and scared and wondering where his people were.

Treading down the gravel to Catherine, Matt took the leash from her hand. "Go lock up your place and grab one of those soft toys Drifter likes. I'll drive." The gentle tone worked, but Matt was saddened by what he saw in the woman's eyes. It was a haunted look he knew well. Jessie was never far from his mind.

Ducking her head, Catherine finally moved, although it struck Matt as a bit unnerving that she didn't run to her dog's aid first. Instead, she was moving as if she were a robot, as if her joints hurt when she walked, although Matt recognized that it was something in the woman's soul that was likely causing the most pain.

Ten minutes later they were on the way to Kensington, to the nearest veterinary clinic Matt could find. It was a silent ride, peppered only with Drifter's tiny whimpers. The puppy was on his owner's lap, but she wasn't looking at him. Occasionally Matt reached over and gave Drifter a tender scratch behind his ear, and he was rewarded with the puppy's sad eyes, filled with love and longing, fixed on Matt's kind face.

At the clinic, it was Catherine's frightened eyes that begged her neighbor for help. Matt had taken the puppy from her lap after he parked and now, in the clinic, with one wary eye on Catherine, he followed the vet into an examining room, absently wondering if Drifter's owner would even join them.

Much later, Drifter was casted up the way Matt expected the puppy would be. Cleared of further injuries, he slept his traumatic experience away on Catherine's lap all the way back to Darnley, and then on Matt's porch swing, which seemed to be the puppy's favorite spot. Idly, after settling him, Matt watched Catherine stare at her dog as she stood at the top of Matt's steps, one hand on the rail and one fidgeting slightly.

She's ready to run, Matt thought inwardly. *She wants to run.*

"You've lost someone." That got her attention. Catherine's gaze moved from her sleeping puppy over to Matt, who was standing by his screen door, waiting, unsure. "Recently, I think."

"I thought you worked in security." The words were spoken quietly, the rhetorical statement timorous and weak.

"I know someone who lost a lot. I used to see that look pretty much every day, in my old life. I guess you could say I know it well."

Catherine's lips moved as she tried to find the words. "My daughter," she eventually admitted. "She was fifteen. Her name was Carly."

Damn. A nauseating ripple crippled Matt. Katy flitted across his mind. He hadn't seen her in a few months. "I'm sorry, Catherine. I'm so, so sorry."

"It was almost six months ago now," she said, and waved a hand absently down towards where Drifter was hit. "A car. She got hit when she was out running." Catherine didn't elaborate. It was enough to get the words out which, in a weird kind of way, actually felt pretty good, as if releasing them brought Carly's vivid presence back to life.

Matt's response was tender. Caring. "You want to sit with me for a while? I have some iced coffee in the fridge. Or we can go stronger."

"Didn't you say at one point that you need to let that man know about Drifter?"

"I should probably ease his worry, yes. I can take a ride down to Twin Shores on my bike." Gesturing to Drifter, Matt added, "Stay here since he's here. Help yourself to the coffee or to whatever else you'd like. I won't be long."

"How about I make us something to eat, Matt? Would you be okay with that?"

"I don't have a lot of food…"

"Oh. Okay." Catherine toed a paint blister on the step. It separated from the step and floated away under the Birkenstock sandal she was wearing.

"It's not that I don't want to, I just honestly don't have anything much. I should have picked up a few steaks or something when we were in town."

Looking expectantly up at him, Catherine tried, "Twin Shores has a camp store. Grab us some steaks and I'll raid my pantry for potatoes. I have some fresh zucchini we can grill as well."

Her small smile warmed his heart, but there was still a huge wall between them, and its name was fear. Apprehensive, Matt nodded. "Okay," he agreed. "All right." Moving down the steps past her, he hesitated just below Catherine. "Maybe you can tell me about Carly. When I get back."

"Maybe." She tried to smile but it came out feeble and crooked. Shifting the tide, she posed a question back at him. "Maybe you can tell me your war story too."

"Maybe." *Some. Definitely not all.*

Biking up the gravel lane, then turning left and cycling down towards the campground, continuously passed by an ever-changing parade of trailers and new campers coming in for the week, Matt lost himself in thought. How much could he tell? How much could he share? Not that he wasn't necessarily willing. In fact, it would be liberating to have someone around to listen to him for a change, someone with whom he could swap out the old pain.

The thing about Matt's life, though, was that it had been spent—a lot of it, anyway—with a well-known, well-loved celebrity. With a troubled woman and her troubled husband, who was also a huge star. Then there was Jacob Ryan, and even Kelly Reilly, by virtue of *Mystic Nights* and Matt's brother Michael's association with her. Add in Charlie and Jack Deacon, and everyone else Matt had met over the years…Tom Ryan and other legendary singers…Well, bringing these people up would change whatever tenuous relationship Matt was starting to form with his neighbor and new friend. He would have to go easy.

A few minutes later, Matt found Mac on the beach and gave him the good news.

"Stay for a drink?" Mac asked him, his pudgy hand holding out a beer, but Matt shook his head.

"Tomorrow, maybe? Drifter's mother's making us dinner."

"You got it. We'll be here. We're soaking up as many rays as we can this week. And thanks for understanding, man. There aren't many like you in the world. You sure about that vet bill?"

"I learned from the best. And yeah, I'm sure." That first part slipped out, and Matt almost choked when he realized he'd spoken the sentiment aloud. Clapping his new friend on the shoulder, he waved to the man's wife, who was coming up from the water with a child's plastic yellow sand bucket in her hand. "Nice to meet you, ma'am," he said amicably after Mac introduced the wholesome blonde as Wendy. "How's the water?"

"Cold." Laughing, she motioned towards a boy and girl, maybe seven and nine, crouched over a tipsy sand castle they were building at the water's edge. "Although they don't seem to mind."

Shortly, after agreeing to meet up on the beach the next day, Matt trudged back up the wooden ramp to a thick green nautical rope that segregated the sensitive sand dunes from hundreds of potentially damaging feet. He'd left his bike there, leaning carefully against the rope on the red dirt lane side. Grabbing it, he pondered the few hundred people lounging on the beach today. Mostly families and, in a lot of cases, extended families with friends, he was stricken with the usual longing for the people he'd considered his family for so long. Even Steve and Charlie and their kids had become close to him over the years. Leaving Jessie's direct employ was like divorcing all of them.

When Matt got back to his cottage with the steaks, he was pleasantly surprised to see that Catherine had a salad already well under way. She was quiet, though, and chopped the veggies she brought over from her cottage with a restraint that told Matt she was likely distracted. *Her daughter,* he figured rightly. *And Drifter. She's had a tough day.*

At one point, as she tossed tomatoes on top of an arugula-spinach mix in a white plastic bowl, she looked over at a small framed photograph on the microwave. Matt followed her glance, and his heart clenched. With her knife pointing at it, Catherine said without looking at him, "That's Jessie Wheeler."

He found his voice, but the first few words came out slightly garbled.

"Yes. And the girl in the picture with her belongs to me. I have a daughter, Catherine. One child. Her name is Katy. She's out of school now."

"Ah. She survived high school. Glad to know it." Sighing, setting down her knife, Catherine turned to Matt. "I'm sorry. Of course I'm glad your daughter is okay. So…are you divorced?"

"Starting this right now, are we? Finally? The inquisition?" A tiny fleck of humor danced across Matt's eyes.

Catherine laughed. "Yes. Why the heck not? Let's get it over with."

"I am going through a divorce. Yes."

"Recently?"

"We separated in January. Okay, next. Or should I say, what's your story? Divorced?"

A cloud washed over Catherine's face. Turning away from him, she starting slicing up an English cucumber. "Yep. Oh, yeah. Divorced his sorry ass." She raised the knife and lowered it with a nasty slice of the cucumber.

"Sorry. Remind me not to piss you off."

She chuckled lightly. "Some day I'll tell you that story. Not today."

"When you're ready, Catherine."

Smiling up at him, she said, "I guess you don't get to our age without a few battle-worn secrets, eh Matt?"

"No, I suppose not." Reaching for a knife, Matt asked with a nod towards the salad, "What's next? Red onion?"

"Sure. Thanks."

Only the sounds of happily chirping birds outside, and wafting gauzy curtains buoyed by the occasional sea breeze gust, entered the cottage sanctuary for the next few minutes, until Catherine broke the comfortable silence with, "So how did your daughter end up managing to grab a picture with Jessie Wheeler? Not to mention one that looks like they're best friends?"

At Matt's silence, she looked over at him. A furrow was lining his brow, and he seemed to be trying to work out what to say.

"Where are you from, Matt? Where's home?" she added.

He stared at the red onion, but paused before mobilizing the knife for another slice. "Vancouver, actually," he said.

"So I suppose it's not a stretch to assume that you might run into someone like Jessie Wheeler occasionally. Stars like her are always doing public events, right?"

"Vancouver's a happening spot for film and television projects, yes. And music. Culture in general, I guess." Matt was cycling around the topic at hand but he was not ready to divulge his association with Jessie just yet. Cursing himself for not tucking the photograph away before inviting Catherine into his cottage, he stopped talking and focused on helping prepare their salad.

Catherine washed her hands and moved onto the steak. "Marinade," she said, holding up a container of something Matt assumed to be a homemade concoction. "Okay?"

"Suit yourself." On edge now, Matt pulled out a glass baking dish. "Use this?" Trying to corner right, he asked about Carly. "What was important to Carly?"

Taking the dish from his outstretched hand, Catherine started to drift into a deeper conversation about Jessie. "Music. Your picture threw me. Carly was into music. Jessie Wheeler and Jacob Ryan were her absolute favorites. It broke her heart when they split up and stopped playing together. That last ballad they did..." She chewed her lip and poked holes in the steaks with a fork to let the marinade soak inside the flesh. "It was addictive. She'd come home from school and disappear for a run, always with Jessie's music on. She was listening to a Jessie Wheeler playlist when she was hit by the car. I expect that's why she was hit. She didn't hear the car."

This was a huge admission, and Matt had the sense to recognize it as such. It floored him, though, making him suck in his gut and emit a small shocked sound that got Catherine's attention.

"What?" she asked, focusing her gaze on him.

"N-nothing." Drained, Matt slumped over the counter. This would kill Jessie, to know this about a fifteen-year-old girl. That she died because she was too focused on Jessie's music to realize a car was swerving in her direction; that she was too caught up in the music to get the hell out of the way. Blinking, he wiped a sweaty arm over his brow and pictured Jessie's sad eyes at hearing that tidbit of information, and the hurt on her face as she digested it.

"I don't know if that gives me solace or makes it worse," Catherine was saying. "Whether I should be angry at some singer I don't even know, or whether I should be glad Carly was listening to music she loved when she died."

Matt was speechless. This was too much. Averting her pointed stare, he let his gaze drift over to the photo of Jessie and Katy. Jessie, in one of her happier moments, had her left arm draped casually but intimately over Katy's shoulders. Both girls were smiling widely enough to crack their jaws in two. Jessie's eyes were so bright, so lit beneath the surface by joy in that photo, that Matt had chosen it above all others to take with him on his seemingly endless journey. He remembered the day it was taken clearly—it was a night Katy was babysitting so Josh and Jessie could sneak out to a movie. Matt was about to escort them to the theater while Dan stayed with Katy and the kids.

Katy had come to the house early so Jessie could give her a guitar lesson while Josh cooked dinner; Emily-Grace had sat in with them, learning a few simple chords herself as Jessie and Katy worked on more difficult bar chords. Matt had sat at the kitchen island and chopped vegetables, much as he was doing now, for pizzas Josh was putting together for all of them. The men had joked at the laughter coming from the media room downstairs, deciding that there was more female giddiness coming from the space than actual learning. That's when Matt had followed Josh downstairs and snapped the picture with his iPhone.

Happiness. Joy. Peace. An extraordinary family enjoying a time of sheer bliss at a rare juncture in their lives when all seemed well, for a change. The memory gutted him. Matt closed his eyes.

"Matt?"

A low whimper started from just outside the nearby window.

"I'll go check on Drifter," Matt said rather abruptly. Moving to the door, he sank against the wall, unseen by his visitor, before he knelt before the dog and offered comfort, which he took back in spades when the puppy licked his wrist. "I know it hurts," he said to the animal, and the moist, trusting eyes took him in, and said the same right back at Matt.

In the kitchen, Catherine was astounded. Maybe Matt's daughter was gone too? Otherwise why would bringing up the picture cause such a physiological reaction? Scanning the picture, it struck her funny, though. Jessie

Wheeler's cheek was pressed firmly against Katy's, and it just seemed there was an intimacy there that you wouldn't ordinarily see in a random photo with a star.

She didn't bring the subject up again, but Matt was quiet all through dinner, and hardly made eye contact. Later, he carried Drifter across the lawn to Catherine's cottage, laid him down in his puppy bed, and backed out of the room with hardly a word.

An hour later, Catherine stood in her cottage with the lights out and watched him settle into a camp chair by his campfire, a beer in one hand and a cooler at his side.

"Can't handle my dead daughter," she caught herself thinking. "That's what it was." Quietly, she closed her inside door and tiptoed down the hall to bury her face in a pillow and wish she had never met the good-looking, dimpled man from Vancouver, with all his deep, dark secrets.

Chapter Seven

A few days later, in Calgary, the *Sacred Peace* production team was engrossed in filming a nightmarish scene. A large number of extras had been cast to participate in a choreographed fight scene that involved multiple difficult shots. Charlie was on set, acting in the scene along with both Josh and Shanda, and Charles and Jonathon were hanging around the perimeter, consulting with the director when questions came up about the script or the action. Jonathon had written this episode, which was fine-tuned by the writers in the production's writers' room. Characteristic of his attention to detail, it was intricate and intense.

The script called for a tense standoff to ramp up into a fight scene inside the bar. Josh's character Bobby, the sheriff, ended the scene sprawled out on his back on the floor with a large burly extra straddling him, bent on choking him.

The first few takes were a little rough—not bad overall, but there were details to iron out in such a dense scene. The director, after consulting Jonathon and Charles, started calling for retakes. As the morning wore on and shots changed to reverses and multiple close-ups, cast and crew started to find the work tedious and exhausting. Josh, whose shoulder ached every time he hit the floor, and whose leg pained every time the big blonde guy attacking him jumped on him, was starting to dread each take.

Yet, he was getting through the shoot. Part of the motivation to suck it up and carry on was the simple knowledge that Jessie was coming back from Vancouver today. She would be around to watch the afternoon's shooting, which would take place in a small valley about a half hour drive outside the city. After wrap, Jessie would travel home with Josh. Already he anticipated stopping at the same dirt road where they had paused to make love on their way to Calgary the past Monday morning. Picturing her in his arms, gently rocking over him while he held onto her hips and lost himself in those beautiful blue eyes, Josh missed the First A.D. call, "First positions, please!" on the newest take.

An elbow in his side jarred him as the entire cast and crew snickered.

"Sawyer. Stop daydreaming. Get with the program."

Charlie.

Embarrassed, his cheeks flaming red, Josh moved to his first position and readied himself for another grueling round of street fighting in the *Sacred Peace* bar. Rubbing his elbow, he braced himself for a new onslaught of bruises.

The first part of the take went well. This was Shanda's close-up, so Josh didn't work quite as hard as he would for his own, since he wasn't featured on camera. The down side was that nobody was really watching him while the camera was rolling, with the exception of Arnie, whose hawk-like eyes rarely left his charge.

Standing at the perimeter of the set next to a large orange-gelled 2 K light that towered above him, Arnie had long ago learned that you could never accidentally get caught in the shot if you stuck close to gear. He'd made it his habit to position himself near lights, which kept him out of the camera's way and which usually still gave him a good view of the action.

Today was tough, though, even for a watcher. There were just so many cast in this scene, and even though the current shot was a close-up, this particular director wanted everyone to continue running their action, to avoid missing something that wouldn't cut together in the editing room later. So by the time they got to Shanda's close-up, the team had already done about twenty takes, and Arnie was tense as he watched Josh struggle with increasing pain. Between cuts Charlie was watching Josh too, Arnie knew, but Charlie had his own street fighting to deal with during takes. Biting his lip, Arnie caught Josh's eye at the end of the take, and sent him a shake of the head.

Groaning as he stood, Josh shrugged at Arnie. He was well accustomed to long days of intense shooting. Hours and hours working on one scene would likely end up cut into only a few minutes that would actually make it on screen.

The crew reset, and Arnie growled under his breath. He didn't like the big blonde guy that, increasingly as the takes went on, seemed to be playing rougher. This last take, the extra shoved Josh's head down so hard that Arnie was pretty sure Josh was seeing stars.

"Almost done," the director hollered. "James, one more, please. For 'sound' this time."

A loud rebuke was heard from the boom guy, who didn't want to take the blame for messing up and having to do one more take, but it was in jest. Despite the tired minds and bodies, all of whom were close to being broken for lunch after six long hours of shooting, everyone on the crew got along well, and there were no hard feelings. Josh managed a small laugh too as he repositioned himself at the top of the scene.

The take started off well. Everyone moved through their blocking exactly as they were supposed to. But near the end of the take, there was one glitch that alerted Arnie to the fact that something was not happening as it should. This time when Josh hit the floor, Arnie could see that he lost it for a moment, that the big blonde extra was apparently using this last opportunity to show the star that he was the boss, that he could act, that he could fight, whatever. Struggling against him, Josh regained his equilibrium, but Arnie cursed and went rigid. Trying to see past the haze of murky bodies thrashing around in front of him, he wished he could call out to Josh to see if he was okay, but it would piss everyone off big time if he ruined the take by shouting.

Eventually the path to Josh cleared, and Arnie only took a few seconds before muttering, "To hell with the take." Using his elbows to shove bodies aside so he could pass through, he hollered at Charlie at the same time that he grasped the big blonde by the back of his coat and threw him across the room.

Josh was out cold, the extra's fingerprints imprinted in his neck.

Charlie turned when he heard his name called, and barely missed being pounded when he lost his focus and didn't duck when he was supposed to. When he saw Arnie in the shot, Charlie instantly recognized that something was wrong. As he scrambled towards Josh and Arnie, he heard the director crying, "What the hell? Cut. Cut!"

Arnie waved Charlie towards Josh, but pivoted around on one squeaky clean Nike to grab the blonde extra by the bicep. Charles and Jonathon were clueing in to what happened, and both were now at Josh's side with Charlie. Carter was on set too, and he came running, brushing his long dark hair out of his eyes as he knelt next to Charlie to offer what assistance he could.

"Medic!" called Charles, as Charlie slapped his friend's face and called his name. "Now!"

The set was quickly immersed in a quiet frenzy as the First A.D., technically the safety officer for the production, got on his walkie to call for immediate assistance.

As Josh started to come around, wondering what the hell was going on, Jon strode briskly over to Arnie.

"Jon, call the police," was all that Arnie had to say to him.

The extra, whose name they eventually found out was Alexander, protested vehemently. "I didn't mean to! I was just into it, you know?"

"The police," Arnie growled. "You hear me, Jon?" He was totally overstepping his boundaries as personal cast security, but this cast happened to be the executive producer's biological son, so Jon snapped his fingers and the police were called.

Charlie, kneeling by Josh, was shaking as Josh accepted his and Carter's help and leveraged himself to a half-sitting position against the wall. "Jesus, Josh." Charlie was wiping anxious fingers through the knot on the tie he was wearing as part of his costume, trying to loosen it even though it was already fairly loose. "What the hell happened?"

"You tell me," Josh rasped, fingering his sore neck. "That guy's a fucking ox."

Charles reached for Josh's fingers and removed them from his neck. Studying the red marks, he proclaimed, "Jessie's not going to like this very much. Can you breathe okay, son?"

Meeting his pseudo father-in-law's concerned eyes, Josh swallowed painfully. "I'm fine. It was nothing, Charles. Like the guy said, he just got into it."

A frown lined Charlie's mouth. "On Shanda's close-up? Give me a break. He wasn't even on camera! He should have been easing off."

"Damn straight." Carter clapped Josh on the shoulder before standing and moving to help Arnie detain the culprit.

"He's an extra, Charlie." Josh's voice was gruff, tired. The medics were at his side now, and Charles and Charlie both backed off to let them in. "He likely didn't know any better." His gaze didn't leave Charlie's somber face, though, and as the medics treated Josh's neck with an ice-cold compress and fired questions at him, Charlie put his hands on his hips and turned away.

His eyes locked themselves into the pale eyes of the man Arnie still held in a vise-grip. There was something creepy about the guy, and he was indeed a new extra on the show, but still...in all likelihood he was probably just as Josh said, an extra who didn't know any better.

But what if he wasn't? Could he have typed that note from last week? Could he have somehow engineered the PCP fiasco? If it was him, who was he working with?

Sickened, Charlie caught Charles' grim expression before looking back at Josh. His friend was sitting with his good leg bent, the fingers of his sore arm gripping the knee of his damaged leg, his head back and his eyes closed. Lips pressed into a thin line, it was obvious Josh was in pain long before the big burly blonde put him out.

"Three more weeks," Charlie bit off to Charles. "Then we're done. We just need to get through three more weeks." Chagrined, he changed his tune to, "Josh has to get through three more weeks. And we have to help him."

As if he heard him, Josh's eyes flitted open and he met Charlie's worried stare. There were so many extras on set today...and so many crew. This episode would hit social media as quickly as the PCP crap. Nodding as if he understood, Charlie moved to his assistant at the perimeter of the set and asked her for his cell phone. Fishing it out of her pocket, she gave it to him and he quickly dialed Jessie's number. Charlie had to leave a message, though. Jessie was on the jet and apparently not taking calls.

While Arnie handed Alexander off to the police to be questioned, everyone else broke for lunch.

Still recovering from the shock of their final morning shot, as they were sliding their trays into metal slots for the catering staff to clean, Charlie broke it to Josh that Jessie hadn't taken his call.

Josh mumbled, "She's likely sleeping. They were all going out last night, apparently. The whole tour group."

"I'd rather catch her by phone than have her see this on social media," Charlie said, a dark tone to his words. "I'll try Dan." Moving to make the call, Charlie frowned when Josh covered his hand with his.

"Don't," Josh said. "Tell her in person, or let me tell her if I'm waiting for a setup. She'll lose it, Charlie. I'd rather she's with one of us."

"Dan's with her."

"Dan's not Matt. They're not close like that. He's closer to the kids than he is to Jessie."

"All right." Dropping the phone back in his front jeans pocket, Charlie paused. "I'll watch for her this afternoon, then."

"Thanks, Charlie. Look…I haven't told Jessie about that note. I don't want her to know. And this, today, was just an extra that got carried away. That's all."

"Yeah. I'm sure that's all it was."

"They're letting him go, right?"

"I think so. According to Charles, the cops will likely let the asshole walk. There is no real reason to hold him." Watching Josh for a reaction, Charlie tried to look indifferent. He failed miserably, and Josh swallowed bitterly.

"Just watch out for my high strung wife," Josh demanded as he strode away. "Don't give her any reason to believe this was more than a stupid accident."

"Which is all it was." Charlie exhaled as Josh moved away. "I hope."

Shortly, the cast and crew set out for the hill to finish their day. The afternoon's shots were easier, involving only a few cast, albeit three of them would be on horseback, which occasionally stressed out the camera operator. These riders were very skilled, though, so it was expected the afternoon's shots would go much easier than the shots from the morning.

Unable to stand the pain in his leg and shoulder any longer, which were now accompanied by an aching head and a throbbing neck, Josh acquiesced to Charlie's demands and took a few Advil. Jessie would be along soon. From his position in the valley on horseback, Josh kept looking up to the top of the hill, where Charlie, who wasn't in this scene, stood with

Arnie, keeping a grim-faced watch. After her arrival, Jessie would surely appear next to them.

As Josh expected, Jessie arrived on set hung-over and tired, but bouncing from excitement. The hard work of Vancouver was behind her, the group had made great strides during the initial tour rehearsals, and by all accounts the week at the ranch had gone just fine with Dee, Carlotta, the kids, and Josh when he was home in the late evenings.

Now, she left Dan just behind her to chat with Charlie, who she bypassed so she could go straight to her old friend Arnie and suss him out about Josh's week. Cozying up below the arm Arnie raised for her to squiggle underneath, she sighed at the view before her. At the bottom of the hill, maybe a hundred feet away, was Josh with two other riders—Shanda and Carter, Jessie saw—between takes, waiting for the First A.D.'s relayed cue via walkie to an assistant closer to the cast.

Josh looked up, and Jessie waved. Saluting back, he didn't smile, and even from that distance Jessie could sense a certain tension in his body in the way he sat more rigid on the horse when he saw her.

"Huh," she thought, squinting in order to see him better. "How was Josh's week, Arnie?" It didn't take her more than a few seconds to ascertain that Arnie, too, was tense.

Her old buddy and Downtown Eastside savior raised his shoulders proudly and said, "You need to talk to Charlie."

"What? Why?" Ducking out from under Arnie's arm, Jessie faced him, and glanced behind him to frame Charlie up in her vision as well. Charlie was watching her with ill-concealed nerves.

Stepping past Arnie, Jessie accosted her ex-fiancé. "You know, for an actor you're really shitty at hiding your feelings, Charlie. What's up with Josh? Did something happen with Shanda?" A wave of nausea snaked its way over her stomach. Wrapping both arms around her belly, she raised her chin and waited for the punch to hit her in the gut.

Charlie scanned the action at the bottom of the hill. The cast was still waiting for the camera operator and director to settle on the frame size for the shot, so their cue to move was delayed. Charlie half-expected Josh to rein his mount in Jessie's direction and come charging up the hill towards them.

"I'm waiting." Placing her booted feet a hip's width apart, Jessie's nostrils flared. Her eyes were serious, alert, on fire.

Sucking in a long breath, Charlie fixed her solidly in his gaze, but the eyes that locked onto Jessie were fatigued and pained. Worried. "Jessie, we had an incident on set earlier today. Just before we broke for lunch."

A cold sweat broke out on Jessie's forehead. Shifting her weight, drawing up her shoulders, she asked, "What kind of incident?" By Charlie's anxious demeanor, she knew that whatever happened demanded her full attention. Josh was okay, though, so…no need to freak out. *Count to ten,* she said inwardly, thinking of Matt's old trick to keep her calm. *Keep calm and carry on…one, two, three…*

"We shot a fight scene. One of the extras got carried away."

"Okay, so…someone got hurt? That happened on *Drifters* once. A guy got knocked out in a bar fight."

Charlie sighed and looked away. Out of the corner of his eye, he could see Arnie watching them. Dan, who had moved to Arnie's side to give Jessie and Charlie some space, was giving him a funny look.

"Our ambitious extra had your husband in a choke-hold Jessie. Josh… lost consciousness for a few minutes."

Tossing her head as she took that in, Jessie moved her arms up and crossed them over her chest. Lifting a hand a second later to wrap a tendril of hair around her finger, she aimed her baby blues at Charlie and frowned. "Lost consciousness? Seriously, Charlie?" Afraid to twist around to fix a hard stare at Josh, who she figured would have his eagle eyes on her until he was cued to move, she braced herself. "Tell me more. Really. I can't wait to hear the rest of this exhilarating story."

"Arnie was watching him. He pulled the guy off."

"And?"

"We had medics on set, as usual for big scenes like that. They looked him over. They suggested he go to the hospital but your stubborn husband said he was fine."

"Is he? Fine?"

Oh, fuck I hate lying to her. Jessie fucking knows me. Charlie emitted a low *ppffffttt* and tried to maintain his gaze with Jessie, but he couldn't do it.

He looked past her down the hill to Josh. Relieved, he heard 'action' finally called. Below, Josh refocused on the shot at hand and urged his horse into action.

A low growl brought Charlie's attention back to Jessie. "What the hell aren't you telling me, Charlie?"

Opening his arms, Charlie shook his head slowly from side to side. "That's all, little girl," he told her, lying through his teeth by virtue of omitting the threat only he, Charles, Jonathon, Matt and Josh knew about, unless you counted the scumbag who typed it in the first place, and the police who were still assessing it.

A sharp finger landed in his chest and shoved him backwards.

"Ouch! Jesus, girl!"

"You know more than you're telling! I can see him down there riding, so I know he's okay, but what am I missing?"

Arnie, recognizing Charlie's fear, sauntered over, with a curious Dan close behind. Taking Jessie's elbow, he steered her around to face him.

It was a warm day, and she was wearing a cute halter top that flowed over the top of her jeans. Her arm was sweaty, and she still smelled a bit like all the beer she consumed last night with Kayla, Jacob, and the tour gang. Staring hard at Arnie, she was gulping past this new fear.

"Jessie, all you need to know is that Josh is going to have a few bruises on his neck but he is, indeed, fine. We had a scare, that's all. We called in the police and they had a chat with the extra but in the end it was determined he just, as Charlie said, got carried away."

"By trying to choke my husband. It was a big scene, you said. How many takes in was this?"

Nobody answered her.

She raised her voice. It came out pitchy and frightened. "Why did nobody see this coming? Why did it get to the point where Josh passed out?" Flinging off Arnie's arm, she cursed and looked away, then threw a last sentence over her shoulder. "Too busy playing actor instead of producer, Charlie?"

Charlie grimaced and wisely chose not to respond to the biting comment. He had long ago learned that when Jessie was in this kind of mood, rising to the bait she tossed his way only served to escalate them into nasty fights.

Below, the director had called 'cut.' Josh was once again focused on the action at the top of the hill.

"I can't wait for this to be over." Jessie's angry declaration was aimed, like a well-placed arrow, staunchly at Charlie, who buckled slightly under the pressure of the threat to Josh that he knew about but felt he couldn't share with the guy's wife. "I'm sorry, Charlie," Jessie was adding. "I know this show is your baby, but I want my husband safe by my side. I would like to stop worrying about Shanda wanting to fuck him, and about people 'accidentally' strangling my husband and lacing his goddamn chowder with PCP!"

At that, she stormed around in a wide circle and took in Josh on horseback below. Swallowing past the ache in her stomach, which seemed to be creating an increasingly large raw hole there, Jessie scanned her eyes over his environment. He seemed safe enough; there were lots of crew around, and Carter, a super-experienced rider, was nearby. No cougars were in the immediate vicinity, and no bears either.

"One breath at a time," she told herself, with Matt's wise, tender voice in her mind. "One fucking second at a time."

Arnie, Dan and Charlie left her alone to watch the rest of the current shot. After the director called, "Cut, that's a keeper," the crew had to change lenses and camera position.

Josh pissed off the head wrangler by immediately taking the opportunity to ride up the hill to his wife. At the top, he leapt off the horse by swinging a leg forward over its neck.

Charlie, visibly relieved since the task gave him something to do, vaulted ahead to take the reins of the frisky animal, which freed him from Jessie's infuriated, concerned scrutiny.

Josh, in his sheriff's jacket, shirt and tie, pants and boots, topped off by a sun-faded brown cowboy hat worn low over his brow, almost stopped Jessie's heart when he took her arm and led her ten paces away from any crew who might be inclined to listen in.

"Jesus, you look good in that outfit." Blinking with approval, Jessie ran her palms over Josh's damp chest and leaned in for a sweet, lingering kiss. "Not much wonder Shanda loses her mind around you."

Josh didn't respond to Jessie's playful flirtation, which he knew damn well was mostly voiced just to ease the tension. He jumped right to the issue at hand. "I've got about five minutes," he told her, wiping a sweaty strand of hair off her face and once again aching for time alone with her on the dirt road on the way back to the ranch. That halter top was simply adorable on his wife's gorgeous dancer's body, the way it flared over her jeans like that, which in turn draped over the worn brown cowboy boots she loved to wear, even in this heat. Josh made a mental note to tell Dan and Arnie to give them some space on the way home.

Slowing his heart rate by refocusing, he insisted to Jessie, "Tell me what you need to tell me."

A quick downturn to her lips revealed to Josh that his wife was going into royal Jessie Wheeler pout mode. A flip of one of her boots onto its side accentuated the childish gesture. Peeking up at Josh from underneath moist eyelashes, Jessie sighed and let her hands slide down his chest and stomach to his belt.

Josh gulped and let his head shake just the slightest bit. His lips parted and he inhaled.

"I know that look." Jessie shoved her right hand a little further down past his belt buckle and grabbed it, hard. She yanked him towards her as her eyes narrowed. At the same time, her left hand came up to his neck to study the red marks, the bruises, that had formed there. "I want sex too," she told him. "But I want it for the rest of my life with you, you big dork. What the hell's going on with this production that twice in two weeks you're being treated by medics? And why the hell didn't you go to the hospital when the EMTs asked you to?"

"I'm sure Charlie already filled you in, Jessie. I won't bother recapping what he said. But I'm fine. See? Look at me. All I can think about right now is taking you to that dirt road and doing X-rated things to you."

"How X-rated?" Her frown flipped over for a second but quickly returned as she deflated entirely. "Jesus, Josh," she moaned. "Why do we always have to be so fucking scared all the time?"

"You say it all the time, little one." Josh lifted her fingers and brushed his lips across the backs of her knuckles. "We can't live our lives in fear. We just have to choose joy now, and live in the moment."

"Oh, take your fucking Yoga 'live-in-the-present' schtick and stuff it where the sun don't shine. Josh, I was hoping to come back to Calgary and relax, not come back and start worrying all over again!"

"Then relax. Stop worrying."

Someone from below hollered up to Charlie, who groaned and, with the horse in tow, approached Josh. "Go," he said, holding out the reins. To Jessie, he said, "Let's go to my trailer and have a drink. This loser's going to be another hour or so."

"Meaning another two hours." Jessie touched her husband's hurt neck again before letting her sad eyes focus back on his worried brown ones. "Josh, be careful down there." The words were a whisper. "I love you. I can't wait to just go home with you and cuddle up with our kids."

"And maybe stop somewhere on the way home?" A sad upturn to the corner of one of Josh's lips brought a little smile to Jessie too.

"Of course. That's a given, cowboy."

"Too much information, you two." Gesturing with the reins, trying to urge Josh to take them, Charlie moved to sidle away, somewhat pacified now that Jessie's mood seemed manageable.

Leaning into Josh for a kiss, Jessie's giggle tickled Josh. "Charlie's just jealous. He's never gotten over losing me to you. Like I'm such a prize."

"You're a prize, Jessie. Don't ever forget it. Every day I'm with you I have to pinch myself. Every day with the kids is a bloody miracle."

"You did get a scare today." Stepping back from him, Jessie frowned. Josh did appear pale, all right, underneath the red flush brought on by the hot day. "C'mere, babe," she said, and lost herself in his husky, earthy, horsey scent, almost knocking his hat off as she buried her face in the coveted, cherished hollow of his sore neck. "This heat's gotta be bugging you, Josh. Do you really need to be wearing that jacket?"

Josh inhaled her scent, too. The lavender was as strong as ever, but the après-beer smell threw him. "I'll take it off when I get a longer break," he replied. His tone hardened a little when he asked, "Good party last night?" as they released each other and he finally accepted the horse's reins from Charlie.

"Great party. Kayla's so happy, Josh."

"Good. That your way of saying Jacob wasn't a problem?" Josh bent in for one more kiss before sliding a boot into a stirrup and hoisting himself up onto the horse's back.

"Jacob wasn't a problem." She blushed. "Jacob wasn't even on my radar. I just wanted to get back to you."

A tiny wistful grin lit up his cheeks.

"Don't make any mistakes," Jessie teased. "The sooner y'all get this shot, the sooner we get to that dirt road, Sawyer."

"You got it." Happy enough considering the fear that still clung to him, Josh reined to the right and galloped off back down the hill, lifting his cowboy hat for a final salute to Charlie as he passed.

"Your husband's got all the women on this set drooling." With a mixture of pride, jealousy, and a deep friendship kinda love, Charlie was watching Josh gallop off. "He makes me sick."

"He makes me happy." Hooking her arm through Charlie's, Jessie pointed him towards the little grouping of trailers she'd passed on the way to the set earlier. "Now where's that drink you promised me? Little hair of the dog, y'know. Think you can muster up some producer clout and get some food brought this way too? I need some protein for that little stop Josh and I are planning on the way home. Lots of protein. Tons."

Charlie rolled his eyes. "Your security must see a helluva lot more than they bargained for, Jess. The way you two talk, you're always going at it. Like friggin' rabbits."

"Sex is one of life's sweetest pleasures, Charlie, when it's with the person you love. And yes, I'm guessing our security does get the occasional eyeful." She blushed, remembering Morgan's admission that he watched her with Jacob one night in New York, and Matt's admission that watching Jessie and Jacob make love on set for one of their films was erotic as heck. "But today we'll send them on their way. We want some privacy."

"I don't think that's a good idea, Jessie. Keep your security close, okay? And maybe just for the next bit, keep the sex in the bedroom." Charlie's earlier jovial chide was gone, replaced by dread.

"What? Charlie!" Stopping, Jessie moved in front of him. "Why?"

"Just...today..." He shrugged, trying to look nonchalant. It didn't work.

A dark cloud crossed over his face. "Humor me, kid. Please. For now, until the shoot is over."

"You're fucking freaking the hell out of me, Charlie."

"Call it a simple precaution," Charlie replied, twisting her around and steering her towards his trailer. "Go home, and fuck your husband til he's cross-eyed. I don't care. Just go the hell home to your fortress in the wilderness. And by the way, I'm jealous as hell."

"Aren't you getting enough, little boy?" Her attempt at lightheartedness was marred by a new bleak reality, but Jessie was trying, which Charlie appreciated.

"Jane and I have an infant son at home. What do you think?"

"Didn't stop us. Ha! Loser."

As they breezed towards Charlie's trailer, their banter was secure in the foundation of a long friendship and a great deal of respect, but there was something at play here that threw Jessie, that she couldn't put her finger on. It was in the sorrow in Charlie's eyes and in the way his voice was filled with a fatigue that she doubted had anything to do with a lack of sleep. Instead, it seemed rooted in what happened to Josh today, and it was echoed in Arnie's wise, pale eyes.

As Jessie stepped up into the trailer, she turned one last time to watch her husband gallop through the shot below. Lifting her hands, she configured a pretend camera, and clicked on what she saw—a man she loved with a desperation that scared her, running free on a horse, doing a job he loved. The father of her children and the center of her being.

The light of her life.

Jessie was numbly, blatantly aware that if Josh departed her life again, the loss of him would have the power to destroy her.

Charlie saw the look, and it shook him to the core. He shivered, touched her back, and gave her a gentle push so she would move inside, where Josh was no longer in view, and where Charlie felt Jessie could maybe, just maybe, feel like her world was somehow under control.

It didn't work for him. He was already afloat on some weird current that was bearing him upstream instead of down.

He stepped inside and, because the day was downright hot, he closed the outer door to the trailer, flipped on the air conditioning, wiped the sweat off his brow, and made his old girl a drink.

Chapter Eight

Matt was watching Catherine when his iPhone rang and emblazoned Charles' name across the screen. Propped up in the sun porch with his feet on a wicker ottoman, ankles crossed, an iPad on his lap, Matt's eyebrows were knitted together in curiosity before the phone rang.

A blue sedan was outside, parked between the two cottages—the landlord. The guy was chatting with Catherine, handing her white envelopes, nodding towards Matt's place. As Matt's phone was ringing, the man was hopping back into his car and backing out onto the lane that ran behind the two places. Matt heard his tires spin on the gravel—obviously he had a bigger, more pressing priority than stopping in for a chat, but that was okay. Matt had work to do and preferred not to be disturbed.

As Catherine glanced over, waved, and went back inside her place, Matt finally took his boss' call.

"Charles. I wasn't expecting to hear from you until tomorrow. What's up?" Always, there was fear associated with the Keating camp when things happened unscheduled or out of order. Matt's heart had started to race the second he saw Charles' name on the small screen.

"We had another incident on set today, Matt. An extra went too far. It's likely nothing, but I felt you needed to know."

Uncrossing his ankles, Matt sat up straighter. In front of him was a lush green lawn, the kind of post-summer rain lawn that left the world in a state of renewal—steamy, damp, fresh, and teeming with promise. Birdsong echoed that promise, and in the Darnley Basin below, the little sailboat, *J & J*, skimmed across the few crests of waves that remained, heeling far to starboard, rewarding its skipper with a rush of adrenalin Matt ached for in this new sedate life of his.

"Tell me," he growled into the phone, wishing to hell he was the sailor cutting through the waves, preferably with a six-pack stashed in the new rainwater surely circling his feet in the open boat.

Charles' explanation was businesslike, unemotional, but Matt knew the man well enough to discern serious concern. What he also perceived was that his boss' unease was aimed more in Jessie's corner than in Josh's, which irritated Matt.

There was nothing that could be done from P.E.I. except step up security around the production. Pissed, Matt stood and used his foot to angrily shove the wicker ottoman onto its side. "I need to be there," he barked at Charles. "I need to talk to the police."

"They don't think there's cause for concern, Matt." Charles was adamant. "There's no point in rushing out here and upsetting Jessie and worrying Josh. The extra swears he just got carried away. There's no evidence to suggest otherwise—"

"No note, you mean."

"Not yet, at least, no. And if you show up out here you know Jessie will find out you're still around and it will only serve to make things worse."

But I need to see her. I need an excuse to see her. "Oh, for fuck's sake." Running a hand through his messy hair, Matt turned his back on Catherine's cottage. His sun porch was lined with windows, and the last thing he needed was for her to see him having a temper tantrum. "What the hell are you calling me for then, Charles? Just to drive a knife through my heart?"

"Matt, you need to be prepared." The alarm in Charles' simple statement left an icy chill on Matt's aforementioned heart.

"So you don't agree with the police. Or the extra, then."

A heavy sigh made its way to Prince Edward Island, where a stunning pink-orange sunset was lighting up the white sand dune hill to Matt's distant right. It seemed *J & J's* skipper was determined to ride out the evening's fading light, to enjoy the perfect ride til the last sunbeam drenched the water and disappeared. The small white sailboat was over on the Malpeque side of the Basin now, on the far side near the channel the fishing boats used to gain entry to their safe harbor. No way was the sailor wanting to lower the curtain on this absolutely serene summer's eve sail.

At least I wouldn't if I were him or her, Matt caught himself wryly thinking. The day had been warm; the temperate salt spray soaking the sailor as he sliced through the waves would be invigorating, welcome.

Charles' response was alarming. "It's no surprise a lot of fans have yet to warm to Josh, Matt. After Jacob…"

"Jesus Christ, Charles. You're the one who has yet to warm to Josh. Why the hell'd you agree with Charlie to cast him? For Jessie's sake? To make her happy?"

"He's a damn fine actor. It was a business decision. "

"Yet you're concerned about the show's audience hating his guts."

"A small portion, Matt, and growing smaller since Jessie and Jacob are singing together again. Josh's low character, as he's perceived in the public eye, will only help us. It's a win-win for everyone, because he is turning in stellar performances every day playing a man like himself, with a lot of personal demons to slay. You saw the clips from the Alberta fundraiser."

A quiet hesitation preceded Matt's next words. "I saw the clips. I just wish I were there to keep an eye on him. You can't imagine what it's like to be this far away…to feel so helpless…"

"Arnie's here."

"Thank Christ. It sounds like Arnie saved Josh's fucking life!" Dropping heavily back onto the sofa, Matt lowered his head between his knees. "I think I'm gonna be sick," he muttered.

Charles took a breath before speaking his mind. "Don't give me some sanctimonious grief over how I feel about Josh, Matt. I care about him because Jessie loves him, yes. I would have been happy to see him go his own way years ago, but I've long accepted that he's not going anywhere as long as she still wants him in her life. And I don't care for you acting like he means any more to you than he does to me, since…" He bit his tongue.

"How I feel about Jessie—or Josh—has nothing to do with this conversation, Charles." Growing more incensed, and feeling powerless, Matt glowered at the frisky sailboat in the Basin below. It seemed its skipper was finally heading to safe port. The bow was pointed into the wind and the mainsail was coming down. "You keep me on your payroll to keep that entire family safe. Josh is a part of that family, and if this role gets to him and he decides to bury himself in drink or drugs again, then I'll still watch out for him. Although it's damn hard to do from a fucking distance." A thought at the back of his mind made its way to the forefront. "How's Jessie handling this?"

Sarcasm fueled Charles' response. "How do you think she's handling this? She lives her life in fear. And she no longer has her rock around to calm her down when anxiety gets the better of her, because you couldn't keep it in your pants."

"Is this a pissing match, Charles? Did you just call me to piss on me with some sense of maligned joy at what might have happened on your set today? Because, knowing you, I can't imagine you'd be happy at the dollars pissed down the toilet if your star was killed just before the end of the shoot. So pardon me if I'm confused as hell."

"Look, I don't need your anger tonight, Matt. I know where it's coming from, but I don't need it. If something happens to Josh…"

"I know. You don't have to say it."

"I need to say it. You knew Jessie was coming to set today when she landed back in Calgary. Charlie took her aside and told her what happened. Truth be told, she handled it better than I thought she would, but I could see the wheels turning. She's got this big shoot coming up in September, in Austin now, a city that's unfamiliar to her, instead of New York—the move had something to do with funding, tax credits or something, no surprise—and the tour for *Sacred Peace* after that. Yet she'd like to grab her husband and disappear. I can see it in her eyes."

"And you can't afford that."

"Jesus Christ, Matt. You're not the only one who loves Jessie and doesn't want to see her hurt. Again."

The *again* was a punctuation mark. An exclamation. It was a final stamp on the difficult, stilted conversation. Inwardly, Matt reeled when he heard it. It sickened him.

"So what do you want me to do, Charles? From here?"

"What I want you to do, Matt, is tell me I'm wrong. Tell me I'm wrong, that what happened today was simply an isolated incident. That we'll get through the rest of this shoot with no more incidents of any kind, especially where Josh is concerned. But if we don't…As I said, I just want you to be prepared."

"To do what? To swoop in and rescue Jessie? She's got lots of potential rescuers. She doesn't need me."

"Jessie mourns you, Matt. She's lost without you. You've been her guardian angel for a very long time."

That brought Matt to silence. Speechless, he realized that Charles was not calling him to worry him. Charles was calling him with the express plea that Matt be ready to come running. Because, as they all knew, Jessie would be lost without Josh. Like the small sailboat now bouncing on the waves without its mainsail for control and guidance, she would be unmercifully tossed to the wind, prey to a whole new darkness.

"It needs to be over," he whispered. "They deserve a happy-ever-after."

"Most people don't get that, Matt. Most people have their share of suffering."

"Jessie's done enough suffering. She's the poster child for suffering."

"Starving children who have lost their parents to AIDS or to war are the poster children for suffering. Jessie would be the first to tell you she's doing okay."

"And the first to crumple up into a bottle of Jim Beam when things bottom up."

"Just be ready, Matt. She might need you. I might need you."

At that, Matt allowed a tiny smile to settle on his lips, at least at one corner. "I'm a flight away. I'm still on your payroll, Charles." The last bit was an attempt at humor. It worked. Matt could sense Charles' relief through the phone line. "I'm sorry for what I said earlier," he added. "About Josh. About what you think of him. That wasn't fair."

"We had a helluva scare today, Matt. Everyone around *Sacred Peace* has grown quite fond of our boy."

"Shanda…?"

Interjecting, Charles said brusquely, "Friends. She's doing okay. They don't spend as much time together anymore, since Carter joined the cast. That was a wise choice—Jon's idea, by the way."

Sighing, Matt settled back on the sofa. Glancing to his right, he saw through Catherine's windows that she was on her computer, intent at something, judging by the way she was leaning forward and studying the screen, her brow puckered and her chin resting on one hand. "Carter's the buffer, huh?" There were two walls and a number of windows between Matt and Catherine. There were miles of land and water between Matt and Jessie. There was also a husband between them, who he knew she would die to save, if she had to.

After he and Charles signed off, Matt rested his phone in his lap and considered the day's events on the *Sacred Peace* set. *I would have strangled the extra,* he told himself, wondering how Arnie had managed not to wrap his thick fingers around the guy's throat. He considered calling him, but a silhouetted figure, backlit by the gorgeous sunset, crossed his path. Catherine was making her way up the steps. Matt waved her in.

"What?" His brow wrinkled for the umpteenth time that evening. She was holding out a white envelope. Grasping it, Matt noticed that it was addressed to him, and that the return address was his landlord's name and address. Instead of totally taking it, he let it hang there between them, his fingers on one side and Catherine's on the other.

"Matt Kelly," she said simply. "This is your receipt. Our busy landlord, who still believes—like most of these islanders, I've discovered—in doing things the old fashioned way, instead of by email, left it with me so he could get to the Ceilidh he was already late for."

"Okay. Thanks. Want to sit?" Matt didn't bother standing. The conversation with Charles had floored and disturbed him to the point of exhaustion.

"Matt Kelly."

Hearing his name repeated got Matt's attention. Using his hands to leverage himself up higher on the sofa, he wrinkled his nose and searched Catherine's face for clues. What the hell had gotten under her skin? The way she was standing there, with most of her weight on one leg and a hand propped up on her hip, was disconcerting. A stark stare wasn't helping soften him towards her on this already troubled east coast evening, which should have been perfect, given the extraordinary beauty just outside his windows.

"Google," Catherine said defiantly. "Ever Google yourself, Matt?"

She waited.

He stilled.

"You know, Matt, for a guy who works in security, I'm rather surprised at you."

He swallowed bitterly and focused an angry stare on her smug face. "I'm not trying to hide. I'm not protecting myself, Catherine."

"The hell you're not." Still standing above him, she took in a breath, switched her weight to her other leg as she turned to watch the small sailboat's skipper drop an anchor, and then Catherine turned back to Matt. "I Googled you. Under the *images* tab, first. You're the top Matt Kelly in the world."

Twisting his lips into a grimace, Matt angled his head away from her. "I'm not interested in hearing about my life from a woman I just met, Catherine. I know all about my own fucked up life."

"The Paris video was interesting. My Prince Edward Island neighbor standing so close to Jessie Wheeler as she sang, kind of threw me. I think the video that got to me the most, though, was the Grammy video, Matt. Both videos, actually. Josh Sawyer throwing you around outside, and then watching you walk on stage to rescue that obviously messed up woman..."

Matt winced, but didn't look back at her. Reaching for a nearby cushion, he wrapped his fingers around one edge and squeezed it, hard. In Catherine's cottage next door he spied Drifter, asleep in a doggy cushion on the floor, having innocent puppy dreams about large bones and long walks on the beach, Matt hoped.

Catherine continued. "You saved her life in New York City. Then at that fundraiser last month, she told the world she got involved with you, and that she lost you because of it. You had sex with her?"

Matt's head whipped around. "Somehow I don't think that's any of your business, Catherine."

She was near tears. "I told you my daughter was listening to her music when she died. You don't know the impact Jessie Wheeler has had on me. Even hearing her name. She was all Carly cared about. Jessie and Jacob, the two of them, their magic, their music."

Slowly, Matt rose and faced her. "I am truly sorry about your daughter, Catherine. I'm glad she had Jessie as an outlet, or as a role model, whatever you want to call it. But what you need to consider right now, after all your…" He waved a hand towards her computer next door, and glowered at her when he looked back at her, "Sleuthing," he glowered, "is that you don't know what Jessie means to me."

"Oh, I think I do know," was her quick response, her voice rising in pitch as she pulled the envelope away from his fingers and tossed it on the sofa he'd just vacated. "I think that on-stage video from the Grammys is pretty damn clear."

"So, what, you and I are no longer friends? Because I'm trying to deal with losing someone who left a fucking great big hole in my life?" The second the words escaped his lips, Matt sucked in a breath. *What the hell did I just say?* he thought as Catherine's eyes started to float. "Oh, Jesus. I'm sorry, Catherine."

"You should be," she retorted, a warm flush instantly blooming across her cheeks. "My daughter is gone. Forever. She is never coming back. Your beloved Jessie Wheeler ushered her out of this world. Your beloved Jessie, whose voice and music was so loud in my Carly's ears that she never heard the car skidding towards her! Your beloved Jessie, with all her money and fame and success, sitting in some expensive ranch home with horses and land and, and…" She was starting to hiccup with the effort it took to say all these things that were tumbling around in her brain like pollen in the wind. "Designer gowns and shoes and three spoiled children, not one but three!" Holding up three fingers, she punctuated the declaration that Jessie had more than she deserved.

"You're out of line, Catherine." Incensed, Matt wiped sweaty hands on his white linen designer shirt, and prepared for battle. "Jessie could care less for fancy clothes and a big house. She hates the whole fame thing. All she wants is her husband and children."

"Oh, poor Matt. That must've sucked for you. Being in love with a woman for years who didn't want you until she lost her pet toy, the guy she used to run to when her husband crashed! And then she wanted you, hey? Because you were the only one there. Is that why?"

"You need to leave, Catherine. You don't know a damn thing about my relationship with Jessie. You don't know me, and most of all, you don't know Jessie."

"I know that she probably used you. For years. You lost your marriage over her, the articles I read said. You gave her your life, and you dove in front of a bullet for her. And from what I read about how she used Jacob and then dumped him for a man like Josh Sawyer, it doesn't sound to me like she was worth it! My daughter died because of her! And you're sitting here hiding and feeling sorry for yourself, dying a little every day until one day you, too, will realize you gave up everything for someone who probably never ever really gave a shit!"

"You got any more bullets you want to fire at me, Catherine? I'm used to it. I can take it." His tone was even and low-pitched. Matt's fists were clenched and his teeth gritted, but he knew where this woman was coming from. "I didn't lie to you about my work with the Keatings and about my personal relationship with Jessie. I just didn't see the need to explain any of that to someone I just met. And I've already spent too much of my evening analyzing how and why people feel the way they do about Josh who, may I add, I have a lot of respect for, and who I consider a personal friend. So do yourself a favor, walk away from me tonight. When you've had some time to process the fact that you know nothing about myself, Jessie, or Josh, then come back and I will tell you what the media chooses to leave out."

Brushing by her, Matt stormed out of the sun porch and made his way up the stairs to his loft bed. Flinging himself down on his stomach, he hugged a pillow and waited for the sound of her footsteps to disappear. The closing of his screen door, and then hers next door, which was quieter but still discernible, was his cue to let go. Shoulders heaving, he cried in a way he hadn't since the day he read the stalking journal Jessie left under her mattress years ago, during Deuce McCall's reign of terror.

Jessie Wheeler. Her name would always be associated with pain—in his life, in Catherine's, in Charles and Dee's. Yet she had this beautiful aura, this amazing light that attracted people to her, to her films, to her music. Her essence was formed by sadness, but her soul tried to believe in hope. She was a rare individual with a heart of gold and the talent to bring her beautiful spirit forward, to share it with others.

So why did it hurt so much to hear what Catherine said about her? That Jessie used him, and Jacob before him?

It hurts because it kills me that Catherine believes Jessie's music had anything to do with the death of her daughter.

It hurts because I am helpless when it comes to loving Jessie.

It hurts because I miss her.

And that's all.

There was an orange cast to his windows now, as the sun made its final descent into the Gulf, just beyond Bird Island off the coast of Cabot Beach in Malpeque. Another day was being laid to rest but Matt didn't see the sun dip into the salty depths tonight. Hugging his downy pillow tighter, he curled up his knees, closed his eyes, and begged the sweet forgiveness of sleep to still the ache as, next door, Catherine did the same.

Hours later, in the Kananaskis, three hours behind Matt and Catherine's east coast existence, Josh brought his wife to him, kissed away her fears, and loved her in the safety of their ranch bedroom. Later, grateful for the chance to hold the woman he loved in his arms as she slept, he lay awake and watched a calm peacefulness come over her worried features. For some unbidden reason Matt crossed his mind, and Josh found himself wondering if he had done the same—if he had lain awake and watched Jessie sleep, that night when Matt and Jessie had finally come together as lovers.

It's never enough, Josh thought. *The perfect moments don't last. Physically loving her, holding her...these are finite things. She's like that song you can't get enough of, that you play over and over and over in your car, that you just want to climb inside and soak up until you reach nirvana. You don't want to hit the stop button. You don't want to turn off the music.*

Consoling himself with the thought that he got to have her longer than anyone, Josh brushed his lips against the forehead he held dearest and, while on the east coast Matt dreamed of the one night the universe gave him, Josh dreamed of the nights he prayed he had left.

Chapter Nine

A full moon hung over Darnley the night after Catherine figured out who Matt worked for. Luminous and spiritual, patches of grey on a glowing pale light, it was a weightless Christmas ornament suspended in a summer sky. It was a gift.

Stoking a new campfire, Matt watched as orange sparks snapped their way to freedom. He kept a long, thick poker stick by the fire. After each prod of the burning campfire wood, he'd developed the nervous habit of sticking the poker's ashy tip into the red earth lining the metal fire pit surround. Matt was a stickler for safety. Anything to keep things under control, to keep some semblance of organized life within his grasp.

The moon was so visible here in this serene place, without artificial city lights to steal its thunder. There was a twinkling red and green sparkle in the sky at the opposite end of the Darnley Basin, over the Gulf of St. Lawrence. Talking to Mac on the Twin Shores beach earlier today had determined that the colored blinks likely denoted a planet. Planet stalking, celestial eavesdropping; this was something not done in Vancouver. The stars on Matt's radar there were the human kind, with two feet and heartbeats.

Now, Matt aligned an App on his iPhone with the stars popping out into the inky sky as the night grew steadily darker. Sinking into his camp chair, he leaned back and took the time to appreciate the universe and all its wonder. It was humbling to be here on the planet, alive and well and in the grasp of something bigger than himself. The simple knowledge took the pressure off of worrying about Josh and, by association, Jessie and the kids.

A voice startled him, and Matt sat up. "Have you figured out which one is Orion's Belt?"

"No," Matt said, and pointed at an overhead light moving through the sky. "But according to this flight App I've got here…just a sec." He paused to switch from a celestial navigation map to a flight App. "That plane is flying direct from New York to Amsterdam. It's at 35 000 feet and it's an eight hour and twenty-five minute flight. It's flying at 312 knots."

"You can see all of that on your phone?"

"You wouldn't believe what I can see from my phone. It would shock you."

"I don't want to know." Pausing, shuffling a toe in the grass, Catherine waited while Matt studied his phone and stared up into space.

After a moment, he slipped the phone onto a small wooden table on his left and gestured towards the camp chair next to him. "Sit, if you want."

She did, and since she had Drifter pulling on his leash anxiously whining and trying to get to Matt, she handed over the leash's looped handle. Matt took it, lifted the puppy, was careful not to jar his casted leg, and set him in his lap. A wide smile crested Matt's face as the puppy started licking him.

"That's really disgusting," he laughed. "What were you eating before you decided to wash my face with your tongue, Drifter?" Reaching for his phone again, Matt selected the photo App and snapped a pic of the puppy. With one hand, he managed to text the photo to Josh with the note, *for the kids*.

Catherine watched him do it. "Did you just send that to your daughter?"

"No," he replied honestly, setting the phone back down and trying to restrain the overexcited puppy. "I sent it to Josh. I already emailed him a note about Drifter. He got a helluva kick out of the name."

"I'll bet." Wrinkling her brow, Catherine reached for the thick poker stick and absently started playing with the fire, moving wood around and trying to bring the flame up. "Surreal. You sent a picture of my dog to the guy who starred in the show Drifter's named for. A show that starred Carly's favorite singer."

Sighing, Matt finally got the dog to settle down on his lap. Drifter watched the fire while Matt scratched him behind the ears. "I've been thinking about how you feel about Jessie, Catherine. You need to separate what happened to Carly from the woman you blame for her death. She could have been listening to anyone."

"I don't completely blame Jessie Wheeler. I blame the kids at school who bullied my daughter and made her want to escape into music and running. The problem is that it's all jumbled up together in my head, and like it or not your old lover is a part of that."

"One night, Catherine. That's all I got with her. And you need to let that go, too. Like I said, there are things you don't understand."

"I spent the morning looking up stuff about Jessie and her life on the Internet." With the stick, Catherine lifted a piece of wood from the top of the fire. It sizzled and landed with a crash, startling Drifter, whose ears perked up as ashes spat into the sky.

"So now you know the media's perception of her, and of what she's been through."

"I watched a lot of her videos too, and some concert footage. I see why Carly loved watching her sing with Jacob Ryan. They were magical together."

"They *are* magical together," Matt corrected her. "Jacob and Jessie bring out the best in each other when it comes to music."

Setting down the stick without pushing it into the dirt, which Matt forced himself to ignore, Catherine looked over at him. "I saw some pretty cool back-stage footage, too. A documentary, I guess. A short one, like fifteen minutes long. Josh was in it."

"And?"

"You were there too. It was shot in Chicago. Part of it was Josh arriving with their older two children. Jessie apparently had the youngest with her on the tour. She seemed pretty relieved to see Josh show up with the older two."

"She's away from the kids a lot more than she'd like to be. When Dylan was a baby they sometimes separated the kids for short times to make things easier."

"I thought she kept the youngest with her because she was touring with Jacob. And he's the littlest guy's father, right?"

"You were on the net. You tell me."

"Ha. Funny. So you're going to test me now to see what I read compared with what's true?"

"You'd be surprised at the garbage that's out there."

Exhaling slowly, Catherine sat back and stared into the glowing coals at the base of the fire. Reaching next to her, she grabbed two more pieces of split wood and placed them perpendicular to each other inside the fire pit. Slightly damp, they spat and sputtered as they started to dry out.

"Matt, I like you. You and I…well, I like your company. I think for a bit I hoped maybe that…well, maybe that…" She sighed again, and pulled at the black Yoga capris she was wearing, adjusting them over her knees. "I think I thought maybe you were this lonely guy who might be looking for female companionship. I've decided that I'm right about the lonely part but…maybe not about the companionship part. And even if you were looking for company, I guess I'd have to say that now that I know who you are, and what kind of life you live when you're not hiding out in some rented cottage on the east coast, I was way off base. I'd be dreaming to ever think I'd fit into your lifestyle."

Glancing over at Matt, she noted that he was watching Drifter chew on a small piece of wood. Was he listening, digesting what she was telling him?

Matt caught the vibe that he was now being watched. Shifting himself up straighter in his seat, he let his gaze drift over to her. Catherine caught her breath when their eyes met, and she wondered what he was seeing.

"You've let your hair down here, though," she told him quietly. "You always wear the same ratty blue sweater and the same plaid shorts. Your hair's a mess. In the documentary, Jessie called you Spike and when the filmmaker asked why, she said it's because you always gel your hair up into little spikes. I don't think she would recognize you the way you look tonight."

"I didn't see the point in gelling my hair today. I was in and out of the water five times this afternoon." A tiny grin lifted a corner of Matt's lip.

"I'm just saying that you don't seem like the same man I saw in that documentary. In those pictures."

"I'm not. I left that world behind. The one where you need to look perfect, to…be perfect."

"I read about Josh being choked to the point of losing consciousness yesterday, on the set of his new show."

Matt shrugged. "There are risks in action shows. He's been hurt before. That's why he gets the big paycheck." His heart picked up its pace. Catherine saw his eyes flicker.

"That's why you were in such a great mood last night."

"Charles had just called before you came over. So yes, I wasn't at my best. I'm sorry. The news threw me. Then…"

"I threw you."

"Can we call it square and start again?"

"Seeing as you don't have a lot of friends here, and your new buddy Mac, the puppy hitter, is leaving soon, I guess we can stay friends."

"Friends, is it?"

"I'm a dowdy teacher from Ontario. Yes, friends. I don't need to have my heart broken by some trendy Vancouverite whose heart is already taken."

"I'm not that trendy. It's all smoke and mirrors." Laughing, Matt reached down and pulled a beer up out of the padded cooler at his side. "I've got beer and I've got some of those fancy colored drinks women seem to like. Pick your poison."

"Got any Smirnoff Ice?"

"Yep." Grabbing one, Matt twisted off the cap and handed it to his friend. He opened the beer and took a deep haul on it. "See?" he explained. "I don't even have glasses. I'm not near as cool as you think."

This time, Catherine laughed. A few minutes later she posed a question that had been on her mind since the moment she clued in that Matt was deeply connected to Jessie Wheeler. "Matt? Do you think…" Picking at the corner of the label on her moist bottle, she leaned forward and avoided his gaze by choosing a vibrant flame to focus on. "Do you think I could get a message to Jessie? Just…you know…on behalf of my daughter."

Matt took another drink before answering. His words emerged slowly, cautiously. "The thing is, Catherine…I'm not really in touch with Jessie. I'm only in touch with Josh, and only occasionally."

"You talk to Charles Keating." Her eyes darted back to him.

Matt saw the deep need there but he was silent. He looked down at Drifter and let out a long breath but said nothing.

"You don't want her to know where you are."

"She knows I'm in P.E.I. It's not that."

"Oh. I get it." Catherine straightened. "You don't want to hurt her."

His silence was her answer.

"What do you think I'm going to say? You bitch, you killed my daughter?"

"Catherine, don't...that's not it."

"No, it's okay, you're likely right. I mean, what would I say?"

"Take some time to think about what you would like to say. I'll see what I can do, Catherine, okay?"

She slumped. "Okay. That's fair."

"And you're right about one thing. But not the other."

"Hmmm?" The soul light in her eyes had flickered out with the renewed remembrance of a lost daughter. When Catherine fixed Matt in her gaze again, he softened, grasped his beer bottle with the left hand that he had previously wrapped around the puppy on his lap, and reached out a hand to brush his fingers against her cheek. She drew in a breath, closed her eyes and let him.

"You're right in that I don't want to hurt Jessie. Never again do I want to be responsible for hurting her. She was everything to me for a very long time, Catherine, and in many ways she still is. If you and I are going to be friends on any level, you need to understand that."

"And the other thing? The one I'm not right about?" Opening her eyes, Catherine laid her left hand over his and melted in the tender way Matt was looking at her now.

"You're not a dowdy teacher. You're a smart, beautiful woman who, I think, hid for a long time behind a daughter you were trying to protect. Maybe now it's your turn to show the world that fighting spark you're always quick to pull up from the depths and fire at me."

Lowering her hand with his entwined in hers, Catherine brushed a thumb over his skin, which was cool and damp from his beer bottle. "Well, my dog likes you," she mumbled, suddenly rather terrified, and feeling her world start to spin at the way those solemn hazel-grey eyes had locked her in their pale gaze. Electricity shot up her spine and landed in a secret place in her heart and in her body where she hadn't felt anything besides loneliness and pain for far too long.

Carefully, Matt lifted Catherine's fingers and kissed the back of her hand. "Drifter's got it all figured out. You nurse the part that's sore, but you don't let it keep you from living. Maybe he's trying to teach us something with that broken leg of his."

"This place isn't real, Matt. We're both in hiding here, in Prince Edward Island. Drifter's just a weird coincidence." Catherine was emphatic. The real world awaited just outside their door. Anything that might happen between her and this amazing man at her side would be nothing but a brief fantasy.

"We're not in hiding. We're in healing. Okay? One day at a time."

"Okay." For once, Catherine's smile was wide and genuine. Sitting back, she took a drink of the Smirnoff Ice she knew Matt had bought just for her, and she settled back to watch the fire. They held hands until the slow movements of his thumb against hers drove them both to distraction. Rising, Matt handed Drifter to her, and he put the fire out with the plastic yellow watering bucket he kept nearby. Then he placed a hand at Catherine's waist and led her up the stairs to his cottage. In the loft, he took Drifter from her and laid him on a big padded chair in the corner of his bedroom, and scratched the puppy's ears until Drifter laid his chin on his good paw and faded into sleep.

Catherine had ducked into the washroom. When she emerged into the cozy starlit bedroom, nervously raking fingers through her wild sea-breezed hair, Matt turned from Drifter and faced her.

"It's been a long time for me," she murmured to him, shaking away the disparaging thought that the last woman he was with could very likely have been Jessie Wheeler, which was freaky for all kinds of reasons. "I don't know if I even remember how to do this."

"Your hair smells like wood smoke." Taking her in his arms, Matt smiled at the woman whose steady friendship (which included a puppy who loved him unconditionally) was a surprise light in his life. Breathing her in, he let his hands rest on the unfamiliar hips. "I'm nervous too, Catherine," he added with a wry grin. "But I'm sure we can figure out what we're supposed to do."

A memory of his surreal night with Jessie came back to him. He'd been terrified that night—his desire, percolating for a very long time, was over the top. The night was unrealistic in terms of any kind of future dream of being with her, which made it more incredible in its intensity. Jessie had asked him if he was scared. Yeah, he'd been scared. Tonight was different, more…attainable. Realistic. He and Catherine didn't have the depth that came from years of trust and friendship, but they were building something together that was starting from the bottom and working its way up. They were building something genuine, with hope for some kind of future together, maybe, although Matt supposed it was presumptuous to consider that at this early juncture.

Catherine let her hands land on Matt's body, on the waist of the plaid shorts she complained earlier that he wore all the time. He was wearing the blue sweater too; P.E.I. August nights were generally cool. They had yet to kiss, and both anticipated the first touch of lips on lips with shivering bodies and trembling hearts. When it happened—when Matt touched his lips to hers, he took her chin in his thumb and forefinger and held her steady, because Catherine was ready to collapse from want and need.

Their kiss lasted long enough for the intensity to build, for Matt to touch his tongue to hers when she parted her lips enough to let him in. Her small moan was welcome. Matt let her pull the blue sweater over his head and drop it to the floor at their feet before he laid his palms on her back and, in one fell swoop, lifted her sweater and T-shirt over her head.

Shy, Catherine balked when he reached for the clasp on her bra. "I wasn't planning on...I know it's not real pretty..."

Ducking his head, Matt pushed away the thought of Jessie in the exquisite rose-grey silk designer dress, of untying it at her neck and bringing it slowly down over her breasts. That wasn't real, none of that night was real, *it was all just some dream I conjured up,* he told himself in order to place himself here, in this moment, with this nervous woman who Matt desired fully and completely.

"You're beautiful," he whispered to her, planting gentle kisses at her neck and down onto the salty tasting skin of her naked shoulder. His tactic worked. She moaned and let him reach back and undo her bra. Catherine's breasts were larger than Matt was accustomed to between petite Julie and athletic Jessie, and Matt found them erotic and enticing. Fingering her, brushing his lips over her, he found himself almost desperate for the next step, but he knew this woman was fragile and frightened despite how much she obviously wanted this too, and so he forced himself to handle her gently, to let her lead him in terms of her comfort level.

When she finally led him to his bed, and laid down on her back, Matt bent over her and kissed her—long, passionate, sweet kisses that held a hint of urgency but that didn't overwhelm Catherine, who let her trembling fingers explore the muscular back and shoulders underneath Matt's grey T-shirt. When she moved her long fingers around to his chest, and bent her head up to take a nipple in her mouth and tease him with her tongue, Matt felt she was ready for a little more.

Gently, he took her hand and placed it over his shorts, and gave her a little pressure to show her what he wanted. Unbuttoning his shorts himself, he stopped and knelt above her so he could haul his T-shirt over his head. Before he laid back over her, he asked softly, "Are you okay with this?"

Accompanied by a few deep swallows, Catherine's nod was almost desperate, and she raised her hips so he could pull her Yoga pants down. She grabbed his hand, though, and halted him, and Matt willed himself to stop if need be. He would not be pulling a Jacob here tonight, taking what he wanted from a woman not willing to give it.

"I'm just...like I said, I wasn't really thinking...I mean, I waxed for the beach, but..."

Laughing aloud, Matt's eyes lit up. "Catherine, I like you. You have a beautiful body. Let yourself enjoy it. I'm not judging you. I promise I will never judge you."

That last bit secured his heart within hers for its ability to gently move them forward in a way that felt comfortable for her. Years without this kind of intimacy with a man was frightening, and definitely moved Catherine outside of her comfort zone, what little comfort zone she ever had with sex in the first place, that is, which wasn't much, given her past partners—a cheating husband who treated sex like she owed it to him, and a university boyfriend who didn't care for anything except pleasing himself.

Letting go of her waistband, Catherine laid back and closed her eyes. *It's now or never,* she thought, and since Matt didn't get up and run screaming from the room, she felt like she could relax a little. She tensed when his tongue touched her and he settled between her legs, letting his own little moan escape as he started to pleasure her in a way Catherine had rarely experienced in her lifetime.

"Oh, God," she moaned, gripping the pillow behind her as he moved over her. "Is this really happening?"

When she started to come, Matt moved up over her and let her rub and squeeze him against her before he went inside and showed her what it was like to be loved by a man who made sure his woman received as much pleasure as she wanted when it came to the physical lovemaking between a man and a woman.

It wasn't an out of the stratosphere union by any means, but it was a good, solid, comfortable place to start and, when it was over, and Matt lay on his side panting beside his partner, he had the sense that it was only the beginning of discovering this woman's body and the pleasures it could bring to both of them.

"Oh, God," she breathed again as she started to come down off her orgasm. "You're good at this."

Laughing, he ducked his head and kissed the top of her ear, which peeked out from behind her tousled longish brown hair. "So are you."

"I have a lot to learn." Blushing, Catherine ran a hand down over Matt's strong shoulder, which she had once staunchly admired from behind the window of her cottage while he hung clothes on the line.

"I have time." A silly grin lit up his face. "I like you, Catherine. You're funny and sweet and, I guess you already know, a bit of a spitfire. And like I said before, your dog likes me. I hope we can get to know each other more while we're here this summer."

"I'm here until Thanksgiving," she told him softly, tracing his chest with a finger. "I go back to teaching then. I'm on bereavement leave until after that weekend."

Kissing her fingers one at a time, slipping them into his mouth and savoring the taste of her, Matt smiled. "Then we've got more time than I thought. Let's go exploring. I haven't seen this island yet." He almost added *Jessie raves about it,* but he fought off the thought. He did, however, consider that he would swing by the nursing home in Clinton to see Jessie's mother, and her old friend George, if the guy was still around.

"I've heard of some good restaurants," she murmured happily. "But Drifter might not be welcome."

"If he's not, we'll stick to the dairy bars. There are tons of those around here. I hope the little mutt likes ice cream."

Snuggling up together, they chatted idly until sleep took over and, with her hand in his, they drifted off as, overhead, the sky started to lighten and a new pink dawn welcomed the east coast of Canada to a whole new day.

Chapter Ten

For about a week in mid-August, dramatic thunder and lightning storms raced through the Kananaskis Country, offering a respite from the interminable heat but shaking the Sawyer ranch and frightening the Sawyer children. One afternoon, Jessie gathered the kids in the sun porch, pulled Dylan onto her lap, and snuggled David and Emily-Grace under her shoulders, one on each side. Together, as they watched theatrical forked lightning stir up the skies, they munched on warm chocolate chip cookies they'd just baked. Jessie and Emily-Grace did their share of screaming as the thunder crashed and roared around them, but their fright turned to raucous laughter and good-natured teasing by the boys until all four of them stuffed their fingers in their ears and squeezed their eyes tightly shut while the thunder raged.

"Is Daddy scared of the thunder too?" David asked at one point. Josh was his hero. In David's little-boy eyes, he had a big, tough daddy who wasn't afraid of anything.

Emily-Grace tuned him in. "Daddy's not scared of the thunder, but he knows not to go riding in the lightning. Right, Momma?"

"You bet," Jessie agreed with a forced smile. "Daddy knows to be careful around thunder and lightning, but it doesn't mean he's afraid of it."

"Is Daddy afraid of stuff?" Wide-eyed, David was twisting a finger in the hem of his T-shirt.

Jessie wrinkled her nose at the nervous gesture and took his small fingers in hers.

Emily-Grace jumped in again. In denim shorts and a pink T-shirt with a gauzy ballet-style hem, ever the girly-girl, she was sitting cross-legged now, facing her mother and the boys. "No, David, Daddy's not afraid of anything. He can't be. Ever."

"Why do you say that, honey?" Jessie lifted her hand from David's fingers and wrapped her arm around his small shoulder.

"Because he's the one who is supposed to take care of us." Pointing an index finger into her chest, Emily-Grace added, "Of me. And of you guys." The finger waved in the general direction of the rest of the Sawyer family. "So he can't be scared of stuff. He has to be strong." The small shoulders caved noticeably. "At least, he's supposed to take care of us." She fixed her piqued eyes on her mother's face. "He doesn't always do a good job of that though, does he, Momma?"

"Uhhh..." Stunned at the new direction this candid conversation with her children was suddenly going, Jessie shook her head at her daughter. "I think Daddy does a very good job of taking care of us," she said carefully, assessing her daughter for clues of what to say next, and how to say it. "Don't you, honey?" To David, she said, "Sweetheart, Daddy does get scared sometimes. Everybody does. It's okay to be scared sometimes. Big strong daddies can be just as scared as mommies."

As if to prove her point, the sky unleashed another spectacular display of lightning, which was soon followed by raging thunder. All four Sawyers screamed, more because it was now fun, and they dissolved into fits of laughter afterwards, although Jessie's laughter was more subdued this time as she studied her somewhat pensive daughter.

"Momma, I heard Grammie say that." Emily-Grace wasn't laughing as hard this time, either.

"What'd Grammie say?" Narrowing her eyes, Jessie made a mental note to have a chat with Deirdre about what to say and not to say in front of the children.

"She said she wished you married Charlie because he's a better man than Daddy. I wish you did too. Me and Stella would be sisters."

"Oh." There were no words. Jessie's mind was now firing its own invisible lightning, all of it aimed at the glamorous Deirdre Keating.

"Grammie doesn't like Daddy very much, does she, Momma?"

David and Dylan were silent. Taking this in, they looked to their mother for guidance. Dylan was a bit young to understand, but he got the gist of the conversation, and David's small Josh-face was wrinkled in confusion.

Tears stung Jessie's eyes. She removed her arms from around her children and sat up straighter. "You listen to me, Emily-Grace," she started slowly. "David, Dylan..." *I have a feeling we will be having this conversation a lot over the years.* "Kids, there is no daddy on this planet who is a better man than your daddy." Eyeing Dylan carefully, she sighed. "Except maybe Jacob. Since he's kinda like a second daddy to all of you." Looking back at her daughter, who seemed to be holding her breath and waiting for her mother to say the right thing, Jessie said, "Sweetheart, you and I have already had a few talks about Daddy over the last little while. You gotta cut him a break. Do you remember..." Catching her breath, Jessie wondered how much she dared say to this sweet girl. How much was Emily-Grace ready to hear? And David too, what could he handle now—was he old enough to understand? "You remember the Langley house, Emily-Grace?"

"Yes, Momma." The serious eyes were bottomless wells, filled to overflowing with blue-eyed wisdom and understanding beyond the child's age. Emily-Grace barely blinked, and did not lose her mother's gaze.

"Well, then. You are old enough to know, honey, that it was not my choice to move us there."

"I know. Stella and I were talking about it. She said we were kidnapped."

Glancing at David, Jessie inhaled slowly. "Which means, kids, that someone else decided we should live there for a while. Away from Daddy."

She waited for the kids to digest that news.

"That's when Daddy got sick." Emily-Grace and Jessie may as well have been alone. She needed to understand a time that only came to her in bits and pieces. "So after, we mostly lived with Grammie and Grampie, and with you and Jacob. Because Daddy couldn't take care of us."

"And...?" Jessie was testing her now.

The pale eyes of her daughter were the most serious Jessie had ever seen them. David and Dylan were, uncharacteristically, completely silent and watchful.

"He wasn't sick in the normal way, was he, Momma? Daddy drank too much beer. Charlie and Jacob drink beer, and so do you. But Daddy gets sick from it, so he doesn't drink it anymore."

"Emily-Grace...I think this might help you understand. Honey...when we were living in the Langley House, your daddy didn't know where we were. Can you imagine what that would feel like? We knew we were okay. But your daddy didn't know that. Every day he got up and went through his day without knowing where we were. For a long time."

"He was scared." This came from David. Jessie bent down and brushed her lips against his forehead. At the same time, she used her sleeve to wipe away a tear.

"Yes, honey, of course he was. So," she looked back at her daughter. "He drank a little too much beer because it helped him feel better. But he learned that beer just made him feel worse in the end, so after a while he went to a place that helped him learn to stop drinking it."

"Rehab." Emily-Grace was stoic. Her eyes were still locked on her mother's. "A lot of actors go to rehab. Daddy's been there a lot of times."

Jesus Christ. Deirdre, we're going to have words.

"Yes," she managed. "It's like a hospital. And it made Daddy better."

"And so we moved back in with Daddy." A sigh heavier than the dense air outside escaped Emily-Grace's chest. "Momma?"

"What, honey?"

"Stella said Daddy might start again someday. Drinking beer. Because he has gone to that rehab hospital a lot of times already and it will probably happen again."

"Why does Stella think that?"

Emily-Grace sensed her mother's rising anguish. She shrugged her shoulders and didn't answer.

"Your Daddy won't drink anymore. You know how I know that?"

"How, Momma?" This was from David. Emily-Grace was already a nonbeliever.

"Because, kids, your daddy does not ever want to live away from us again. Not for a long time, anyway, just for little breaks when we both have to work, that's all. I also know that because we will help him by giving him all kinds of love. Starting tonight. Starting tonight when he comes in that door I want to see who can give Daddy the biggest hug."

Emily-Grace looked away.

Reaching out a finger, Jessie tickled her. Another loud crash of thunder rocked the ranch house to its core, but this time nobody screamed or laughed.

"What?" Jessie asked her quietly.

The small head turned and Emily-Grace raised her shoulders. Her voice was small. "You know what I do to help me go to sleep, Momma?"

"What, sweetheart?" Jessie held her breath as David and Dylan listened closely.

"I make Charlie my daddy. It used to be Jacob but now it's Charlie."

"Ahhh." Jessie forced herself to respond. "Because you and Stella are so close. You'd like to be sisters."

A slow shake of the head was the little girl's answer. "No, Momma. Because me and Stella are like sisters anyway. No, do you wanna know why?"

Jessie's answer was a sacred whisper. "Yes."

"Because I'm not scared of Charlie. He never drinks too much beer, and he never yells. He's a star as big as Daddy and he's never gone to that rehab place. Not once. And he's only ever nice to people. He doesn't lose his temper the way Daddy does."

"Some day, baby girl," Jessie started, realizing as she spoke that this conversation—and Emily-Grace's influence on the younger children—would impact the way David and Dylan perceived their father for likely the remainder of their childhoods. "Some day you will look at your father differently. You will see him the same way I do. Which is with nothing but love and understanding, because that is what he deserves."

"Grammie says you only see Daddy through rose-colored glasses. You don't see the real him."

"Oh, is that what Grammie says?"

"Yes."

"Honey, I've got news for you. I am the only one who really sees your daddy for who he really is. You are his daughter. You need to stand back and have a good look at him, Emily-Grace. You need to remind yourself that he has had a lot of struggles in his lifetime, and that he is a strong man deserving of our respect because he has overcome those struggles. What's Charlie ever had to overcome? Nothing! Nothing, baby."

"He lost you, Momma. And Grammie says it almost destroyed him."

"Oh, for Pete's sake. Grammie says, Grammie says, Grammie says...I'm gonna call Grammie and tell her to keep her opinions to herself!" Grumbling, Jessie lifted Dylan and set him on the floor. Standing, she turned one last time to Emily-Grace and David, but it was clear by the way they looked back at her with serious expressions that this battle was lost. "You know what Daddy's scared of the most, David?"

David didn't answer. This whole conversation frightened him more than the thunder and lightning.

Emily-Grace did, though. Without missing a beat she said, "Losing us. Again."

"Yes. So we..." Jessie pointed a finger at all of the children, but her eyes were a little wild now. Afraid. "We have to prove to him that he is deeply loved. By all of us. So he is never that scared again. So he never reaches for beer again. Ever. Okay?"

Only Dylan answered, and his "Okay" was a quiet murmur.

Frustrated, Jessie stomped her foot. "You're his babies," she railed to Emily-Grace and David. "He loves you so much! Is it too much to ask to just love him back?"

Emily-Grace and David shared a look. Finally, Emily-Grace stood and bypassed her mother, on her way back out to the kitchen where the oven timer was beeping. A new tray of just baked cookies was ready to be removed and set out to cool. Over her shoulder, she tossed back at her mother, with an air of stubborn defiance, "I love him, Momma. But I still wish you had married Charlie."

"Jesus Christ," Jessie mumbled under her breath. "Seriously, Dee?"

Filing away the intention to call her the first chance she got to speak unobserved and unheard by her children, Jessie followed her daughter out to the kitchen. As she helped Emily-Grace remove the cookies from the oven and then slide them onto a cooling rack, Jessie pictured Josh at the studio, working, living in the skin of a Sheriff named Bobby. Spending his days around a cast and crew who had grown to love and respect him as a man as well as an actor.

She wished she could reach out to him and just hang on for dear life.

Because nothing was going to likely hurt worse in Josh's lifetime than the harsh judgment of his own children.

Catching Emily-Grace's eyes, she frowned. The child was setting a half-dozen of the biggest, best looking cookies aside, on a separate plate. She was heading over to Stella's later, for a play date.

"Are those for you and Stella later?" Jessie asked.

"No." Emily-Grace blinked wisely back at her mother. "These are for Daddy."

Oh. Okay. "All right," Jessie said softly. "We won't eat those." Reaching out, she picked up another half dozen cookies, and she smiled at Emily-Grace. "Here, honey," she said, bending to retrieve a Tupperware container and placing the cookies in it. "Why don't you take these to Charlie?"

A wide smile creased Emily-Grace's face. She wiped a hand over a darkening blonde ringlet, to swipe it off her sweaty cheek. Accepting the Tupperware, she nodded.

"He'll like that, Momma. Thank you."

"You, my child, are very, very welcome." With a flourish, Jessie swept her daughter up in a hug. Kissing her cheek, she breathed, "And thank you."

Chapter Eleven

Sacred Peace took weather cover indoors in the studio during the week of continuous thunder and lightning storms, but eventually moved out onto location to grab some climactic river shots a few weeks before the end of the season one shoot.

Always appreciative of nature and the beauty of his surroundings, Josh was standing at the crest of a cliff overlooking the fast-moving Kananaskis River early one morning while the crew hurried around setting up the camera along with large white silks on metal frameworks to soften the light. The ever-necessary craft service table was also just about ready. Greg, the slender token Newfoundlander on the crew, was piling it up with essentials meant to keep the large crew happy. As he worked, coffee, tea, toast, fruit, bagels and chocolate were being consumed almost as quickly as they were placed on the table on this misty Alberta morning.

Josh had already commandeered a banana and some oj. He'd slept in this morning, preferring to snuggle his wife's warm body than take time for breakfast at the ranch. Now, he was waiting for Greg's partner in the craft service truck to whip him up some eggs and bacon. According to the First A.D., since the cast and crew had already blocked out their scene, he, Charlie, Carter and Shanda would have about forty-five minutes to chill before the crew would be set up and ready for a rehearsal with camera.

A lot of crew were milling about now, some rushing, and some, like on-set wardrobe and hair, relaxing until they would be needed when the camera was ready to roll. The other cast were either in their trailers or getting some finishing touches done on their hair or wardrobe. Josh, apart from the occasional crew who wandered by to admire the foamy river below, was alone, just beyond an expanse of trees.

As he stood back a few feet, careful to watch his footing to safeguard against a fall into the rushing water twenty feet below, Josh reflected on the months to come. His and Jessie's schedules would overlap for two weeks in September. She was starting a new film in Austin, Texas—switched from NYC, which she was less than thrilled about—that would keep her busy up to a week before the *Sacred Peace* press tour. They had decided to move their three children back to Vancouver during that time, where they would stay with Deirdre and Carlotta, until Josh finished *Sacred Peace* and moved back to Vancouver as well. This way the children could attend school at West Point Grey Academy, and move back to the UBC house with Josh until the press tour started.

The entire family would then go on tour, bringing with them extra security as well as a ton of schoolwork and a tutor. The tour, which would include concerts featuring Jessie and Jacob, and tons of interviews with the media for Josh as well as other cast, would only last six weeks, at which point both Josh and Jessie planned to take a break just to be with their children and enjoy some time as a family. *Sacred Peace* would be starting up again in March; prior to that, both Josh and Jessie were considering film projects for the first few months of the following year. On top of this were the usual awards shows and fundraisers, and the occasional concert or outdoor festival for Jessie.

Josh was exhausted just thinking about it.

Still, by all accounts, *Sacred Peace* was going to be a stunning series. The first half of the season was already edited and ready for delivery to the network. Josh had watched the first three episodes with Charlie, Jonathon, Charles and Shanda, one Saturday night after a short day's shoot. At Charles' condo in Calgary, they had ordered dinner and, apart from Josh, had consumed more than a few drinks as they sat on pins and needles to see how their hard work compared with the early vision of the show on paper.

Josh didn't normally like watching himself on screen. The love scenes with Shanda were especially tough to take, for the difficult feelings both still occasionally had to fight, but overall the results were dramatic and heartfelt, cinematic in visual scope, and compelling in terms of story. Now, pleased at the memory of what they'd screened that night, Josh allowed a small smile to form on his lips as, below, the fast-moving glacier fed river announced its presence with a foamy rush and an adrenalin-fuelled hum.

Someone from the craft service truck called his name. Josh, across the clearing and beyond the small copse of trees, was far enough away that he barely heard the call. As he turned to tilt an ear to clarify that it was his breakfast that was ready, and his name that was being called, something crashed into him and he spun backwards on unbalanced boots.

Clawing at empty air, Josh had a sickening feeling. Safety was always key on this set, and he knew to stand back from the edge of the cliff, but whatever hit him had propelled him far enough forward that suddenly Josh was staring at the sky with nothing between it and the roaring ice-cold river but his falling body and a rush of crisp, cool air. Twenty feet later, he hit the water with enough force to almost knock the breath out of his lungs. Swiftly, Josh was completely immersed and gasping from the sudden jarring cold. Frantically, he clawed at the water and pedaled his feet. In the heavy cast boots his character Bobby wore, he was quickly being pulled deeper underneath the frigid water.

Oh fuck, this isn't good, he thought with a desperation that fed him with the sudden need to defeat the elements. Above, he thought he heard Arnie yelling but Josh couldn't be sure. The section of the river in which he found himself submerged was fast-moving, whitewater in places, and the roar was deafening. *Maybe I just wish I heard Arnie,* he told himself, as he fought to untie first one boot and then the other, and lever them off his feet while, at the same time, holding his breath and trying to get a grip on how far he was from shore.

It was August—summertime—but the Kananaskis was an icy glacier-fed river. It was deadly, dangerous in a very short time due to the risk of hypothermia. Already Josh could feel his brain start to go muddy on him; his fingers were struggling with the boots, but finally both were off, left to sink to the bottom of the river to maybe be rescued later by crew or, more likely, left to the pebbly bottom forever.

Frantic, Josh managed to suck in a breath when losing the boots enabled him to propel himself to the surface. He wasn't wearing a jacket but his pants were heavy—his fingers would not cooperate to undo his belt.

Oh, Jesus, he thought wildly. *Stupid me. I should have known better than to stand so close to the edge like that.* Arnie hadn't been far away, but Josh was cursing him now, wishing his security hadn't drank so much coffee and had to take a leak. *Who shoved me?* was his next random thought. Clearly, the push was intended to make him go over the edge. Josh, who had been staring downwards at the river, had no clue who was near him at the moment he was pushed. Now, he shoved those harried thoughts aside and focused on survival.

A strong swimmer, fit and healthy since his injuries from the horse-toss were, for the most part, healed, Josh made for the bank of the river. His arms felt like lead, though, and his legs were heavy. He had been in the mind-numbing cold river more than a minute already. There were no signs of crew or anyone down this low, at the surface, who were able to help. He was on his own.

A pool of whitewater ahead propelled him fast over rocks that bruised his body and made him miss his first attempt to secure footing in the shallows. Cursing, afraid he was going to black out or lose all ability to move his arms and legs, Josh went under again, and fought to claw his way to the surface as the rapids spun him around and around, tossing him like a rag doll in a washing machine until they mercifully spit him out.

Jessie, he agonized. *The kids. If I survive this I have to tell her we need a plan. We need a plan to keep them safe; they need someone to watch over them if I'm no longer around.*

A chilling new thought took root. *Maybe they'd be better off without me...*

Josh's thoughts deteriorated quickly in the freezing cold of the mighty glacier-fed Rocky Mountain river. Another foamy white spin; all he could see were flashes of trees dotted on the river's perimeters; all he could hear was own inner voice screaming for help. In reality, Josh couldn't muster up any true voice. Under he went again, smashed his left knee against an underwater rock, and grabbed at—nothing. There was nothing but roiling river water to grab hold of.

Mustering up some renewed fight in his quickly weakening body and spirit, Josh started to pray. *Please God, get me out of this. Please God, Jessie and the kids...they need me. Get me out of here.*

As quick as the last eddy sank him, it tossed him out. Numbly grasping at something, anything, Josh's hand made contact with a low lying tree branch suspended over the river's edge. Managing to wrap an elbow around it, Josh hung on until his fuzzy vision told him he could maybe shimmy across it to shore, or at least to shallower water. But it was his sore, recently repaired shoulder that was taking the strain. Moving the shoulder was doable, but not achieved without pain, with all his weight and the rushing river adding to the task. Screaming in his head, his long hair dripping and obscuring his vision, Josh forced his left hand up to the rough bark of the branch, so he could use it to take his weight and shimmy over the right hand, in a slow, treacherous gamble to make small gains and reach the shore.

Ten minutes had passed since he was pushed off the cliff, and Josh was losing the battle. He could feel his hands slipping. The rush of water was fighting for dominion over his body, trying to haul him back into its murky depths. In the end, the water won and he slipped back underneath the surface, noting with a strange numbed alacrity that there was a peacefulness under there, where the sun's rays reached him and halo'd his vision with a softly nuanced glowing light.

He closed his eyes and stopped fighting.

A thick hand reached in and grasped Josh's shirt. The hazy figure attached to the hand hauled him roughly to shore, screaming his name and cursing at him as he dragged Josh's body to safety.

Arnie.

Struggling to open his eyes, Josh fixed his gaze on the man. Arnie threw him on his side on the smooth pebbles at the river's edge. Absently thinking he should fight against him, because Arnie was now ripping off Josh's shirt while someone else hauled off his pants, Josh just closed his eyes again instead.

Arnie's long-sleeved Henley was being pulled over Josh now. No one had jackets on; the summer morning had started out cool but had rapidly warmed. Now someone was lying behind Josh as he spat out water from his lungs; a small body was wrapping itself around him, loaning him what heat and energy it could.

Shanda.

Josh recognized the feel of her body from their love scenes. Arnie, too, was holding him now, pressing Josh against his chest as he tried to inject warmth back into the too-cool body. Someone arrived with blankets; they tossed them over Josh and then a woman from wardrobe engineered one underneath him. Shivering profusely, Josh almost quaked his way out of them, but Shanda and Arnie were not letting go.

In the murky distance Josh heard rumblings that told him the set medics were close. He tried to open his eyes and focus on Arnie, who was hollering at him to stay awake, but it was futile. Josh stayed conscious, and although he could hear everyone around him, there was no way his foggy brain could make his lips co-operate and respond.

Slowly, a new warmth sourced through his body, though, and Josh started to come around. When he finally managed to keep his eyes open and focus on Arnie, the man Jessie knew as the Downtown Eastside angel was halo'ed in the earlier light that filtered through to Josh from the sun above. Arnie's cheeks were damp; droplets from his short hair were dripping over Josh's chest and landing on his cheeks like tears. Arnie's pale, gentle eyes were worried and afraid, and he was trembling.

"S-sorry," Josh finally managed to mumble. "Too close…to cliff…"

Relief washed over Arnie's face but it was quickly replaced with a deeper fear. "Josh, you better just be one accident prone son-of-a-bitch," he muttered. "And you better be warming up."

Closing his eyes, Josh turned his head away.

Jessie was humming happily in the ranch kitchen, rolling out dough to make cinnamon buns today, her trusty helper Emily-Grace at her side, when both she and her daughter stopped cold. The radio was on, tuned to their favorite Calgary pop station, and the announcer was suddenly telling the listening audience that actor Josh Sawyer had just been pulled from the icy Kananaskis River. Purported to have fallen over a twenty foot cliff, he was hypothermic and beat up from the rocks. He was being transported to a Calgary hospital but was reportedly conscious and responsive.

Jessie froze, and stared at her daughter, whose eyes were wide.

Emily-Grace spoke first. Filled with fright, her words emerged with a tragic undertone. "Momma, is he saying Daddy? Is that what the man is saying?"

Fear gutted Jessie. Without answering her daughter, she hollered at Dan, who was outside playing basketball with David while Dylan tended the horses in the barn with Gary.

"Dan!" Sprinting to her bedroom, Jessie grabbed her purse, then ducked back towards the kitchen to hug her daughter. "Daddy's fine, honey. The announcer said so. But Momma's going to the hospital to bring him home."

Tears were now running down Emily-Grace's pale cheeks. Standing at the island on a blue Rubbermaid step, she was holding the rolling pin in one hand, oddly suspending it above the half-rolled dough.

"You and Dan finish these. I'll call you the first chance I get. Daddy will love these warm cinnamon rolls when he gets home. I love you." With a big squeeze, Jessie went running.

Outside, she hugged the one son within sight and ran to her Mustang, screaming at Dan over her shoulder. "Dan, call Arnie and tell him to call me! Or get Charlie to call! Emily-Grace is inside alone!" Jumping into her car, she started the ignition as Dan vaulted up alongside and hauled open her door. Yelling at him, she fought to close the door but he wouldn't let her.

"What's going on, Jessie? Tell me! You're not going anywhere without me, not in this panicked state!"

"You need to stay with the kids, Dan! You and Gary, one to watch them and one outside on security! I just heard on the radio that Josh got hurt and I need to go! Let me go!"

"Hurt? How!" Dan held fast to the door.

Frustrated, Jessie started kicking it as big tears flew down her cheeks. "Let me go! Fuck you, Dan! Fuck you!"

It didn't cross her mind that little David was close by, twisting his fingers and also starting to cry as he realized his world was once again spinning out of control.

"Emily-Grace is inside, she heard too. She needs you. I'll be fine. Please, just let me go and get a hold of Arnie or Charlie. Or Charles. Please, Dan, please!"

One last hard well-placed kick and she managed to get him in the crotch.

Doubling over, Dan yelped, and Jessie took off, narrowly missing her small son as she backed up the car in a frantic rush to get away before Dan recovered and went after her.

It wasn't ten minutes after she squealed past the gate before her phone rang.

"Arnie," she yelled into it, fighting the highway noise in the open car, "what the hell?! Why did I have to hear this on the goddamned radio?"

"Someone on the crew must have tweeted it." As always, Arnie's was a voice of calm in the wilderness. "Jessie, Dan says you've already split."

"Is he okay? Arnie, just tell me if Josh is okay! Please!" Frantic, Jessie put the pedal to the metal and passed a BMW going well over the speed limit.

"He's doing okay. He's conscious, Jessie. I'm right behind the ambulance. Josh is being transported to Calgary for observation. *Sacred Peace* is going ahead with other shots and some quick rewrites."

"I don't give a fuck about *Sacred Peace* and its goddamned rewrites! What the hell happened?!"

"I don't...we're not sure. He went over the cliff into the river, that's all anyone seems to know at this point in time. He's being treated for hypothermia."

"And where in goddamned hell were you when this happened?!"

"Look, a man drinks coffee, occasionally he needs to piss. Jessie, I can't stand next to him and hold his hand 24-7!"

On her end, Jessie sensed the desperation and apologetic worry in her old friend's voice. She eased off.

"Okay, look Arnie, where's Charlie? And Charles? I know Jon is back in Vancouver."

"Charlie and Charles were in a Skype meeting when this happened. Charles was at his condo in Calgary, and Charlie was in his trailer at the location. Charles is meeting us at the hospital, and Charlie is with Josh in the ambulance."

"How close are you to Calgary?"

"Twenty minutes. Slow down. There's no need to get arrested or skid off the road. You're not far behind us, and Josh was doing okay last I checked. He was talking."

They signed off, and Jessie slowed down a bit, but in her adrenalin-fueled state she felt she could have run to the hospital faster than her car was taking her.

At the hospital she found both Charles and Charlie in the emergency waiting room. She trusted that Arnie had switched off with Charlie and was with her husband. Without hesitation, Jessie rushed Charlie. In her favorite angry Jessie move, she shoved him back against the wall.

"You shut that production down!" she screamed, to the shock and amazement of everyone in the waiting room. "No more of this! No more scary bullshit that is apparently targeting my husband. You shut it down!" Twisting around to Charles, she cried out at him as well, as Charlie tried in vain to reason with her. "You hear me? Shut it the hell down!"

Charlie grabbed her elbow and shook it to get her to listen. "Jessie, take it easy, will you please? Josh is okay. He was awake and talking up a storm when we got here."

The last part was a stretch, but Charlie was desperate to calm Jessie down. Charles glanced up at the main desk and strode over to ask for a private room to wait in, his face pale and his hands shaking.

"Josh never talks up a storm. I doubt he's talking at all. Charlie, this is insane! You need to do something. He could've been killed!"

And you weren't even there to see it, to feel the panic, Charlie thought, reliving the fear of the ten minutes Josh was in the river. *Thank God.*

Terrified, Jessie shook off his hold on her. "Where is he? I want to see him!"

"They're warming him up and running some tests just as a precaution," Charlie answered, trying to project a measure of calm in his voice. "They said he'll likely be released in a few hours. Someone will come get us when we can see him. Just hang tough for now, Jess."

"Where's Arnie? Is Arnie with him?"

"He went out to the parking lot to try to head you off at the pass. I told you, Josh is having tests. They'll come get us when he's back."

"He shouldn't be alone, Charlie! Josh shouldn't be alone."

Charlie had no answer for that. Sighing, he wrapped an arm around Jessie's shoulders and tried to pull her close, but she shoved him away.

"I want both you and Charles to tell me you are shutting *Sacred Peace* down until you know what the hell's going on. Promise me!"

Grabbing her elbow again, and squeezing hard, Charlie steered his vociferously protesting friend towards a room a nurse led them to.

Inside the room, which was some kind of sterile meeting room with a central table, and chairs for a dozen people, Charles, who was just ahead of them, turned and growled loudly. "We had one written threat, Jessie, one. And there's no proof that the choking incident or what happened today were any more than weird accidents."

Jessie's eyes widened and she stood stock still. "What do you mean you had one written threat? What the hell are you talking about, Charles?"

"Oh, Jesus, here we go," Charlie moaned, turning in a small circle before stopping to face the two of them, hands on his hips.

Grim-faced, Charles frowned. "We had a note. One. It pointed at Josh as a possible target. But that was after the PCP laced chowder. Nothing else has been found since. There's no reason to believe—"

"Charles! Do you mean to tell me there was a written threat against Josh and you carried on as usual all this time?" The blood drained from Jessie's face as she steadied her shaking legs by resting her butt on an arm of one of the chairs in the glassed-in space.

"Today was likely a fluke, Jessie. He got too close, he got dizzy or something."

"No. Josh is not stupid. He wouldn't just randomly tumble over a cliff into a river where white water rafters and kayakers have been known to drown from the effects of hypothermia, for God's sake!"

"Jessie, calm down. People are watching."

"I don't care! I don't care if the Pope sees me cursing and swearing! You just told me Josh has been named a target by some maniac! Again! Tell me, Charles, at what point do he and I get to live in peace? At what point do we get to feel safe? Ever?"

Watching, Charlie could barely contain his fury and anger at the universe for granting his friends so much grief. Today could have been an accident, but then again it may not have been. *Time will tell,* he thought. *Maybe we'll get another note.* In the meantime, he could barely handle the angst in Jessie's eyes, the worry in her closed fists and in the way she turned from them and hung her head on the table.

Slowly leveraging herself up after a moment to collect her wits, Jessie stood and faced them, these two men she loved like family. "You shut this production down," she demanded with a low growl, pointing a trembling finger at them. "And call me when you hear how Josh is doing. I need a drive."

Charles stood in front of the door and blocked her way. "Jessie, no. That's not an option, the way you're feeling right now."

Swinging past him, kicking at the door with one toed boot, Jessie hissed between her teeth. "What I'm feeling right now is furious that two people I love dearly, whom I thought I trusted, have put their stupid television show ahead of my husband's safety! The way I feel right now is so pissed that I could put both of you through that glass window. Let me go, unless you feel like finding yourself in one of those emergency rooms getting stitched up! Call me when you know he's okay."

Jostling past Charles, Jessie shoved open the door and disappeared into the waiting room and then out into the bright Calgary sunlight just beyond.

Charles moved to follow her, but Charlie grabbed his arm. "No. You know her. She needs some time to cool off."

"She's alone, Charlie. She's not safe."

"This is Calgary, not L.A. or New York. She's never been named as a target. She'll be fine."

His worried eyes said that he couldn't verify that, but Charlie knew Jessie well enough to know she would only lose them if they tried to follow her. Dropping into the chair she'd just vacated, he fixed a hopeless stare at Charles, and wondered about the heavy price continuously exacted upon his friends for the sake of success in the heady world of entertainment.

Chapter Twelve

Gabrielle Daoust was trying to calm her two-year-old son when she wandered through Calgary's Chinook Centre Mall and spotted a woman she was certain looked familiar, hunkered down over a white takeout coffee cup in a chair just outside a Starbucks on the main concourse. Handing the squealing boy to her husband, she said, as the woman looked towards the sound and her pale eyes met Gabrielle's darker ones, "That looks like Jessie Wheeler-Sawyer."

"Gabrielle…" The husband's name was Jeff. He was a nice guy, but already annoyed at his son's temper tantrum, which started the second they left their vehicle and which showed no promising signs of abating. "If it is, I'm sure she wants her privacy after what happened today."

"Why is she here and not with her husband? Hmmm. You know me, Jeff. I need answers."

"This is not the time, Gab. It's really not." Their son was attracting a lot of attention with his screaming and wailing as he tried to escape the prison of his father's arms. Gabrielle was completely unconcerned.

"Back in a few minutes." Discreetly, she turned her back to the woman she thought was Jessie, and hit record on her iPhone, which she tucked into an exterior pocket in her purse in the hopes that it would record without sounding too muffled. "Sorry, Jeff. But if that's Jessie…" Eyes alight, she touched her son's sweaty forehead and swung around.

"Great." Secretly, though, Jeff was amused. His pretty wife, with her dark, straightened hair, a pear-shaped almost squat figure, and a confident stride, constantly amazed him. He was her opposite, tall and blonde. They were a fun couple, popular amongst their friends, usually happy and easygoing. Now, Jeff chuckled despite his annoyance, set his son down, and took off after him down the hall while Gabrielle did her thing.

Seated, Jessie straightened when she saw the short young twenty-something woman approach. *Crap,* she thought, reaching up to pull a red and white ball cap down lower over her ears. *So much for my disguise.*

Gabrielle stopped a comfortable five feet away. "Hey, Jessie," she said with a casual wave. "I hope my son didn't upset whatever you were doing. He's quite the little firecracker."

Gazing past her, dark circles under her eyes, Jessie watched the boy's father chase him into a Build-A-Bear store. She would have smiled if she could have mustered up the energy.

"What's his name?" she managed.

"Tyler. For my dad."

"I don't mind screaming kids. I'm kind of used to them."

"Dylan, huh? Your youngest?"

Before she answered, Jessie contemplated the woman standing in front of her. She seemed okay. Her pleasant eyes exuded a kindness that Jessie found comforting even though the gal was a stranger. She wasn't pulling out an iPhone and taking pics, nor did she seem to be scrambling for an autograph.

Sitting back, taking her Starbucks caramel macchiato with her into her lap, Jessie replied, "Yep, Dylan. I guess everybody knows he's got a mind of his own. That video from Pacific Center, right?"

"Mmm, I saw four videos from that day. It must drive you nuts."

"Don't you have anything better to do with your time than watch people like me fuck up?" Jessie's shoulders sank.

"You make my ordinary life much more interesting." Sticking out a hand, Gabrielle introduced herself. "Gabrielle. That was my husband, Jeff."

Apprehensive, but taking the woman's hand, Jessie said, "A J name. Good." Furrowing her brow, she angled her head up at Gabrielle and asked, "Or is he one of those G-E-O-F-F Geoffs?"

"Nope. He's a good old J."

"Good one." A little sulky, Jessie held up her coffee as a toast. "Here's to our special guys whose names start with J." Lowering her voice, she leaned forward conspiratorially. "They're very special people."

"I know they are." Inwardly, Gabrielle was tickled. Jessie was far more open than she expected her to be. Hesitating, she gestured to the chair opposite Jessie. "I know this is forward, but may I sit? You look like you could use some company."

"Have at 'er." Using her foot, Jessie pushed the chair out for Gabrielle. "But I should warn you, I may not be the best conversationalist at the moment. You'll have to do all the talking."

Realizing that was a warning of sorts, Gabrielle softened, and nodded. "I understand," she said, and glanced around.

"I'm alone," Jessie told her rather bravely. "I skipped out. I was pissed."

"Hmmm, I've heard you do that on occasion."

"You would too if you were me. Trust me. Especially today." Wrapping an arm around her belly, Jessie deflated almost entirely and peered over at Gabrielle with sad eyes.

"What's happening, Jessie? On that set? What happened today?"

"I don't know yet. He was having tests done when I got to the hospital. I haven't had a chance to talk to him yet." The blue eyes were floating.

Watching her, Gabrielle's heart skipped a beat, and Jessie had to stifle the urge to climb into the young woman's arms.

What is it about you? Jessie wondered. *You have some safe aura.*

"He's okay, though?" The words were spoken slowly, with sincere compassion.

"So they tell me. As okay as someone can be after falling fully clothed twenty feet into a glacial river, I suppose."

"Fallen, huh? He tripped and went over?"

Jessie's eyes narrowed, and she clutched her Starbucks cup tighter. "To be honest, I don't know."

"And he was choked a while ago? And before that, the PCP thing?"

Tilting her head, Jessie stared at her tablemate. "Who are you, Gabrielle? Why are you curious about what's going on with my husband and all his weird little accidents? Are you with the media?"

Hesitating, Gabrielle admitted, "I might be. On some level." She waited to see how Jessie took this.

Jessie accepted the sketchy non-committal information with a grain of salt and a shrug. "All right then. I suppose you have questions. Ask away."

"I only have one."

Surprised, Jessie sat up straight again and took a sip of her warm beverage. "It must be a good one."

"It's about your husband."

"Don't ask me if he's good in bed. I'm getting a better vibe from you than that. I'm expecting something more…earth shattering."

Tossing back her head, Gabrielle laughed. Down the hall, her husband was just leaving the bear shop with his son. He smiled when he saw a slight upturn to Jessie's lips. "Atta girl," he said, too far away for his wife to hear, but it was worth saying anyway. At least Tyler was somewhat settled now. The little guy reached for his father's fingers and led him to another store across the hall.

"Earth shattering…well, it may not be earth shattering. I'm just wondering what you think about all this negativity surrounding Josh, since you came back to him. I know you've lost fans as well. That's gotta hurt on a personal level." Inside, Gabrielle's stomach was jelly. *Never let them see you sweat,* she told herself as she fixed a gentle smile in Jessie's direction.

"Ah ha. I knew it. Although you're right. That's not even remotely earth shattering. In fact, it's old news. I don't know why anyone still cares."

"Neither do I. But I'm curious as to how much it bothers you."

"You don't want to know why I chose Josh? Usually that's what people want to know. That whole temper thing, you know?" She said 'temper thing' with a mocking scowl, which echoed her pissed off frustrated, terrified mood.

Gabrielle caught the vibe and said softly, "I know why you chose Josh. I've been watching you from the beginning, Jessie. It's not hard to see how much the two of you love each other."

With a sigh, Jessie leaned forward and placed her elbows on the table. Slowly, she twisted her Starbucks cup around and around, and stared numbly at it while she answered. "Thank you for that. If you're sincere, then you're rare."

"I think those of us who are crazy in love with our men recognize it in each other."

"That's nice. I'm glad you have that." Jessie picked at the white sticky label stuck to her cup. "I've loved others too. Just…it's different with Josh. I can't even breathe when I think about the possibility of losing him." Looking up at Gabrielle, Jessie fought back a new round of tears. "So as far as your question goes, I think you already know the answer."

"It bothers you. A lot."

"Only in that I can't stand to see him hurt. I don't care what other people think, I don't care if fans choose Jacob over him. It's their choice. Jacob makes great music. He and I make great music together. He and I will always love each other. But Josh is everything to me and I'm…" Unable to help herself, she swiped at fresh tears that escaped from the corners of her eyes, and aimed her gaze at a large painted 'flat white' hot beverage advertisement in the Starbucks window to her right. When she felt a little more composed, she told the stranger across from her, "I'm actually terrified of what's been happening on set. I'm probably going to get in shit for telling you this, but I was just told that after the PCP thing in the chowder, someone left a note that threatened Josh. As if he hasn't been anyone's target before, like, always."

A flush of anger swept up and across the kind Gabrielle's cheeks. "Again? What are you thinking?"

"I don't know! Everything, I guess. Someone connected to Nadia or Morgan or, or even my old stalker, Deuce McCall. It's not like there's nobody in our collective past whose death might not need avenging, in some deranged person's eyes. I don't know what to think. Charles thinks it's likely just a coincidence, today and the choking thing. I'm not so sure."

Wringing her hands, Jessie stared at her phone. Charlie was calling. "One sec," she said to Gabrielle, as she snapped it up and turned sideways to answer. "Charlie?"

"He's being released, Jessie. Where are you, are you okay?"

"I'm fine, I'm…" She glanced at Gabrielle and managed a tiny smile. "I'm having a Starbucks with a friend. I'll be there in twenty minutes."

"You've got the Mustang? I take it you want to drive Josh home. Want me to get Arnie to switch off with you? He said he drove to set in the King Ranch with Josh today. It's cooling down out there."

"August evenings. Yes, tell Arnie to hang on and he can take the Mustang.

He'll love that since he's staying at the house while you guys shoot on the river. I'll be there in a bit."

"Charlie?" Gabrielle couldn't avoid the smile that widened across her face. "I love my husband, but Charlie's my celebrity crush. He has been since forever. Since the two of you made that movie in Curacao years ago."

"Well, here's your scoop on Charlie. He's every bit as amazing as you think he is. Sorry." Jessie smiled too, a sad little attempt at a smile, anyway. "Although I'm super pissed at him right now."

"Because…?"

"Because I want him to shut the production down until they figure out if there's still a threat against Josh, or if these last two things are just a strange coincidence."

"But he won't because it'll cost him."

"Of course. Tons of money. But he shouldn't be putting the production ahead of my husband's safety."

"Maybe he doesn't see any real reason…?"

"Do you think I'm just freaking out because I'm scared? That I can't see the whole picture?"

"I wouldn't presume to know, Jessie. I can't imagine the pressure you guys have always lived under. But I suppose if the show doesn't get another note, then maybe it was just a one-off and your hubby just happens to be in a risky profession. But…"

"But what?"

"But there are a lot of angry fans still around. Angry about you choosing Josh over Jacob."

"I know." Sighing, Jessie finished her caramel macchiato and paused before standing. This woman just had a rare light about her that Jessie found comforting. "So I guess what we agree on is that there is no shortage of people who want to see harm come to the man I love. I swear, Gabrielle. If something happens to him…" She couldn't finish, and just shook her head instead.

With a sad smile of her own, Gabrielle stood and extended a hand to Jessie. "I'll say some prayers for you, sweetheart. And uh, Jessie? Next time you decide to hide in public, switch the hat. I'm from Prince Edward Island. I recognized the Summerside Western Capitals hat before I realized who was under it. It's become common knowledge that you often wear that hat when you want to be incognito."

"Oh, crap. I suck. It was all I had in the car today." Taking it off, Jessie handed it to Gabrielle. "From me to you. Give it to your husband."

"Are you kidding? No!" Gabrielle paused, and Jessie managed a grin. Fishing a black sharpie she kept for autograph purposes out of her bag, Jessie signed the crest on the hat. "You deserve it," she said. "You were actually kinda nice to talk to."

Biting her lip, Gabrielle had one last thing to say. "Look, Jessie, I'm real glad you are as sweet as everyone always says you are. Because. . .you should know. . .I'm a celebrity blogger. I've got a few million readers. And I'm real honest."

"Oh. Oh, shit. Now I have to think about everything I just said to you." Flustered, Jessie knit her brows together as she picked up her paper cup and dumped it in the nearby compost. Absently, she fished after it and tossed the lid in a bin marked 'waste.'

"If there's anything you don't want me to repeat, send me an email." Stretching out her hand, Gabrielle motioned toward a small lime green card with black print that floated between them.

"Nah. I'm an honest person too, Gabrielle. Put it out there that I'm scared for my husband. Maybe it will soften people towards him."

"At the very least, I can get an army of other bloggers and fans to switch the hate tide, Jessie. Some have already written Jacob Ryan off anyway, for what he did to you after his fiancée was killed."

"You can write that I take at least some of the responsibility for what happened. Jacob crossed a line, but he and I have made our peace. He's happy now. He's real happy."

"You know, if there's ever anything you guys want made public, I'm on your side, Jessie. I get a good vibe from you."

"Same." Jessie's eyes lit up. "Would Jeff with a J mind if you visited the *Sacred Peace* set? To meet Charlie, of course." She winked.

"I think my knees just went weak. Jeff's used to my crush on Charlie. He'll just roll his eyes and want to come meet Shanda Ellis. And you, of course."

"I'll set it up." Jessie held up Gabrielle's card. "I'd give you my personal email but I really don't know you. I hope you understand. If you really want to reach me at any time, I'm on Facebook as Rachel Sandy from Nova Scotia. Kay? R-A-C-H-E-L."

"You're really something. Can I give you a hug?"

"I was going to ask you for one. Of course. Take a picture too. With the hat if you want."

They took a selfie before Gabrielle turned to Jessie and asked, "Any final thoughts?"

"Hmmm. Yes. I'm just a person who loves her man the same way every other gal loves her guy. I just want to see Josh and our kids happy and safe. That's all. That's my main goal in life."

"Me too. Now go take him home. Stop hiding in the mall and go love him."

"You too, Gabrielle. Go love your man. Thank you."

When they parted, Jessie couldn't help but watch Gabrielle cross the floor and take her husband's hand. Jeff soon had a big smile on his face and a happy wave for Jessie. Tyler was snuggled up in his arms munching on a cookie. Jessie's heart ached for the simple life she figured they were leading.

Pulling up to the hospital twenty minutes later, Jessie found Josh leaning alone against the far wall of the small room where she had left Charlie and Charles earlier. Arnie was conferring in another corner with the two producers and, thankfully, someone had the decency to pull blinds down over the glass so the guys had some privacy. Everyone turned to look at Jessie when she stepped inside the space, but apart from giving Arnie the keys to the 'stang, and taking the keys to the truck, she only had eyes for her quiet husband.

Charles tried to say something to her as she fixed her gaze on Josh and waited for him to make his way over to the door, but Jessie air-palmed Charles and didn't meet his eye, nor did she make any pretense about how she felt about Charlie at the present time, choosing to ignore him as well.

The only words she spoke were said to Arnie, voiced without losing her gaze on Josh, who didn't have the energy to muster a smile, and who was wearing fresh jeans and a vintage button up shirt Charlie had retrieved for him from their Calgary condo.

"Arnie, don't follow us," Jessie demanded. "Go straight to the ranch and check on Dan and the kids, please. We'll be along in a bit."

"You got it, Jessie." Arnie, too, was rather pissed at Charlie and Charles and their inability to take action as far as the production versus Josh was concerned. They didn't have another note, but as of an hour ago they had Josh's quiet word that he'd been literally pushed over the edge today. No one from the set was admitting to seeing a thing, though. Everyone rushed to the cliff edge so quickly after Josh went over that whoever did the pushing got lost in the shuffle, which was likely exactly what had been planned.

Josh didn't stop in front of Jessie, and she didn't expect him to. As he left the room he held the door open for her and she slipped through it, then they left together, hand in hand.

Arnie stepped out behind them to holler where the truck was parked, but they didn't acknowledge that they heard. The quiet man shoved his hands in his pockets and watched them go.

They found the truck the 'new tech' way, by clicking on the car finder button twice, so the horn sounded and the direction indicators flashed.

Driving out of the city, Jessie and Josh didn't share a single word. In the truck, Josh simply closed his eyes and sank down into the passenger seat as the horrifying memory of the fear that coursed through him as he sputtered and choked his way through the frigid river debilitated him.

Reaching over to him, Jessie wrapped her fingers in his but she kept her eyes on the road ahead. Determined, swallowing past the angry tears that hovered beneath the surface all day when they weren't blatantly coursing down her cheeks, she pulled off the highway when she reached the dirt road where she and Josh had stopped to make love before she flew out to Vancouver for the tour rehearsals.

Sliding the big truck to a stop, she left the ignition on a setting where she could play music, and she selected an iPhone playlist that featured ballads by the metal band Metallica. The restrained opening E Minor arpeggio—the open low E followed by the open G, B and high E—of their most famous ballad, *Nothing Else Matters,* melted in her ears as she moved sideways over the middle console to straddle her husband's lap.

She faced him as the ballad built and filled the cab around them.

Roughly, she used her thumb and fingers to thrust Josh's chin up, to make him open his eyes and focus on her. The pain in his eyes shattered her;

he was equally bereft at the agony in hers. Mixed with anger, Jessie's usual diaphanous gaze was hard and a deeper blue than usual. A sheen of moisture covered both of her eyes—her own private river, a safe one for Josh to climb into, to disappear into. As she bent forward to start biting his lip, to feel his wet mouth under hers, to taste the blood she roughly drew from him, Jessie closed her eyes, but not before Josh saw flecks of hurt and worry cascade underneath the surface.

She took him with a desperation borne of impending loss, something Jessie knew well. Rocking her hips forward to start them off on a path of desire that accelerated quickly, Jessie bit harder on Josh's top and then bottom lip, placed her hands on both stubbly cheeks, and moaned with her need to feel his physical body respond to her, warm and wanting.

Josh could taste his blood too; he wiped his tongue over his lips before he opened his mouth wide and tilted his head back to let Jessie thrust her tongue as deeply into him as she could.

There was a dampness on his cheeks, he wasn't crying so Jessie must be, Josh realized. It hurt him to the core, seeing her like that, desperate to join her body to his on this day when an icy river fought with him over the right to his life.

Josh put his hands on her hips, but Jessie moaned and told him, "No," before she removed his hands and held them, wrists together, above his head. With her free hand, she ripped open the snaps of the plaid shirt Charlie had brought Josh to wear; it was an old yellow plaid one he liked, a favorite for its soft brushed flannel. Lifting the white T-shirt beneath it, Jessie pulled both up over her husband's head, and then she let go of his wrists and dropped the shirts on the driver's seat. She let his fingers graze her elbows while she worked at unbuckling his wide leather belt, her pace hurried and frantic now, new sobs starting in her throat in remembrance of all the times she ached for him and couldn't have him; at all the times they were separated because some diabolical idiot had it out for them, for...him.

The belt loosened, Josh helped her out by raising his hips so Jessie could usher his jeans down; he moved to undo her jeans but she shoved his hands away and did the work herself, pulling her jeans and panties off all the way, her brown boots too, so she could have the freedom to widen her legs and ride him uninhibited by such a mundane thing as clothes.

Josh sank further into the wide leather seat as his wife took every bit of him into her and bent forward to suck hard on his lip as her pleasure increased. Josh, too, was moaning now with the intensity of his wife's lovemaking; more than anything he wanted to roll her over and drive himself deeper into her, and hold her wrists above her head while she clenched and came around him, but he couldn't. For the second time that day he was prisoner to another living force's wants and needs, but this time it was okay, this was the way it should be. Grabbing her hips now, pressing her further down onto him, he groaned and floated somewhere above them as Jessie grabbed at his hair and sucked harder and harder; as she moved to his ear, his neck, his shoulder, finally coming hard onto him while her teeth left red marks in his flesh.

Jessie's tears were coming harder now too; like a waterfall they drenched Josh with their capacity to love him, to cleanse him, to communicate her love for him through simple salt and water.

"I can't stand it," she was sobbing as she rocked her hips to absorb every last bit of the pleasure that came from loving him and as Josh, too, climaxed. "I can't stand it. Loving you…it destroys me, Josh. It always has, and it always will."

Around them, the Metallica ballad built to a whole other climax, sweet guitar and husky voices hitting notes that satisfied on one level but failed to reach nirvana, to completely heal. Jessie had the music on so loud that the truck shook. The drums and electric guitars pounded in her ears, driving the rawness of her pain to a whole new level that the choice of music greedily took from her soul. To her, *Nothing Else Matters* was an angry song, a song about wanting, about needing, the love of another; it was beautifully constructed and performed but was angry and raw nonetheless. Like Jessie and Josh's lovemaking, the metal ballad's wailing guitar and painful, haunting lyrics were enmeshed in each other; they drove home the point that often things that are simply beautiful sometimes *hurt.*

Music hurt. Love hurt. Loving this man beneath Jessie hurt, because with him it seemed there was always a risk of loss. Jessie was a guitar and Josh was the percussion. Together they were close to perfection, apart they were just individual parts of a lost whole. As in the Metallica ballad, even when joined they could never be enough. Their life on the planet together could never reach a state of perfection. Too many parts of their souls had already been lost, stolen from them in bits and pieces, in other affairs and in the treachery of others, and even just in too much time apart.

Climaxing together in Josh's truck on a back road in the Kananaskis Country of Alberta, near the river that almost stole Josh's life today, was simply not enough. The sexual release was not a glue that could hold them together, instead it was an agony that tried to tear them apart for its inability to sear away the losses that came before and that threatened to hang over them until they caved. Clutching her man to her chest as she clenched and cried out and sobbed around him, Jessie's pain was barely heard above the feral music marking this new knowing; in her head, though, she heard every word she screamed in terrorized fear.

One day you will be gone from me forever. One day I will no longer hold you in my arms, I will no longer make love to you. One day we will no longer be together. Forever. And I can't stand it.

Josh, coming down from the agony and ecstasy of the unexpected emotion Jessie was pouring into him, pressed her sweet body close to him and breathed her in. His breath was still ragged, his blood was still pounding in his ears.

"Sweet Jesus, that was fine," he gasped, pressing his ear against her chest so he could hear every beat of her heart, so he could feel her warmth as it soaked into him. He rocked her as, somewhere west of them, the sun melted behind a bank of clouds, behind a jagged mountain peak.

The sky darkened.

Jessie's body stopped shaking as her sobs eased, but Josh kept rocking her anyway, the way he rocked all three of their children as babies, and even now when they needed his comfort. Jessie's arms were wrapped so tight around him that Josh didn't ever want her to let go. But eventually the truck cooled and the Metallica ballad playlist ended. The silence, after the heavy pounding, was welcome, but it was also shocking in its scarcity.

Lifting her hips, Jessie reached over and opened the passenger door. Slipping off her husband's lap, she grabbed a box of Kleenex from behind the seat, and stood by the side of the road to clean up. Tossing the soiled tissues into the woods, she apologized to the environment and prayed the tissues would compost quickly. Pivoting around, she took the jeans and panties Josh handed her, and then her boots, putting them on one at a time by leaning her feet up on the running board of the big truck.

Josh was dressed again. Leaning back against the truck, ankles crossed, he watched his wife buckle up her belt. When she was ready, they stood apart, just out of reach, and contemplated who they had become and what they meant to each other. No words, no love song could fill that silence, the one that came with a need bigger than two people, than a family, than a planet, than a universe, could ever hope to comprehend.

"It's too big for us." Jessie lost herself in the liquid brown eyes she loved, in the man who stood so casually nearby, whose very essence brought her to her knees again and again and again. "This thing. Us. It's too damn big."

"We promised ourselves, Jess. After McCall, after Morgan and Nadia. We said no more fear. We said we wouldn't let fear get to us."

"But it is! It is getting to us. But this is the thing...I can't live my life worrying about you every second of every day, Josh. It's crippling!"

"Then wipe the slate clean. Start again."

"How?" Throwing her arms out to the sides, Jessie faced him with a new desperation. "How, Josh? After everything we've been through? Charles and Charlie won't pull the plug on *Sacred Peace*. You know they won't."

"They can't. Come on, Jessie. You know they can't. If someone wants me dead, they'll find a way to make it happen, here or in Vancouver. Stopping production will only let the idiot win."

"So. You *were* pushed today."

Momentarily silent, Josh uncrossed and re-crossed his ankles. "Yes. I was."

"By who?"

"I have no fucking clue. I was staring out at the water thinking about you. Wishing I was home in bed doing sweet things to my wife."

"Lovely. That helps."

"Look, Jessie. There are only a few weeks left on this show. Everyone's tired. We all want it to be done. I'll be careful not to put myself in a vulnerable position again. I'll be fine."

"Don't make promises you can't keep, Josh. Just fucking don't."

"C'mere." Reaching out to her, Josh pulled Jessie close and sighed as her body gave in to him. "I don't want to scare you, Jessie, but I need you to promise me something, okay?"

In his arms, she tensed. Her muffled voice came from his chest. "Why don't I like the sound of that?" Raising her head, she backed off a little and looked at him.

"Jessie, little one...You know there are no guarantees. I could drive out to Calgary tomorrow and get nailed by a transport truck. So could you, for that matter. We need to soak up the time we have, every minute, every second. We can't take a single moment for granted."

"We already live that way, Josh. And then we go our separate ways to work on shows. We pretty much suck at keeping promises." Sniffling, she shrank and curled up into herself as Josh smiled and wiped away new tears with his thumbs.

"So cute," he mumbled adorably, his eyes alight.

"Stop making me want to take you all over again. Stop making me be so damned deeply in love with you!"

"Never." The word was simple beauty and pleasure all on its own. Hugging her, Josh added, "Now, will you listen? At what I need you to promise me? And don't freak out. It's just a precaution." Taking her cheeks in his palms, Josh waited until Jessie nodded up at him from underneath sopping wet eyelashes.

One more sniffle, and she nodded again. "Okay. I'm listening. Speak."

A deep sigh preceded Josh's wish, which was aptly punctuated with forlorn, glistening eyes. "Jess...if this goes sour...if something happens to me..."

"No." She struggled to get away, and he grabbed her shoulders and forced her to listen.

"Jessie, I mean it. It could happen. Now listen. Are you listening?"

She stopped struggling and refocused on him, new tears trailing slowly down the damp cheeks.

"I want you to go to Matt. That's what I want. Go to Matt because he has always been there for you. For us, for the kids. He loves you. He's pretty much always loved you, I think."

"Josh, Matt knows I am nothing without you. I'm a piece of dirt on the ground without you. Why would he want that? Why would he want me like that?"

"Because, little one, didn't you hear me? He loves you. That's why. You have to promise me you will go to him. Promise me so I won't worry the next time..." He gulped, and looked away.

"Is that what you were thinking today, Josh? While you tried to get the hell out of that freezing river? You were worrying about me and the kids?"

"Hell, yeah." Grinning stupidly, he looked back at her. "If I was gonna die today, I sure as hell wanted my last thoughts to be of my beautiful wife and my amazing kids."

"This isn't helping." Melting back into his chest, Jessie closed her eyes and wrapped both arms around him. "No more bad and scary stuff, okay? Let's just stay here forever."

As if on cue, inside the truck Jessie's cell started to ring. She groaned and ignored it, but Josh reached behind and grabbed it.

"Charles," he said, holding it out to her.

"Fuck him." Jessie turned her face into Josh's neck and exhaled. She felt him smile under her warm breath as it tickled the hair at the base of his neck.

Josh answered anyway, and Jessie growled menacingly at him. "Yep, what's up Charles?"

Tuning out, Jessie moved away from her husband and sauntered around the truck. Pulling herself up into the driver's seat, she waited for Josh to get off the phone and climb into the passenger seat before she started the ignition.

"Is he pulling the plug?" she asked.

"Nope. He just wanted to know if we were home yet. Dan called him. The kids are getting anxious. I guess Arnie's not there yet."

"Oh shit, yes. I scared the shit out of them today. Josh?" She locked him in her frightened gaze. "Emily-Grace and I heard it on the radio. That you were pulled out of the river."

"The pleasures of social media, huh?"

"I suppose so. Someone Tweeted it, I guess. Or Facebooked it."

"Well, let's put it behind us and go see our kids, huh Jess? I really need to see our kids."

Wistful, Jessie leaned towards him for one final brush of her lips against his. Then, settling back against the big truck, she sent Josh a diabolical grin. "More Metallica?" she asked.

"Yeah, about that. That was crazy. In a good way. But maybe we should play something a little more, uh, less painful? Like how about some nice, easy country. Kenny Chesney or Keith Urban. I'd even do Alan Jackson if you were up for it."

"Country smuntry." Talia crossed Jessie's mind. Talia, who was no longer on the planet. She shivered. "No country," she declared. "Compromise. Colin James."

As *Into the Mystic* filled the cab, she pulled a U-turn and headed back towards the highway. At her side, Josh smiled and pictured cuddling up with Jessie and all three of their children while he read as many bedtime stories as the kids wanted.

"Heaven," he mumbled sleepily as Jessie turned left onto the highway.

"Don't get any ideas," she scowled, misunderstanding his meaning. But Josh didn't hear her. Between his rough ride in the cool river, and Jessie's desperate lovemaking, he was wiped out. He was asleep before Colin James sang the final verse of the treasured song, and snoring by the time Jessie hit the replay button.

As she drifted west into the setting sun, Jessie remembered that she hadn't answered him earlier. Now, she took his hand and brought Matt's gentle eyes to mind.

"Yes," she said softly to the wind as it zipped past the truck. "Matt. Sweet Matt."

And somehow, knowing Matt would likely always, in one way or another, have her back, Jessie was able to relax into the music, and make her way home.

Chapter Thirteen

Alin was the tallest member of her family, which resulted in relentless teasing from her younger brother.

"Your contribution to life is to be that person in the grocery store who everyone asks to get bottles off the top shelf for them."

Alin had different ideas about her larger purpose. Tonight, as she strolled around the Sawyer family ranch an hour west of her home in Calgary, she felt called to be a protector. Twenty-three years old, she had applied to the RCMP—the Royal Canadian Mounted Police—but there were hoops to jump through to get into that organization. So far, she had already done a successful written test, and was waiting for a call to do the physical component of the application process.

Athletic by nature, Alin was a star basketball player in both high school and university. When the security firm she worked for sent her to the Sawyer family's ranch, she was thrilled to find a basketball net installed down by the barn. It certainly helped to pass the long nights strolling the grounds, which was her preference over sitting down by the gate checking Facebook all night long. That usually made her sleepy, and even doing jumping jacks and planks and sit-ups didn't help much once the sleep bug got through to you on your all night shift.

There was something sacred about being awake when most people were sleeping. These summer nights were warm and cozy, and the ranch, although much more ordinary than Alin had expected it to be, given that its owners were wealthy celebrities, was an ideal place to act out scenarios from her future life as a law enforcement officer.

As she patrolled the barn, the house (being careful not to look in the windows and frighten the occupants, or see something she shouldn't around the area of the master bedroom in the far southwest corner), and the other outbuildings where gardening supplies, extra outside furniture, and sometimes Jessie's Mustang and Josh's Harley were stored, Alin pretended she was apprehending criminals of the worst kind. Drug lords, rapists, money launderers, the Mafia…they all came through the Sawyer ranch when Alin was on duty. In reality they were only shadows, or sometimes a hoe or a rake left leaning up against the shed, but they stood in for the bad guys just fine. And when Alin shot, she never missed, each shot accented with what remained of her light East Indian accent in a low *kapow,* which was a remnant of having only her younger brother Patin to play with when they were young and still living in India.

Now, she looked up at the stars and sighed with the beauty of it all. Her uniform was as black as the solemn and mystical night sky, her hair darker than all, wound up in a tight bun that hurt tonight. Always cautious to make sure she was presentable and professional, in case she actually got to see one of the famous Sawyers close-up, Alin tucked every tail of her ironed shirt in perfectly, and shined her shoes before every shift to make sure there were no visible scuff marks.

It was three in the morning, and she had just come up from the gate after doing her hourly check-in. Arnie was asleep in the house, in the guest room. Alin had conferred with him at midnight, after Josh and Jessie went to bed. Each night when she was on shift walking the grounds, Arnie spent fifteen or twenty minutes with her, showing her Jujitsu moves or Karate holds and defenses. Alin soaked up every second of his informal training. Arnie was a boxer, too, and she had already made plans to meet him at a gym in Calgary to learn what she could.

"You have potential," he had told her earlier tonight. "Have you ever thought about doing private security for a living?"

"No," she told him with an almost fierce determination. "I want to go all the way with the RCMP. The only thing I don't want to do is the musical ride they do on horseback. Large animals are not my thing."

"Too bad," he had said with a twinkle in his eye as he headed to the screen door to tuck in for the night. "I think you would be great. Josh and Jessie are always looking for someone they can trust to travel with them. It can be an exciting lifestyle."

True, Alin felt her senses light up at the idea of travelling with a celebrity family she knew had been through a lot in their short time together. And although she rarely even got to see Josh or Jessie apart from the occasional wave at the gate, it was easy to see they were good people. Often, Alin watched the whole family playing together in the yard—basketball, soccer, even baseball sometimes. There was a lot of love there. The children were happy, but still…there was a pall over the family that came from a tragic past. It had increased over the last few weeks, due to weird accidents happening on the set where Josh was working.

Josh. Alin's friends were nuts about the fact that she got to work with him, that she got to hang out at the ranch to help protect him and his family. Sure, Alin wasn't carrying a weapon, but her supervisor at the gate was. She was more of a, well, a watcher. Always looking for intruders, crazy fans mostly, she'd been told when she got the gig, which she got mostly for her athleticism. As yet, she had never spoken to Josh Sawyer, but he always nodded in his serious tragic, sad, unsmiling way when he passed her. Was she afraid of him? Did all those rumors about his temper make her nervous? Maybe a little, but Alin was made of tough stuff. She had to be; her brother had pounded her head into the basement's cement floor regularly until he got old enough to realize he could really hurt her. And she was from an immigrant family. She'd had to be tough because her unusual smell and strange clothes and weird accent—which, to Alin, were all perfectly normal—made her a target for teasing amongst her classmates and friends.

It was quiet tonight. Only the whisper of a Kananaskis breeze rustling through the trees created the occasional stir. The leafy swishes sometimes encouraged a whinny from one of Josh's two horses stabled in the small barn on the eastern side of the ranch, kitty-corner across a dirt clearing from the rambling one-story home.

Alin made her way closer to the barn and grabbed the basketball. Already tonight she'd 'pretend shot' two fictional Columbian drug smugglers that took her an hour to find as she patrolled the place. Shooting baskets would pass some more time, although she would have to be careful not to let the ball hit the ground. After all, the Sawyer family of five, plus Arnie, was sleeping, and Josh had an early call so both he and Arnie'd be up and about by five, likely. Then either Dan or Sam or sometimes both would land at the ranch around the time Alin's shift would end at seven.

Josh's King Ranch was parked close to the basketball net tonight, its nose snug against the barn where the horses were resting. The Mustang and SUV were on the side opposite the barn door. Alin wrinkled her nose. *Hmmm. Can I be sure I won't accidentally miss the basket and have the ball smash Josh's truck mirror or something? Yeah. Sure. I'm good at this.* She was a bit nervous, but after the first few shots, Alin was feeling very comfortable with her shooting, and soon she was 'pretend-shooting' from an all-star RCMP basketball team somewhere, maybe in Montreal, or Toronto, instead of 'pretend-shooting' criminals.

A light crunching sound got her attention just as she was gaining her stride. Footsteps? Behind the barn? Voices too, were there voices? Whipping her head around to give her a 360 degree scan of the area, Alin grasped the basketball tightly between her hands and held her breath so she could hear better.

I'm dreaming, she thought, and was ready to try for her twelfth consecutive basket when the horses started shuffling in their stalls, accenting their heavy feet on the wooden floor with what seemed like anxious neighs and whinnies.

Alin put a finger on the mic clip on her black jacket. But then she hesitated. A few nights earlier, the supervisor, a greying black man in his sixties, had warned her not to bother him unless she was sure there were issues. Alin figured it was because he liked to doze off once in a while. So tonight she decided to investigate the source of the noise before bugging him.

Likely one of the barn cats, she figured. *Woke up the horses and annoyed them. As long as it's not a cougar or a bear. Big animals and me? Not friends. Not friends at all.*

Creeping softly around the back of Josh's truck to the large closed sliding door of the barn, the blood started to pound in her temples as Alin contemplated what she might find on the other side. Slowly, she drew the door open wide enough to let her body in, and then quickly wider after a frozen pause. It took a moment for her eyes to adjust to the dim light, but there was something bright in one, no two, corners. It was sparking in fresh straw, and it was orange, the color of…

"Fire!" she cried, her voice barely audible at first as the shock of what she was seeing momentarily crippled her. When awareness clicked in she screamed much louder, and then louder again, turning her face back towards the ranch house as she yelled, where she knew some open windows might transmit her cry. "Fire! Fire!"

Racing deeper into the barn, Alin stared at the shuffling, frightened horses. "Oh, shit," she breathed, watching the flames lick and spit near the back of the small structure. The fire had a clear path to where the two scared animals were penned. Alin knew there was no way in hell she would have time to race back to the house to wake Josh or Arnie. Speaking quickly into her mic clip now, she mobilized her supervisor into action.

"Fire, call 911, now!"

Sucking in a breath, mustering up whatever courage she could find while staring into the terrified eyes of an animal she knew could easily trample her, Alin hauled open the stall door of the first horse and grabbed the animal's halter. She thought about letting it go, but who knew what would happen to the horse if it took off and a cougar got it, the way one got Blue? Then Josh would be out two, or maybe three of his beloved horses.

"Universe, hear me, I need you," she pleaded as she tried to gain control of the horse, which wanted to stay in the place it knew as a safe haven. "Come with me, horse," she begged, and finally managed to lead the animal at a half run around the truck towards a lead clipped to the outside of the nearby corral where she'd seen Josh tie the horses on occasion. She hoped that by the time the barn went completely up in flames someone else would be awake to take the horses somewhere safer, more removed, because soon there would be huge fire trucks and fast-moving police cars roaring up the lane.

Screaming "Fire!" again, Alin stopped to grab a baseball-sized rock that she found near the base for the basketball net. Silently thanking David for gathering rocks to try to throw into the net earlier this evening, she pitched it at a window in the sun porch. The rock shattered the glass instantly. Setting her sights back on the open door to the barn, Alin mustered up one last mammoth bout of courage and launched herself inside.

Everyone in the house was jarred instantly awake when the window smashed into smithereens. Arnie was the first out of his bed; the first thing he did was run to the children's bedrooms to make sure they were safe. Leaving them scared and crying in their beds, he sprinted across the open concept living area to Josh and Jessie's bedroom.

Josh was on his way out of the door, hauling jeans up around his hips and zipping up the fly. Leaving the button undone, he hollered behind him at Jessie, "The kids! Let's get them out of here!" At that point, all he'd heard was the lone word 'fire' and a window shattering, so he had no clue where the fire even was.

Roughly, Arnie grabbed his left shoulder and propelled him forward. The fire, its wicked tongue now licking angrily at the roof of the barn, was clearly visible. "It's the barn," Arnie ascertained, his voice a quickly rising crescendo.

A quick glance around, and both he and Josh were fairly certain the house, at least as far as they could see, was okay. Jessie was at the bedroom door now, jeans on, pulling a white tank top over her bare breasts. She sprinted for the kids' rooms, meeting Josh's petrified gaze just before he took off behind Arnie for the barn, grabbing worn cowboy boots and shoving them on his feet as he hopped his way outdoors.

Bare-chested, Josh ran for the barn. Whipping around and running backwards to eyeball the house and be sure it was not on fire, he caught a glimpse of one horse clipped to the corral. Dancing nervously, its ears were pricked back; it would soon get away if it had its way.

"Oh, fuck," Josh cursed, vaulting to the door of the barn with Jessie's terrified screams, as she ran from the house, now in his ears.

"Don't you go in there! Don't you go in that barn, Josh!"

"With my luck lately, this isn't going to end well," he growled at himself, but Arnie was already inside and Josh knew the city man did not have any comfort level with horses, especially scared ones.

Just as he got to the door, Arnie was running out. "It's too late, Josh. Stay the hell outside." Shoving him, Arnie pushed Josh backwards so hard that Josh slipped and landed on his back on the hard ground, which didn't do his sore shoulder any good.

Grimacing, he jumped up, pushed Arnie aside, and headed for the open barn door. He could hear the horse whinnying in fear, and there was something else...a voice, pleading loudly with the horse...a girl...the East Indian girl was on patrol duty tonight.

"Oh Jesus, Arnie. That girl's in here...!"

Inside, Josh started coughing right away, and he had to shield his eyes from the brightness of the fire. Alin was pleading and begging the horse to come with her, but it was backed into a corner and, apart from rearing up in fear, it was not budging. Grasping Alin's arm, Josh shoved her towards Arnie, who grabbed her waist and propelled her out of the barn. Arnie came running back in, but by then Josh had kicked the first stall door shut to prevent an animal from re-entering, as horses will do, thinking of the barn as its safe place, and he grabbed the second horse by the halter. Calming it as best he could, Josh talked the animal into trusting him, then led it through the clearest path he could find to escape the flames and make freedom.

Outside, he was coughing so hard and his eyes were watering so bad that he had to give the halter to the first hand that reached for it—Arnie.

Across the clearing by the house, Jessie could tell by the horse's anxious movements that neither Arnie nor Alin were going to be able to hold it, and Josh was bent over coughing, so she set Dylan on an Adirondack chair next to his crying siblings, ran over to the horse, and grabbed the halter from Arnie.

"Come, Toby," she begged the horse, leading it around Josh's truck towards the corral. Opening the gate, she let the horse go free, then detached the first horse's halter from where Alin had attached it and sent it running inside the corral as well. Pacing, Jessie put her hands on her hips and took in her surroundings. The house seemed fine, the other outbuildings seemed fine, but the barn was quickly being consumed.

"There's no serious wind," Arnie said to her. "Thank God. The house should be safe."

Throwing a look to the kids, Jessie started to make her way over to them. Passing Josh, she grabbed his elbow and forced him to come with her. Alin was there too, shaking from the shock as her supervisor started running up the lane.

Josh loosed himself from Jessie's grasp and wheeled around. He stopped.

Alin suddenly found herself staring into the sorrowful chocolate eyes she'd only seen close-up in movies and on the Internet. Trying to avoid looking at the man's muscled bare chest and unbuttoned jeans, she blinked and focused on the angry lights flashing in his eyes.

Jessie and Arnie both stopped moving to see what she had to say. Trembling, Alin raised her shoulders and waited.

"Never go into a burning barn," Josh growled at her, jabbing a finger in her general direction. "That was just plain stupid."

"Josh, easy." Jessie walked back towards him while David made his way into Arnie's strong arms. Emily-Grace had Dylan by the hand now, refusing to let him go towards the adults and hence towards the scary barn fire.

"I didn't…it was just starting. It happened so fast." Alin paused before firing back at him. "You did."

The nerve on Josh's cheek was twitching as Jessie laid a calming hand on his bare back. The muscles beneath her fingers were vibrating.

Josh let his eyes dart to the hopeless vision of his burning barn in front of him. They had yet to hear fire trucks.

"They're my horses," he said with righteous indignation. "Not yours."

Alin swallowed past the bitterness in her throat. "I wasn't going to stand back and let them burn. I was hired to protect all of you."

"For what, twenty bucks an hour? Jesus. You could have been killed." Josh pointed towards the rafters that were already starting to crunch under the flames circling them. "Those rafters are coming down any second. Your name's Alin, right?"

"Y-yes." This man could be scary when he wanted to be, but there was a soulful hurt deep in those eyes that softened Alin's fear of him.

"Are you hurt, Alin?" Stubborn, she shook her head, but she'd been holding onto one arm when Josh spoke to her.

Reaching out, he pulled her arm towards him. A gash in her jacket revealed blisters forming on the skin underneath.

"It's not bad," she tried. "It's just a flesh wound. A piece of burning wood…" She let the sentence trail off.

Recognizing the line from the Monty Python film, Jessie half-smiled, but Josh was pissed. Arnie, in the meantime, set David down next to Emily-Grace, moved quickly back across the clearing, and jumped into Josh's truck. Grabbing the keys from under the visor, he moved the big rig up the yard near the ATVs. He was coming back for the Mustang when Josh dropped Alin's arm, gave her a hard look, and started over to help. The Harley was already secure in its distant building. The fire trucks were going to need space.

Heading towards the SUV, Josh spoke sharply over his shoulder to his wife. "Jessie, can you see to Alin's arm? Arnie and I need to take a walk around the property after we get the vehicles moved." Josh spun back around, hesitated, fixed Alin in his steady, solemn gaze, and managed a quiet, "Thank you."

Alin's voice was a croak as her knees went weak. "You're welcome, Mr. Sawyer."

"Josh," he replied, and let a worried attempt at a smile filter through before he pivoted back around and jumped into the Lexus.

"Crazy girl. You think you were in some action flick or something?" Jessie stepped forward and touched Alin's good arm. David was at her side now, pulling at her jeans, sobbing. Scooping him up, Jessie snuggled him against her chest and soothed him as she led Alin to the big chairs where Emily-Grace and Dylan were waiting.

"I'm sorry, Mrs. Wheeler, um, Sawyer. I knew he already lost one horse. I couldn't let him lose the other two."

Easing into a chair with David on her lap, Jessie said, "Jessie, please. Just call me Jessie." With a sad smile she added, "Josh has that effect on people who know him. We would all do anything for him." She sighed, and Alin noted the wistful sorrow that crossed the pale blue eyes. "I hope he didn't frighten you too much. What could have happened...the thought of it...it scared him. Us." Bending around David, Jessie reached for Alin's hand. "May I?"

"Um...I guess." Wincing, Alin let Jessie take a closer look at her burn.

"I know how bad that hurts. I had a few of my own not so long ago."

"The Langley fire. I remember."

"You must be a tough cookie, Alin. I should get something for that. A cold cloth, maybe? I have some good stuff for burns too, hyaluronic acid, all the way from Prince Edward Island."

In the distance, sirens were finally audible. Jessie's shoulders sank from relief. The men were now walking around the property, making sure there were no other fires being started, perhaps waiting to consume the house.

"I'm okay. I'll wait." Alin stood to go. "I should do some checking too. It's my job."

Jessie's voice was soft and friendly. "I think Josh would want you to stay with us for the time being. You've done your job. Is that okay?"

Alin's cheeks flushed pink. Jessie Wheeler-Sawyer was asking her to stay and sit. A quaking child—Emily-Grace—was leaning into Alin's good side. There were fresh tears on the little girl's cheeks. All three of the children were silent now, though, which struck Alin as a bit odd. Alin touched Emily-Grace's arm and smiled sadly at her. "The barn can be rebuilt, honey," she said. "The horses are okay."

"I don't know if Precious is okay." Twisting her fingers, Emily-Grace had more to say. "I was wondering if you saw her in the barn."

"Precious is the striped orange barn cat, right?"

"Yes. Did you see her?"

"No, honey, not in the barn, but I saw her earlier. She's quite the mouser. She was up by the trail. It looked like she was hunting."

"Emily-Grace, Precious is probably just going to stay away for a little while. Until things settle down. We've got some big ole noisy fire trucks heading our way. Kids, you'll like that, huh?" Jessie's explanation and attempt at easing the children's minds seemed to work, but Emily-Grace's eyes stayed locked on the perimeter of the barn. Jessie trembled at the mountains of orange flames eerily reflected in her daughter's eyes.

Turning to Alin, Jessie studied her closely. The young woman really was in pain, judging by her bright eyes and tense posture, but she was apparently too tough to admit it. She was immediately likable. And now Emily-Grace was half-sitting on the girl's lap. The child rarely took to adults she didn't know. Something about Alin was comforting, friendly. Strong.

"Did you see anything?" Jessie finally got up the nerve to ask, just before the emergency vehicles, with their blazing lights and roaring sirens, came careening up the lane. "I mean...how did it start?"

The worry in Jessie's eyes derailed Alin a bit. She shook her head. "No. I'm sorry, I was playing basketball. Um...Oh, I probably shouldn't have been... I had just finished patrolling the grounds..."

"It's okay. I'm sure the nights are long and boring. A little basketball's not a bad thing."

Grateful for Jessie's understanding, Alin bowed her head, but she let her good arm rest around the shoulders of the little girl who seemed to need some comfort while her barn crackled and sputtered in bits and pieces to the ground. "I didn't see anything. I heard a noise, and then the horses started moving around. It was odd. I thought maybe one of the barn cats was bothering them. I went in."

"You have a good arm."

"The rock? I'm sorry about your window. I figured the barn would be toast by the time I ran up to the house to wake you. It must have terrified you, to be woken out of a sound sleep in such a way."

"You did the right thing, Alin. You're a quick thinker."

"I'm sorry I didn't see anything. I think, though...I'm pretty sure I heard voices. Two people. It was so dim, though...I wasn't sure they were real."

"So the fire was set." Jessie pressed her lips into a straight line. "I can't say I'm going to be sorry when *Sacred Peace* is done shooting." Tears threatened, but she was learning strength from Alin. Holding the tears hostage, Jessie refused to set them free.

Chapter Fourteen

For the next while, they sat together and held the children, who eventually drifted back off to sleep in their arms. EMTs treated Alin's burn and, when Josh came back around to the clearing, a few small spots on his shoulders and back as well. After questioning Alin, the police tried to convince her to go to the hospital in Canmore but she said she would stay with Jessie and the kids until Dan or Sam arrived, and told them she would drop in to emerge in Calgary when she got back to the city.

Watching the fire do its nefarious work, they all ran through scenarios about what may have happened as Josh and Jessie's barn settled into ashes. A new orange started in the skyline just beyond the wreckage. It began as a thin line on the horizon and was soon a brilliant, wide ribbon marking a new day, a new hope. As the sun peeked up over the crest, both Jessie and Alin pondered the polarized opposites of their last few hours—an orange that destroyed, an orange that marked the new.

"Will you be okay?" Alin asked Jessie after Dan arrived and, shocked and saddened, lifted the sleeping, curled up Emily-Grace and took her inside. "I should go. My parents will be worried if they hear about this on the news."

"I know the feeling." Jessie handed David to Josh, while Arnie took Dylan. She rose and stretched. She and Josh both faced Alin with a quiet, respectful air.

"Alin, I'm sorry if I was gruff earlier," Josh apologized. "Our family...we've been having a few trials lately. The thought of what could have happened..." He trailed off as David winced and squiggled in closer to his father's warm body.

Josh had slipped inside the house and fished out a T-shirt to put on, which

Alin was grateful for (*My friends will have a field day with this,* she thought). He was still ruggedly good-looking, though, with that piece of hair falling over his ear like that…she shivered.

"It's okay," she said truthfully. "I know you were scared. I'm sorry about the barn and about all the things that have been happening to you guys. I wish you well. I'll see you next time."

"Can I have a hug?" Jessie asked, and gave her a gentle squeeze. "For all we know, honey, you saved our lives. All of us. They could have been going for the house next."

By then, Josh knew that Alin had heard voices, and they had found accelerants—gas cans—behind the barn. Empty.

And more behind the house. Full.

"Stay in touch," he told her, taking her phone from her and inserting his personal phone number under an alias—Toby MacDonald. Toby for one of the horses, and MacDonald because it was such a generic name. "Don't share this with anyone. And if you need anything…ever…call us. Okay?"

Alin left on cloud nine despite chiding herself for not catching the perps instead of letting the Sawyers' barn burn down.

Jessie watched her disappear down the lane to climb into her car, which was parked in a field by the gate, before she followed Josh inside the house. They settled the kids for a few more hours of sleep before dropping down onto the wicker loveseat in the sun porch to watch the investigators and a few remaining firemen at work.

Tucking herself under Josh's arm, Jessie said what both of them were thinking.

"Alin was out there alone. With maybe two very dangerous people."

"She looked like she could hold her own, Jessie. But still…I know. Suddenly all kinds of people are at risk because of us."

"Did you see Emily-Grace take to her? She never does that."

"Alin seems like a nice person. Arnie said he's already tried to talk her into working with us full time."

"She applied to the RCMP, she said. That's her dream."

"Well, if she changes her mind…she's already been screened. And I just have a good feeling about her."

"So do I. I'm going to send her some of that hyaluronic acid from Quannessence in P.E.I. It helped my burns."

Josh tapped his fingers on the arm of the loveseat. Jessie straightened.

"What?" she asked.

"You're going to hate me."

"What." This time it was not a question. It was more of a growl.

"You need to pack up the kids and go, Jessie. You can't be here any longer, with some asshole or assholes running around trying to scare us. I'm not even going to go into the 'what ifs.'"

"I'm not leaving you. I refuse on principle to leave you, Josh. Not yet. I have to go soon enough."

"We're talking one week here, Jessie. One week early. You have to go then anyway, to get the kids settled at La Casa before you leave for Austin."

"One week is seven days too many. I'm not leaving you." Snuggling deeper into Josh's side, Jessie sighed and laid her head on her husband's lap. She scrunched her face into his belly and would have sobbed if simple exhaustion and fear hadn't robbed her of her senses. The world felt dull and grey despite the brilliant sunshine now outside their window, ushered in by a stunning sunrise.

"Yes, you are. I'll get the kids packed up. Get some sleep because you'll be the one dealing with them when they wake all rowdy and raring to go."

"If I go, you're coming with me. Charles and Charlie will shut *Sacred Peace* down now, anyway, after this latest crap." She didn't say it out loud, but Jessie felt in her heart that now that the nasty element was targeting the Sawyer home, where Jessie and the kids lived, instead of just Josh, the men would have the sense—drawn from fear—to close down the production. They could always pick up the last two episodes anyway, in a month or so, if the person or people causing all this trouble were identified and arrested, as Jessie prayed they would be. Surely the accelerants left behind the barn had fingerprints. Surely the perps left footprints, tire treads.

Josh's silence pissed her off but Jessie was too beat to argue with him. Snaking her arms around his waist, she breathed him in and closed her eyes. Shortly, she was snoring lightly.

Charlie and Charles arrived together from Calgary, having given hasty instructions to the director as well as to the first and second A.Ds. to shift the shooting day around. Jon was still in Vancouver, but he was flying in later in the day to supervise production. The guys found Josh wide awake on the wicker loveseat in the sun porch, rubbing his stubble and staring out at the remains of his smoking barn. Tuckered out, Jessie was sound asleep in his lap. Arnie was outside chatting with investigators, and Dan, as per Arnie's instructions, was patrolling the back and side of the house near the kids' rooms.

Assured that Jessie was snoring, Charles sat on the antique wooden trunk Jessie'd moved in as the Sawyer family coffee table, and faced Josh. Charlie exhaled deeply and took a seat on a wicker chair in the opposite corner.

"I haven't called Matt yet," Charles started. "He'll lose it. He'll want to come back."

"He'll want Jessie and the kids back in Vancouver, that's what he'll want." Josh scratched his head, moving slowly so as not to wake his exhausted wife. Outside, Gary was pulling up, ready to care for the horses. *Boy, is he in for a surprise,* Josh thought. Moving his hand to his mouth so he could chew on a nail, he looked over at Charlie. "Can you or Jack find someone to trailer the horses back to Southlands? Your dad was taking them for the winter anyway."

"Yeah, sure." Absently, Charlie shook his head at the carnage outside. His vision was disrupted by the shattered window in the sun porch. Gesturing towards it, he raised his eyebrows.

"Security," Josh said. "A young East Indian girl. She fired a rock to wake us up and then she bolted for the horses. She very likely may have saved us all."

"Very likely?" Charles asked.

Josh sighed and rubbed his forehead with his fingers. He touched Jessie's hair but she didn't stir. She was snoring enough for him to know she was truly lost in dreamland. "We found gas cans behind the house, too. Not just behind the barn. The ones behind the barn were empty. The ones behind the house…not so much. The girl…Alin…likely scared the creeps away by rousing us when she did."

"Jesus Christ." Charlie went white. "Where behind the house?"

Josh hesitated. "Our bedroom," he said without looking at Charlie. "Right behind our heads."

Charles stood and turned away from Josh. The creaking of the trunk as he rose startled Jessie, and she stirred, moaning as she woke and her harsh reality took hold.

Josh tried to smile down at her. "Hey, little one," he said tenderly, touching her cheek with the backs of his fingers as she rolled over and blinked sleepily up at him. "We've got company."

Groaning, Jessie leveraged herself around and up, and leaned back against the loveseat, stretching widely and frowning at the devastation of her perfect view across the clearing outside. Since the river incident a week ago, she had not spoken to either Charlie or Charles. Now, she glared at each of them in turn, and scooped her fingers into Josh's on his lap.

"I'll have the jet ready for you just after lunch, Jessie," Charles said as he turned back to face her. Steeling up his courage, he prepared for a battle he was determined to win. He looked old, tired, but that didn't deter his spitfire singer.

"Don't bother. Unless you and dickweed over here," she gestured to Charlie, "decide to shut down production like I asked you to before things got more out of hand, I'm not going anywhere. I'm not leaving my husband."

Beside her, Josh sank into the cushion, closed his eyes, and tilted his head backwards. Under his breath, he counted to five. "This is not about me, Jess," he told her as he blinked his eyes open and stared dejectedly at the ceiling. "This is about the safety of you and the kids."

From his corner, Charlie chewed on his nails and just watched. He couldn't take his eyes off the woman he was once a week away from marrying. Jessie would do anything to protect Josh. He very much doubted she would have ever done the same for him.

"The production will continue. We're a few weeks away from wrapping our season." Charles now had rosy red spots high on his cheeks.

Fidgeting in her seat, Jessie swallowed. There would have to be a point where she would need to back down. The man had already had one heart attack. Pushing herself up off the loveseat, she glanced towards Josh and squeezed his fingers as she walked away. As their hands lost touch, his dropped to his lap, empty and drained. Hers fell to her sides, and then a little behind her, as if she needed to reach for him even as she walked away.

Josh rotated his head back towards Charles and watched the man as his eyes trailed after the woman he'd made famous, who he thought of as his daughter. Charlie, too, was watching Jessie, Josh noted. They were both terrified of losing her. Of something happening to the children. They would have her on that jet today if it meant they had to drag her there kicking and screaming. *Me? Do they care about me?*

As if they could read his mind, both men looked at Josh at the same time, which Josh found disconcerting. Blinking, swallowing past the choking feeling he'd felt in his throat ever since he ran into the burning barn, he raised his arms in surrender. "I'm here," he told them, his voice raspy and flat, exhausted and devoid of emotion. "I'm not bailing on *Sacred Peace.* And I think I know someone who can talk Jessie into going back to Vancouver. Give me some time, will you?"

Standing, Josh reached for his iPhone from where he'd set it on the antique trunk. Nodding to his bosses, he left the sun porch and went to find Gary, first of all, to fill him in. The screen door banged behind him.

Leaning against the doorframe of their bedroom, Jessie crossed her arms and watched him go. Josh's shoulders were slumped, and Jessie wondered if he'd had words with Charlie and Charles. Letting her gaze drift sideways into the sun porch, she met Charlie's concerned stare. With an upside down middle-finger salute, Jessie telegraphed her anger and disapproval of his choice to continue shooting *Sacred Peace.* Spinning around and pulling off her white tank top as she moved, she marched into the bedroom.

Charles and Charlie were never surprised by Jessie's games, and both couldn't help but notice that she wasn't wearing a bra under the tank top, which made sense since she likely had dressed in a hurry when the fire broke out. This action of hers, though, stripping partially down in front of Charlie, was obviously meant to send him a very clear message. *I chose Josh. I choose Josh.* It was a kick in the pants, hurtful even after all this time, even after marriage and Jane and children.

Jessie stopped a few feet past the doorway, crossed both arms over her breasts, and counted to ten before she moved again. Swallowing bitterness and anger at Charlie's refusal to choose her husband over his TV show, she let him see what he was missing—a bare back, sexy low cut jeans, and boots. Tossing her hair, she turned back to him, arms still crossed, aware that Charles could see her too, but simply too done in to care. Her fiery glare in Charlie's direction was punctuated when she uncrossed her arms and let him see it all—the perfect breasts he used to love to lick and tease, the body he used to sink himself into. The soul he tried to love but failed desperately at back when they were together, mostly because Jessie was too far gone to open herself up to anybody back then. No, she hadn't let anyone in until the soulful, sad Josh stepped into her life, a timeless boy in a shiny contemporary sterile bar.

Charles turned away, unsure, knowing that on some level Jessie's actions went back to that old choice—Josh over Charlie—and how Charlie was choosing *Sacred Peace* over Josh's safety now.

Straightening, Charlie watched her. Letting his eyes fall over the body he once loved with a desperation that went largely unanswered, he had to fight a quick surge of surprise desire that tripped up the insides of his legs and landed in his groin. His lips parted but his eyes hardened.

Jessie's voice rang out as she widened her stance, brown booted toes pointed in, bare breasts exposed as she raised her arms so as to display herself fully and completely for him. "Is this how you get back at me, Charlie?" she asked, her voice quaking. "After all this time? Is this how you get even with me? You know what he means to me."

Standing, Charlie faced her but he didn't move towards her. Not yet. Licking his lips nervously, he wondered if Josh could see the vicious game his wife was playing now.

In the bedroom, Jessie tilted one booted foot over on its side, cocked her head, sent Charlie an erotic 'come hither' stare complete with half-closed eyes, and lowered one hand to her jeans. Unbuttoning the top button, she ripped down the zipper and thrust her hand inside.

"Jesus Christ." Charlie almost moaned, but he was getting angry now. As he strode towards his ex from eons ago, she started to move her hand, and lowered the jeans.over her hips, which she started to move rhythmically towards him as she sucked on her bottom lip.

At the door to the bedroom, Charlie paused and swallowed as he framed Jessie in his vision.

"You still want this, Charlie?" she asked him, cheeks flushing pink as she widened her legs a little more to give herself room to play. "I'll trade you. Shut down the production so I can take my husband home alive and standing instead of in a fucking box, and I'll give you all you want."

"You're off your fucking rocker, Jessie." Charlie was white. His voice was low, husky, and his hand was on the door but he was trembling, unable to make his arm move to shut the damned thing.

"I mean it," she said, trying for a low, sexy *purrrr* but failing miserably in her worry and grief. "You know what sex means to me. Fucking nothing. I've traded it before, I can do it again. It's love that matters to me." At that, new tears streaked down her face, and more than anything, Charlie wanted to take her in his arms to kiss away the pain. At the moment that her first tear splashed its way onto the floor, he realized that it was love that mattered to him too.

"I'm sorry," he whispered to her, and her hand stopped moving.

Jessie hung her head in shame as a new wave of convulsing sobs started to overtake her. "Don't ever speak to me again," she demanded. "Neither you, nor Charles, nor Jonathon. None of you. All this time you kept him close because of me. Or to serve yourselves because you know he's a brilliant actor. But you don't give a shit about Josh. None of you do, and none of you ever have. I fucking hate all of you."

Crumbling, Charlie was helpless. He just stared at her, half naked, erotic as hell as far as he was concerned, with her hand still shoved down the front of her jeans and her legs wide apart. Lonely and hurting and scared, vulnerable and ashamed of herself, of her past, of who she was and felt she always would be.

A hand moved past Charlie. It grabbed the door and slammed it shut, but not before Charlie saw a wretched hurt settle across Jessie's face, and swim across the pale eyes Charlie usually saw aimed at him with love and friendship.

Slam. It was loud enough to wake all three children.

Charlie turned, half crumpled and utterly defeated. The first thing he saw was worn cowboy boots. Forcing himself more upright, he nodded at the figure in front of him.

Josh, in faded jeans and a white T-shirt, fixed a hard, angry look at Charlie. "You think it matters to me what all of you think, Charlie? About me?" he asked him. "You think I haven't long ago figured out that I'm just along for the ride, for wherever it might take all of you? I know what the world thinks of me, what it's always thought of me. I know people attach themselves to me because I have certain skills that I bring to the table, but that everyone still thinks I'm just a wildcard ready to combust at any moment. I also know that the beautiful woman in that room sees more in me than any of you combined ever will."

Twisting around, disgusted at Charlie's futile attempt to hide an obvious desire for his wife, Josh moved to go, but after six steps, he turned and fired one last dagger. "I told you I wouldn't bail on you. I'm better than that. Jessie has made me a better person. I'm seeing this thing through. But if I do end up in a box, it's not you who she'll run to. It's not you, it's not Jacob, it's not even Steve, as a friend or whatever. It's the man I'm about to call, whose word is gold, whose wisdom is cherished, and who both of us trust to always do the right thing by us. You? I know you try, Charlie, but your judgment is clouded by the almighty dollar. You're too easy to seduce. You, and Charles over there, who has pimped Jessie out for years. Don't even get me going about Jon, my 'dad.'"

As Josh stormed away, Charlie sank to the floor and buried his head in his hands. "I'm gonna be sick," he groaned, as a small body landed in his lap.

Dylan.

"Where Daddy go?" the little boy asked the man he knew well, who was often at their home, who Daddy worked with these days. Dylan took Charlie's face in both palms in an attempt to get his attention.

Charlie sighed at the sight of the cobalt eyes of another man who lost to Josh. "Your daddy is a better man than the rest of us put together. You know that, Dylan?" Wrapping his arms around the small body, Charlie hid his face in Dylan's hair so the child wouldn't see him cry.

Chapter Fifteen

Josh slipped into the corral and paced at the far end, out of sight, while inside the ranch house Jessie sank to her knees in the shower and sobbed at the futility of a decision she felt was completely unacceptable. She considered calling Dee and trying to talk some sense into her—Jane too, maybe. Maybe the women would see things the way Jessie did. Maybe the women would understand that pain could only go so far before a person disappeared forever, the way Jessie's mother did.

Outside, Josh stared at Matt's name on his contacts list. It was now just after nine a.m. Alberta time, which meant it was noon on the east coast. Was it a warm day in P.E.I.? Would Matt be down on the beach where cell phone service was most certainly sketchy?

"Please be there," Josh begged the man. "Please answer."

Backing up against the split rail fence, where Josh could see the house from underneath a treed canopy, he used his arms to leverage himself up onto the top rail, and he tapped the 'call' icon.

In Darnley, Prince Edward Island, Matt was packing a padded cooler bag to take down to the beach. He'd just dropped in two Smirnoff Ice for Catherine and two locally brewed Gahan Brewery Sir John A. MacDonald Ales for himself, when his cell rang. Catherine was next to him, slicing tomatoes for sandwiches. She saw the caller ID before Matt did, since the phone was resting on the counter next to her.

Furrowing her brow, she glanced at Matt, who spotted the name on the screen and frowned at a call from Josh at this time of the day. Picking up the phone, Catherine silently handed it over to Matt.

Letting the cooler settle to the floor, Matt accepted the cell from her outstretched hand and took it to the sun porch where, he later realized, Catherine could hear every word.

"What's up, Josh?" he asked, alarm coloring the serious tone of his work voice. Raising an arm so he could run fingers through his quickly growing hair, Matt ran his hand back and forth over the no longer short spikes, his elbow stretched out to the side as he did so. Quiet then, he fixed his gaze on the crystalline blue sparkles of the Darnley Basin laid out in front of him as Josh described the devastation of the now smoldering barn in the hot, dry Kananaskis Country of far off Alberta.

From the kitchen, Catherine watched Matt sink to the sofa and hang his head in his hands. "What now?" she murmured quietly, recalling the last call, the one that came from Charles describing the river incident which, she had figured from Matt's pale cheeks that night, Josh was lucky to have survived.

Now, Matt was listening carefully.

"I have a stubborn girl on my hands," Josh was saying to him. "She needs someone she trusts to pound some sense into her, Matt. I know she'll listen to you."

Matt had not spoken with Jessie since leaving months before. Hearing her voice again...his throat constricted as Josh read into the silence.

"Will you talk to her? Please?"

It took Matt a bit to muster up the courage, but once Josh threw in how angry Jessie was at the two Charles', he relented. Through the phone, he could hear Josh's footsteps on hard-packed dirt, and could almost feel the man's fear at the reign of terror that seemed, yet again, to have commandeered his life.

At the ranch, Josh let the screen door slam behind him as he moved towards the closed door of the master bedroom. He ignored the long faces of Charles and Charlie, who were trying to entertain the kids while passing a phone back and forth to settle various upset *Sacred Peace* personalities.

David tried to stop Josh, but over the line Matt heard Josh calmly say, "One minute, little guy. Just give Daddy a minute and I'll come play cars with you." The ordinary words from a father to his son floored Matt, given that Josh's and David's worlds were apparently not even close to ordinary today.

Josh twisted the handle and pushed open the recently slammed door of the bedroom just as Jessie was exiting the shower. She was towel drying her hair as she made her way into the room.

Challenging him, because she figured Josh was there to lecture her for what she did to Charlie, Jessie stopped and braced herself for an onslaught.

Instead, Josh held out his phone. At the same time he said, "Put some clothes on," which Matt overheard and which caused him to close his eyes and moan.

Apprehensive, upset, thinking maybe it was Steve on the other end of her husband's phone, Jessie took the towel down from her hair and wrapped it around her body. Taking the phone, a questioning look crossed her shower-rosy cheeks as Josh watched her.

"Hey," she said into it, sitting on the edge of the bed and staring at the floor.

At first, Matt was unable to voice a single word. Hearing that small *hey* from Jessie's lips was like receiving manna from Heaven. A small wounded bird she was, all her pain, anger, frustration and fear wrapped up in that one tiny word.

Just as Jessie was about to lift the phone away from her ear and hand it, with a questioning look, back to her husband, she heard Matt's voice.

"Hey back," came the trusted duskiness of the man who had been Jessie's guardian angel for so long.

"Oh, Jesus." Closing her eyes, Jessie pinched a corner with two fingers but tears, always so close to the surface these days, leaked out anyway. "Matt."

Struggling too, Matt managed, "Rough day?"

From the P.E.I. kitchen, Catherine watched this man she was really just getting to know as a lover and a friend cave at, what? All she knew was that it had to do with his old world. With a chaotic and agonizing Jessie and Josh world.

Over the phone, Matt heard the small timorous voice that brought such beautiful music to the world say, "We lost our barn, Matt."

"I know, sweetheart. Josh just told me. I'm real sorry."

"There's been...a lot of bad stuff again, Matt. Someone's trying to scare us."

"I know. I know, Jessie, I...Charles calls me sometimes."

Her heart skipped a beat. "Oh. I didn't know." Glancing up, Jessie saw Josh back out of the room. He closed the door behind him. She moved to a deep wicker chair in the corner and pulled her legs up so she could wrap an arm around her bent knees. Sniffling, she said in a hurt sing-songy kind of voice, "I'm glad you're in touch. That's good, right?"

Ignoring the comment because Matt didn't want to reveal more than he was ready to say, he jumped into Josh's purpose for the call.

"Josh says you're being stubborn, Jessie. He's worried. You need to take your children and go back to Vancouver."

Studying a broken nail, Jessie emitted a small *ooommpphhh*. "I can't," she finally said to him. "I'm scared, Matt."

"Of?"

"Losing him again. To Shanda, or to this maniac that Charlie says left a threatening note after the PCP crap. Who likely shoved him over a cliff into a freezing river, who likely burned down our barn. And who maybe choked him too, I don't know!" She was crying openly now.

His heart breaking into a million helpless pieces, Matt conjured up the strong voice he always used with Jessie during tough times. Rising, he did it by leaning against the side wall by the entry to the sun porch, one arm raised above his head, the forearm placed against the wall for balance. He had totally forgotten Catherine was anywhere near. "I know," he told his old charge. "But Jessie, you have to consider your children."

In the kitchen, Catherine sucked in a breath at the name. Matt was talking to Jessie Wheeler. The notion floored her. Gripping the kitchen counter, she paled and strained to hear.

Matt was continuing. "This person has gotten way too close to your family. You need to be somewhere more contained. You know this, Jessie. You don't need me to tell you this."

"If I go it means giving in to the fear. I don't operate that way, Matt."

"You're giving in to the fear by staying at the ranch and watching over your husband, which you know is pointless. You can't save him, Jessie."

"Fuck you, Matt. I have to try. Nobody else is."

"Jessie, listen to me. You know the guys can't shut down the production. They're all doing their best to try to help Josh, to eliminate the threat, and they'll do even more now. Josh says they're cutting down to just necessary crew, and they're screening the ones they keep. Perimeter security is being tripled. You can't say they're not trying. You have to trust them."

"I trust you, Matt. You're the only one I trust. And you're not here. I need you here."

Closing his eyes, Matt turned his head so his cheek could rest against the wall. Catherine was floored. Matt was pinching away tears.

"I can't be there," he was saying. "You know I can't. But Jessie..." He hesitated. *Should I tell her?* In the end he decided to ease her fears the best way he knew how. "I'm still on Charles' payroll, kid. I've been watching over you all along. I'll never let you go."

Her sharp intake of breath calmed him. "You're still working for Charles? You're still coordinating our security?"

"With Ulysses too, yes. I just can't be there with you, as long as..."

"As long as Josh is here," she cut in. "Jesus, Matt. Everybody wants him gone. Even you. What am I supposed to think?"

"I don't want him gone. I know how hollow you are when he's not with you. I know how embedded you are in each other."

"I'm embedded in you too, Matt. God, I miss you."

"Go to Vancouver. You say you trust me. Let me help 'Charles squared' keep your husband safe while they finish their show. Even Josh wants to stay, Jessie. He doesn't want to let this guy or girl win either."

Considering his request, Jessie squeezed her eyes tightly shut. Opening them and peering outside, she wondered why investigators were wandering around her backyard. Reaching up, she twisted the blind closed. "If I go, Matt..." She drifted off.

"Hmm?"

"I know you can't guarantee his safety."

"I'll do my best, kiddo. You know I will."

"Can I...can I call you from Vancouver?"

Matt paused, and winced. Watching him, Catherine was immobile. This conversation was breaking her new man. "I don't think that's a good idea," she heard him say.

"I miss your voice, Matt. I miss our chats."

"Not now, Jessie. Not for the next bit, okay?" His voice caught. "Not unless you really need me. Then you can call."

"Like I did before, huh? When Morgan and Nadia kidnapped us. It was too late then, Matt, for you to save us. You were too damn far away."

A slow *ppffftt* prefaced his next comment. Matt rubbed his forehead with a thumb and forefinger as he said words with the power to crumple both of them. "I'll always care for you, Jessie. I'll always be in your corner, even if just from a distance. But I can't have you in my life the way I want you to be in it. I can't hear your voice. I can't see you."

"So you replaced me with a dog." She tried to laugh but it fell flat. "Drifter. Good name. Josh showed me the picture. He's adorable."

"I didn't name him."

"So…who did?"

"A friend." Matt couldn't look up at Catherine, but she got the gist of what he was saying. Of what he was omitting.

"Oh. I see. What's her name?"

"Not now."

"She's there."

Matt stayed silent.

Trying to sound carefree, Jessie gulped out, "Are you happy?"

He paused. "What do you think, Jessie?"

"Fuuucckkk, Matt. You suck."

"I love you, kid. I better go, okay?" He was breaking down now, and so was Jessie on her end. This conversation had to be over. "Promise me you will pack up those children and go."

"Okay." He could barely hear her past the thick emotion in her throat. "I will. Promise me you will keep watching over us."

"I will."

"Take care of your new friend, Matt. Treat her right."

"I will. You know I will."

After a prolonged silence, Jessie tapped 'end' without saying goodbye. She sat back and stared at the floor, letting the phone drop limply to the chair cushion.

Waiting, Matt heard the line close down. Groaning, he leaned his forehead into the wall and tried to breathe.

Jessie made her way to the bed, and lay down on her side with her back to the door. Ten minutes later, she heard the door click as Josh pushed it open. Lying down behind her, holding her, he whispered, "I'm sorry. For everything. For all this craziness. And for you losing Matt."

"I'll go. I'll go, Josh. I just need a few minutes to…to…" She buried her face in the pillow as her shoulders shook.

Josh moved to go, to give her some privacy, but Jessie reached behind her and grabbed his arm. Pulling it around her, she clung to his hand like a desperate child clinging to a doll, while in P.E.I. Catherine moved past Matt and went down to the beach alone.

Chapter Sixteen

By the time Jessie got the ranch house sorted out and cleaned up to a level she felt would do until she got back for a weekend to do a final run through, it was officially evening. Josh helped when he wasn't outside working with the investigators, or doing whatever cleanup he could manage with the help of Gary and Charlie. Charles, too, was pressed into service to help entertain the kids and keep them out of harm's way.

Jessie stood by Josh at the Lexus SUV and got the kids into their seats, then turned to give the Mustang a final look of longing. The vehicles would all be driven or shipped back to Vancouver within the next few weeks; same with the horses, when Josh and Charlie were able to coordinate a suitable wrangler and a time to load Toby and Misty.

Arnie, with Dan as passenger, would follow the SUV. Charles and Charlie would leave shortly as well in Charlie's Porsche, a bit behind the others, in order to give Josh and Jessie a little space.

Now, though, Josh gave Jessie's shoulders a little turn and pointed her towards the guys. Both men were standing by the corral, chatting idly with Gary. Charlie, with one foot up on the bottom rail of the split rail fence, both elbows bent over the top rail, kept tuning out of the conversation. The defeated looks he kept sending over to Jessie were starting to entertain Josh, but Jessie was still pissed.

"I'm not going over there," she said, flipping back around to her husband, hiding behind the big SUV.

To his credit, Josh planted his feet a hip's width apart and lifted Jessie's chin so she had no choice but to look at him. He melted at the sad eyes aimed in his direction. "Jessie," he demanded, unable to disguise his amusement at Charlie's dejection, "you can't leave mad. Those guys would do anything for you. They've been helping us here all day while everyone on the *Sacred Peace* set was losing their minds trying to get some kind of a day shot without me."

"Hmmm, if I'm mad, I can leave mad," was Jessie's nervy answer, complete with a childish foot stomp and petulant crossed arms. Daring Josh to cross her, she sent him a glare infused with ache, which gave her the effect of a stubborn three year old.

"You're spending way too much time with Dylan." Reaching for her, Josh puffed up his cheeks and blew the air out as he hugged her, burying his face in his wife's sweat-damp hair. "Go. Don't leave them thinking you hate them."

"Maybe I do."

Leaning back, taking her cheeks in his palms, Josh gently chided her. "No, you don't." He tried another tack. "Look, Jess, things are fine on *Sacred Peace*. In fact, they're really great, apart from all this other weirdness. We've almost got our first season in the can. The kids are healthy, Charles is having great checkups, Charlie and Jane have a new son...Jacob and Kayla are on cloud nine...Carter's got a steady job with *Sacred Peace* now...We have a lot to be thankful for. Go give those two Eeyores some serious hugs so when you're down in Austin feeling alone and miserable, you won't also be consumed by guilt at the way you left them."

"You are way too good for 'Charles squared,' Josh. They don't deserve to have you on their show. You should be out winning Oscars."

"I don't need more Oscars on my shelf, little one. I just need my family close by, and safe. That's all I ever want."

"So you're sending us away."

"Only for a short time. You'll get sick of me on the tour."

"Never."

Smiling, Josh bent his forehead to Jessie's and let out a contented sigh. She soaked up his warm breath and lost herself in his strength for a moment, then pressed her lips to his neck and pushed him aside.

Striding confidently over to the men at the corral, she forced her gaze on the horses in the distance while, in her peripheral vision, she saw Charlie shove his body away from the fence and lower his raised foot to the ground. Stopping a few feet in front of him, Jessie angled her boot over on its side, and shoved both hands in her back jeans pockets.

Charlie bit his bottom lip and shrugged his shoulders. "I won't try to tell you that you were wrong in there." Gesturing with his head towards the ranch, he added, "About Josh, I mean. Because I know your stubborn ass won't listen."

Charles started up beside him while, at the SUV, which was parked in front of the home to facilitate packing, Josh walked to the back and sat on the bumper, facing them.

"Charlie, take it easy," Charles said as he laid a strong hand on Charlie's shoulder.

"I don't care." Jessie's response was meant for Charlie. "I don't agree with what you're doing, and I won't pretend that the world is all sunshine and roses when it isn't."

"We have no choice," Charlie told her, placing both hands on his hips and staring into the despondent pale blue eyes he once planned to make his forever. "The whole thing's a speeding train, Jessie. Calling a halt now would be suicide for *Sacred Peace*."

"Give me a break. Either one of you could float that production for a while if you needed to. Hell, I would pay the whole damn bill myself if it would guarantee Josh's safety."

"The best thing you can do for Josh, Jessie," interrupted Charles just as Charlie was about to open his mouth to speak, "is let him finish the season. We're stepping things up to the point where he is going to be annoyed as hell with us for having so much security on his tail, and he's promised to start staying at the condo to keep himself more contained."

"So someone can't, what, run his truck off the highway, or shoot him when he's out for a ride, you mean? Wonderful. Now they can just plant bombs in his building."

"Enough, Jessie. You're sounding like a spoiled princess. The simple fact is there is no way anyone can guarantee Josh's safety, least of all you." Charlie's face flushed a deep crimson.

Fixing an angry glare on him, Jessie removed her right hand from her back pocket and gave his chest a shove. "Thanks for that, Charlie. You don't think I realize I'm the one who continually causes him pain? That he would have been better staying with Michelle, maybe, or fucked-up Nadia, even? At least then he'd be in his own cotton-balled world and not the target of some pissed off Jacob Ryan fan."

Taking the bait, Charlie marched forward and roughly grabbed Jessie's arm as she whipped around to go.

"Ouch!" she cried, trying to yank her arm away.

"Do you honestly think taking him to your bed every night in Vancouver is going to make him less of a target? Holding him and playing your little sex games with him are not going to change a damn thing. They didn't before, and they won't now. The only way to fight these creeps, as all of us have learned, is to be as prepared as we can be when they strike. Blaming Charles and Jon and I for keeping *Sacred Peace* going is like blaming God for rain. It might cause a flood, but the earth will dry up without it. Josh needs this show. He needs the friendships he's made on it, he needs the challenge the part gives him, and he could use the damn awards and fan support when it airs to ease some of that crap that you leaving Jacob unleashed on him!"

"We've already established that it's all my fault, Charlie, that everything that hurts Josh is my fault. Maybe you can just let me wallow in that on my own and not rub my fucking face in it every chance you get, huh?"

Charles stepped in and tried to pull Charlie's arm off Jessie but he was unsuccessful. Frustrated, he growled at them. "That's enough, you two. You still fight like a couple. Stop it. The kids are watching."

Charlie leaned in to Jessie. Eyes blazing, he spat at her, "Speaking of rubbing your face in it, that was a really shitty little game you played earlier. I've long ago gotten over everything I lost when you made it abundantly clear you'd rather be fucking Josh than me!"

"What you lost? Like what, your excuse to have a different woman in your bed every night?" In an infuriating singsong voice Jessie tossed in, "'Oh poor Charlie, he's so damn lonely he better go find a sexy warm body to hold instead of trying to understand the messed up woman he's got!'"

Seething, Charlie fired back. "That's low. You were just this singer in her own damn bubble, hiding behind songs that made millions; the more songs you wrote and hid behind, the more millions you made and chucked into your bank account, and the further away you pushed me—"

"You and your fucking money. I'm so sick of you and your goddamn attachment to money and prestige, Charlie! You and your goddamned black Porsches, a new one every year!"

"It was never about the money, Jessie! Goddamn it!" At that, Charlie threw her arm down hard enough for Jessie to wince. Rubbing it, she sucked in a breath at the sheer loss floating in the usually intelligent, gentle eyes peering back at her from behind moist lashes. It was as if by his frustrated pronunciation Charlie was exposed to a base common denominator, to a base level that suddenly stripped all of his usual pretensions away and left his soul naked in front of her, for a change.

Jessie felt herself wither even further. Wanting to curl up and sleep forever, she tried to wrap her arms around her belly to keep herself from cracking into a thousand pieces. So many people hurt, all because of her deep love for one man.

Charlie read her like a book. "Jessie. When you and Josh are happy, the rest of us are good. You need to understand that. It's like you light up the darkness, you know? The way you love him...We see it, we honor it, and we cherish it. What you have bleeds into the rest of us. The light...it seeps in. What you did earlier, it brought back a lot of old shit that I don't really like remembering. I know I sucked as a boyfriend in those days, but at the time I had no idea how to reach you." He lowered his voice and slowed down. "You need to know now that I will never sink so low as to use you for sex for any reason, even if it is just to get to hold you in my arms for one more night, knowing everything I know about you now...knowing we're closer now than we ever were back then."

Taking her in his arms, moving her arms away from her stomach and wrapping them around his waist, Charlie finished what he had to say by closing his eyes and whispering it in her ear. "I love you more now than I ever thought possible, Jessie. You don't think I know what I lost? I know. I see it every time I watch you with him. It's not about your body, it's not about sex, and it never was. It's about this beautiful, crazy, spoiled woman I'm holding right now. The one with the power to lift up an entire world after some nut jobs shoot up a lineup outside a concert hall in Paris. The one who forgives the people who hurt her entire family because she knows they did it out of some misguided pain of their own."

Standing a step back from her now, Charlie bent forward and kissed his old girl on the forehead. He could see that she was swallowing back tears, and it made his eyes lighten up a little. "Jessie, I would throw myself in front of a truck to save Josh if it meant I would always see you happy. But I cannot shut down my TV series and throw a bunch of people out of work, knowing that this idiot can just as easily follow Josh to Vancouver. Even if it meant I could hold you again, and love you again. Take your babies home, and let Charles and me look after your man the best we can. Okay?"

"Charlie…" Melting into the old familiar chest, Jessie let Charlie move in closer and hold her for a few extended minutes. That little gesture, allowing him in like that, did more for the two of them than many years of shared barbecues and smiling attempts at forgiveness.

Watching them from the back of the Lexus, Josh swallowed and straightened. Without being able to hear what they were saying to each other, some of it apparently hostile, Josh was humbled. There was some serious love there, between the two; there always had been, even back in the days when Josh and Jessie first got together, when Jessie was struggling with her engagement to Charlie while falling head over heels in love with Josh.

After a bit, Jessie pushed herself back from Charlie. The man standing in front of her now was not the Charlie she knew these days, the one married to Jane, with two children waiting for him today at the Calgary condo. This was the old Charlie, the one who tearfully handed Jessie back her freedom the day he saw her sing Amazing Grace at Terri's funeral; when she was lost in Josh's steady strength on that difficult day.

"I'm sorry," she whispered to him now, apologizing for, well, everything.

Softening, he sent her peace and love with a tender kiss on her forehead. "Me too," he said. "Go now, before I can't let go."

A final squeeze between good friends, and Jessie moved sideways to hug Charles too. "Do you think you could see if the East Indian girl, Alin, would consider working with us?" she asked him. "Emily-Grace really took to her. Even if it's just for a little while until she gets into the RCMP, or for special times."

"I'll ask," Charles promised. "Give my best to Deirdre. Tell her I'll be home in a few weeks."

"I will. We'll drink some wine with Carlotta and bitch about our men. No worries."

Charles' laugh was genuine and very, very welcome.

"By the way, Josh sent me over," Jessie told the two of them as she held Charles' hand. "Just so you know. He's the guy who keeps me coming back to everyone I try to shut out. He's the guy who makes everything better. Take care of him. Please. I beg you."

Looking past her over at Josh, Charlie was further humbled. Despite everything Jessie had screamed at him in anger earlier, Josh had become someone Charlie cared a lot for. He was the kind of friend who always had a listening ear, who was a casual buddy to go horseback riding with in the woods and through Alberta's crocus-lined meadows, he was the guy to call when you needed help to move your dryer at home. Josh was always ready and willing to help with whatever, even if it meant finishing out a TV series that had been Charlie's dream and passion for a few years now, but which might mean more nasty accidents or threats to Josh's safety.

Now, from across the clearing, Charlie took a closer look at his friend. Leaning against the bumper, Josh was playing with something he grasped in his hand; it was a piece of wood he was carving with a small penknife he'd pulled from a pocket. His longish hair was falling forward over his cheek; like a curtain, it shielded him from the world the way it always had, with the exception of the few times Josh had cut it shorter for film projects, which Charlie sensed made Josh feel exposed and vulnerable.

The day was still warm. Josh had changed into jeans a little less faded and beat up than the ones he wore all day to pull stuff from the fire that he thought was worth saving. Like Jessie, he had stuffed his feet into pointed toe cowboy boots, scuffed and dirty, but old and comfortable. A tight cream-colored Henley, all three buttons undone, fell over the jeans, but Josh's wide belt buckle, delicate engraved silver from some western outfitter in the states, was visible. Charlie couldn't deny it—even his male eyes could see the rugged good looks that likely captivated Jessie in the first place, and Shanda too.

Hell, I wouldn't have cast him if he wasn't good looking, Charlie thought with a twinge of jealousy. But there was so much more to Josh Sawyer than just good looks. He was so bandaged up that his very essence begged to be saved. Yet, was he strong? Hell, yeah. Inside and out, although Josh himself likely didn't think so.

Yeah, Charlie thought. *Jessie was wrong, today.* Like a lightning strike, it hit him just how much he did care about Josh.

His eyes drifted back to Jessie. Inside them, she saw a solemn promise settle. But first, there was a final thought, from Charlie's lips to her ears. "Josh is my friend, Jessie. He was my friend long before you came into my life. I love the guy. I really do. I'll watch out for him. I promise you."

Like a rainbow was passing over it, Jessie's face lit up, all Technicolor relief. She nodded, her throat too choked up to form words. A quick swipe with fisted knuckles, and she erased any semblance of tears at this difficult parting.

To her back as she walked away, Charlie tossed a gem that Jessie laughed at, and decided to store away in her memory bank for future use. "How about I sell the Porsche? Would that convince you that I don't care about money? I'll get a rusted out Camry. Or a Corolla. Or maybe an original Volkswagen Bug from the 70's. Do they still sell those?"

Wheeling around to walk backwards, Jessie shook her head at him while Charles toed the dirt and started to follow so he could say goodbye to the children he considered his grandkids. "Charlie, the day you sell your Porsche is the day I commit you to a straitjacket and a rubber room. I'll see you."

Turning again, she slowed when she spied Josh standing to greet her. He was holding something out to her. Taking it, Jessie inhaled slowly, and angled her head to study it more closely.

"It's a cross," he told her. "It's meant to keep you safe." Folding up his penknife and tucking it into his front jeans pocket, he turned the small piece of wood around in her fingers to show her what he'd carved in the back, at the bottom.

"J heart J," Jessie read, tearing up again. "God, I need to get away from you so I can stop crying 24-7."

Grinning shyly, Josh reached back to the bumper and pulled up another hand carved cross. This one, too, had the tender inscription on the bottom.

"J heart J," he remarked happily, his usually solemn brown eyes alight. He held it against his chest. "This one's for me."

"C'mere," she murmured, and pulled him close. "I'll share mine with the kids."

"They all have something of their own. Emily-Grace wanted a sheep, and I did my best although I think it looks more like a cow. David got a tractor and Dylan, of course, got a horse. He's the cowboy in the family."

Accepting her hug, Josh's warm arms were such comfort that Jessie closed her eyes and dreamed she could stay in the exquisite moment forever. But soon, they were on the road, then at the airport, and then her husband and the SUV were just dots on the pavement as the jet keened off into the clouds and set a course for the western sunset.

Chapter Seventeen

Matt found Catherine on the beach, but it took some searching.

She was settled on a camp chair wedged into warm white sand, half hidden behind a jagged point of sandstone rocks, much farther down the beach than their usual spot, which was either at Twin Shores or Thunder Cove, depending on their moods and on the day.

Panting from the effort to trudge through the deep sand, Matt reached for the cooler as soon as he dropped down on the bright green and blue neon striped blanket laid out at Catherine's feet for the purpose of post-swim 'must dry off' tanning sessions.

"You really made me work for this," he told her not unkindly as he zipped open the cooler, removed a beer, and untwisted the cap. A lengthy slug of the cool beverage helped settle him physically, but the silence from his beach mate was disconcerting.

"Catherine," he started, grazing a finger over her bare toes. "Please tell me you're not the silent treatment type. I'd rather you just yelled at me and got it over with."

A quiet murmur alerted Matt to the fact that Catherine might talk if he continued to encourage her. She'd likely been stewing since his noon phone call, and it was now two in the afternoon, so Catherine was either likely super pissed or super sad, and not anywhere near the middle, which was where Matt really wanted her to be.

"What?" he asked quietly, stretching out on his side with his beer and looking up at her.

"I don't want to do this, Matt. Anymore."

"Do what? We're enjoying each other's company, Catherine."

A hard stare landed on him. If it had been a stone, Matt would have been knocked out. He frowned.

"I figured that's all it was," she steamed. "A neighborly liaison. Easy sex."

"Don't forget that cute puppy sleeping in my air-conditioned loft at this very moment." A tiny smile lighting up his eyes, Matt scooped up a handful of sand and let it fall through his fingers. Repeating the gesture, he laughed at Catherine's serious grimace. "You're overthinking this, Catherine. We're good together, you and me. I have no idea what I'm doing or where I'm going after the cottage closes down at Thanksgiving. I'm open to ideas, and I hope at least one of those includes you."

"I think what you'd really like to do is go back to Vancouver, Matt. If you could, you would."

Watching the white sand grains filter through his fingers, Matt pondered that. "It's not an option," he said without looking at her.

"I gather that. But what if it was an option?"

"It won't be. I've accepted that. I knew that the second I kissed her in Brussels. I knew it was over."

"Your affair?"

"My...career. The way it was, at least. I don't think twenty-four hours counts as an affair."

Catherine took a drink of her second Smirnoff Ice. Wriggling in the camp chair, she gazed out at the small waves breaking over the shore, their white crests foamy as they *shussshed* over the wet sand and tried to fight their way back out to the cool blue of the Gulf. Pressure on her bladder made her consider a quick swim, but there was a big wind yesterday and so the water, all stirred up, was colder than normal today. Instead of moving, she reached for a bag of barbecue chips sticking out of her beach bag. Thrusting a hand in, she munched away without offering any to Matt.

"Pardon me for being a pig, but I'm not really part of the tofu and wheat grass crowd," she fumed.

A heavy sigh escaped Matt's lips. "I guess it's not a stretch to assume that comment was a dig. My only question is, was it meant for me or are you out to get Jessie? Because you shouldn't crush someone you don't even know, Catherine. Especially when she's not here to defend herself."

"She's a superstar. She probably hasn't had a barbecue chip since she was eighteen."

"She barely had anything at all when she was eighteen. Jessie was living on the streets, trading music and sex for slices of pizza."

"Touché. She's made up for it. The sex part too, apparently."

Sucking on his bottom lip, Matt tipped his bottle back and drained it. Standing, he wiped sand off his hands and reached in the cooler to withdraw a second beer. "When you're ready to talk in a reasonable manner, come see me," he said, a darkness settling over his face. "And by the way, Jessie inhales barbecue chips. They must be some kind of beach hangover left over from her P.E.I. days."

Digging his toes into the sand, Matt bent over to grab the flip-flops he'd carried down the beach with him earlier. He moved to go, but Catherine's voice stopped him.

"It's not so much your...affair...or even your obvious love for her that scares me, Matt. It's just her. I don't know if I can stand the idea of...her... being a part of your life in any way at all. My daughter..." She let the terrible memory drift off.

Sighing, Matt turned back around and faced her. "I can't tell you what to think, Catherine. Jessie is, and always will be, a part of my life in one way or another. I can't imagine being fully and completely separated from her, ever. I tried before, and it didn't stick. I feel responsible for her. Not just her safety...her. Her sanity, sometimes."

"That's what today was about? Calming her down, I take it. Something else happened?"

"Somebody lit a fire at their ranch and burned their barn down in the middle of the night. They were planning to do the same to the house..." He had to stop and gather his senses. The notion was chilling. "But a woman on the local security team heard something in the barn, and discovered the fire. She woke everyone and likely prevented the second fire from being lit. Jessie needed to get herself and the kids the hell out of Alberta but she wouldn't go. She was refusing to leave her husband."

"She's scared for him."

"She lives her life in fear of losing him, Catherine."

"I lost someone." Overcome, Catherine kept her gaze on Matt. "I'm still here."

"Do you want to be?" he asked softly.

"With you? Yes. Alive? On the earth? Some days I'm not so sure. I don't blame your girl for being scared. Living life without Carly...is a nightmare."

"Catherine..." Matt moved towards her, grasped her fingers in his, and knelt before her. "I can't tell you how sorry I am about your daughter. All I know is there is a lot of beauty left in life. What's that old Thoreau quote? 'It's not what you see, it's how you see it.' I believe he's talking about nature, about beauty...that we don't always see the wonders of the earth until we look for them. Even though sometimes they're right in front of us." He smiled, and squeezed her hand. "But I think his words also relate to loss. You can choose to see the world as darkness, or you can choose to see it as light."

"What wise person taught you that?" A tiny smile landed on Catherine's lips, and she bent forward to plant a light kiss on her new lover's very welcoming mouth.

"That's the way Jessie tries to see the world, Catherine. It's not always easy for her. But she tries. Her music is filled with that message. She's all about forgiveness. Your daughter was the wise one, choosing Jessie's tunes."

"She sounds like a very special woman, Matt. Really."

"She has her days." Leaning forward, Matt let a sweet kiss anchor that thought.

Catherine was a salt-of-the-earth woman, and her messy beach hair was dry and tangled. Dried seawater on her skin left it rough, and her toenail polish was flaking and wearing off. Her fingernails? Toast. Chipped, and her cuticles likely hadn't had any attention in a while. Apart from Jessie, Matt's last semi-regular woman was Miranda, a classy, wealthy Vancouver businesswoman who had the money, if not always the time, for regular spa treatments to leave her skin robust and healthy, and her nails spit-shined and perfect.

Sometimes Matt caught himself studying Catherine as she peeled potatoes or mixed a salad. *What do I see in her?* he wondered. In his heart, he knew. She was the opposite of the women he was used to, for the most part. But she also brought Jessie to mind. Jessie, who only cared about her nails when some public event demanded it, who wolfed down barbecue chips by the handful, leaving crumbs, well, everywhere. Jessie, who knew loss on a deeply personal level, and whose sometimes despairing eyes came to mind when Matt studied the hurt in Catherine's eyes.

Now, bending before Catherine on the beach, kissing her, letting the kisses escalate, Matt wished they were back at his cottage, or at hers. Anywhere not quite so public.

"I have to pee. Really badly." Catherine was talking while she kissed him, which made Matt laugh.

"Time for a swim?" he asked, a mischievous glint in his eye.

"Definitely time for a swim, since we're at Thunder Cove and there are no facilities in the immediate vicinity." She was laughing now too. "But you'll have to swim far away from me, at least at first."

"It's a big ocean. Come." Standing, wincing at the creaking in his knees, Matt extended a hand.

Taking it, Catherine rose and walked hand in hand down to the water with her new man. "She asked about me, on the phone. I could tell."

"Mmmm. She was curious. She liked that you named your dog Drifter."

"Matt?"

"Yes?" They were at the edge of the water, and he groaned when the cool Atlantic Ocean nipped his toes.

"It's strange how things work out sometimes, don't you think?"

"You can say that again. Are we really going in there? Why's it so cold today?"

"It's either that or pee in the sand. I'll take the ocean. Wimp."

"Who's the wimp?" Matt took off running, leaping over the waves and soaking up the heat and beauty of this late summer day. Catherine was right behind him. The ocean cooled Matt off in all the right places, until he got a chance to love his woman properly in the peace and privacy of his cottage a few hours later.

At one in the morning, Matt kissed Catherine and eased out of his bed. "Meeting," he told her. "The time difference between here and the west coast is a pain in the ass."

Charles and Charlie should be at Charles' Calgary condo by now, according to a message Matt received earlier from Charlie. Ulysses, four hours behind in Vancouver with Deirdre, would be in on the Internet meeting, as would Jon. Catherine wished him well and left him to it, but from Matt's loft bed she heard every word.

"Surreal," she told herself, wondering for the umpteenth time whether she should trust this man with the gentle, wise eyes not to break her heart at summer's end. Listening to him in work mode, his voice serious but even and controlled despite the fear she could hear behind every sentence, and in the timbre of the other men's voices, she ached for him to be true and sincere. "Carly, did you have something to do with this?" she asked her daughter's spirit as she pulled the duvet up to her chin. "Are you trying to tell me something?"

From downstairs, she heard a voice she knew to be that of Charlie Deacon, an actor she had admired for years. Charlie was thanking Matt for convincing Jessie to go, to get on the jet and take the children back to Vancouver.

"She's moved into La Casa for the time being," Charlie was telling him. "Apparently there's quite the reunion happening, huh Ulysses?"

A new voice Catherine determined was this Ulysses character said, "Carlotta broke out her favorite cheeses, and Dee pillaged the wine cellar. So, yes. You can probably hear them, they're in the front room getting loaded."

"Just what you and Dan need, three drunk women on your hands." Matt's voice was tired, gravelly, but Catherine thought he sounded relieved.

Suddenly a new voice came over the computer. A woman. Catherine crept to the edge of the bed, leaned on the rail, and looked over the edge of the loft space. Jessie was in the frame, both arms wrapped around a good-looking black man's strong shoulders.

"Hey, Matt," she was saying, almost with contempt, it seemed, a glass of wine teetering in one hand. "I didn't know y'all were meeting tonight. It must be past your bedtime in red mud land."

Sitting back, Matt was quiet. But he'd clicked on the image of Ulysses and Jessie and made it fill the frame of the computer, so that he could no longer, at least for the moment, see Charles, Charlie and Jon. After a minute when nobody said anything, which Catherine found curious, Matt said a quiet, "Hey, Jessie."

She held out her glass to him. It waved a little unsteadily, and she almost tripped, but Ulysses grabbed her forearm, which was still snug around his neck. "I'm here. I came back to Van."

"I see that."

"The kids are glad. I think they were scared. That whole 'barn going up in flames with the horses inside' thing freaked them out."

"Jess…" The simple word was a warning.

"Oh, fuck off. I know. You don't want to talk to me. You don't want to see my face or hear my voice. I heard you. I'll respect that." Ulysses swallowed uncomfortably and looked away as Jessie's voice got soft and her eyes moistened. "I just thought you would like to know that I listened to you. I'm here. I might just stay drunk and high for the next six weeks or so, but I'm fucking here, Matt. Okay?"

Their earlier call had been just a phone call. Seeing Jessie on this live Internet call floored Matt. It unsettled Jessie too. Speechless, Matt had to remind himself that other people in on this meeting could see him. Catherine, though, saw him raise a hand out of frame as if he wanted to touch the screen.

Finally he spoke. "Jesus, Jessie. I wish you wouldn't…I don't…"

"I know." Wavering in the frame, she raised the glass to her lips and took a long drink. "And I know why all of you are meeting tonight. You're going to talk about Josh, right? Ulysses and Dan have us nimbots under control, and maybe Alin will join us for a bit. So we're good. So no talking about me and the kids, y'hear? Just Josh. Please."

Even from up in the loft, Catherine could see the desperation in Jessie's eyes. It was reflected in Matt's.

God, she completely derails him, Catherine thought inwardly, almost stunned at Jessie's capacity to floor Matt. There was definitely still something at play between the two. The intensity of the way they were looking at each other, all these miles apart, was both shocking and humbling.

Jessie's voice cut into Catherine's thoughts. "You shoulda seen me trying to drag Dylan away from Josh. It was torture, separating the two of them again. My monster child's got some crush on his daddy. I had to promise him a sing-song on the jet." Jessie paused for a sip of wine. "We sang all the way home. All of us except Dan, the big party-pooper. He read the paper. Emily-Grace played guitar. She's got a knack, that one. Already knows how to lose herself in music when she can't deal. David mostly curled up into a corner with that brow-beaten teddy bear of his and watched us. I got a few smiles out of him, though."

"Jessie..."

"I know, I know, y'all have work to do." But Jessie had a little more to say, even though Charles, too, came through and gently asked her to let them hold their meeting, which she blatantly ignored. "You know what he told me, Matt? What Josh told me after he got out of the hospital, after the whole messed-up river thing? After he almost died?"

Unable to answer, Matt just sat in numb silence, but Catherine saw him wipe an eye. So did Jessie, who swallowed and spoke with a thick sorrow Catherine knew well.

"He told me to go to you." She pointed the far edge of the wine glass towards the monitor. "If something happens to him. He said I should go to you."

Up from Matt, Catherine gasped, and he turned sideways to meet her anxious stare. In Vancouver, Jessie straightened, stood and disappeared from the screen, and then bent back down so Matt could see her again when he looked back.

"Hey! Oops, I guess you're not alone there, Matt. Josh must not have considered that you might find someone else to warm your bed. Silly Josh. What was he thinking?" Her voice changed, it got lighter, high-pitched. Forced. "Can I meet her? Come on, Matt, bring her to the computer."

"This is not the time, Jessie. We have things to discuss."

"Uh huh. And I can see that you're already tired. Must have been a good workout, Matt, assuming she's in your bed. Or wherever." She giggled.

Cutting in, Charlie was getting frustrated. "Jesus Christ, Jessie. You're drunk and you're out of line. Go away."

Her eyes flicked to another area of her screen, where Charles and Charlie, or one of them, was visible. A second later Jessie's eyes darted back to Matt. She opened her mouth as if to speak, but she couldn't quite seem to muster any words.

Matt pulled her back to him. He may as well have sent her a rope, a lifeline.

His words were sheer understanding. "You look beat too, Jessie. Maybe you should put the wine down and go snuggle up with your kids."

Watching him, she teetered a little more. Ulysses' arm tightened on hers. "I will, Matt. I swear." Unmoving, she barely blinked. "I'm afraid to go," she finally managed, her voice a croak. "I haven't seen you in so long. I thought you were gone…from all of our lives. Until this morning, I thought you were gone forever."

Knowing now that Catherine was listening, and watching, Matt spoke quietly. "Never. I told you that."

"I will see you again, Matt."

"Yes. Some day, kid."

"Not too soon, because that would mean…" She bit her lip.

"Not too soon, Jessie. We'll make sure of that. Tonight we'll make sure of that. Go. Please."

"I wrote him a song. On the jet, with the kids' help. Charles will like it."

"Josh is a lucky man."

"One of these days I'm gonna write a song for you, Matt. Just for you."

Everyone was silent. In the loft, Catherine sat back and hugged her stomach.

"Okay," Matt finally said. "I would like that."

"I'm gonna call it *Watch Over Me*. It'll be like I'm begging for you to come back."

Charlie broke in again. "Jessie, I'm going to end this call if you don't…"

"Oh fuck off, Charlie. I'm leaving." The eyes had flicked away again. Now they locked themselves on Matt. "Bye, Matt. Luv you. Please tell your new lady that she's got the best man on the planet. She really does."

Not counting Josh, Matt whispered under his breath. *Not counting Josh.* "Bye, Jessie. I love you too."

When she finally disappeared from the screen, and from the room, judging by her receding footsteps, it was a full five minutes before Matt felt composed enough to really participate in the meeting, and even then he only felt half there. It was a strange and rather unreal situation in which to find himself, working out extensive security for Josh while still aching to be around Jessie, the best friend and brief lover he desperately missed.

Two hours later, Matt finally crept back up the loft stairs to bed. He found Catherine sleepy-eyed but awake. This time, instead of giving him the silent treatment or being angry with him, she pulled him close and held him.

"I'm so sorry, Matt. I've been so wrapped up in my own pain I've completely failed to recognize yours. I guess there are different kinds of loss. I'm so sorry."

He couldn't answer. The meeting had been exhausting and worrisome, and the exchange with Jessie at the beginning was completely draining. Matt's body started to shake, and he buried his face in Catherine's messy beach hair while he tried to regain control.

"It's okay," she told him. "I understand. It's okay, Matt."

Holding him in the half-light of the white moon creeping in the window, Catherine allowed a few tears of her own to escape. But tonight, instead of crying for her lost daughter, she wept for the man trembling in her arms.

Chapter Eighteen

Charlie sucked in a breath and exhaled deeply. The director of *Sacred Peace's* final episode had just called 'Cut' for the last time on season one. Charlie's baby had come to fruition and, best of all, the last bit had been unremarkable in terms of new attacks on Josh or on the set in general. Nor were there any more 'weird' accidents. All that was left was a few hours of hard drinking tonight and an official formal wrap party the next night. Then Charlie would happily send Josh back to Vancouver, to his kids. There would be time to worry about season two over the long winter. Coming up there would be some travel for the press tour, since season one was premiering at the end of September, but Charlie figured it would be easier to contain and monitor Josh on a more one to one basis than on a busy TV set.

The next night, Josh and Charlie were lighthearted and acting like teenage goofs while they got ready for the formal wrap party, which was being hosted at the same hotel where the Alberta Children's Hospital fundraiser was held back in July. The guys dressed in the Calgary condo they'd agreed to share when they needed to be in town. Jane was there too, having left her children with the visiting Jack and Lydia, along with extra security, in Canmore. When Carter and Ashley dropped by the condo, they made their way as a group to a waiting limo outside and were swifted off to the party.

At the hotel, Josh dropped into a seat next to Shanda and draped an arm around her shoulders. She was dateless tonight, and happy to be Josh's informal 'plus one.' Handsome Carter and the demure, glowing Ashley settled into seats at the table too, to Shanda's left, soon to celebrate the arrival of a new baby, and Jane and Charlie tucked into chairs to the right of Josh.

"We did it, Josh," Shanda said happily, raising a glass of wine to Josh's water. "I plan to get roaring drunk."

Josh pointed to her glass. "A sip of wine, a sip of water. Unless you plan to be carried home tonight."

"Water won't slow me down tonight." There was something in her gaze that softened Josh.

He smiled. "All right. I'll carry you home. But I'm leaving you on the doorstep."

"And you call yourself a gentleman." Her pink lips widened playfully as she laid a hand on his thigh. Their friendship had deepened over the course of the shoot, and even more so after Shanda's re-commitment to the show back in July. As lovers on *Sacred Peace*, a lot of time was spent in each other's company and in each other's arms. What that meant was a mutual respect and a kind of love that both had come to cherish. It also granted them certain casual intimacies that, at the table, Jane noticed.

Turning her head to Charlie at one point while Josh's and Shanda's heads were bent together to share some private joke, she raised her eyebrows.

He shrugged. "They're okay. They've established boundaries."

"Boundaries? She's well on her way to oblivion tonight, Charlie."

"Josh isn't." Charlie waved a hand at Josh's water glass. "He'll be okay."

Sitting back, Jane, in a crimson red designer dress, crossed her arms and sent Shanda a look of warning. Shanda caught the look and backed away from Josh, who turned to Jane in his black dress shirt and formal jacket, and sent her a questioning look.

Jane just looked away, but Josh and Shanda both got the message and eased off.

The evening was like a burst bubble. The pressure was off. *Sacred Peace* would go to editing, at least the episodes remaining would—the first half of the season was already complete. For the most part, though, the tension was gone. Everyone was happy and sad at the same time, a close-knit family about to part ways until season two would go to camera next spring.

After dinner—after awards, a blooper reel, and a lot of laughs—a live jazz and blues band took the stage. Midway through the night, Josh gave Jessie a call.

He caught her just off set in Austin.

"Hey, Josh."

Even over the phone line Josh could hear the wistful tone in her voice. "Hey, little one. How's the shooting going today?"

"It's fine." Rising from her cast chair, she made her way past the craft table and past an electric hauling a heavy 2 K light, to the far corner of the soundstage where she was working. Facing the corner and ducking her head, she traced a wooden truss and turned an ankle over. "How's the wrap party?"

"Great. Miss you, though."

"Live band?"

"Yep. Blues, mostly."

"Anyone I would know?"

"Local group, so no, I doubt it."

"You dancing?"

"Some."

"Okay. Glad you're having fun."

Josh sighed. "Everyone's getting pretty loaded. I won't be staying late. I want to get to the ranch early and start packing things up for the drive on Monday."

"Is Arnie driving with you? Or behind you?"

"He's coming with me in the King Ranch. We're towing my bike in a trailer. The Lexus and your Mustang are already gone. I'll call you tomorrow to see if there's anything else you really want me to grab."

"Charlie's staying?"

"Yep. Lots of wrapping for him to deal with, but he's flying out in a few weeks after he closes up the Canmore house. He's pretty wired."

"I bet! First season of his own show under his belt."

"You okay?"

"Oh, I dunno. I get tired of this. I don't know anyone and they all treat me like I'm someone I'm not. I just put my head down and work."

"I know the feeling, Jess. A few more weeks and we'll be together again."

"The kids will be glad to see you."

Josh didn't answer right away. Shanda had crept up to him and was pulling his hand so he'd go dance with her. He laughed and yanked his hand away.

"Josh?"

"Sorry, Jess. Look, I should go. I'll say my goodnights and head out."

"I'm being called to set anyway," she lied, ennui and loneliness thickening her words. "Call me tomorrow."

"Jessie Wheeler-Sawyer," Josh grinned into the phone, pushing Shanda away. "Biggest star on the planet and lonely as hell."

"The air's thin up here at the top," she sighed. "Sometimes it's hard to breathe."

In the background on Josh's end, Jessie heard Shanda's distinctive laugh. He laughed too, and Jessie heard him move the phone away and tell her to leave him alone. Straightening, she stopped moving the finger she was tracing with.

"I'm sorry, Jess. Shanda's loaded."

"Grrreeatt. And I asked her to stay on the show why?"

"It's fine. I'm fine. I'm sober as hell. I can handle her. Besides, Jane's watching me like a hawk." Josh chuckled lightly.

"All right. Go play while I work. Call the kids in the morning, okay?"

"I will. I love you, little one. Always and forever."

"Always and forever, Josh." In her pocket, Jessie fingered the small cross Josh had carved for her. "See you soon, cowboy."

After they disconnected, she stood and leaned her head against the truss until a frizzy haired A.D. tiptoed up behind her and asked her to come to set. Shoving the cross back in her pocket, Jessie turned, forced a sad smile, and followed her.

At the party, Josh let Shanda lead him to the dance floor. The song playing was a slow tune, a waltz, so they chatted while they danced.

She started by tucking Jessie's favorite piece of rogue hair back behind Josh's ear.

"That bit of hair is off limits." With a twinkle in his eye, Josh pushed her hand down.

"Since when?" Shanda fought his hand and moved the hair again. At the same time, she brushed a thumb against his cheek. He shot her a 'look.'

"Since I just got off the phone with my wife."

"Your wife. Yes. I was hoping since she wasn't here tonight that I could pretend I was your wife." Her eyes dancing, Shanda beamed up at him. "I'd say that would include fifteen minutes in a broom closet with you, but I know that's not happening."

"A broom closet, is it? I'm more partial to a King-sized bed. More room to play."

Shoving her pointer fingers in her ears, Shanda tilted her head back and laughed. The light caught on her blonde curls, giving her a sexy Marilyn Monroe playfulness. "Too much information! Let me just rewind and erase that image, shall I?"

"Hey, you started it!" Josh pulled her closer so as to avoid an older couple, a few of the series' regular extras, who were slow jive-dancing around the floor. He moved his hands to her small waist and smiled into Shanda's pretty eyes. "It's been great working with you, Shanda," he told her with a readily apparent sincerity. "Really great. You're the best."

"Thank you," she replied, taking his tie in her fingers and playing with it. "You're pretty damn awesome yourself, Josh Sawyer. Let's do this again a few more times."

"At least ten," he grinned. "Although I hope the next few seasons don't have any extra added attractions to spice things up the way season one did."

"What, you didn't like the free trip down the river?"

At the cloud that washed over him, Shanda's shoulders sank. "I'm sorry, Josh. That was thoughtless. That day…" Sucking a breath in between her teeth, she shook her head. "It was a nightmare. Terrifying. I thought…we all thought…" She couldn't say the words, but moved closer to him and wrapped her arms around his shoulders. Burying her face in his neck, Shanda held on tight.

To her right, Jane, in Charlie's arms, tensed. Charlie looked over. Josh seemed confused. Sad. The earlier light in his eyes was dim. Charlie hesitated when he saw Josh place a hand behind Shanda's head and press her to him.

Josh was whispering in his co-star's ear. "It's okay, Shanda. It all turned out okay." Her response was to hold him tighter. They finished the dance that way, dancing much closer than they should have been, and Josh had to duck his head to avoid letting anyone see desire cross his face, flushing over his cheeks and making his eyes dusky and warm.

As the song came to an end, Shanda looked up at him. "You know what I wish?"

Nervous, Josh passed his tongue over his lips and waited. He was still holding her, both hands at her waist.

"I wish things were different. I know where I stand. I think I love your wife as much as you do," she managed a small laugh, "but I still wish things were different. I'm drunk, so I know I'm going to say something I'll regret in the morning, but Josh?"

"I'm listening." He was, too, his brown eyes serious and rather intently focused on her.

"I wish I could have felt you inside me. That's what I wish. Just once. Just once so I could feel as close to you as…" She swallowed. "As close to you as it's possible to be close to a man. That's what I wish."

The waltz was over and a new, fast tune had started. Around them, couples moved and laughed, dancing away the stress of the last many months of long days and hard work. Josh stared at Shanda, and told himself she was just drunk. Blinking, he sucked in a breath and glanced away, catching Charlie's warning eye.

Shanda's voice and her soft touch on his cheek pulled him back to her. "I think about it sometimes. What it would feel like to have you moving over me and…inside me. Holding you…" The pretty eyes were wet now, and the dim light in the space gave her the effect of a silent film starlet, in her clingy low black dress and high heels. "I even thought about asking you to do it, to take me all the way one day…under the sheets, on set. Nobody would ever know the difference."

"You're right, Shanda." Josh finally found his voice. "You're drunk."

She reached a hand down and gave the outside of his pants a gentle push, which she repeated slowly, her eyes not leaving his face. Josh swallowed painfully and moved her hand away. "One night," she whispered. "One. Please."

Shaking his head, Josh held her wrist away from him. "One night destroys friendships," he told her. "One night would be the end of us." Matt crossed his mind. "We've been over this."

"Ah. You want it. You want it too."

Frustrated, Josh looked back over at Charlie, who could see his entire season two go up in flames if Shanda rethought her decision to stay with the show. Sending Charlie a quiet *help,* Josh turned back to Shanda.

"Shanda, listen to me. I'm not going to give you some speech about waiting and some day the right guy will come along for you."

"You're my right guy, Josh. You're my only guy."

"No. I'm not. If I was, I wouldn't be married to someone else. No, look. This is what I have to say to you, as your very good friend. You need to enjoy every moment. You need to choose to enjoy every moment. Find ways to deal with the loneliness. Find a friend willing to sleep with you if you need that. But you need to understand that it's not going to be me. It's not ever going to be me."

"Once," she begged him, using her free hand to steady his cheek so she could kiss him. Josh didn't pull away. He had tasted her many times and many ways over the duration of the shoot, and the feel and taste of her skin was intoxicating. Parting his lips, he let Shanda tongue him.

Nearby, Jane shoved Charlie towards him just as Josh relaxed his hold on Shanda's wrist. Shanda started to rub him again, in earnest this time, before she moaned and lifted both arms up around his shoulders.

"Once," she breathed again and again. "Once, Josh. Please. Please please please."

In his peripheral vision, Josh saw Charlie curse and make his way past a few couples towards them, but he didn't pull away. Instead it was as if he was under some spell, lost in Shanda's lustful gaze and in the power of her luscious lips and tongue to build hot desire in him.

Charlie was kind and understanding. Taking Shanda's right arm, he removed it from around his friend's shoulder. "Come on, sweetheart," he said tenderly. "Time to start on the water, I think."

"No," she whined. "Charlie, let me be. Let us be." Standing there in front of Josh, she sent him a look of silent desperation as she shook Charlie's arm off.

Ten feet away from Josh, Charles, too, was watching this little interplay happen. A nauseating memory of seeing Josh with Nadia, and hearing about him years ago on the Virginia set with the female crew passed over him. So, too, did Jessie's sad voice on the phone from Austin earlier that day. A corner of his lip turned downwards in disgust, but he remained still. Charlie was handling this. Charlie was Jessie's protector.

"He wants it," Shanda said to Charlie, unable to lose Josh's burning gaze. "Jessie doesn't need to know."

That was it. The one word that had the power to break the connection. Like a loose wire, it sizzled into Josh's heart and mind and sent his confused feelings for Shanda into the dark, musty corners from where they'd appeared in the first place.

"One day in season two then, maybe," Shanda whispered to him. "Promise me."

"No," Josh murmured, but his eyes were still soft and tender. His hand was still on her waist. "I wish you would see that…I can't. I won't risk losing her again."

"Oh, fuck Jessie. Seriously, Josh. I respect her, I do, but…look at what she's done to you. All these things that happened on set this season, they were all because of her, you do realize that, right?"

"Enough, Shanda." Charlie grabbed her arm again, a little roughly this time.

"Because she chose you over Jacob! Isn't that right, Charlie?" She took a step backwards and wobbled on her high heels. Charlie gripped her arm a little tighter. "Maybe if you let her go the prick would stop trying to hurt you!"

"Shanda?" Charlie asked quietly. "Do you know something about what's been happening? About who has targeted Josh?"

Whipping her head around to Charlie, Shanda went grey. "What? I—no! No, of course not!"

"Then how do you know the threat we received was from a fan of Jacob's?"

"I—because…I just assumed, that's all. It makes sense. The whole world is pissed at Josh. Hell, I was pissed at him before I knew him."

"If you know something, you need to tell us."

"Charlie, I just asked the man to fuck me. Do you think I want to see anything bad happen to him? Like, ever? I love him. I love him," she added a second time, crumpling under the wine, the emotion, the pressure.

"Then love him from a distance. Let's go." Adamant, Charlie started to lead Shanda away.

Josh stopped him. "Charlie," he said with a firmness he knew would get Charlie's attention. Charlie stopped and looked back at him. "Let me just…"

Josh let out a breath and bent forward to brush his lips across Shanda's forehead. "Look. I love you back, okay? But make your peace with us before season two, Shanda. I thought we were already there, you and me. Maybe we are when you're sober, I don't know. Have a good break. I'll see you around for some of the press stuff in a few weeks. Okay?"

She leaned in and pressed her lips against his again, while Charlie still clung to her elbow. "What if we asked Jessie to join us?" Her eyes were dancing now, though, in a misty, sad kind of way. At his low chuckle, she laughed out loud. "Bye, Josh. I'll see you. Heartbreaker."

As she left his line of vision, Josh pocketed his hands and stared at the floor. If Charlie hadn't come along, would he have? Could he have? Clearing out the cobwebs, he shook his head, then raised his chin to meet Charles' livid stare.

Eyes flashing, Charles moved towards him. "I admit that you did well during the season, Josh. Shanda's a sweet, beautiful, kind woman. But you scared the shit out of me tonight."

"Jesus, Charles, cut me some slack. I don't need you watching my every move. She was drunk, that's all."

"Yes, and men much stronger than you find their way into the beds of women like that every day, whether they want to or not."

"I don't need to. My wife takes good care of me in that regard."

"You think I'm stupid? You think I just fell off the turnip truck?" Charles was much too close to Josh now. Josh backed away a step. "I'm a man, Josh. You would have been out that door in a second if Charlie hadn't come along."

"No, Charles. I won't lie and say she's an easy woman to walk away from, but I would not have gone there with Shanda." *I don't think...would I have? No. No way.*

"Okay, but you just let her shove her tongue down your throat here in front of everyone. Arnie spent the last ten minutes running around shoving peoples' cell phones in their pockets for them."

Oh, Jesus. Josh swallowed. "Well, if it wasn't videos, it'd be you, wouldn't it be, Charles? When do you plan on telling Jessie, tonight while she's on set in Austin, or at some point tomorrow?"

"I wish...I just wish..." Eerily, Charles' words were parroting Shanda's from earlier. Only Charles' were vicious and angry.

"What? That I died in that fucking river?" Josh bent close to Charles and spoke in a low, hurt tone. "For all I know, you've been engineering all this shit that's been happening to me. Because we all know that you, more than anyone, wish to hell Jessie'd stayed with Jacob. Or Charlie, before that. Don't we, Charles?"

Leaving Charles standing alone to anxiously wipe his chin whiskers, Josh stormed out of the room, passing Arnie on the way. Staring at the floor, Josh clapped him on the shoulder and didn't break pace as he moved by him. "Time to go, Arnie. Let's blow this popsicle stand."

Charlie saw him leave. Handing the wobbly Shanda off to Jane, he sprinted after Josh and caught up to him in the hotel lobby. "I don't know what you said to Charles, Josh, but the guy's white."

"Fuck off, Charlie. It's been a long night." Grumbling, Josh started to move away but Charlie grabbed his elbow and threw him around to face him.

"Go see Jessie, Josh. Fly out tomorrow. You can fly back in a few days and pack up."

Looking up at him, Josh was surprised to see serious worry cross Charlie's face. "Do you know something I don't, Charlie?"

"All I know is that Shanda's not leaving until Monday. And apart from Arnie, I think you're alone at the ranch all day tomorrow."

"Give me a break, Charlie." But the fight was gone out of Josh's voice.

"Look, man." Charlie pointed to himself. "I know you don't want to hurt Jessie. But you put a woman like Shanda in your bedroom and you won't limp away. You're talking to a guy who swore time and time again that I would never hurt that girl...and I lost her over my inability to walk away from an easy lay. And Josh, let's face it. Shanda is not just any woman. Hell, on some level probably she doesn't even understand, she likely feels she deserves some time with you." Charlie chilled, and started to back away from Josh, but he stopped just a few feet away. 'I'm going to work on getting Charles to agree to cut her loose before next season, Josh. You're not super human, man. None of us are when it comes to a woman like that, one that's in love with you. One that maybe...you kind of love back."

Bitter, Josh pressed his lips together and tried to focus on Charlie. "Do you think he—Charles—will tell Jessie about tonight, Charlie?"

"Hell, yeah. You know he will. Go see her, man. She gets it. She knows. You know she knows."

"About Shanda, you mean."

"Nah. Well yeah, but no. I mean about this love thing. That it's not some cut and dry formula thing where you just love one person and can easily forget about the rest of the people who come into your life."

Gazing at him, Josh thought, *least of all you. I know.*

Nodding, he saw Charlie's shoulders droop. One more look to Arnie, who half-waved to Charlie, and Josh walked away.

Pivoting slowly around on one shiny dress shoe, Charlie tucked in his loose shirttails as he made his way back to the small ballroom where the *Sacred Peace* gang was celebrating. Jane was waiting for him there. Shanda was off in the corner sitting on the camera operator's lap now, laughing, both arms draped loosely around his neck.

Opening her arms, Jane's eyes lit up when Charlie stopped at the doorway and surveyed his TV family. His gaze landed on her, and the corners of his lips curved up. Making his way to her, he lifted her and swung her slowly around, kissing her as her feet reached the floor.

"Thank God for you, Jane," he told her. "Thank God for you coming into my life and straightening out my stupid ass."

"Do you think Josh is okay?"

"I think Shanda has a power over him that scares him. But yes, he'll be fine."

"How do you know?"

"Because I'm about to walk over to Charles and ask him to gas up the jet for Josh so he can go see Jessie. And I'm about to ask him to start thinking about letting Shanda go. No season two for her."

"What?" Jane swayed slowly with her husband, enjoying the feel of his warm body against her.

"She's too much of a wild card, Jane. She's too close to him."

"Any woman is too much of a wild card around that man. Every woman in this room is in love with him."

"Every woman?" Charlie raised his eyebrows.

"Most women." Jane laughed, and playfully punched her husband in the stomach.

"Ouch."

"You'll have trouble finding someone as easy to work with as Shanda, Charlie. Who you can trust not to try to seduce your star."

"Hmmmm." Charlie smiled.

"What? Who?"

"I know one woman I would trust around Josh. Who is easy to work with when she's not having hissy fits...and when she's not being childish...and when she's not smoking or dumping Jim Beam down her throat, or when she's not on tour..."

Her face fell. "Jessie? Really, Charlie? You can't bring Jessie in here to star with Josh."

"Why the hell not?"

"Well, for one thing, she and Josh are, and will always be, Kate and Billy from *Drifters*."

"And the other reason?"

"I hate to say this, Charlie, they're our very best friends, but..."

"What?" His smile upended itself.

"They're volatile, honey. It's like...always a struggle for them. Everything. You bring her onto your show and something happens and you no longer have a show."

"Shanda's as much a wild card as Jessie, in that regard."

"No, Charlie, she isn't. Josh doesn't love Shanda the way he loves Jessie. If he loses it and goes to bed with Shanda some day, he'll be able to walk away from her. Or still work with her, I think. And Jessie will have to forgive him because, well, in some weird way maybe she owes him a free pass."

"Or two." Charlie grimaced.

"But if you bring Jessie in here, suddenly your show changes in a way that might not work—don't forget the whole uproar from Jacob's fans—and suddenly Josh no longer has a place that's just his. I think he needs that, Charlie. Even though you and Charles are all about Jessie, she's not a part of this cast. *Sacred Peace* is Josh's playground."

"When did you get so wise?" Charlie murmured into his wife's slender neck. "And let's not forget that *Sacred Peace* almost got Josh killed, too."

"*Sacred Peace* didn't almost get him killed. Some mentally ill person did. I'm hoping he or she is long gone by season two."

"So am I, Jane. So am I."

Charlie pressed his wife against him and held on for dear life. In a minute he would go see Charles and suggest sending Josh off to Austin to see Jessie in the morning. But for now his wife smelled like roses, and her arms were warm and loving. Inhaling deeply, he buried his nose in her neck, and thanked God for the long ago day he went looking for Jessie on Vancouver's Downtown Eastside.

Chapter Nineteen

Jessie was on set when Josh arrived. The film she was working on, a contemporary story about a woman investigating a century old murder, was less emotional for Jessie than the Brussels film, which would be premiering within the month, but it was still a raw visit into parts of herself that Jessie found left her drained. Now, as Josh crept quietly into a space just off set where he could see her but where she couldn't see him, he was immediately concerned.

For one thing, she was pale. Hungover, maybe? When he talked to her last night he didn't think she'd been drinking. She was on set at the time, so it wasn't likely, but Josh knew she was lonely and quite often she retreated into her old fave, Jim Beam, if loneliness and despondency converged. Without him, without the kids, Jessie was her old lonely self on film sets where, as she had told him, people didn't know her. She was like that when she started on *Drifters*, he remembered, as he watched her fiddle absently with some prop piece, an antique pitcher, while she waited for the gaffer to instruct one of the electrics to move a light. Yes, she'd alienated herself when she first joined the *Drifters* cast. It was Steve who first pulled her in, who took the time to try to get to know her, to bring down Jessie's walls.

The lost look in her eyes disappeared when the First A.D. called, "First positions, rehearsal for camera, everybody."

Jessie looked up at the A.D., and Josh ducked a little further behind the sound mixer's cart, where he was trying to remain unseen so he wouldn't throw off Jessie's rhythm or the rhythm of the crew. They were shooting in a built set on a soundstage. This one was designed to be a Victorian home, and so it was dark and dimly lit, which made it easier for Josh to hide.

It was a good forty-five minutes before the camera rehearsals were finished (they did two) and the first shot was completed, which took six takes because the older actor playing opposite Jessie kept forgetting his lines and had to have them fed to him more than once by the script supervisor.

Jessie was released so the cinematographer could reset for her close-up. Watching his wife, Josh could sense her loneliness and gloom instantly return. Knowing her, he figured she would head for the craft table, grab a snack and maybe a coffee or water, and slink either back to her trailer or to a cast chair just off set until she was called again. As she started to move, he was saddened to see that Jessie lowered her head, shoved her hands in her pockets, and didn't make any attempt to meet the eyes of anyone on the crew. Instead, she slinked by everyone and stepped out of the back door of the set.

There, she stopped. Josh hadn't taken his eyes off her. Jessie had finally looked up to get her bearings, and spotted him. Leaning a shoulder against the exterior of the set, parting his lips slightly in a small *hello,* he watched her lift her chin, see him, and settle back on one ankle. Jessie moved her head slowly from side to side as the happy realization set in that he was there, in Austin, with her.

Shoving himself away from the wall, Josh moved towards her, his boots sharp and staccato-y on the wooden floor. Relief was obviously washing over his wife. Jessie was powerless to fight the surfeit of emotion rising in her chest and in her throat, and now displaying itself across her face, at the sight of the man she was terrified to leave in Alberta a few weeks earlier.

"Hey, little one," Josh said, taking her in his arms and hanging on tight. "It's okay. I'm here. I'm in one piece."

"God, it's good to see you." That was all Jessie could manage at first, as his simple presence settled into her bones.

Her husband's spirit, those beautiful moist, tender chocolate eyes gazing into hers, and his big hands on her hips, had the instant power to turn Jessie's mood around. Feeling suddenly playful, she wrapped both sets of fingers around his engraved silver belt buckle and poised her pale eyes up at him. "So I saw on Twitter that you got a pretty good going over from Shanda last night, until Charlie pulled you away."

The memory of the desire that encounter had wrought almost brought

Josh to his knees. "What, no 'hi Josh, I love you, I miss you?'" His eyes were dancing. *I know a good way to deal with that desire...*

"Did you actually get through the season without sleeping with her?" Jessie frowned. "Not counting when the cameras were rolling."

"Hey. None of that. You know I did."

"Stronger man than Charlie."

"He slept with Shanda?"

"No, you dork!" Jessie swatted him. "At least I hope not. But he would have in the old days."

"She was drunk, Jess. But I shouldn't have let her kiss me. I'm sorry."

"You didn't sleep with her?"

"You already asked me that."

"It's serious shit. I needed to ask twice." The childish, petulant Jessie was back. It was her frisky side, and Josh felt a weight rise off his chest just to see this woman emerge to replace the sad, lonely one who stepped off set a few short minutes ago.

"How much longer?" he asked her, brushing her hair back off her face and longing to play-bite those perfect lips. "Just close-ups?"

"With him?" Jessie tossed her curls in the direction of her co-star. "Mister 'I couldn't remember my lines if you gave me an inner ear monitor and shouted them at me?' Likely hours. Do you want to go back to my suite and hang out?"

"As if. I want you in my sight." Taking her hand, Josh led his wife to a quiet corner, where they were able to sit undisturbed until she was needed again.

Six interminable hours later, Jessie was released for the remainder of the day. In the elevator on the way up to her suite at a local hotel, she held Josh's hand and ordered Arnie and Dan to take some time off.

"Go get some steaks. You're in Texas! It's steak or taquitos. Local security lives outside my door. And we're not planning to leave the hotel."

Arnie glanced at Josh, who turned a little red and shrugged. "We'll call you in a few hours, guys. We're good."

"Let us sweep the suite first. Deal?"

"Deal."

By the time the guys were gone, Josh was starving. Standing before Jessie, he tossed a question at her. "Which first, food or play? You choose."

"You have to ask?" Blushing like a shy schoolgirl, Jessie lifted the bottom hem of her husband's T-shirt and pulled it over his head. Dropping to her knees, she let kisses land all over his chest, and took the time to give each nipple a squeeze and a gentle suck as well. Looking up at him, she sent him a diabolical grin and undid his belt.

Josh raised his hands and laughed. "Good enough," he said, "but since you're making me wait, I'll expect the best steak in Austin after this."

It wasn't long before he lifted her from her knees, turned her around, and put his hands on the waist of her jeans and eased them down. Jessie bent over the foot of the bed and rested her forehead on a forearm. Gently, Josh entered her and loved her, rubbing her breasts and fingering her nipples with one hand as he moved, and placing the other hand on a hip to help keep her steady.

"Is this okay?" he asked her, panting as sweet waves of pleasure swept through his body, always hyper-aware of any triggers from Jessie's Deuce McCall days that might come back to haunt her. By the sounds of her moans and groans, though, and the way she pushed back against him to increase her pleasure, Josh wasn't especially concerned, but he knew enough to move at an easy pace and not take his wife too roughly this way.

Her, "Oh God, yes," satisfied him and brought forth a low chuckle before Josh leaned in and kissed her shoulder.

"My beautiful girl," he murmured tenderly before their lovemaking heated up to a point where the only sounds they made were exclamations of desire and pure, perfect satisfaction.

In bed afterwards, her hair mussed up on the pillow and one leg thrown over Josh's, Jessie sprawled half over his chest. "I can't tell you how glad I am you're here," she whispered. "Josh, this is the loneliest set I've been on in years."

"Why?" he asked, bringing his free hand around his body to pull her closer as he basked in the afterglow.

"I don't know. I know a lot of it is my own fault. I've been so worried about you."

"I'm good. *Sacred Peace* is wrapped and all is quiet on the western front."

"Yes, but you still have to go back to the ranch."

"I do, yeah, but I won't be alone. Arnie will be with me. We'll get things packed up and drive back to Vancouver together in a few days."

"I don't even want you driving." Jessie put on her best pout and buried her nose in his bicep.

"I can't curl up into a ball, Jess. I'm not going to turtle my way through this. It seems like whoever was causing trouble gave up, anyway."

"Duh, cause he or she had to run the friggin' gauntlet to get to you. You have less security now, doofus."

"Worrying isn't helping, Jessie. It solves nothing. Come on, you know your Bible."

"Trust me, Josh, I pray. I pray all the time. Sometimes I pray so much I think I'm becoming OCD. The more Hail Marys I pray, the safer I figure you are. That kind of thing."

"My sweet Catholic girl. Then stop worrying. Mary's looking out for me."

"I'm such a role model for the Catholic church. Duh. At least I can say my prayers are genuine. They're very heartfelt."

"I know they are, little one. Don't be so hard on yourself. You're one of the kindest, most generous people I know. I'm sure Jesus has your back."

"And yours," she whispered.

"Or the universe or, I dunno, the Dalai Lama or Buddha or whoever. They're all sitting around having tea right now saying 'that Jessie girl sure prays hard. She's paid her dues. Let's do right by her now.'"

"By keeping my husband and children safe? Hell, yeah!"

Josh laughed and started to speak but Jessie leaned up over him and placed a finger over his lips.

"Probably I shouldn't have said 'hell,' huh Josh?"

"Probably not. Sadly, I've heard you say much worse, Catholic girl. Jess?"

"Mmmmm?"

"About that steak?"

Jessie rolled fully on top of him and placed her knees on either side of his hips. "Awww, my sexy cowboy's hungry. I suppose I should do something about that."

Her mischievous grin alerted Josh to the fact that Jessie likely wasn't considering ordering food any time soon. In another twenty minutes, though, leaving her dazed and very happy on her back on the bed, he ordered it himself.

Jessie had the next day off, so she and Josh poked around the city with Dan and Arnie. By the time she had to go back to work, it felt like old times. Unfortunately, part of the whole old times thing was having to let go.

A hired driver from the production drove the four of them to the airport to meet the jet. By the time they arrived, Jessie had already crashed again. The short trip found her staring outside the window of the Lincoln Navigator, her nose pressed to the glass, her left hand firmly tucked into Josh's right, resting on his thigh.

At the airport, Arnie had a few words with Dan while Josh squared Jessie on to him and placed both hands on her shoulders. "You are strong, little one. A few more weeks on this film and I'll see you at home. In the meantime, Deirdre says the kids are doing great, they're happy as clams. Your new friend Alin is coming to Van this week for a while, which has our daughter stoked. In the meantime, Kayla's working with Emily-Grace on her dancing, and Jacob's got the guitar and piano lessons under control. Even David's taken an interest in piano, apparently."

"But school's not going so good."

"They'll have a tutor on the tour. We'll deal. One day at a time."

"Maybe if I start to suck, the production will fire me. They can replace me with some other princess diva."

"Speaking of princesses…how about you suck it up, princess? Come on, Jessie, don't be looking at me with tears in your eyes. I won't be able to stand leaving you. I'll be miserable for the next few weeks. And think what this does to Arnie! Tough as nails on the outside, but inside, the man's a pile of mush."

"I hate this. I want to come home. I miss my babies."

"I know you do, Jessie. And I think…" Sighing, Josh took his hands off her shoulders and placed them on his hips. He looked away.

"What?"

Chewing on his bottom lip, Josh let his gaze flit back to Jessie. "You miss your old buddy Matt. You're not used to being on a production without having him around."

The casual comment was a knife thrust in the gut. Jessie sucked in a breath and almost doubled over. "I have Dan," she tried weakly, averting Josh's gaze by focusing on a crack in the asphalt.

"Dan the man, huh? Mister all-business quiet guy who does better with kids? You miss your friend."

Jessie had no answer for that. Crossing her arms, she fought back the urge to have a complete meltdown because she knew that would throw Josh off entirely. And, when all was said and done, she did not want to be responsible for sending him home worried sick about her, reflecting on that awful time when he was in such rough shape that he pretty much pushed her into turning to Matt.

Knowing his girl well, Josh just pulled her into his arms and stared over her shoulder at Dan and Arnie. Dan was watching them; his large arms the size of tree trunks were crossed, but he kept looking at his watch. Jessie was already going to be late for her call.

"All right," Josh started, his voice husky. "We've established what the problem is. Now go find someone on set you can be friends with, and indulge in some post-wrap girl talk over Mai Tais or whatever the hell they drink in Texas. I'm fine because Mother Mary is watching over me, remember? I'm going to pack up the ranch with Arnie, drive home, and hug our kids. You will rock this film with Mister 'feed me all my lines,' and you'll be home in a few weeks."

"Lawn Darts. I've been drinking Lawn Darts."

"Not funny, Jessie." Josh frowned.

She stomped her foot. "They're a riff on the Negroni."

"Which is…" Raising his arm uselessly, Josh let the words fade away. "Forget it," he said, but pointed at her foot. "You stomped your foot."

His light jibe accomplished what Josh hoped it would. Tossing her head, Jessie smiled and wiped a few strands of windblown hair out of her eyes. "I did. Indeed."

"I'll see you." A last kiss on her forehead, and Josh forced himself to walk away. "Arnie," he called over his shoulder. "Let's go."

Arnie dropped a moving one-armed hug around Jessie's shoulder as he passed. "I'll watch out for him, Jessie."

"Um-humn." Pressing a thumb and forefinger to the corners of her eyes, Jessie just nodded and watched her husband mount the few steps to the open door of the Keating jet.

At the top, Josh gave her their usual 'I love you' salute—a finger to the eye, a hand over the heart, a sweeping flourish away from the lips.

"I love you too, babe," Jessie murmured, sending Josh back the same loving visual message.

Turning, Josh disappeared inside the jet, but it killed him to leave her. As he dropped into a seat and waited for Arnie, he cursed at the futility of their busy careers.

Outside, Jessie stood stock still until Dan made his way over to her. Tentative, he told her they needed to get going, but she shook her head and watched the steps fold upwards and meld themselves into the jet. When one of the guys on the tarmac gave her the evil eye (*obviously a Jacob Ryan fan,* she thought), Jessie let Dan slip an arm around her waist and lead her back to the big black SUV.

The jet turned and motored down the runway, taking Josh and Arnie away, and leaving Jessie alone in a city that frightened her, and that felt alien and, in some ways, even feral. Just the other day there was a shooting in a downtown bar. Three people were killed. Texas still carried its old wild west vibe of yore and that, perhaps, was one of the reasons why, that night after wrap, Jessie got roaring drunk on the mini-bottles in her well stocked bar, smoked a bit of weed Dan grudgingly rounded up for her from a crew member on the film, and placed a call to Matt.

There was a second reason too. Already depressed and miserable when she got back to her suite, she sat down to check her email while she waited for Penne Rigate a Quattro Formaggi to be delivered by room service. She scanned through the usual stuff first, which included a note from Steve to say hi, another from Jacob checking details on the upcoming tour, and one from Deirdre with pictures of the kids lined up at the kitchen island in La Casa, lightly dusted in flour while baking with Carlotta (which brought tears to their mother's eyes). Then an email that she thought (hoped) might be junk mail, since she didn't recognize the sender, jumped out at her.

Whore, the subject line read. There was an attachment. A morbid curiosity got the better of her. Jessie opened the email. A line at the top, in a small black font, read *'You should have stayed with Jacob.'* Poising a finger over the mouse, Jessie counted to five before she got up the guts to open the attachment.

It was a video, about twenty minutes long. Vaguely, Jessie recognized the people featured in it. She also immediately knew the branding—it was from Caryn and Eric's studio on East Hastings.

"Well, it's not like I figured you disappeared forever," she thought randomly, watching a young, naive version of herself get seduced by a good-looking twenty-something guy she remembered as Luke. There was a girl in the video too. Jessie only made about a half dozen films for Caryn, and she clearly recalled this as the first. The sheer nervousness in her questioning eyes confirmed it, as did the way the girl led her to a sofa and gave her directions.

Jessie clicked 'stop' before the film played out too far. This was an old version of herself in the dark days when she lived on the Downtown Eastside with Caryn and Eric, at a time when she went by the stage name Emily Wheeler. Interestingly enough, the memories associated with the making of the films didn't sicken her so much as the sheer existence of some nefarious past that Jessie remembered was her attempt at coming back to life after the horror of Sandy's murder at the hands of Deuce McCall. No, the filmmaking she recalled as nerve-wracking at first, but in actuality quite pleasant overall. Jessie was a willing participant—Caryn never forced her to do anything she didn't want to do. The video was a clean, erotic romp with two partners she trusted. In some ways, Jessie credited her time on the Downtown Eastside with teaching her how to enjoy her body, which paid off today in spades in a healthy relationship with the man she loved.

A vicious mind was behind the sending of this video to her, though. The sender was a generic fkl411@freakshow.com.

"What do you want from me?" Jessie wondered. The idea that whoever sent the video might make it public crossed her mind. Sitting back in her chair, Jessie let her hands drop to her lap. Really, in her heart, the way she was feeling today, she didn't much care if the film went public, if the people in her close circle or even her fans saw it. As far as she was concerned, it was consensual sex with willing partners, and it put food in her belly at a time when she had none. Caryn's studio gave her a safe place to belong at a time when she rarely had the ability to speak, after what she'd witnessed in Charleston. But...she had children to consider now.

"Hell, I figured you'd show up some day," Jessie told herself again, admitting inwardly that this was not a surprise. Looking down, she started playing with her fingernails, ending with a quick intake of breath and the nails of her right hand forming crescent moons in the back of her left hand. The images of her children in Deirdre's email were forefront in her addled mind. Flour-covered, laughing, happy. Innocent.

"I don't deserve you. You deserve a better mother than the one you have," she sighed.

At that point, she slammed shut the lid of her MacBook, and paced the suite. Normally she would send something like this to Matt, to get him to find the identity of the sender and deal with it. But this was an erotic film featuring Jessie at a young age. It was likely buried amongst a gajillion other videos on some deeply buried porn site, yes, and in it she was under the name of Emily Wheeler and not wholly recognizable as the woman who became the singer and actor Jessie Wheeler. If people saw it, Jessie figured none of them would be looking for her, or recognize one of the young actors in it as her.

Someone had, though. And they did a malicious thing by sending it to her, which was a whole other cause for concern because Jessie's email address was private and supposedly secure.

What to do? Wringing her hands, Jessie considered sending a one liner to Matt, maybe, instead of the entire email. That might do. But...no. Everything had changed with him after they got close in Brussels. After they had sex, and a magical night and day together? That memory was sacred to Jessie, and she knew it was to Matt as well. How could she destroy what little relationship they had left by sending Matt something that might change the way he felt about her, or worse—seem like some kind of tease? Judging by the way Matt reacted to her the two times she had contact with him lately, Jessie figured she had no choice but to keep him out of this loop.

Dan? I can go to Dan. But...no. The big man was serious security. It was like after he made the mistake years ago that got Josh abducted by McCall, Dan was afraid to let his guard down, to get close. Their communications were official and formal, for the most part. Josh? *Nah-ah, no f'ing way. I will not hurt that man any more than I already have.*

There was nobody left. Exposing herself this way to her friends was not an option. Sitting down on the foot of the bed, Jessie sank lower. By the time the knock came at her door announcing the arrival of her dinner, she was already half in the bag.

By the time she was staring at Matt's contact info on her iPhone, she had, in all her glorious drunken logic, caved, and sent him the video.

Chapter Twenty

Matt had just helped Catherine make a s'more when Jessie broke down and called. Outside at the campfire, under a luminous moon and glorious stars too numerous to count—including, tonight, a number of dreamy falling stars—he was licking gooey marshmallow off his fingers when his cellphone, which was resting on a small white plastic table at his side, lit up.

Jessie, it read. Blinking, he stared at it before looking sideways at Catherine who, at that moment, was wide-eyed and unnerved at having been caught by her new man with a mouthful of breaking graham wafers, warm marshmallow, and melted chocolate, all of which were leaving sticky trails on the corners of her mouth.

"Take it," she tried to say, the words coming out muffled with cotton. "I'll be back." Rising, she headed inside to wash her mouth and fingers, and to try to somehow more gracefully swallow the gooey fireside treat without Matt's gorgeous eyes on her.

Swallowing nervously, Matt lifted the phone. Immediately, he knew taking Jessie's call was a mistake, but what could he do? He'd told her she could call if she really needed to. Maybe this was an emergency. The thought gutted him. He bent over his knees and wiped his forehead as sweat broke out in little beads.

She spoke before he even said hello. "Matt?"

"Yeah. I'm here. You okay, Jessie?"

"S-shure. Shure, Matt. I'se fine."

He paused. *Oh, shit.* "You've been drinking," he said, his heart sinking.

"Y-yep. Been drinkin'. Had a leetle weed too."

Closing his eyes, Matt rose, startling Drifter, who was asleep behind his chair. Leaving Drifter whining for him, lashed to a small post Matt had hammered into the ground, Matt started walking towards the Darnley Basin. He stopped at the edge of the low cliff and stared at the lights of the cozy homes and cottages across the small bay on the Malpeque side.

He didn't speak until he stopped moving. "Jessie, why are you calling? What do you need?" Matt's voice was gruff. Brusque. Defensive.

Jessie recoiled. "I jus wan-ned to hear your voice, Matt." She was so drunk she was struggling to stay awake. In her suite, she was sprawled crookedly across her bed, feet sticking out over one side. She wanted to suss his mood out before she mentioned the video.

"Where's Dan?"

"I dunno. Fucking the maid, who knows and who cares."

"You can't make a habit of this, Jessie. Calling me when you've been drinking."

"Don't…forget the weed."

"Calling me after Josh leaves. Right? He left today?"

Speaking slowly so she could get the words out, Jessie managed, "Ahhh. Matt's jealoush. I like it when you're jealoush, Matt."

"I'm not…Jesus, Jessie. Get it together, will you?"

Even as inebriated as she was, Jessie clearly understood Matt's anger. It reverberated inside her like a yoyo, bouncing back and forth around her insides until she had to roll onto her side and curl up into a little ball.

From P.E.I., Matt heard her start to softly cry. Groaning, he rubbed a hand absently back and forth over his hair. "Jessie, come on. What the hell am I supposed to do, kid? Tell me what I'm supposed to do with you."

"I just…I'm in this film, Matt."

"I know, kid. In Austin."

"'Course you know." It was a whisper that Matt had to strain to hear. "You're watchin' over me still. Not that one, though. Not that film. Thas…not the one I mean."

Missing the point, partly because Jessie was hard to make out and her voice was so small and quiet, Matt referenced the project she was working on. "So what about the film, Jessie? What's the problem with this film? Is it paying you too much? The cool twenty mil has you feeling guilty?"

Oh, shit. He's still so angry. This is not the time... She went with, "It's lonely here. Without you. Without my friend."

Weak at the knees, Matt sank to the earth. Behind him, Catherine was just coming back out of his cottage. She made her way to Drifter, gathered the dog in her arms, and wondered what the latest Keating / Sawyer crisis was about. She prayed Josh was okay.

"Jessie...we knew this would happen. If we...well, we knew. That's all. There are consequences to every action, and this is ours."

"Consequences? Why should one night be a fuckin' life sentence, Matt? One fuckin' night."

Her sobs were hard to take. Matt straightened up his shoulders and played hardball as, in the Basin below, the little white sailboat flashed its 'J & J' at him every time it bobbed up on a crest and was illuminated by the moon.

"Because it is, Jessie. Because we got too close, that's why."

"Because we luff each other, thass why. You can luff more than one person, you know."

"Being lonely is not enough reason to call me and remind me of how I feel about you, Jessie. Missing your husband is not enough reason to call me and smash my heart into a million pieces all over again."

"Stop bein' so angry...at me all the time, Matt," she slurred. "We spent years together...without me climbin' into your bed. Years. You forget...'bout all that?"

"You know the drill, Jessie. I collected a paycheck. I was paid to be there." Rubbing his forehead with his fingertips, hard, Matt gasped at how much it hurt to say that.

Jessie was silent as she took in his harsh truth. When she spoke, her entire body was trembling with hurt and anger. "You fucking ash-hole. You fucking ash-hole, Matt."

"You can't call me like this, Jessie. I guess Jacob wasn't available? Who's next on your list? Charlie? Or Steve?"

"You mus...really...hate me. Huh, Matt?" Sniffling, Jessie held the phone to one ear and tried to keep her eyes open.

"Leave me alone, Jessie. Okay? Let me do my job and stop calling me."

"S'okay, I will," she managed in a forced sing-songey drunk voice. "Cuz you know what, Matt? I really...hate you too."

It was a full two minutes of silence before Matt ended the call. As far as he knew, Jessie had not tapped on the 'end' icon the whole time. He could hear a muffled sobbing; likely Jessie's face was pressed into the bed covers or into a rug on the floor or into her sleeve, wherever she happened to be. It broke his heart anew.

More than ten minutes later, he felt Catherine's presence behind him. By then he had used his own sleeve to wipe away yet more tears shed for the love of a woman he felt could never be his.

"I'd ask if you were okay but I don't think you are," she said, sitting on the grass next to him and wondering why he was so fixated on the little white sailboat bobbing on the water below them. "Did something else happen?"

Holding the phone up, Matt decided to be honest. "Jessie. She was drunk. And high, I guess."

"Oh. She really is a handful, isn't she, Matt?"

"Don't let fame fool you, Catherine. The superstars who walk amongst us are the loneliest people on the planet. And Jessie's at the top, so I guess that makes her the absolute loneliest."

"She has a husband, Matt. One she is crazy in love with. And three beautiful children."

"Yet she is alone in some random hotel suite in Austin, Texas, worried sick about her husband, drenching her mind with alcohol to numb the pain. It just feels like..." He sighed. "It feels like it did that summer she was being stalked. She abused herself a lot then, too. It's what she does when things get too tough to handle."

"Is it a problem? Does she need to go to rehab?"

"No, no...it's not like that with her. It's more of a casual thing. Something usually sets her off." Considering that, he wrinkled his eyebrows but finally chalked up Jessie's night of self-medicating to her loneliness in Austin. "Catherine? You never ask about her. About my life watching over her, before. Most people are curious."

"How about we don't share our war stories? How about we just pretend everything is perfect? That the woman you guarded and cared for isn't the same one my daughter was listening to when she died."

"You remind me of her."

"I can't imagine how. These abs haven't seen the inside of a gym in a while."

"I think…you're just kind, Catherine. You're a kind, caring soul."

"So are you, Matt." She tucked her arm into his and laid her head on his shoulder. "Do you think about them all the time, Matt? Do you worry about them?"

A strange choking sound got caught in his throat. "Worry about them? I live my life in fear for them. Josh—well, as you've figured out, there are still people out there who have it in for him. I worry about him."

"So I guess by default you also worry about her."

He didn't answer. And that was his answer. After a bit he said, "Look, why don't you go inside? I'll put out the fire in a bit. I just need to sit for a while."

"Oh. Okay. You sure you don't want company?"

"I just need a minute."

"Okay." Remaining at his side, though, she looked back at him. "Hey, Matt? Can I ask you something?"

"Sure, Cath. Anything." Distracted, he stared out over the Basin, at the ominous wispy grey Halloween-like clouds now passing over them, hiding the twinkling stars from sight.

"I was thinking…when I go back to London…I know Jessie Wheeler is playing a show in Toronto. With Jacob Ryan. That promo show for Josh Sawyer and Charlie Deacon's new television show, right?"

Alert now, Matt paused, and folded his elbows around his knees. He flicked his gaze to the dark blades of grass peeking up between his feet. "You want to go."

"Yes. I do. I suppose I want to know what all the fuss is about. Why Carly was so enamored with the two of them."

"I don't know, Catherine. Do you think that's such a good idea?"

"It might help sort things out in my head for me, Matt. It might make things easier…with you."

"You've been pretty clear about your feelings for Jessie."

"There's more, Matt, I…I think I'd like to meet her. Do you think you could arrange that?"

Matt almost gasped. Forcing himself to try to remain somewhat stoic, he picked a blade of grass and stuck it between his thumbs like his father used to when he and his brother Michael were children. Pressing it to his lips, he blew through it and tried to make it whistle, but the sound that emerged was more of a mute cry from a sick cow than an actual shrill, sharp whistle.

He dropped the blade of grass and exhaled slowly as he wiped his palms on his jeans. "I don't want the two of you to meet."

"Why not?" The question wasn't defensive. It was carefully and quietly asked.

"Because what you want to tell Jessie will hurt her. And she's already been hurt enough. That's why."

"You don't know what I'm planning to say to her."

"I think I do." Still averting his gaze from Catherine's questioning eyes, Matt added, "She doesn't need to hear that a teenage girl listening to her music couldn't hear a car that killed her. Jessie's music is about healing. It's not about causing pain."

"But that's the truth, Matt. That's what happened. Why shouldn't your rock star lover know the truth?"

"Don't push it, Catherine. Don't push your luck here."

"Is that a warning, Matt?" Pushing herself up, Catherine looked down at the man she was well aware already had her heart in his palm. "I thought Jessie was your past. I was hoping I might be your future. We can't start a relationship that pits us against each other right from the get-go."

"Then you should consider not using my position with the Keatings to score concert tickets, Catherine. How many do you want, enough for all of your teacher friends? Enough for your whole damn high school? I suppose I could just ask Jessie to show up at your school, but the way she sounded tonight I can't guarantee she'll be sober."

Standing over him, Catherine's heart sank. *I have someone to look out for, too,* she told herself as she lifted a hand to her lips and chewed a nail. *She just happens to be dead. And like it or not, Jessie Wheeler was the last living connection to Carly. Hers was the last voice my daughter heard.*

"I'll be inside," she said abruptly as she turned away.

Her footsteps were slow, hesitant, as if Catherine was a little afraid to leave

Matt by the edge of the cliff, but it wasn't high enough for him to get badly hurt if he hurled his despondent self over, so she kept walking. Matt didn't come in for about an hour, and this time, instead of holding him, Catherine let him turn his back to her when he came to bed, and she drifted off to sleep without his skin so much as even touching hers.

The next morning dawned grey and cool. After a light breakfast of a poached egg on toast, Matt started to scroll through his emails, but when he saw Jessie's name on the incoming list, and the subject line *whore,* he determined he wasn't in the mood to deal with her just yet. Rising from the computer, he decided a good way to beat out some frustration was to go for a morning run up to the end of the Lower Darnley Road to the old schoolhouse with the broken glass angel. The obviously angry email from his drunk superstar charge could wait.

He asked Catherine to come, and got rather annoyed when she declined.

"I'm not a runner, Matt," she told him, as if she were daring him to challenge her. As if she were testing him to see how many differences between them would stand in their way of becoming a long-term couple.

"You might like it," was his candid response. "How will you know whether or not you like running if you don't try it? Carly liked it. She got something out of it."

"That's low, Matt." Twisting away from him, Catherine bent over the dishwasher, her way of saying *go away.* "She got dead out of it. That's what she got."

So he went, at a fast pace that Jessie would have loved. Catherine would have just slowed him down, anyway. To Jessie, as to Matt, running offered a certain freedom. The so-called 'runner's high' was the real deal. Once your lungs were engaged and got into the rhythm, your legs beat naturally down a chosen path.

These days when he ran, Matt made a certain concession, for Catherine's sake. No longer did he take music along.

"There's never a guarantee of safety, about anything," he had said the other morning as he kissed her before he left the cottage. "But out of respect for you, and for your daughter, I'll leave the earbuds at home when I go running."

"Thank you," she had murmured, grateful, remembering now that small kindness as she scratched Drifter's ears and watched Matt go, a lonely figure on a gravel lane, lost in Keating / Sawyer thought and worry, she supposed.

With Matt off for an hour and the dishes cleaned up, and anxiety and energy to burn after the tension of both last night and this morning, Catherine puttered around the place. Cleaning the bathroom was easy, throwing laundry in was a breeze. While she waited for the washing machine to do its thing, she slid into the chair at the corner desk, and laid her hand over the mouse.

The big iMac computer lit up like a Christmas tree, albeit in pale blues and pinks as a beach background slipped into view, no doubt selected by the cottage's owner, since the computer was part of the rental.

Matt's email program was still open. Catherine caught her breath. There, in clear black letters, was the unopened email from Jessie.

"No, no, don't do it," she chided herself, holding the black arrow over the email. "He'll know. There's no way he won't know." But she couldn't help herself. The subject line was far too enticing.

What Catherine found shocked the hell out of her. Furrowing her brow at the *You should have stayed with Jacob* line, she licked her lips nervously and clicked on the video link. *So this is porn,* she said inwardly, watching a young Jessie settle back on a couch while both a twenty-something blonde woman and a handsome, dark-haired young man used her as their plaything.

She was near the end of it when Matt's feet jogged up the steps. Standing, turning to him, her face a weird shade of green, she was trembling.

Matt's eyes darted to the screen. "You're watching porn, Catherine? At ten thirty a.m.? Someone's feeling frisky."

"She sends you porn videos? Of herself? That's the kind of relationship you have with Jessie Wheeler? Why does it make me think you've been sleeping with her all along…"

"What? Jesus, no." Moving past her to the computer, Matt stared at the image Catherine had frozen on the screen the instant she heard his footsteps on the stairs. A young Jessie, on her back, her face turned to the side, eyes closed, a blonde woman's lips on her cheek, that same woman's hand cupped over Jessie's left breast. A boy's hands at her hips, Jessie's left hand over his.

A wider scan revealed the source—Jessie's email. The disturbing subject line. In his haste and quickly growing rage, Matt did not see the one line warning, nor did the fact that the email was a 'forward' catch his eye.

He turned to Catherine. "You opened my email." Suddenly he needed a whole new run.

Pointing a finger at him, she was equally incensed. "She sends her old porn to you! What kind of man are you? What kind of woman is she?"

"She was upset last night. She was drunk and high and lonely! Obviously she was exercising a clear lack of judgment, but Catherine, that's not your business! You have no right to be opening my personal email. What the hell were you thinking?"

"Honestly, Matt?" she replied, seriously quaking now. "I don't know. I don't know what the hell I was thinking." A quiet pause, and she scooped Drifter up in her arms. His poor casted paw stuck straight out, and his eyes drooped at his beloved Matt as she backed out of the room.

Matt didn't try to stop her. What he did do, before cleansing off the sweat from his run in a warm shower, was call Charles. Before he did that, he brought the cursor back to the beginning of the video and watched Jessie in her first film ever until the midway point, when things were heating up onscreen and he was experiencing a physiological reaction that disturbed him.

Cursing again, he was near tears by the time he got Charles on the line. An image of a dusky-eyed Jessie was frozen on screen; her back was arched and her hips were raised to meet the tongue of the young man while the woman's lips suckled a nipple.

In Calgary, at 7:35 in the morning, Charles was already up to his eyeballs in work. Charlie sat across the desk from him. The two were trying to wrap up *Sacred Peace* by completing piles of funding paperwork for the federal and provincial governments.

Charles grabbed the phone after the first ring. "Matt," he barked. "What's up? When are you moving back to Vancouver?"

Matt skipped the pleasantries. Even Charlie could hear his angry words as Matt bit them off.

"You need to tell your girl to wisen the hell up, Charles. Jessie called me last night. She was so drunk she could hardly talk. You don't want to know what ended up in my inbox this morning."

"I have a feeling you're about to tell me." Sitting back in his high leather office chair, Charles focused a steady gaze at Charlie, who had his ankles crossed over a nearby chair and a laptop on his lap, which he closed as his eyes narrowed at Charles. Even secondhand, he could hear Matt's voice shaking. A rarity in cool Matt Kelly world.

Over the phone, both Charles and Charlie listened to Matt's revelatory explanation. "An old porn film of Jessie's. She must have gone digging last night. We were both pretty pissed at each other when she hung up the phone. I suppose this is her way of getting back at me for asking her not to contact me."

In Prince Edward Island, Matt was rubbing his forehead over and over as he paced his living room. The dingy day hung over him. His stomach was ready to heave up the earlier poached egg on toast. Dropping onto the computer chair, he winced painfully.

"Call her off, Charles. I can't talk to her anymore, at all, and I don't need these kinds of emails showing up in my inbox."

"Are you sure, Matt? You're angry. Just give it some time. I'm sure she'll settle down once she's off this film."

"And back with her husband, you mean. So she gets regular sex and doesn't have to fantasize about the one night we had together. And shove it back in my face and…" He stopped, and drifted off, but his inner voice was weeping *break my heart all over again.* "You remember what we were talking about in your office the day you had your heart attack, Charles? What you were saying about Jessie?"

Charles' heart sank as he met Charlie's curious eyes. "I remember, Matt."

"Well, you're right. It's true. She will always be that whore from the Downtown Eastside. No amount of Givenchy or Chanel or designer Zuhair Murad gowns will ever change that. I'm sick of her and her vicious games."

"Matt," Charles started in a soft tone as Charlie sank into his chair and buried his forehead in his hand, "go easy. You don't think I know the sound of a man with a broken heart? We all know Jessie's got some twisted notion of herself that comes out when she's alone and feeling lost. It doesn't mean she's—"

Matt rather soundly cut him off. "She is who she thinks she is. And who she leads others to believe she is. Call her off me, Charles. I can't handle her right now."

Staring at his screen, at an image of Jessie that Matt swore he would never seek out, Matt was crushed. This, to him, was the last straw. *She sent me a film of herself in the kind of ecstasy I experienced in person. She wants me to suffer.* It was the first time in his life Matt actually felt something akin to revulsion and maybe even hate for a woman he'd loved, first as a client and friend, and then as a lover, for so long.

"All right, Matt. I'll talk to Jessie. It'll have to be over the phone, though. Charlie and I are up to our eyeballs in wrapping this show."

Hanging up a few minutes later, Charles sighed and sank deeper into his chair, causing it to squeak in protest. "Well, Charlie," he said, sounding tired and defeated. "Looks like our girl really crossed a line this time."

"She's a piece of work, Charles. I'll give her that. I don't know why she would do this to Josh, though. It doesn't add up. He said they had a perfect weekend together."

"Why would she want to hurt him and torture Matt at the same time, you mean?"

"Exactly." Running a thumb and forefinger over the stubble on his chin, Charlie shrugged. "I really don't know. Drinking, I suppose, can push lonely people in all kinds of bizarre and unwelcome directions."

"Let's face it, Charlie. When it comes to Jessie, she's not exactly your typical individual, is she?"

"If you mean she's got a past that none of us can deny, I guess so. I still don't get why she'd go digging for some old porn films that Caryn promised us would never see the light of day, though."

"Maybe Jessie had them all along. Did you consider that?"

"Why? For what purpose?"

Charles shrugged. "We just found out, didn't we?" Leaning forward, he said in his usual businesslike tone, "What time is it in Austin? Why don't we finish this form and then I'll give her a call?"

"Do you want me to call her, Charles?"

"No, son. I think this is one time Jessie needs a good rap on the knuckles. I've never heard Matt so angry with her. And I've seen him angry with her plenty of times. No offense to you, but you can be a softie around Jessie. Either that or the two of you will have each other shot and killed over the phone line. I doubt the Austin producers would appreciate that from their star today."

"Okay. But Charles? Let me know how it goes?"

"I will. And Charlie, I don't think this is something Josh needs to hear from us. If Jessie or Matt wants to tell him, fine. Not us."

"You got it. Let's get to work, Charles." Opening his laptop, Charlie tried to focus, but all he kept seeing were Jessie's sad eyes, and Matt's hurt heart.

In P.E.I., Matt settled back against his chair and pondered his shaking hand. Standing so abruptly that his chair fell over, he marched into the shower, and leaned against the wall under the spray. He stayed in the shower for a good twenty minutes, barely moving, before he finally had the energy to shut it off and turn around to face what remained of a dismal day.

Chapter Twenty-one

Checking her email in the morning, before reporting to set for a late call, Jessie had the sick feeling she'd messed up last night but she couldn't remember exactly why. The alcohol remaining in her system seemed to be somehow connected with her East Hastings work experiences as well as with Matt, for some weird reason. Vaguely, she remembered calling Matt but the gist of their 'chat' wasn't at the forefront of her consciousness. All she really knew was how she was feeling, which was a combination of a weak sick-green, combined with a general sense of self-loathing and regret.

The remainder of the night before had been spent on the floor in the expansive shiny-tiled suite washroom, her pale cheek resting on the cool floor in between bouts of stomach-crunching vomiting. Now, as Dan texted her to see if she was ready to make the trip to the studio for her noon call, Jessie found herself completely immobile.

Rounding up some fight with which to face the day, she texted him back with one hand and searched her emails with the other. Dan had a key card to her suite. Jessie heard the door click open the second her eyes landed on the old erotic video in her inbox. Clicking on it, she peeked desperately at the left column, where the initial email info was stored. A tiny curved grey arrow facing to the left gave her stupidity away.

"Oh, Jesus," she groaned, clicking on it. "I sent this to Matt. God, I'm stunned."

Overhearing her, Dan strode to a stop ten feet away. "Are you okay, Jessie?" Surveying the suite, he caught sight of last night's detritus—clothes on the floor, a room service dinner tray, a number of small empty bottles of Bourbon. An ash tray…

"Nope," she answered, curling up into herself on the chair and hugging her belly.

"Did you have some breakfast?" Dan asked, relieved to note that she had showered, at least.

"Hell, no. Not this morning."

"We should go, then. You're due on set in ten minutes and it's a thirty minute drive."

"Oh, fuck. This day's really going to suck." Extending a hand, Jessie allowed Dan to ease her up out of her chair. "Dan, I need a favor," she said as they moved towards the door. Grabbing her bag from the floor on the way, which caused her to pause and reconsider leaving the suite, she eyeballed the washroom and waited for a new attack of nausea to pass.

"What can I do for you, Jessie?" he replied, concern washing over his chiseled Scandinavian features.

"I need...Dan, something happened last night."

He scanned the room. "I see that."

"Not that. No, ummm...Some idiot sent me a video. Something I kinda hoped maybe didn't exist anymore. One of mine from, uh, from the early days. On the Downtown Eastside."

Illumination crossed his face. He held open the door of the suite so she could pass through. "Okay. I understand."

"There was kind of a threatening message attached. I should have come to you, Dan, but I..." She shrugged as they walked down the hallway. "All those years with Matt, you know. I'm sorry, but I called him. And I think I might have, um, also sent him the email. With the video. So he could figure out who sent it to me in the first place."

"Okay, Jessie. I'll look into it. Can you send me the email?" A red blush bloomed across his cheeks. "You can delete the attachment. Just send the person's contact info."

She held up her phone. "Sent," she said. "Attachment included. I don't really give a shit, is the thing, you know?"

"You should," he said quietly. "You should give a shit, Jessie."

"I don't. Everything...all these years...it's such a struggle, you know, Dan? Living the way we do, running here, running there. No real privacy, everyone knowing our business...trying to keep things afloat with Josh, who I would give my life for. My life, Dan! It's just my kids...our kids...if this gets out, we might as well pull them out of school forever. Because the thing is, the rest of the world doesn't really get the sex thing. How erotic and beautiful it can be, I mean, between consenting partners. I'm not talking about the bad stuff here."

"I understand, Jessie. I'll call Matt and we'll see what we can figure out."

"He's not going to be very fond of me today, Dan. I have a vague memory of telling him I hate him."

"Somehow I doubt that's the truth, Jessie." Dan smiled, and gestured for Jessie to enter the elevator. She did, but closed her eyes and sank to the floor as it started to descend.

Dan called Matt after he deposited Jessie on set for blocking.

In P.E.I., Matt stared bitterly at Dan's name on the phone before he answered it.

"Five rings," Dan said. "Did I catch you on the beach, you lucky sunuvabitch?"

"It's freezing here today. The only thing I'll be doing on the beach is tossing balls for a puppy." *If his mistress lets me,* Matt grumped, closing the lid of his personal laptop, which he was using in the sun porch to compose a half-serious resignation letter to Charles, more to let off some steam than to actually consider sending it.

"I just walked Jessie to blocking. She had a late call today."

"Better you than me. I might've taken her highness' head off." Matt was stretched out comfortably on the sofa, with his feet up on the coffee table, the laptop on his lap. Wiping a hand over his face a few times, he sighed and set the small computer aside.

"She figured that. She gave me the heads up."

"I called Charles. I don't want her contacting me, Dan. You should know that, in case she gets stupid again."

"Fine, Matt. Although *you* should know that Jessie seems pretty remorseful this morning. She's not in great shape."

"She oughtta be remorseful. I hope she's sick as a goddamn dog. I hope she vomits all over the set today."

"Wow." Dan was thoughtful. "She really did a number on you last night."

"Dan, between you and me, she sent me one of her old videos. Some... porn she did years ago. Catherine found it."

"Catherine being..."

"My new lady. Or maybe my old one now, I'm not really sure at this point."

"Oh. Matt, uh..." Confused, Dan stood back and watched Jessie as she blocked her scene. Usually she was prepared for each and every scene but today she was clinging to the day's scene sides as if they were a lifeline. Every few moments, she lifted the papers and focused on the words on the page.

"What, Dan?"

"She's wondering if you found out anything about that video. About where it came from. Who sent it to her. Jessie didn't want to try asking you again herself, on account of telling you she hated you, apparently."

An electric zip ripped down Matt's head and sizzled at the base of his neck. At the same time, he froze. "What did you say, Dan?" His voice was suddenly low and serious.

"The...porn video. Jessie wants to know if you had any luck finding out where it came from."

Vaulting up, Matt made his way to the large iMac computer in the cottage's main living area. Opening his email program, he found the message from Jessie. Sucking in a breath, he clicked on it and took a closer look. Clearly it was a forwarded message. Clearly the line about Jacob was a warning. Clearly that was why she got drunk and high last night. She was afraid and upset, and missing her security blanket. She was missing her Matt.

"I'm such a dick." Sinking into his chair, Matt stared at the address from the original emailer. "Is she okay today, Dan?"

"Not so much, no. I'll keep a good eye on her today, Matt. I promise you."

"I know you will, Dan. All right, I'll get on this right away. I'll be in touch when I find out where it came from."

"Will you call me or..."

"I'm not calling Jessie. You'll hear from me, and likely from Charles today as well. Have a good day, Dan. Watch over our girl."

"Will do," Dan said, and disconnected as Jessie grabbed the first A.D.'s arm and rather hurriedly left the set in the middle of blocking, which left everyone at loose ends until she returned.

"Restroom," she mumbled as she rushed by Dan. Crunching on a lip, Dan eyed the assembled, annoyed cast and crew before he turned to follow her, where he stood twenty feet away from the washroom to keep an eye on her.

In P.E.I., Matt, too, was sick to his stomach, but more at his hasty 'it's all about me and my pain' reaction to Jessie when she called the night before. "I told her to call me if she really needed me," he muttered angrily at himself. "And I totally blew her off."

Almost as if he were trying to make it up to her, he poked away at figuring out who sent the vicious email in the first place. In the end, he called Dan with the news that it had come from some random middle-aged computer hacker in Kansas. The local police picked the guy up within the hour but quickly determined that he was a porn junkie who got a kick out of discovering Jessie in the old video, and who thought he would try to get a rise out of her. As far as they could tell, the man had not released the video to a wider audience, nor did he seem to have any connection with the goings-on in Alberta that had made Josh a target.

But by the time Matt reached Dan, and Charles after him, Charles had already almost disemboweled Jessie.

He caught her at lunch, just as she was settling into the small table in her cast trailer with a light avocado-spinach salad and garlic toast.

"Jessie, how's your day going?" Charles started, in a brusque tone that immediately raised the hackles on the back of Jessie's neck.

"Uh..."

"I hear it's a bit of a tough one."

"Uh...yes..."

"I had a call from Matt this morning, Jessie. An hour later I had a call from Philip."

Philip was the executive producer on the Austin film.

"Oops. Okay. Yell at me. You can't destroy me any more than I already feel destroyed today, Charles. I can take it." Pushing her salad and toast away, Jessie leaned her forehead into her hand over a bent elbow, and sighed.

"I'm having hotel staff clear the bar in your suite today, Jessie. And Dan is being ordered to stop getting weed for you."

"Fine. Hey, how'd you know?"

"Matt. If I had known all these years..."

Interjecting, Jessie sniped at him. "I can get weed if and when I want without any trouble, Charles. But I don't need it. Last night was not the norm."

"I'm relieved to hear that. Philip—"

"Oh, fuck Philip. He's got bigger problems than my one hungover day. His male lead can't remember a single goddamn line."

"What about Matt? I've never heard him so angry."

Jessie dropped her forehead to the table. "Just tell him it won't happen again, okay Charles? I should have gone to Dan."

Charles' intuition perked up. "Why Dan? Am I missing something?"

With another heavy sigh, Jessie filled him in. At the end she added, "I panicked. With everything that happened with Matt last spring, I didn't know what to do. I thought I would have a drink and think about it. I screwed up."

"According to Dan, the woman Matt's been seeing found the video, Jessie. He's incensed."

"Oh! Oh." *Okay, so he's putting her before me now...as it should be.* She swallowed and blinked a new round of tears away. "That sucks."

"Yes. You need to start putting others ahead of yourself, Jessie. This me-me-me focus has got to change. You're being paid millions to do this movie, and Matt's heart is already in pieces on the floor. Use the right channels from now on. Dan first, or me. Leave Matt alone."

"Okay." *And how much are you making off of me while I shoot this film? Or off my music for Sacred Peace, or off my husband, who almost got killed on your production? The guy that sent the video was absolutely right, but we always knew that, didn't we? I'm such a whore.*

Jessie had a moment when she wanted to scream at Charles, when she wanted to pack everything up and just walk away, from the film, from Austin, from him and Deirdre. But she reminded herself that she had already done that. The only thing that was different this time was in knowing in her heart that she wanted to pack up Josh and the kids and take them with her, so they could all escape her seemingly corrupt world of fame and money and grief.

"I have to go, Charles," she said, and hit 'end' on the call before he had a chance to say goodbye. She stayed immobile, her head on the table, until a slight movement brought her iPhone and headphones to her so she could close her eyes and drown away the rest of the miserable lunch hour in music.

In Calgary, Charlie was leaning against the doorframe of Charles' office. "How did it go?" he asked warily. Judging by the red spots high on Charles' cheeks, his talk with Jessie hadn't necessarily gone well.

Throwing up his hands in frustration, Charles said, "She hung up on me. It's as if she doesn't understand that she is being paid a lot of money to do this film. As if she doesn't understand how much her little game with Matt has hurt him. Has hurt us, all of us, really."

"She knows," Charlie offered quietly, moving to go. "To her, what's happening now is no different from what happened in those films all those years ago. She just gets a bigger paycheck now, Charles. That's all. She's still somebody's toy." Slapping the doorframe, Charlie emitted a small *pfffttt* sound, and started to go.

Insulted, Charles called him back. "And Matt? How do you explain what she's doing to him? You heard her on that Internet meeting a while ago. Talk about toys. He's hers. In Jacob's absentia, might I add. And let's not forget what she did to you at the ranch the day the barn burned."

Charlie ducked his head back in. His eyes were dark and somber. "It's not up to me to explain what goes through her head, Charles. All I know is I can strip away all the extraneous shit that comes with that girl—all the sad past, the tragedies, the sex videos and photos, the stubborn, childish behavior—and I'm left with an image of the beautiful soul I fell in love with. Or I can leave all that shit—and guess what? The way I felt about her—the way I feel about her—doesn't change. And I'm not talking sexually here, Charles, like I want her back, or any of that bullshit. I'm talking about the woman who has become a very dear friend. Is she insecure? Is it always rainbows and butterflies with her? No. But she deserves better than to be left thinking she means no more to any of us than big paychecks. That her mistakes aren't redeemable."

With that, Charlie walked away, leaving Charles to consider the homeless waif he and Deirdre rescued from the Downtown Eastside all those years ago, and the broken spirit she still carried with her every day.

Chapter Twenty-Two

The next morning, Matt was up before the sun. The night had been sleepless overall. Visions of Jessie paraded through his mind all night long; 'come hither' eyes and a sexy body dared him to take her in one way or another, but every time he went near her the Jessie in his dream kept changing back to the young, timid, voiceless girl he saw in the erotic video. It frightened him. Lust and desire were one thing; focused in the wrong direction on a woman he couldn't have was quite another. Seeing that woman as she was years ago, frightened and barely speaking after witnessing the murder of her teen boyfriend, was another thing altogether.

Waking in a cold sweat at four in the morning, Matt considered the vulnerable part of Jessie Wheeler, which colored her music and made her that much sweeter, in his opinion.

"I'm a man who takes care of people," he told himself as he lay alone in his bed. "She's got this 'help me' layer that just cries out to me. I can't help but want to save her, to carry her away to some deep, dark cave and love the hurt away."

Rolling onto his side, he propelled himself up to a sitting position on the side of the bed, and sat for a minute before standing. "May as well go for my run," he thought. Glancing out of the big loft window, Matt saw the expanse of stars that always humbled him in this peaceful island paradise. There was virtually no light pollution out here in Darnley, on the island's north shore. The stars now were vivid and alight, too numerous to count. A stunning sunrise would make itself known soon. Yawning, Matt pushed his fatigue away. A jog would be just the thing to clear his head, and maybe later he would put one of the cottage's kayaks in the Basin and paddle over to Malpeque Harbor to see the fishing boats at anchor.

"Vancouver drivers could take a lesson from Malpeque fishermen," he thought as he tied his runners. As a paddler Matt had, more than once, found himself having to move out of the way of the fishermen's big lobster boats. He was strong, so it was never an issue to paddle away from their narrow channel, but still, they always throttled down as they passed. Usually they waved, too. Kindness personified, the people on this island were. Sometimes Matt wished they wouldn't slow down—he relished the idea of pointing the bow of his small watercraft into the waves so he could play in them, although the first time he tried it outside the Basin, off the main beach, where the waves were generally bigger, he was quickly and soundly swamped.

Matt's run was invigorating. He was so pumped by the time he got back to the lane leading to his cottage that he ran on by it and continued down the Lower Darnley Road to the campground, Twin Shores. A quick run to the right, to the area known by the locals as the 'old' part of the park, led him towards a number of heavily wooded campsites set off from cozy red dirt lanes with quirky nautical names like Keel Lane, Lighthouse Lane, and Pier Lane. The friendly signs brought a smile to his lips.

At the shore, he slowed down and caught his breath by placing his hands on his hips and wandering down the wooden ramp to the white sand beach. Already there was a family on the beach—a mom, a dad, and two small children, a boy and girl maybe five and seven. The sun was well on its way up by now, pink and orange and glorious and stunning, melting into the sky like heated wax from a candle's warm flame, spreading its wings over Darnley and offering a kind of almost spiritual peace sought by people the world over. The kids were on their knees digging in the sand, molding whatever creations their innocent hearts desired; the adults were holding hands as they dipped their toes in the cool Atlantic. Squealing, the woman was obviously delighted with this time to play.

Watching, Matt had to fight the sorrow that often waylaid him when he saw families together. One thing that always struck him as funny was that when the sadness hit, it was usually Jessie and Josh and the kids who he pictured in place of the real families on the beach, or in a grocery store, or wherever. It was never his own. Really, he hadn't spent enough time with Julie and Katy to ever really feel they were a family. Distance always got in the way. Jessie always got in the way.

No, when Matt spied on families like this one here, today, he replaced their faces with the idyllic Sawyer family from Vancouver, only he wanted them to be ordinary and undisturbed by the combined angsts of their fearsome past. In reality, the Sawyer children would not grow up without scars inherited from their parents. They would not build castles on a beach anywhere in the world without a constant overriding fear—of abduction, of overzealous fans, of paparazzi yanging for a close-up photo of Josh and Jessie's famous family.

With a heavy sigh, Matt toed a hole in the sand and spun himself back around to walk up the wooden ramp. He broke into a light jog to make his way back to his cottage, and was surprised to see a light on in Catherine's place when he got there. Slowing, he was even more surprised to see the back of her SUV open, and her stepping over to it with an armload of puppy things, including a soft round bed Matt had bought Drifter after his broken leg fiasco.

"Catherine?" he asked, noting that the vehicle was already half-packed.

"Hello, Matt. How was your run?"

"Fine. You're leaving."

"Yes. I'm done here. I have nothing left."

Reaching for an elbow, he prevented her from moving back into the cottage. "Running away is not going to solve anything, Catherine."

"I'm not interested in being in love with a man whose sole purpose in life is to protect a woman who doesn't really seem all that interested in his protection, Matt. And I don't like the way I feel when I look into your eyes and see nothing but fear and worry there, for a man and a family who could choose to back out of the spotlight if they're so damn scared."

"Catherine, think this through. You and I and Drifter are off to a good start here."

Catherine's voice rose to a higher pitch. "Are we, Matt? You're the one who is not thinking things through. Jessie, Jessie, Jessie, I'm so sick of hearing about this woman! You are so hurt by her that you tell her not to contact you, but you still take her calls and she's still on your email list. You have spent how much of your life being devoted to this woman and her family? To the point of losing your own, isn't that right, Matt? Is that not devotion?" Stepping forward, she yanked at his T-shirt. Drawing it down hard over his shoulder, she brushed her thumb across the New York bullet hole scar. Now, her tone was a tearful whisper. "Is this not devotion, Matt? How can I compete with that kind of love?"

"It's not a competition, Catherine. Jessie is not an option for me. She never was."

"Ah. I see. But if she was…an option, I mean, if that's what you want to call it."

Matt's heart sank like a stone. By omission, and by not calling a spade a spade, he'd just told Catherine where his true feelings lay. In that split second, he saw himself spending the rest of his life alone. The love he had for Jessie was not comparable to anyone else—because they all loved her in their own ways. Charlie lost her, Steve adored her, Jacob…well, that was an intense musical connection that became a physical craving…a soul thing… Josh? *Where do I start with Josh,* Matt wondered. Josh was built into Jessie's soul. The damage the two of them had faced alone before they met, and then together, had staunchly sealed their need of each other.

So where do I fit in? Regarding Catherine now with sorrow and loss, Matt could feel Jessie's essence in every pore of his body. After all their years together, she was so wound up in who he was now, as a human being and as a man, that Matt couldn't see past her. Their love was not based on lust or desire, although it had come to that eventually, which surprised no one. No, what they shared was a deep connection based on friendship and trust. The kind of friendship and trust shared by soldiers who have been to battle. The kind of friendship and trust that comes out on the other side of bloody, battle-weary wars.

"We had a summer fling," Catherine was saying to him now, although Matt barely heard her as a new pulse started in his ears, almost drowning out her words and the whining of the puppy at her feet who was craving attention.

"We did." Matt was lost for words after he spoke those two. They were a realization, and an ending, of something special that had barely begun.

"You're really something," Catherine breathed twenty minutes later when she was packed and ready to go. "You're a very special man, Matt Kelly, guardian and protector to Jessie Wheeler. Maybe if you had been running with my daughter you could have saved her."

"Jessie saved her, Catherine. I know you don't see it that way, but to a bullied teenager, Jessie's music is everything."

"It's just a damn good place to hide. That's all it is, Matt. That's all it ever was and that's all it will ever be."

"If you say so."

Matt took her phone from her and opened up the Notes App. He typed in his Vancouver address and his email. She already had his phone number. Handing the cell back to her, he said, "If you ever need anything, I mean anything, Catherine, you know where to find me."

"Maybe we'll meet again here every summer, Matt. We can have a summer fling every year."

That drew a smile. "You got it," he replied, bringing her to him for a final hug. Bringing Drifter to his chest, he was surprised to find himself sniffling. "You take care of each other, y'hear?"

She left with no further fanfare, just backed her vehicle out of the small driveway, pointed it towards the main lane, and drove away. Hands on his hips, Matt watched her go. Ten minutes later he, too, was packing up.

Matt drove to the airport that evening and caught an all-nighter to Vancouver. Saying goodbye to Darnley and his peaceful refuge was as hard as saying goodbye to Catherine and Drifter, his partners in crime for the last almost two months. As he turned left towards Charlottetown at the end of the Lower Darnley Road, he realized he had not dropped in to see Jessie's mother or Jessie's old pal George. Instead, he and Catherine had lingered on the beach, kayaked until they were salt-sprayed and sunburned, barbecued almost every night, took Drifter for long hand-in-hand walks on the beach, explored the island, and shared fresh seafood at expensive restaurants and cheap but cozy dairy bars.

Leaving peaceful Darnley behind him now, terribly unsure about what the future would bring, Matt almost cried. The cottage had provided a sweet refuge from a harsh reality that, just plainly, hurt. What would he do back in Vancouver besides schedule meetings with Charles and Ulysses at times that would hopefully keep him from running into Jessie?

At least she would be going on her six-week tour soon. The entire family was travelling, and the new girl, Alin, would be joining the usual contingent to help cover some of the slack from Matt's physical exodus. Matt would continue to coordinate from behind the scenes. From Vancouver. Alone.

The ocean stretched to the left beside him for a while as he drove along the north shore of Prince Edward Island. It was getting dark now. A blue-black twilight guided him along the rural stretch to the small city airport. The sky was quickly becoming brilliantly starlit; the heavens were suddenly enchanting and mysterious. Rolling his window down, Matt tilted his head to hear the east coast waves crash over the beach for the last time. Haunting, their depths unknown, they followed him, chasing him back towards the airport, all the way towards Vancouver...

All the way back home.

Chapter Twenty-three

"Jessie, can you get off that thing and help me with Dylan? Packing for a little kid who insists on bringing every toy he has is impossible." Josh's heavy footsteps made their way to the open door of his and Jessie's bedroom.

Looking up at him, Jessie chewed a nail, tilted her head, and tried to hide her smile. Glowing, she gave up and tossed the iPad she was studying on the bed. "C'mere," she purred. "Jesus, you look good. Are you really all mine?"

Burying his frustration was easy for Josh when Jessie gave him *that* look. Growling adorably, he crossed the room and straddled her on all fours, forcing her to lie back on their bed. Giggling, she pushed his long hair back over his ears and tugged at his jeans.

"Please," she begged. "Now, before the kids come in."

"The kids are in Dylan's room trying to choose his toys for the tour, Jessie. They could pop in any second."

"In the bathroom, then, worry wart. C'mon, let's hurry."

Laughing, Josh leaned on his forearms, tenting her in the safety of his musky Josh smell. "Tonight at the hotel, little one," he vowed. "I promise. You're insatiable, by the way."

"Aw, yeah, dork! You come in here with faded jeans, an old brown leather belt, cowboy boots, and a white long-sleeved cotton shirt under your blue T-shirt and you question my sudden lust for you? Love the strategically placed holes in the thighs, by the way. I'm gonna lose my mind on the jet."

Raising his eyebrows, Josh bent down and lovingly kissed his wife. She moaned and rolled her eyes before wrapping her arms around his broad back and pulling him fully down on top of her.

"Mile high club, maybe?" she begged. "I can't wait til I get to the hotel, cowboy."

"Gimme a minute." A diabolical grin and a quick check on the kids later, and Josh grabbed his wife's hand. "Bathroom, now."

Inside, Josh pushed the door closed and locked it. A wide smile cracking his jaw, he lost himself in the blue eyes he loved as Jessie's body melted into his. She was wearing jeans too, as faded as his, with her own strategically placed holes, but Josh was quick to pull them down past her hips. Slipping a hand between her legs, he soaked up the little mewls escaping her mouth and landing in his ear. When she gasped and delicately bit his earlobe, he lifted her up on the countertop so she could spread her legs wider and let him go inside.

"Good thing you had a head start," he teased her as he moved, pulling at a nipple he was fondling between his finger and thumb. "Kids'll be at the door any minute."

"Shut up and focus!" Eyes alight, Jessie bent her face into the hollow of his neck and planted kisses.

His breath ragged now, Josh didn't have to be told again. Their timing was perfect. Just after they climaxed, almost perfectly in sync, a small knock came at the door.

"Daddy! I know which toys now! Dawid and Emiwy-Gwace hepped me!"

Stifling her giggles by shoving her face into Josh's shirt, Jessie didn't answer, but Josh managed a rather out-of-breath, "Okay, little buddy! I'll be right there. Give me one sec."

Pushing Jessie away from him, he laughed outright. "That was close."

"That was perfect." Dreamily, she stroked his chin and cheek, and let her mouth close over his for a long, lingering kiss. "I love you so much, Josh. Thank God for the next six weeks."

"Yep. I'll second that. Love you back, Jessie."

An hour later, they were at the jet. The kids were as excited as their parents to be going on tour. As soon as they were seated, Emily-Grace snuggled up to her mother's side and grabbed her securely around the waist. She buried her face in Jessie's slim tan leather jacket.

"Hey, what's this?" Jessie asked, a note of concern in her voice and questions in her eyes.

"I hate school so much. I'm glad we're getting a private tutor again."

"I'm sorry, honey. School's a challenge when you're only there part time. I don't know how to fix that yet, but Daddy and me are working on it."

"It's easy, Momma. Take me with you when you have to work, like we did with Daddy's and Grampie's TV show."

"School's important, sweetheart. You make friends at school."

"Stella's my friend. I'll just hang out with her."

"You can on this trip, Emily-Grace, but Stella won't be on every show or tour."

"She says she'll be living in Canmore every year for the next ten years because our daddies really rocked *Sacred Peace*. They're gonna shoot at least ten seasons of it, she says."

Cringing, Jessie prayed not, if the next few seasons were anything like season one, with all its injuries and rather questionable 'accidents.' "I don't know, baby," she answered honestly. "I just don't know. That will be up to the people who watch the show, and the network executives who help finance it."

"They'll love it. Daddy's the star."

Hugging her daughter tightly to her, Jessie murmured, "I'm glad to see you are happier with Daddy these days, honey. He tries so hard just to love all of us." Her heart swelled, and she twisted her neck just a little so she could see Josh on the couch behind her, with Dylan on one side of him and David on the other. Josh was buckling the kids in, but he caught her adoring look and grinned happily back at his two girls.

"I love Daddy," Emily-Grace told her mother now, curling up her legs and giving her one of her heart-melting serious Emily-Grace looks. "He just confuses me sometimes."

"Get used to it, sweetheart. Loving people can be very confusing a lot of the time. Trust me on that one." Jessie planted a tender kiss on the top of her daughter's head and took a moment to buckle her in.

Carlotta and Deirdre eased into seats across from Jessie and Emily-Grace, facing them. Charles touched Jessie's shoulder as he walked towards the back of the plane to sit with the guys, Dan and Sam included. Jessie noticeably cringed when he touched her, and she looked away.

Ulysses dropped into a seat across the aisle, where he could indoctrinate the new girl, Alin, who had delayed her physical test with the RCMP to help out with the *Sacred Peace* press and concert tour. Jessie couldn't help but sigh at Matt's absence. Often, that was his chosen seat on the Keating jet.

Jacob and Kayla were flying out on a later charter with the rest of the tour group. Charlie and his family, including Jack and Lydia to help with their children, as well as Jonathon and Giselle, would be on another flight. Trucks with gear would meet them at the various stops on the six-week tour, which included concert venues as well as television stations across the states and Canada to promote the new show.

Jessie's Belgium film had just premiered too. She and Josh had travelled with Charles and Dee to its European opening, followed by a New York weekend to usher it into the North American market. By all accounts, it was stunning and tormented, its heartbreaking subject matter and the bluegrass music soundtrack coalescing to create a perfect haunting blend. The addition of a compelling story and gorgeous, original cinematography, with dramatic production design, was making the film a Golden Globe and Oscar frontrunner. Jessie's name had been all over the entertainment news the week of the premieres.

Halfway into the flight, with the little boys in total rapture over their grandfather's storytelling ability, and Emily-Grace getting to know Alin, Josh moved up to sit by Jessie. Draping an arm comfortably around her shoulders, he smiled in total contentment as she snuggled into him, wrapping a leg around his and encircling an arm around his waist.

"Sigh. Pure serenity," she said, closing her eyes.

"Yep. Perfection." Josh, too, closed his eyes, but not before leaning his head over hers and taking her fingers in his. "Hey, Jess?"

"Mmm?"

"What was it you were reading this morning that was so serious?"

"And there it goes. See that, Josh? That's our perfect moment flying out the window, thanks to a shot of reality."

"Sorry, Jessie. I don't mean to pry. You just seemed really into whatever you were reading."

"Yeah, you do. You mean to pry. But you might wish you hadn't."

"Shoot. I'm ready."

Lifting her head away from him, Jessie settled back against her own wide leather seat. Gazing down at their entwined fingers, she tried to sort out what to say. "I was reading a blog, that's all," she said in the end, bringing one booted foot up and hanging her leg casually over the armrest. "Remember that woman I told you I met at the Chinook Center in Calgary last summer? Gabrielle?"

"The one who came on set to meet Charlie?"

"Yep. That's her."

"What about her? She seemed nice. A little star struck around Charlie, but I accept that I can't always win over him. Although I don't know what she sees in him."

Giggling, Jessie pushed the sobering thoughts from the blog away until Josh brought her back to them.

"So...what was in her blog today that was so serious?" Avoiding Jessie's eyes, he stared at their hands and waited for what he knew wouldn't necessarily be good news.

Jessie felt his grip on her fingers tighten. It broke her heart that Josh was so used to bad news that he was mentally preparing himself for what was coming. "Well, back in the summer, she posted an article that questioned what was happening to you on set. The so-called accidents."

"I recall. You told her that Charlie admitted there was a threatening note."

"Only one. Gabrielle suggested that if it was written by some crazy Jacob Ryan fan, she could whip up an army of social media supporters to change the tide of fans' distaste of me."

"Of me, you mean. Of you choosing me." Josh sighed and sank deeper into his seat, while across from him, Deirdre clued in to the fact that Josh and Jessie's conversation had taken a serious turn. She watched them carefully, hoping for nothing but good fortune on this six-week tour.

"Whatever. Same old, same old," Jessie grumbled. "What I was reading today was just some of what I guess you would call active conversation about the whole thing. About us. It got heated over the last few months, really polarized, with some fans in our corner and some in Jacob's. It hasn't helped matters that Jacob announced his engagement to your sister. Talia's fans are also pissed. So Gabrielle responded today with a scathing reprisal for the naysayers, telling them to leave us all the hell alone to live our lives however we see fit."

Josh was silent for a minute as he took that in. "How much power does she have?"

"Seems like a lot, but Josh, people are crazy. None of them know us, yet all of them are passing judgment."

"Good thing we learned a long time ago not to read celebrity blogs. Right Jess?" His twinkling eyes aimed in her direction eased the tension somewhat, and Jessie groaned.

"I know. It's just that I met her and I liked her. She seems really fair. I saw something on Twitter and I got curious."

"Twitter now too! You're digging your own hole, little one."

"Ouch." Shivering, Jessie fought off a sudden chill. Countering, she half-joked in her best Yoda voice, "Please to not use such morbid metaphors, oh wise one."

"You know better. Jessie, you can't go looking at that crap."

"Face it, Josh. If someone's got it in for us, they're going to surface at some point."

"What's this? We're fine. We got through season one."

"And now we're embarking on a press tour. With our children. And Josh…" She drifted off.

"What? I'm listening." To prove she had his full attention, he angled his head more in her direction and tightened his hold around her shoulders. Jessie continued to play with the fingers of his left hand while she pondered how to tell him what else was worrying her.

"I know there were full gas cans found behind our bedroom. The night of the barn fire."

Chewing his lip, Josh considered that. "Someone on the Calgary security team was paid to let them through. We know that much. The kid admitted it."

"Yet another ruined life because of us."

"The way I hear it, he was pretty remorseful. He couldn't stand living with the guilt. Maybe this will be his one and only crime. And Jessie, nobody got hurt."

"Who told you this, Josh? And why is this the first I'm hearing of it?"

Again, Josh paused. "I met with Matt and Charles last week."

Jessie caught her breath and stopped playing with her husband's fingers. "Matt's back?"

"He's back. Yes. He moved back to the condo he bought after he and Julie split."

"Oh. I see." Her hands broke out in a cold sweat. "Is he…coming on this tour?" She couldn't look at Josh.

"Not that I'm aware of." Studying her, Josh was sorry he brought up Matt's name. "You were going to find out one way or another," he said. "I figured you would do better hearing this from me."

Jessie looked over at Deirdre. "You've seen Matt?" she asked. "I suppose you've had him to dinner. Without me."

Nobody spoke, but Dee gave Josh a sympathetic look.

Shuffling in her seat, Jessie glanced over at Josh. "It's not what you think," she whispered. "I would just like to see him, you know, to make sure he's okay." A new thought occurred to her. "So what's this new woman of his like? Oh, the puppy! Did you meet the puppy? Drifter?" Trying to sound normal, Jessie's voice was anything but. Aware of this, she closed her lips and shut up.

"No puppy," Josh said. "No woman, either."

"Oh. I'm sorry."

"I'll tell him you said so. I'm sure he'll be thrilled you care." The sarcasm was grating.

Wincing, Jessie reached her right hand up and snagged his other hand in hers. "Enough. Let's move on."

"Agreed." Josh pulled his arm away from her hand, using his damaged right shoulder as an excuse to change his position, but when Jessie stole a glance at him, he was looking away from her, studying the new girl as she played with Emily-Grace.

Curling her body back into his, Jessie laid her cheek against his shoulder, wrapped both arms around his, and disappeared into sleep.

Chapter Twenty-four

With the exception of a bout of food poisoning that swept over all three Sawyer children and both of their parents, the tour was unexceptional in terms of unplanned incidents. Now on TV, *Sacred Peace* was receiving great acclaim, the press meetings were slick and professional, and the concerts, featuring Jacob and Jessie with a small group of dancers and skilled musicians that occasionally included newbie Casey on the drums, were outstanding, in large venues that all sold out within an hour of going on sale.

The final concert date was set for December 1st in Toronto. In London, Ontario a week before, Catherine opened an envelope delivered to her at the High School where she taught English. Inside, she found a single concert ticket to the sold out show. No note, no return address. Just one simple paper ticket.

She considered not going. In the end, her curiosity got the better of her. The concert was on a Friday night. Taking a personal day from school, Catherine boarded Drifter with a friend, dressed in her best jeans and wool coat, and made the two-hour drive to the large city. Too nervous to eat anything, she skipped dinner and wandered the first shopping mall she found when she got to the city, until it was time to go to the venue.

Will I see Matt? she wondered. *Will he be there?*

She doubted it. The two hadn't necessarily parted on good terms. The ticket was an out-of-the-blue complete surprise. Still, she half-hoped Matt would be sitting next to her. Finding her seat on an aisle next to an excited thirty-something couple, she scanned her area. No Matt. A great seat, five rows from the front in the VIP section, but no Matt. Alone, Catherine settled in to watch the show.

Since leaving Prince Edward Island, she had tried to control her growing fascination with Jessie Wheeler, but it was tough. Jessie was ingrained in Matt, and vice versa, this much Catherine knew, so studying up on Jessie was like getting a secret glimpse into Matt. Occasionally she found images of him that earlier sweeps of the Internet had missed, but mostly she found that articles about Jessie did not include Matt by her side. Usually her most recognizable bodyguard was a tall well-built man of Scandinavian features. Had Matt called him Dan? Maybe. In some of the newer photos, especially those where paparazzi had captured glimpses of the Sawyer children, a dark-haired Indian girl was visible. Pretty, and very tall and athletic, Catherine wondered if she was filling in for Matt, at least as far as a physical replacement went.

At least one thing was certain—Jessie was still with Josh, and the two looked more in love than ever during any public appearances. Gone were the angry, sad eyes that seemed to haunt them in photographs from early in the year, around the time of Talia's death as well as the Grammys. Now, Catherine thought, in most pictures they seemed completely lost in each other. Even when carrying their two youngest children, they were often joined somehow, with a finger in a belt loop or protectively around the other's waist.

The anticipation at the concert venue was almost unbearable. As time went on, Catherine was dealing better with the loss of her teenage daughter. A new support group helped. Surprising herself, Catherine had watched a lot of Jessie's music videos. They were easy enough to find on YouTube. Sometimes, when she was really missing Carly, she put earbuds attached to Carly's iPhone in her ears and selected the Jessie Wheeler playlist. On those days, usually the lonely weekends and holidays, she lay down on her daughter's bed and cried out her pain. And sometimes, Jessie's music healed. Sometimes it helped. Sometimes it helped with the loss of a good man, too, a man who was close to Jessie. Sometimes Jessie's music brought Catherine back to endless warm summer nights that started by a Prince Edward Island campfire and that ended in the arms of that very good man.

Now, Catherine was about to see Jessie perform live. She would not be some video caricature. The woman on stage would be the real deal.

Swallowing past her nerves at the emotion she was sure to have to defeat in order to get through the night, Catherine tensed when she heard a low hum start throughout the concert hall. It increased in intensity when a few lights started to play around the stage area. Then the curtain came up, and Jessie Wheeler, with Jacob Ryan beside her, was exposed.

As one, the crowd stood and cheered their appreciation. If there were Jacob and Jessie naysayers in this crowd tonight, or Josh and Jessie naysayers, they were not visible, nor could they be heard.

Why am I here? Are you trying to tell me something, Matt? Are you here?

The question was sent telepathically, and it was received.

Matt was in the audience. He'd flown alone to Toronto for this, the final concert of the *Sacred Peace* tour. He, like Josh and Charles and Dee, and all of the old *Drifters* gang, which included Charlie by default, was a sucker for Jessie's live shows. It killed Matt to coordinate her security and yet miss all of the performances. Did Charles know he was here? Yep. But just Charles. No one else did. Matt stayed out of the way, in a seat far away from where he knew any of the others, including Catherine, would be sitting.

He made a request to Charles at a quick meeting before the show, though.

"I need a favor."

"Of course, Matt. Anything," Charles had replied.

"I need you to let a woman go backstage after the show. To meet Jessie. Not in the public group where the contest winners and VIPs will be, though. This woman needs to meet Jessie in private. In her dressing room."

Charles had hesitated, but only for a brief second. "Of course, Matt. Give me the details. I'll let Jessie know to expect her."

"Charles...make sure Deirdre is there, okay? And Josh. And give Jessie the heads up that it might be emotional. But please don't tell her I set this up. Okay, Charles?"

"All right. Consider it taken care of."

There was a lot of adrenalin pumping through the theater now as Jacob and Jessie launched into their first tune. A multi-media display behind them pumped up the energy of the show, as it had during the Alberta fundraiser. Josh's larger-than-life captivating appearance on screen—with Shanda, nonetheless, who was here tonight as well—in unison with his wife's surreal music, had the audience under more than even the usual dreamlike Jessie and Jacob spell. Matt and Catherine were both goners from the first note. The rest of the audience may as well have been floating above the city, so buoyed were they by the exquisite gift they were handed on this cool Toronto night.

Jessie's chosen outfit near the end of the show was a tight pair of glistening black pants, accompanied by a similar black halter top that opened in the back, tied behind the neck, and flowed over her waist. Matt almost lost it when he spied her on stage in it, in a top very similar to the one from the dress he had so erotically untied from around her neck months before. What brought him to his knees, though, was her introduction to her first song after changing into the outfit, which showed off her curves in a very pleasing way.

From the stage, with a nervous and melancholy smile aimed at the general audience, she said, "So this next song is a departure from the *Sacred Peace* soundtrack. I wrote it for a special friend of mine who is no longer in my life the way I would like him to be. The way he used to be. I hear he spent some time snuggled into a cottage in my beloved Prince Edward Island last summer. I hope my island took good care of you, Matt. I hope it did a good job of watching over you."

The announcement left Matt almost unable to breathe. Fighting back intense emotion, he dug his nails into his thighs as Jacob launched Jessie into the song with some gorgeous slow guitar picking. The song was reminiscent of Bob Dylan's *I Believe In You.* In a perfect assimilation of music and lyric, it built to a sweet, satisfying climax that brought to mind Matt and Jessie's sensual night. Considering their fight on the phone the night Jessie got drunk in Austin, and that they hadn't been in contact since, the song left its imprint deep in Matt's spirit. In the verses, the lyrics begged him to come back, yet the chorus was a soulful goodbye. The ending was clear—no regrets, no more sorrows. Jessie's message to Matt was one of love for the past, and trust for the future.

Catherine was spellbound. It was impossible to clearly hear every melodious word as it was sung, even though the theater was utterly silent with the exception of the music coming from the stage. She got the drift, though, of what Jessie was saying to Matt, and it stung while it healed, which was how she figured Matt would feel too once he heard the song. Jessie was a powerful communicator when it came to speaking through music. She knew how to reach the unreachable people in her life, and she did it well.

After that almost spiritual gift, there was one song left. Catherine and Matt (and everyone present) wondered how Jessie managed to perform it without losing her mind, but not only did she perform it, she brought the place to its feet with a rousing standing ovation before the final strains of the song had petered out. It was the heavy ballad she and Jacob had first played for Matt and Charles at the Robson Street studio, accompanied by the same *Sacred Peace* video montage featured at the Alberta Children's Hospital fundraiser.

Unbeknownst to the audience, Josh was watching the entire show from stage right. Matt figured that out when Jessie stared off into the wings with a dreamy, challenging, almost sexual smile. Recognizing the song immediately, Matt knew the audience was in for something special, since he'd streamed the fundraiser live. Now, though, already completely debilitated from Jessie's musical message to him, he inhaled for strength and settled in for a crazy ride. Every pore in his body was on high alert; the music was powerful enough, but adding the visuals made the experience insane.

Jacob started, as he did in Alberta, with guitar strains in a minor key that were supported by a second player further upstage and closer to Jessie. By the time Jessie stepped to the microphone after the silent interchange with her husband, the background visuals had started. What hit home with the audience were the scenes featuring Shanda; how could Jessie separate what was happening with her husband on screen from her life with Josh at home?

As the song hit its peak, a sweet, wailing guitar reached a perfect suspended high note that gave the listener a satisfying resolution, and then it collapsed, the on-screen images echoing it as it played out…Josh with Shanda up against the wall the day she orgasmed in front of the crew, her turning back to face him as the climax eased into a denouement, the wall holding her up, her palms wide open against the wall for support…staring down at her actor-lover in confused shock infused with wonder and unexpected afterglow as Josh sank to his knees, clutching her against him as he moved down her body…Shanda grasping a handful of Josh's hair and pulling it back from his face as he looked up at her, as if in prayer…in worship...both of them breathing with exertion, completely lost in some dreamlike abyss.

The song's climax was instrumental. Matt and Catherine watched Jessie turn to the screen to view the spectacular sex scene play out. It amazed both of them that she kept a straight face and managed to come back to the mic when she needed to. To both of them, in fact to everyone present that night, it was just another way Jessie Wheeler was worthy of their respect, but only Matt, because of Charles, had any inkling of the background story and the angst Shanda's admitted love for Josh caused Jessie. He was humbled and floored at her poise.

Just as the encores were starting, Catherine felt a shadowy presence at her side. A uniformed usher, a young woman with her hair pulled up in a tight bun, bent to her ear and spoke to her.

"Is your name Catherine?"

Startled, Catherine looked up. "Yes?"

"Will you come with me, please?"

"What? Why?" It hit Catherine like a bullet. Matt. She was being escorted backstage. "I don't...I don't know..."

The usher, who was making an effort not to block anyone's view, was already moving away. Catherine had no choice but to follow her.

The backstage area was surreal.

The dancers and musicians were all on stage for the encores, but the place was still humming with crew, media, and assorted contest winners. Terribly unsure, Catherine's eyes darted around in search of Matt, in case he was in fact somewhere nearby, but there was no sign of him. The usher took her directly to a room marked with a digital sign—Jessie Wheeler.

She almost collapsed.

"I don't know about this," she said to the usher.

Smiling warmly, the girl replied, "This is a great honor, Ma'am. Jessie is a very special woman. All of us had the chance to meet her earlier. You'll love her."

At that, the woman knocked on the door to Jessie's dressing room and gestured to urge Catherine to go inside. Alin and Carlotta were there with Dylan, Emily-Grace and David, who were deemed too young to see the *Sacred Peace* videos and so were kept backstage.

Approaching Catherine, Alin held out a hand, which Catherine hesitantly took.

"You must be Catherine. We were told to expect you. Welcome. My name is Alin. This is Carlotta, who works with the Keatings in their home. I'm a special friend to the Sawyers."

"Special friend? You mean security?" By Alin's small nod and hesitant smile towards the kids, who didn't hear the remark, Catherine realized her error. "Oh," she said quickly, clapping a hand over her mouth. "I'm sorry. I probably shouldn't have said that."

"We try to keep the kids as relaxed as we can but I'm sure they know what's up." Alin smiled. "Have a seat. Jessie is meeting with contest winners shortly but she won't be long."

Fascinated by where she found herself, Catherine nodded numbly and eased down onto a large sofa against the side wall. It wasn't two minutes before Dylan was in her lap.

"I have a new dinosaur," he told her, proudly showing off a small plastic dollar-store dinosaur. "He's a T-Wex."

"He's very handsome." Catherine caught her breath. *Surreal.*

"Would you like something to drink, Catherine?" Alin was very gracious, quick to recognize her guest's discomfort.

"No, uh…thank you, uh, Alin. Alin, is…would…would Matt be around?"

"Matt?" Alin studied the woman's face, taking note of the earnest expression. "No," she said. "I'm sorry, he didn't come on the tour. To my knowledge he isn't here."

"Okay." Catherine's face fell. Trying to smile past her nerves, she tuned in to the program sound being piped in to the large dressing room. It seemed the show was over. The cheering was loud and raucous. She tried to focus on the little boy moving a dinosaur around on her knees, and waited.

Chapter Twenty-five

Meeting the contest winners and VIPs was always an adrenalin-fueled, exhausting rush. Leaving the small conference room afterwards, Jacob draped an arm loosely over Jessie's shoulders and brushed his lips against her cheek.

"Fantastic show tonight, Jessie. It was really something. The energy out there was unreal."

"I think I was suspended on the ceiling looking down during most of that show." Using both arms to hug him tightly as they walked back towards their dressing rooms, with Josh and Kayla joking around behind them, Jessie shook her head in surprise. "Sometimes I wonder how I got so lucky, to be able to stand on stage with you and belt out tunes like that."

"Magic."

"You got that right."

"Especially with images of your husband on screen right behind me. Although I take pleasure in knowing that in some of them he's having sex with another woman."

Throwing her head back, Jessie laughed outright. "I take no pleasure in that. However, I do take pleasure in knowing I had a lot of amazing sex with the man I'm actually sharing the stage with. That helps."

"We're twisted, Jess." Jacob's eyes were wide, his expression suddenly solemn, but it was in jest. Tickling him, Jessie soaked up his obvious happiness.

Near her dressing room, she stopped to give him a big bear hug. "Try to get some sleep. Big day at the Toronto Zoo tomorrow."

Kayla scooted up and jumped on his back, and Jacob held his arms out to the sides so she had to cling to him with both arms and both legs. Snuggling into his neck, her words to Jessie came out muffled. "Did you see this man on stage? I don't know if it's the guitar or the tight jeans but I can guarantee you he will be very, very tired at the zoo tomorrow. But it'll be a happy tired, I promise."

Jessie blushed and avoided Josh's eyes. "Uh—yeah. Too much information, Kayla." A quick visceral memory of her own nocturnal post-concert highs with Jacob assaulted her sensitive parts and she almost moaned out loud, but when she looked into Jacob's eyes a happy peace passed between the two of them instead of the old, sad longing. Sidling forward, Jessie kissed Kayla's cheek and gave Jacob a quick peck too. "I love you guys. Thanks for a phenomenal show."

Jacob put his hands under Kayla's legs to help support her on his back, and he swung around and piggybacked her towards his dressing room. Jessie and Josh rolled their eyes at each other when they heard him say, "Start now? Lock the door."

"I don't wanna know," Josh grinned at Jessie, pulling her towards him for a sweet hug. His voice softened and he gazed adoringly into her eyes. "You were incredible out there tonight, little one."

"So were you, Mister 'every-woman-and-most-of-the-men-in-the-audience-are-in-love-with-me-now.' That sex scene with Shanda drives me insane."

"Hey, we've talked about that. We're good, remember?"

Jessie pressed her forehead to him and slipped the fingers of both hands behind his belt. "I'm not talking about being jealous," she purred. "I'm talking about how fucking hot it is. I get to take you home. Don't tell me I am not going to be the luckiest woman on the planet tonight."

Chuckling, Josh pressed her to him and whispered a few plans for later in her ear, which had Jessie's face fairly bright pink by the time she turned, her hand in his, and opened the door to her dressing room.

Across and behind them, about fifty feet away behind the excited crowds of people rushing up and down the hall, tucked behind a trolley full of gear cases, was Matt. His eyes had scanned the hallway as he waited for them to come back from the gathering with the contest winners, and eventually settled on the foursome, who were flanked by Dan and Ulysses, local security, and Charles, Charlie and Deirdre bringing up the rear. Watching Josh and

Jessie share their little moment before they went into the dressing room was satisfying on many levels, and gut wrenching on others. No couple deserved joy and happiness any more than these two did. In his heart Matt knew that—it was just that his soul cried when he admitted it.

He leaned against the trolley, and considered what to do now. Nobody knew he was here, with the exception of Charles. When asked if he planned to attend the concert, he had just studied his desert boots and shook his head. It wouldn't do to see Jessie anyway. She was so happy; at least she would be until she met with Catherine, Matt figured rightly. To see him would add an extra layer of angst and, likely guilt, especially with Josh in the room. Matt and Jessie had not eyeballed each other in person since the day at the hospital when her fingers trailed away from his. The only words they had spoken since were infused with hurt and loss and, that last time, a frustrated anger.

The overriding question now was whether Matt could stand the idea of being this close to Jessie and not talk to her. Catherine too, would need some support, and Matt had come to care enough for her to want to offer that. He felt a little like he had thrown her to the wolves, bringing her backstage like this. Jessie too, for that matter. But Catherine had asked for the opportunity to meet Jessie and say her piece, so in the end Matt appeased himself by thinking he was only giving her a final gift that would maybe facilitate some healing.

Leaning deeper into the trolley, he tried to duck his head away from a group of Jessie's dancers who would easily recognize him, and he waited rather impatiently while he considered what was happening in that dressing room, and whether he ought to make an appearance.

Catherine, who stood when Jessie and Josh entered, scanned Jessie from head to toe, and quickly decided the singer was perfect in every way. Fit, beautiful, talented, remnants of stage glitter on her sea-pearl eyes and high on her cheeks...No wonder Carly and millions of others were infatuated with her. Unfortunately, the effect it had on Catherine was to make her feel inferior and, well, frumpy, in size 32 jeans, practical lace-up boots, and a warm winter coat. Clutching at the plaid scarf she wore loosely around her neck, she blinked and waited for the blood to stop pounding in her ears so she could speak.

Thankfully, Jessie spoke first.

"Hello," she said, also a little apprehensive at the mysterious secrecy of this meeting. Her playful attentions to Josh went by the wayside rather quickly when she discerned the high emotion evident in the woman's puffy eyes and somewhat pink face. Extending a hand, she moved slowly forward. "Jessie," she offered. "It's a pleasure to meet you."

"You might change your mind about that," Catherine blurted out, as the door opened and Deirdre came into the room. Josh and Jessie tensed.

Josh left Jessie's side with a gentle squeeze of her fingers and a silent *I'm here if you need me,* after shaking their guest's hand and saying a quiet, "Hello." Moving to the far end of the room, he scooped up David and playfully tossed him over one shoulder. Alin approached him. Together with Carlotta, they ushered the children into an adjoining room to give Jessie some privacy with her guest.

"Momma needs a few minutes with this nice lady," he told them.

Josh made his way back a minute later, closing the door behind him. He stood at the back of the room by the craft table and pondered Catherine's purpose here.

Catherine, discerning that Jessie had been told nothing, back-pedaled and reached out a hand. "My name is Catherine," she said. "With a C."

"Would you like to sit?" Apprehensive, Jessie lifted a hand and waved lightly towards the sofa.

"No, no, actually." The words came out quick and guarded. "Thanks anyway."

"Okay." Waiting, Jessie faced her, but she couldn't resist the nervous temptation to twist a ringlet in her hair, which Catherine found interesting. "I figure you must have something to tell me," Jessie managed, trying to sound friendly. "I don't usually meet people in my personal dressing room after shows."

"To be honest, I didn't know I was meeting you. I asked if it could be arranged, but…I didn't think this was happening. The person I asked obviously had second thoughts."

"Oh. Uh…who? Who did you ask?"

The innocent query took Catherine by surprise. It also had the duplicate effect to make her feel like an intruder. Bristling, using ammunition she felt quite certain would hurt Jessie based on the little she knew about hers and Matt's interactions, she said his name. "Matt Kelly. An old friend of yours, I think."

That startled everyone in the room. Jessie's eyes flitted over to Josh as he straightened in curiosity. Forcing herself to look at this woman again, who Jessie thought was really pretty in a natural sort of way, she mumbled, "Oh." Legions of unspoken thoughts passed between her and Catherine. Their essence was a man who meant a great deal to both, and whose name spoken in a dressing room after a moving, passionate concert, had the power to turn the air a compressed grey and bring a stilted stillness into the conversation.

"Now that I'm here, I—" Catherine stopped short. After witnessing Jessie's dramatic performance, after watching her pour her heart and soul into her music, after listening to her music endlessly after the last few months, after emptying her tears and loneliness into her daughter's bed day after day and night after night, she was swept up in a vortex of confusion and loss that completely disabled her. The concert tonight was the pinnacle of all that, of months of learning about Jessie, only a little through Matt because it was like he was hiding her, protecting her from Catherine, or more likely from his heart. Generally, he had barely spoken about her. The rest of Catherine's investigative work had been done via the plethora of information available about Jessie on the Internet, through gossip pages, YouTube, blogs, and readily available official newspaper and media reports. Now, with Jessie in front of her, perfect and sweet and a little bit scared, a woman who had suffered more than most people, Catherine was rendered speechless.

Bowing her head, she let tears fall to the rug beneath her feet.

Jessie stopped twisting her ringlet and stared helplessly at Josh. Deirdre stepped forward.

"Catherine," she said with a tenderness that Jessie, struggling with how to handle this, appreciated, "come and sit. Can we get you a drink? Some wine, or herbal tea perhaps?" Taking Catherine's elbow, she started to move towards the sofa.

Shrugging her off, Catherine said sharply, "No. No. Please, I…" Sighing deeply, she looked up at Jessie but still couldn't find a way past the brick wall of emotion to speak.

Jessie caught Dee's eye and sent her a quiet *Okay, I got this.* Dee let her hand drop from the woman's elbow as Jessie started slowly.

"Are you from P.E.I.? Because I know that's where Matt was for a while."

It helped. Talking about that serene restorative province and the special time Catherine spent with Matt there helped.

Jessie saw the light come over her eyes, and she exhaled slightly. *Leave it to beautiful, healing Prince Edward Island,* she thought.

"No, not exactly," Catherine started, managing to get a grip. " I spent six weeks there last summer, that's all. I rented a cottage."

"In Darnley." Jessie's voice was quiet.

"Yes. It turned out your old friend had rented the cottage next door."

"He's not my 'old' friend, as you say." Feeling defensive over her relationship with Matt, Jessie's nostrils flared slightly. "I hope he's still my friend."

Amused, Josh ducked his head and grinned, a cascade of hair falling over his cheek and hiding his reaction from Jessie. Grabbing a carrot from a veggie tray, he munched on it as he listened. He sobered at Catherine's response to Jessie's little hot-tempered spurt.

"From what I gleaned from Matt, Jessie, you were much more than just a friend to him. The man I knew was a man trying desperately to let you go."

Raising her chin, Jessie fought a rising panic. *No,* she screamed inwardly. *Never.* She planted her feet more securely and faced off against this frustrating woman. "Why are you here, Catherine? What is it you need to tell me that Matt apparently endorsed?"

"My daughter," Catherine choked. Retrieving her smartphone from her pocket, she opened a photo and handed it to Jessie. "Her name was Carly. She was bullied in school. When she had a bad day, she would go running after school. She was fifteen when a car slipped on a patch of ice and ran her down."

"Oh, Jesus. I'm sorry." Jessie stared at the picture. The girl peeking out at her was a freckled long-haired beauty with big glasses. All gangly innocence and perfection. Jessie handed the phone back, still confused as to what this could possibly have to do with her. Unless Matt was involved with this woman (it seemed unlikely, they weren't at all the same kind of person) and just thought meeting Jessie might help her somehow. But there was another layer here, somewhere. Jessie could feel it coming.

In the end, it was a direct hit between the eyes; it was an arrow in the heart.

Catherine's voice was thin and tired. But it was still accusing. "She didn't hear it. The car." Gesturing to her ears she added, almost eerily casually, "Earbuds. She was listening to music. Loudly, if I know my daughter."

Jessie took a step back the second the words were spoken. "My…my music," she discerned.

Whatever stale air was in the room got sucked out on the dying hopes and dreams of a mother who had wanted the best for her child—safety, happiness, peace and joy. Deirdre pressed manicured fingers to her lips while, at the craft table, Josh went rigid and made ready to bolt over to his wife. But the damage was done. Hearing the terrible truth, which ripped through her veins like icy water into a warm river, made the blood drain out of Jessie's face as something in her died.

"My music was responsible for a child's death."

"My child." Catherine pointed to herself as months of anger and grief came to the surface in front of the woman who Catherine couldn't stop herself from blaming. In her heart was a new truth that she had to set free as well. That a man she had come to love in a very short time was also gone from her life because of Jessie. This woman was to be reviled.

Yet…the blue eyes were floating now. The pretty bare shoulders in the glitzy halter top, which likely cost more than six months of Catherine's car payments, were trembling. This woman knew pain. She knew tragedy. She knew loss. She knew hunger. She knew the throbbing, incapacitating curse of loneliness.

"I want so bad to hate you," Catherine gasped, half choking. "But I can't."

Raising her arms and backing a few more steps away, Jessie challenged, "Hate me. I can take it." She left her arms out wide.

Catherine idly thought she wanted to take flight.

Josh met Deirdre's eyes. They'd be picking up these pieces for a while. "Fuck, Matt," passed quietly across Josh's lips. "What the fuck were you thinking?"

Catherine heard the subdued, angry words. She twisted around to look at Josh briefly before aiming her hard, heartbroken gaze back at Jessie. "Matt didn't want me to come here, to see you. To tell you. Because he didn't want me to hurt you. He can't stand to see you hurt."

"Matt would never hurt me." The words were a whisper, spoken on the only trail of sanity Jessie had left as her world spun anew.

"No, but you hurt him. And he hurt me."

"You were a couple? The puppy…Drifter…"

"Is mine. Although I think he thought he was Matt's for a while."

Jessie rallied, and shifted her stance. "What happened with Matt and me is between us, Catherine. And if Matt hurt you, I'm sorry. You can blame my music for what happened to your daughter, if you want to, but you can't say I had anything to do with Matt and you."

"You destroyed him. He has nothing left because of you. He lost his home, his wife…his daughter too, in some ways, since he never seems to see her. His job is not the same. He lost his dignity and he lost himself along the way."

"That's enough, Catherine." Deirdre touched her elbow again. "I think it's time for you to go."

Josh was frozen, hearing this. He didn't need the reminder, either, of the horrible isolating days that led to Jessie turning to Matt—her friend, her comforter, her protector. That led to all of them losing a good friend, a man they all depended on for so long. Dropping his hands to his sides, he closed his eyes and turned his head away.

The door opened behind Jessie but she was too stricken to notice it. This night had been so incredible, so perfect. It seemed everyone was finally happy. Safe. Her fists clenched and unclenched as she tried to breathe. "Well," she managed to croak, "I guess he got even then, didn't he?"

It hit Catherine like a lightning bolt. Her face contorted into confusion as she pondered that. "You think that's why he arranged for me to see you? To use me to get back at you? I thought you said he would never hurt you."

"I guess," Jessie breathed, raising her chin defiantly in a desperate move towards self-preservation, "if you hurt someone bad enough they might find it in themselves to drive their own knife in some day."

At that, Catherine let her eyes drift over Jessie's shoulders to Matt, who was standing inside the door with both hands buried in the pockets of a navy cashmere coat that landed mid-thigh over expensive jeans. The hair that earned him the nickname 'Spike' from Jessie was perfectly gelled and teased. Now, his leather desert boots placed wide apart, he crunched on a lip, nodded just slightly, and aimed moist pale hazel-grey eyes at Catherine, who only knew the rumpled beach bum version of him, and who found herself completely breathless at the impeccable, distinguished man now standing before her.

Jessie caught Catherine's look, which was an odd flickering of surprise, adoration, and sheer desolation. Letting her shoulders sink further, wiping a shaking hand over her eyes, Jessie fixed her gaze on a spot on the floor as she turned slowly around to face Matt for the first time in months.

"It's okay," she said to him, her voice barely discernible, the pale eyes covered in a misty sheen she was too numb to release. "I get it." Melting in the hurt she still saw in the gentle, caring eyes she loved deeply, Jessie had to reach for Deirdre in order to steady herself. Nervous, immobile, she licked her lips, found some inner haughtiness, tossed her curls, and quite succinctly built herself a whole new wall.

"This is not about me, Jessie," he clarified. "Or how I feel about you. And it's not," he looked at Catherine, avoiding the hard angry stare Josh was firing at him, "about how I feel about you, Catherine. It's about a mother who needed to know why her daughter," he paused, and took in a deep breath to find the strength, "loved Jessie Wheeler so much. So that mother can let you go." Glancing back at Jessie crushed him but he let himself go there anyway.

The wisdom and strength in his words were infused by the raw, feral dominance of the truth. Letting go had to happen…by Catherine, and by Matt. It had to happen because both of them had been lost in Jessie for far too long—lost in her music, in her illusory life, in her strength, in her capacity to see the goodness in people, in her light. In her essence, and in the tragedies that seemed to come from loving her.

Matt forced his eyes away from Jessie's still body and let them land on his summer lover. "Catherine, I sent you the ticket so you could see the kind of power this girl has over people. I think you can honestly say that everyone who saw the show tonight left suspended, changed. I think you can say that your daughter's love for Jessie was genuine, based on respect for Jessie as a person, and for the music that comes from her soul. Carly didn't die alone, Catherine. Jessie carried her home."

His eyes flicked back to Jessie. "You were right the first time. I would never hurt you. This wasn't about hurting you. It was about helping a bereaved mother get past her pain." At her shocked look, he said, "I was standing outside the door." Brushing past her, he took Catherine in his arms and pulled her close. She was sobbing now, quietly, letting it all go...the months of pain. The loss. The losses. Matt's arms were strong, his spirit even stronger. "Thatta girl," he whispered to her. "Thatta girl."

Jessie, alone, was staring at the floor where Matt had been standing. When he brushed by her, she had lifted an arm with some leftover instinct that told her he was coming to her. His scent was there, in the hair gel, in the cashmere coat, in his aftershave. It still floated on the air Jessie was breathing. Pivoting slowly around on one boot, she braced herself for what she would see—Matt's strength holding up a woman who blamed Jessie's music for her daughter's death. It was too much. That old hole in the bucket had been ripped solidly open and left jagged and raw. Its fresh, red jaw was gaping somewhere deep in her belly, challenging her to sink to her knees anew.

No, she told it. *I am stronger than that now. I may bend, but I will not break.*

Looking up, she saw Josh's eyes on her, questioning, wondering where he fit in right now, in this agonized new pain surrounding his wife. Jessie covered the distance to him by padding up on her toes, so she wouldn't disturb the embrace that turned her vision muzzy and grey.

Josh took her in his arms and held on tight.

"I'm here," he murmured, pulling her head down so she could cry unnoticed. "I'm here, and I'm not going anywhere. I will always be with you now, Jessie. You're not alone. Whatever life throws at you, you're not alone."

A muffled, "Okay," came from somewhere under the mess of curls and tears. "Okay."

The door clicked shut while Jessie was buried in Josh's saving grace. Jessie's head snapped up. Matt and Catherine were gone. Matt...was gone. Again.

"Fucking bastard," she said to Josh and Dee as she wiped a hand across her eyes. "He never fucking says goodbye."

Letting go of Josh's hand, she disappeared into the washroom to wipe away the glitter from the show, and locked the door behind her.

Chapter Twenty-six

The trip to the Toronto Zoo was part of *Sacred Peace's* efforts to grant the children who were along for the tour a rousing thank-you for their patience and support during the endless interviews, rehearsals and performances. Jessie and Josh weren't the only two adults who had their children with them. Stella was along for the fun, and her baby brother Lucas, too. There were also two couples on the crew who had children, and who brought them along. Jessie and Jane had chatted about it—it didn't seem fair to just bring their own kids along and expect other families to be separated. In the end, they gave them the choice, and throughout the tour they were also joined by occasional partners and children, which made for some fun, busy, inclusive family time during a term of hard work and dedication. Whenever possible, family events were organized, fit in amongst the discipline of schoolwork and the occasional chores, which were enforced where possible to keep the older kids from getting spoiled and from feeling entitled.

At the zoo, Jessie hooked an elbow around Carlotta's and walked with her on one side and Deirdre on the other as they approached the penguins. It was cool today, but sunny, and the women were constantly pulling up zippers and wrapping scarves tighter around the kids' necks. Keeping an eye on them was easier than they figured it might be. Jacob and Kayla were uproariously in their element with the Sawyer kids and Stella, and at this moment Jacob had David on his shoulders and Dylan running around his feet, while Kayla told stage disaster stories to the two girls.

Josh and Charlie, who were walking with Jane behind Jessie and the older women, were contemplative until Josh broke down at Charlie's request to explain why Jessie was so quiet and removed today, after the high from the show last night. Explaining Catherine's visit and Matt's brief reappearance in their lives, Josh told them she had hardly said a word today, even to the kids.

"You know Jessie," he said. "She needs time to make her way back from these things."

Jane was appalled. "That woman had the audacity to suggest that Jessie was responsible for her daughter's death?"

"Not Jessie, necessarily. Her music." Josh was quiet.

Charlie, who was pushing his son's stroller, tossed in, "So Jessie. May as well be real here, Josh."

Incensed, Jane added, "Guys, did this woman not stop to consider that maybe, just maybe, her daughter is the one responsible? She's the one who had the music cranked!"

Bearing that in mind, Josh said, "I think it's easier to blame someone else when it comes to these things, Jane. I've been thinking about it, and you know what? Considering Matt's role in this whole thing, I think he set up the meeting because he knew Jessie could take it. Maybe he wasn't sure at first, because Catherine said he told her 'no' when she asked him, but he came through for her."

"I think it was nasty of Matt." Jane's eyes followed Jessie up the narrow pathway. Clearly, Jessie was not in a good place today. She was leaning into Carlotta, almost clinging to her the way a child clings to its mother. Thankfully, Carlotta loved Jessie like a daughter so her padded shoulders were welcoming and comforting.

"I thought so at first," Josh replied, his eyes also locked on his wife. "But I think Matt really cares about Catherine. He obviously thought that introducing her to Jessie would give her closure."

"And?" Charlie was curious. "Besides destroying Jessie in the process, I mean."

"I don't think anyone got closure from last night. I think maybe it didn't go the way Matt hoped it might."

As they considered that, a small hand inserted itself in Josh's. He looked down to see Emily-Grace looking wistfully up at him. "Daddy, I was just wondering if you would like to go see the penguins with me."

"Oh, my heart," Jane breathed to Charlie. There had been so much worry over Jacob and his closeness to Josh's children, and the resolution really just came down to all of them spending time together.

Josh's smile was so wide he thought his face would crack. "Only if you name them all," he teased her. "Every last one."

"Daddy!" Her 'little girl squeal' got Jessie's attention. Turning, she spotted her daughter hand-in-hand with her father, sunlight on the darkening-blonde ringlets and a happy light in her eyes. Swinging her father's hand, Emily-Grace was bouncing. Josh, too, was the picture of happiness with his oldest, often reticent and judgmental, child by his side.

Looking up, Josh caught Jessie's eye, and he straightened and smiled at her as Emily-Grace, Charlie and Jane all started shouting penguin names at him. Tuning them out for a second, he sent Jessie a left-handed *I love you.* She responded by biting her bottom lip and trying to smile back, but it got upended and she turned and ducked her head into Carlotta's wide shoulder.

Emily-Grace was ecstatic, and now Stella was nipping at Charlie's heels. The two girls hauled on their fathers, pulling at them until Charlie passed the stroller to Jane and ran off, daring Josh to follow.

Clinging tightly to Emily-Grace's hand, Josh let her lead him to the penguins, but he made sure they swung near Jessie as they passed. Dipping his lips to her ear, he whispered, "I love you." His warm breath on her ear and a one-armed hug around her waist sealed the tender sentiment.

Then he was gone, off to see the penguins with his daughter and his good friends, with Jacob, Kayla, and the Sawyer boys in hot pursuit.

The family was packing up to head to the jet later when Jessie sat on the edge of the master bedroom bed in this last, endless *Sacred Peace* tour hotel suite. Clutching one of Josh's white T-shirts, she looked up at him and waited for him to stop moving and question her. It only took him a minute. He had been waiting all day for her to come around, to open up to him. Jessie had been quiet and detached throughout breakfast and lunch, and at the zoo, and last night when they went to bed neither he nor she had made any move towards making love as they had been looking forward to after the show.

Now he stood before her, his shaving kit dangling from his hand, and waited for her to speak.

"I think…" She crunched on a lip and pulled Dylan onto her lap when he handed her a dinosaur book and begged her to read it. "One sec, Dylan. Josh… I want to go to London."

"What?" That wasn't what he was expecting to hear. "By that I assume you mean London, Ontario."

"I want to go to that school, where Carly went. Emily-Grace will read with you, sweetheart," she said to Dylan. "How about Momma comes over in a minute?"

Protesting, Dylan slid off her lap, only to face complaints aimed at him when Emily-Grace refused to read. She was designing hair on an iPad Internet App and her current blue streaks just weren't working. David shuffled over to Dylan and grabbed the book out of his hands. Jessie watched as they snuggled up on the couch to read. Alin dropped down beside them to help when David got stuck.

Observing them as they settled, Jessie said, "I just think that I could help somehow, if I went to that school and talked to the kids about bullying. It might help."

"Help you, you mean." Softening, Josh sauntered over to the bed and eased down beside his wife. Taking her hand, kissing her knuckles, he said, "I don't think that's a good idea on short notice, Jessie. We're supposed to leave here in half an hour."

"I'm going to go ask Deirdre. Maybe we can swing it. Dan and I can go."

Josh was silent.

"What?" she asked him.

"Where's Matt, Jessie?"

"How the hell should I know? You're the one who's been in touch with him." A light dawned over her face. "Oh," she said hotly, running a forefinger over her top and then her bottom lip, and nodding. "You think Matt and I are gonna hook up again. You think he's in London? With Catherine?"

"I don't know where he is, Jessie. Today I don't want to know."

"Even if he is there, I don't plan on seeing her. I just want to go to the school and knock some sense into those kids. This whole bullying thing pisses me off."

"All right." Josh tossed up his hands in frustration. "But if you're staying, I'm staying."

"No, Josh, the kids…"

"Hey," he argued, using his fingers to turn her face around to him. "I'm being bullied, little one. I'm, like, the poster boy for being bullied. By the world. I know how much it hurts. I know how terrifying it is."

"Oh, way to melt my heart. For God's sake, Josh. You're killing me here."

A slow grin widened across his cheeks. "I never did get that adrenalin fueled rough sex you promised me. Maybe we can find some time for it if we stay."

"I hate to leave the kids again."

"We just had six amazing weeks with them. They'll be okay for a few days."

"Okay." Smiling sadly, she bent forward and tenderly kissed him. "Let me go break the news to Charles and Dee."

Standing, Josh pulled Jessie up by the hand. "I may as well face that fire with you too," he said. "The kids are fine with Alin. Dan's outside the door."

"I'm sure she loves being a babysitter half the time."

"She wouldn't be here if she didn't."

Ten minutes later, they were inside Charles and Dee's suite, shuffling their feet and looking very much like teenagers in love asking for the car so they could sneak off to have sex.

"What?" Charles was less than impressed already, and he staunchly crossed his arms to prove it.

Jessie did the explaining, which softened things because the Keatings knew how she was feeling today and they were relieved to see her reaching out to them now. What that resulted in was a shared look between the older couple that, although clouded with worry and frustration, was at least amenable.

Deirdre held up her phone. Ulysses was downstairs in the lobby getting their pick-up vehicles organized. "I'll call Ulysses, as well as the front desk about getting your suite extended for a few more days. You can have a rest tomorrow and go to the school on Monday, if we can make arrangements. You can keep Dan and Alin with you. Sam and Ulysses can do the kids' security and Carlotta and Grampie and I can handle feedings and bedtime."

"Just leave school 'til we get home, Dee."

"Your poor children."

"A few more days won't hurt." Josh wrapped an arm around Jessie's waist. "Thank you."

Charles uncrossed his arms and placed them on his hips. He gave Jessie a long look, which she caught and returned.

"What?" she asked him.

"Jessie, Catherine's a teacher at that school."

"Oh." Her brow furrowed. "Oh, and you know this because…?"

"I saw Matt this morning. He and Ulysses and I had a long talk."

"Oh, is he…staying in the hotel?"

"No, he's staying down the road. But we met at the restaurant downstairs."

"At six a.m. apparently, since we were at breakfast there at eight."

"We met while you and Josh were at the hotel gym, yes."

"I suppose he was watching the elevator door for masked intruders the whole time." She swallowed.

"If you are asking if he is still on my payroll, he is, smartie pants." Charles paused. "Look, Jessie, I'll enlist Matt to check in with Catherine and see if she can set things up with the school. Or if she's even willing…" He drifted off.

"To see me again. I hear ya, Charles."

"He will want to be there." Charles glanced at Josh. "Is that okay with you?"

A low *ppffftt* escaped Josh's lips. "Sure. Why not?"

Next, Charles fixed a hard gaze on his singing star. "You and Matt should use this opportunity to make your peace, Jessie."

A slow back and forth turn of her head was her response, along with a somber, "Mmmm. Not happening. He pretty much hates me these days." The spoken admission gutted her. She sighed and cornered right. "How come it's okay for kids to have a lot of love for other people but when adults love more than one person it's taboo?"

"You really have to ask that?" This, too, was from Charles.

Josh looked away.

"I'm not talking about sex, Charles."

"Jessie…" Charles knew about the threatening email and the erotic sex video. Over the years there were numerous signs and warnings that constantly reminded him that, with Jack Deacon's help, he'd plucked his girl from the streets. Now, he felt compelled to speak on the subject they tried so hard to avoid. "I know you have a big heart. I know there is a lot of room in that heart. I know too, that..." He sighed, and averted her stare for a minute. "Well," he continued, "that over the years you have learned to enjoy your body in a healthy, adult way. Especially after... Well, after McCall I can't imagine it was easy getting back to loving yourself again."

"Jesus, Charles, really?" Jessie was rather aghast.

He raised a hand and air-palmed her. "Hear me out. Wouldn't life be great if we could love other people whenever we want with our bodies without fear of complication or remorse, like the kind that hurts and alienates other people?"

"Free love. I think it's been done." Josh's wry response was dry.

"It's still being done. Don't kid yourself into thinking that era is over, Josh. But look at me, Josh, and tell me that you can stand by and let Jessie spend time with Matt alone, or even Jacob still, and not drive yourself insane wondering what the hell they're up to. Even if all of you consented."

Jessie glanced at Josh, and took his hand.

Scratching his head, Josh said, "Lots of couples have open marriages. As weird as it is to be discussing this with you, Charles, it's not what I want." He looked at Jessie and, slightly entertained, grinned at her. "We do well enough on our own."

"We do fine," she agreed staunchly. "I don't want an open marriage, either. But Josh...Charles...I miss Matt. I can't stand not having him in my life. It was torture the first time he left us, when Emily-Grace was a baby, and it's torture now."

"Unfortunately, Jessie, the attraction between you is preventing the two of you from working together the way you used to. Too much has changed. I'm sure your husband agrees." Charles was adamant. His brow was creased in concentration.

"Oh, so that's what you and Matt talked about this morning." Jessie gulped and blinked at him. Beside her, Josh toed the floor and grunted lightly. Shanda's perky blonde curls floated over his mind.

"He was very candid, Jessie. Matt wants the best for you and Josh. Hell, he knows you deserve it. But somewhere along the line, he fell in love with you."

"I know." Suddenly she was blinking back tears. Suddenly Josh stopped moving.

"It was not totally unexpected. Nobody," he glanced at Josh, "is judging either of you. Right, Josh?"

In response, Josh exhaled and looked over at Jessie. "We've talked about this. We're good," he said quietly.

"That doesn't solve anything," Jessie moaned, childishly stomping her foot.

"Jessie, this is what's going to happen. Matt will be around to help sort out this school thing, only because it's last minute and he has access to the woman who can make it happen. Who I think, according to what Matt said this morning about her attitude last night after they left, will be agreeable to making it happen."

"Oh, so she got a good fuck so now she's all happy again?" Wrestling her hand out of Josh's grasp, Jessie folded her arms over her belly and frowned.

"Jessie, this is what I'm talking about." Small red spots appeared on Charles' cheeks and he pointed an angry finger at her. "This has to stop. You and Matt left things in a bad place between you. It's coloring his work with us, and it's got you making drunken phone calls to him in the middle of the night that upset and confuse him."

"What? What the hell, Jessie?" Josh was less than impressed at this new, revelatory information, although he did know about the erotic video that was emailed to Jessie.

"Long story," she growled. "And it only happened once."

"And the Internet meeting? Shall we also include that?" Charles countered.

"You suck, Charles! Twice I spoke to him, apart from the night of the barn fire when Josh put me on the phone with him. And only once did I call him, and that was only because of that stupid video!"

"And because you missed him. You can't be doing that, or I will have to..." Charles sighed.

"Oh, well, I thought you fired him ages ago. So do what you have to do, Charles! I don't fucking care!"

"I'm just saying that he's ready to run, Jessie. To be released. That's all I'm saying. Most of this ball is in your court. Either find some kind of peace with Matt that will allow all of us to keep working together, from a distance in your perspective, or let him go so he can live his life in peace."

"It's not gonna happen." This, surprisingly, was from Josh. He tucked an arm around Jessie's waist but locked his eyes on Charles. "Once you love Jessie Wheeler, your heart is toast. No more peace. Just ask Jacob."

"What?" Shocked, Jessie elbowed him. "Don't be stupid. Jacob's head over heels in love with Kayla. They're great together. He's finally happy. I'm happy. Mostly," she added with a serious downturn to her lips.

"Ha!" Josh looked at her, but he wasn't judging or angry. He was the sweet, understanding, loving man she was crazy about. Brushing back her hair, he smiled sadly. "Jacob will never be over you, Jessie, the same way I know you will never be fully and completely over him. Even Charlie, for that matter, is still putty in your hands. Matt's heart is newly broken. And so is yours."

Starting to protest, she stopped when Josh put a finger to her lips to stop her. "Little one," he said with a tenderness that cut, for its simple truth. "You and I...always and forever, right?"

Teary-eyed, she nodded.

"Like you said at the top of this conversation, there is a lot of room in our hearts to love a lot of people."

"Shanda," she whispered, suddenly understanding.

"Yes. So I know your heart hurts over Matt. But I also think you can find a way to work together that respects our marriage and that respects his feelings. If there has to be distance and a rule that drunk calls are not allowed," he twisted his lip and thoughtfully chewed on the corner, "then so be it. At the same time, Jess...I want you to know that I get it. I know how much you miss him, and I know how much it hurts to have to let him separate himself from us like this. I also want you to know that I want Matt looking after us, after all of us. I trust him to do right by us. But ultimately we have to consider what's best for Matt. What he wants."

"You want me to let him go."

"No. That's not what I want. You'd be even more miserable and then I'd never get sex."

Watching them, Charles groaned and mocked them by putting his hands over his ears. Deirdre was off the phone now, staring at all of them in curious amusement.

Josh inhaled deeply and continued. "Shanda, Jessie, has nothing on Matt. I barely know her compared to your years with Matt. And I think the world of her. So I can't even begin to imagine how much Matt is hurting right now. So I think what I am saying is that I think it needs to be his choice, as to whether he stays or goes. And the ball is in your court, as Charles said, to help him make that choice."

A serious bent settled across Jessie's eyes, flickering there as she pondered this new wisdom from the man who got hurt in the first place by the man whose fate in the Keating employ—and in their lives overall—lay in the balance. "Okay." She nodded. "All right, Josh. I hear what you're saying. And may I just add that I fucking love you."

Deirdre tut-tutted in her condemning Deirdre way. "Is it really necessary to add that expletive in there, Jessie? You swear far too much, honey."

"Sometimes," Jessie smiled, her eyes never leaving her husband's, "a girl just needs a little extra oomph in what she's trying to say, Dee. I apologize if it offends you, but even my love songs aren't enough to express how much I love this man."

Charles lifted his gaze away from the couple in front of him, who were now embracing and sharing a tender kiss, and let it flit over to his wife of many years. His eyes were shining, as were hers. Years of worry for these two had prematurely aged both of them but now, watching Josh and Jessie disappear the way they always did when love got the best of them, was infinitely satisfying and absolutely welcome, swear words or not. Taking Dee's hand, he winked and pointed towards the bedroom.

"I saw that," Jessie laughed, turning back to them. "Still got it, do you Charles?" Swatting him lightly, she bent forward and brushed her lips against his cheek. "I love you, you big goof. Please tell Matt we'll get through Monday somehow and then I hope he'll fly back to Vancouver on the jet with us. We'll talk. We'll find a way to sort this out and make it work."

"Scoot." Dee used both hands to motion Josh and Jessie out of the door. To Charles, she said, "We have about five minutes before Ulysses expects us downstairs. Jessie, Josh, your suite has been extended until Tuesday morning at ten, as has Dan's, and Alin's too, and your rental vehicle that Dan is responsible for has also been extended. We'll be in touch about the school and Matt. Bring your children downstairs so we can start loading them up. Enjoy your evening and a quiet day tomorrow. Now...go. We're down to four minutes."

"Can you make it happen that quick, Charles?" Jessie was in royal form now, a sense of relief having washed over her as she considered her chances to make things right with Catherine, and with Matt as well.

"Get her out of here." Laughing, Charles clapped Josh on the shoulder as he walked him to the door. "See you in ten."

"Oh, now it's ten!" Hugging Dee, Jessie whispered, "Thank you. I love you."

They slipped out of the door, counting down the half hour or so it would take to get their children as well as the kids' things downstairs and packed into the SUVs, and then themselves into their own big bed for an evening of snuggling, sprinkled generously with tender kisses and sweet, sweet love.

Chapter Twenty-seven

"I needed to tell you," Catherine said to Jessie Monday morning at John Paul 2 High School in London, Ontario.

She and Jessie were facing each other, seated in students' desks in Catherine's classroom over the lunch hour. The door was closed to curious students who wondered why a big Scandinavian blonde was standing outside like some grand behemoth, obviously guarding the room. Josh was down the hall getting to know the acting teacher, with Matt for company, and Alin at Matt's side. Alin was picking up a few security tidbits from Matt as well as a few thoughts about her possible future with the RCMP, since the RCMP was a big part of Matt's early career history.

It had taken the morning to get things organized and permissions from the school sorted, although the Vancouver crew had left their hotel before things were finalized in order to make the school on time for an afternoon session with the students. Now, the plan was for Jessie to play some songs and chat with students in Catherine's two afternoon English classes, and for Josh to talk to the drama students about acting, with some serious chats about bullying nestled in between.

Later, both Josh and Jessie would agree that their brief time with these students was not enough. It would lead to worry and concern over their own children, and a series of informative and educational videos down the road, using their careers as leverage for attention and solidifying more support for them as a couple as time went on.

"I needed you to know," Catherine was saying now, much more calmly than she managed to speak after the concert a few nights earlier. "Last spring when Carly was killed I couldn't even tie my shoes for the first few weeks. When the police gave me back her iPhone and I realized she was listening to your playlist when she died, which didn't surprise me because she loved your music, I didn't know whether to laugh or cry."

Taking her hand, Jessie sighed. "You floored me, Catherine. Your daughter was beautiful. I would never have wanted my music to be associated with anything bad, but over the years it has been, from time to time."

"When you and your children were abducted."

"And a stalker before that. A man who got confused about love. It ended with Josh being badly hurt." Her stomach clenched with remembrance, and with the relatively new fears associated with Josh's 'accidents' on the *Sacred Peace* set.

"I'm angry," Catherine admitted. "But I have been taking comfort in knowing that Carly was probably singing while she was running. Singing your songs, your lyrics. She would have been listening to someone while she was running, so I guess I'm glad it was you. Your music gave her great pleasure, Jessie. It gave her peace. I'm sorry I hurt you the other night. You should know that your concert was a very emotional ride for everyone there, not just for a mother missing her daughter."

"Thank you. I think." Jessie wrinkled her nose. "Try being the one on stage belting out those tunes. Or lost in agony writing them. Music is a blessing and a curse, you know?"

"I can imagine! Some of your songs are painful to listen to. I can't get enough of some of them." After a minute, Catherine looked into the understanding blue eyes of her guest. "Jessie, I know you're here at the school to talk to the kids about bullying. But do you know why Carly had troubles? Trouble was new to her, over the last few school years."

"I'm sorry to hear that. And no, I don't know her story."

"She was a young teenager, if you know what I mean. Not into boys, not into makeup and girl chats. Her father was a teacher here too. He…got involved with another teacher. It became a 'thing,' here and at home. Carly was doing her grade nine year here. It was hell for her."

"Oh, shit. And for you too, I can imagine."

"Coming to school every day was like going to hell. People talking about us behind our backs, seeing him in the hallway with this woman…she was my friend. Past tense. It all exploded one day when Carly stumbled across them, kissing in his classroom. She'd dropped in to beg for lunch money. Like I said, she was a young teen. It destroyed her. He and his woman transferred schools, and Carly and I were left to pick up the pieces. The other students had a field day. And so did the teachers."

"I'm sorry you had to go through all that, Catherine. I have a daughter. I can't even imagine."

"I think you can. I know your troubles have led both you and your husband into the arms of other lovers. It can't have been easy on the kids."

Ruffled a bit by that, Jessie held her cool and sighed. "Josh and I seem to have to fight a lot to be together. It has not been an easy ride for any of us, least of all for our confused kids. But we really love each other, Catherine. Ultimately we can't stay apart. And I'm really, really grateful that he feels the same way I do. I know it's a blessing. I hope you find that someday. It's worth the fight."

"Look, Jessie, about Matt…"

Throwing up her hands, Jessie smiled sadly. "He's your business, Catherine. I love him desperately, and I always will, but I want him to find happiness. I can't be with him. Sometimes I wish I could divide my heart in two, but I can't. I went through that with Jacob, and it was hell. Josh will always be my guy."

"He really loves you. I can't…" Catherine shook her head.

"Give him some time, Catherine. I know Matt. There's no way he would ever have granted you access to me in my personal dressing room if there weren't some serious feelings there."

"I don't know."

"The dog, then," Jessie laughed. "It was all about the dog, Drifter. Cool name, by the way."

"Drifter's a mutt. He's incorrigible."

"Then the name really suits. Us *Drifters* actors are all mutts. 'Specially me and Josh."

"I think you're amazing."

Blushing, Jessie shrank a bit in her seat. "I'm just a girl trying to make her way in a tough world. In love with a man who constantly challenges and surprises me. Catherine...what was Carly's favorite tune of mine?"

"The same one I love the best. The one everybody calls *Josh's Song*. It's got a beautiful, inspiring message."

"Ah. No surprise. It's my favorite too. I wrote it for Josh after finding him spaced out on drugs at Charlie's club, the day Charlie asked me to marry him. One look in those sad, lost brown eyes and I was a total goner."

"I think one of the only times I saw Carly smile her whole last year was when I walked into her room and begged her to turn the music down, and she was listening to that song. She kept putting it on repeat. It drove me nuts until I finally, just this fall, really listened to it."

"I have a feeling a lot of parents, and maybe some spouses too, aren't fans of my music when it's blasted in bedrooms and cars."

"Or on earbuds." Catherine smiled wanly. "It's okay. It transported Carly to a better place. The song gave her peace."

"Thank you."

"You write about real things that hurt, Jessie. You help people."

"There's a lot of sadness in my music. I don't have any illusions about saving the world, Catherine."

"Well, I think that's part of your charm. That's what makes you special. I'm glad we met. And I'm glad you could find it in yourself to give me a second chance."

"Me too. We were all emotional after the concert. Thank you for seeing me."

The bell rang then, and Dan glanced in.

"Ready for this?" Catherine asked with a smile. "The onslaught?"

"I'm ready." Standing, Jessie inhaled deeply and wiped both sweaty palms on her jeans. Bending over, she grabbed her guitar from its case, and started to tune. Looking up at the small window in the classroom door, she grinned and gave Dan a thumbs-up.

Catherine stood back and watched her, shaking her head a little in disbelief.

Before the door opened and the first amazed students traipsed in, Jessie twisted around to Catherine one last time. "Do you think we could go to your house after to meet Drifter? I really need to meet him. Josh would love him. Animals take to him like cats to catnip."

"I'm sure it can be arranged," Catherine laughed. "But I'm not making dinner for celebrities accustomed to fine dining. I refuse on principal."

"We'll order in! We're big pizza fans. Or Josh can make us fajitas. He's an awesome cook." At that, Jessie started greeting the kids, who stood stock still as they entered and stared in shock at the famous singer in their midst. With a wave she said shyly, "Hi, I'm Jessie. What're your names?"

She got the afternoon underway with a song she sang by request. Not to her surprise, the requested tune was *Josh's Song.*

"For Carly," she said as she started on the first few notes. She ducked her head shyly at Catherine. "And for Carly's mom."

A wide smile from Catherine was her response. A hypnotic appreciation was the response from the students as Jessie's heart swelled.

I'm in a classroom with a teacher, she thought, humbled right down to her toes. *Can life get any better than this?*

She played the song with heart, singing for a bullied, traumatized fifteen-year old named Carly, and was never more proud to be granted the healing gift of music.

Chapter Twenty-eight

Jessie was standing in the aisle of the jet deciding where to sit when Matt pulled up to the private aircraft. She had to duck to see him out of the small window, but it was worth it. Back to his flawless self, Matt was a GQ model disguised as a guy who worked security. Catching her breath at the sight of her good friend, Jessie almost sank to her knees with relief.

"He's here," she said to Josh as he stowed his laptop for the flight. "He showed up."

Josh, too, bent and glanced out of the window. Cashmere coat open and flowing, his familiar leather messenger bag tossed over a shoulder, Matt was making his way towards the jet. His purposeful stride was either meant to telegraph confidence or to camouflage Matt's anxiety—Josh wasn't sure.

Taking Jessie's hand, Josh used his free hand to point at their usual seats.

"Take the window," he told her. "I'll sit in the back with Dan and Alin."

Humbled and grateful, Jessie touched his cheek. "I love how you always know what I need, Josh," she murmured. "How you always know what I'm thinking."

He'd had his own issues over the years, but when Josh was feeling good he was strength personified. Now, he brushed his lips against Jessie's forehead and couldn't avoid teasing her. "No sneaking off to the bedroom or the bathroom to join the mile high club, Jess. Save that for me."

"Oh, Josh." Waving a hand towards the back of the jet, Jessie adopted a playful banter. "Been there done that so many times that I'm, like, their president now."

His smile flipped upside down.

Laughing, Jessie gave him a gentle push. "With you, you big dork. Only with you." It was a white lie, meant to salvage his feelings. In truth, Jessie spent more time in the back bedroom on flights with Jacob than she did with Josh in all the time they'd been together. Jacob was just, well, that kind of guy. Adventurous and a little risqué. Especially when it came to sex.

"Yeah. All right." Josh's reply was hesitant and defensive. Shaking his head at her, he moved to the back of the jet to the couch just as Matt's feet sounded on the steps.

"Off to a great start," Jessie mumbled, twisting a ringlet in her hair as she pivoted around and pondered facing Matt for what would feel like a somewhat public discussion. A small smile lifted the corners of her lips, though, as she fondly remembered some of the more adventurous flights with Jacob during their times as a couple. Her face pinked up a little but she pushed the memory away and looked up to spy Matt studying her, swallowing nervously and wondering where he should sit.

Yesterday at the school they broke a little of the ice frosting their interactions simply by having to be in each other's company, but the moments were small, painted with a word here or there, mostly. Drifter, at Catherine's home later, helped. His joyful greeting was a balm for the soul. The broken leg was healed and he was all bouncy affection, jumping up on his visitors despite Catherine's mortified proclamations that he never did that. Matt had teased her about getting Drifter to puppy school, which Jessie jealously gleaned was some private joke between them, but overall the dog's presence had given them a safe place to focus their nerves.

Now, Jessie slid in to the window seat Josh had pointed out earlier. Timid, she shoved both thumbs over her front jeans pockets and hunkered up her shoulders. "Sit with me?" she asked Matt. "Please?"

Matt focused on her but he didn't move. This flight was meant to be an opportunity to talk, but having Jessie in front of him after all those days and nights of feeling her loss from his life was almost surreal. Part of him wanted to reach out and touch her to see if she was real.

A peek to the back of the plane revealed Josh chatting with Alin and Dan as he settled into his seat. Josh looked up and caught Matt's eye. A comforting glance towards Jessie told Matt that Josh, too, wanted them to make peace. Furthermore, it cemented Matt's affirmation that Josh was a good, kind man with a wisdom and maturity the world did not give him credit for.

Inhaling between his teeth, Matt made a small suction sound that Jessie found amusing. *Don't be so scared,* she thought, and caught herself remembering the night she approached him in his condo before they made love and asked him if he was nervous or scared. *You act all tough, but you're just a man. You hurt the same way I do.*

Encouraging him, Jessie smiled softly up at him as she eased more comfortably into her seat. Beside her, Matt peeled off his leather bag and the expensive coat, and handed them to Victoria, who had stolen up behind him with her usual grace and soothing floral scent. Wiping his palms on his jeans, Matt took one last glance at Jessie before he sat down beside her and focused his eyes on Victoria as she stowed his things in a nearby cabinet.

"Hey, Matt?" A small voice beside him pulled him back to Jessie.

"I'm here, kid." Inhaling deeply, Matt ran a hand over the barely-there stubble on his cheek but he didn't look at her.

"I'm glad you're here. I've spent way too much of my life missing you."

His silence was his answer, although he did manage a nod.

Jessie continued, as she buckled herself in and handed Matt the buckle at his side so he could do the same. "Do you remember the first time we met?"

"At La Casa," he replied, softening, sinking into the memory. "You were caught up in a whirlwind of change, adjusting to fame and to a crazy new life that I wasn't sure you were ready for."

"And so were you. You had just left the RCMP."

"That's right."

"Why, Matt? Why did you leave policing?"

Considering what to say, Matt finally told her, "There comes a point when you've just seen too much. I couldn't stand it anymore. The violence. The bad stuff."

"You know what I think? I think you were too sensitive for that kind of work. Becoming a bodyguard to some anonymous actor-singer seemed safer."

"At the time." Matt tried to force a smile but it came out crooked. "I remember what you were wearing that day. The way you looked at me. It was like you were saying 'I'm standing at the edge of something bigger than myself here, and I don't know if I am going to be okay.'"

"Pretty much." Jessie sighed, remembering the lonely fear and confusion, and the secrets she was always afraid to admit were part of her life, of her dark past.

"You had this look on your face that captivated me from the start. All haunted and scared, yet wise, I think. As if you'd lived a thousand lifetimes and knew so much more than the rest of us."

"I saw the same look in you, Matt. That first day. I saw a man who looked sad to me but he was hiding it under all these layers of professionalism, I guess you could call it. You wanted to prove to the great Charles Keating that you could handle his new young singer slash actor."

"He wasn't worried about you at that point as far as your little independent rebellious streak." Thoughtful, Matt added as he accepted a coffee from Victoria, "He and Deirdre were concerned about whether you could handle the fame they knew was coming your way. Their little orphaned waif." Coloring a bit at his take on the image of Jessie back then, all vulnerable and scared, Matt wrapped his hands around his coffee cup and soaked up the warmth.

Jessie accepted her latte from Victoria and smiled her 'thank you.' "What I remember most about meeting you that day was your eyes, I think. I was scared because you were this impeccable dresser, this rich guy who put his hands on his hips underneath his jacket, put most of his weight on one leg and studied me kind of sideways-like, as if you were trying to figure out whether you wanted the gig or not. At the beginning I figured you only took it because you needed something short term. You never thought it would last, did you, Matt?"

"I didn't want the gig. Not really. Not until I...Well," Matt shifted in his seat and cleared his throat. "Not until I looked into those beautiful blue eyes of yours, Jessie. I felt like you needed someone to take care of you, and it was quickly apparent that Charlie was failing miserably on that account. I know Charles and Dee were trying, but I felt like neither of them really understood you. All they knew was there was a beautiful soul in their home who was desperately craving love and acceptance but who, on most levels, was absolutely unreachable. I don't know, I just knew that you needed a rock. And all of a sudden I needed to be that rock."

"I was scared to death of you at first. You and your fancy clothes and your bossy orders." Chuckling, Jessie took a sip of her latte. "Except for that sadness. I always wondered where it came from."

"Michael was a big part of it, losing his family the way he did. Not having anyone to talk to, always having to be the big tough police officer..." Matt drifted off.

"You had Julie then."

"She was good at a lot of things, Jessie, but she wasn't someone to vent to, most times. I don't think I really felt like anyone understood me until I heard your music. Me and millions of others on this planet, I guess. Somehow you manage to validate what all of us are feeling. You make us feel understood."

"I just write and sing what I feel, Matt."

"Then you're very honest. Aren't you, Jessie?"

As she pondered the hidden meaning in his comment, Jessie sipped on her latte and waited until the jet was airborne before she spoke again. This time, her voice was lower, her intentions clear.

"I suppose I'm a little too honest, Matt. Aren't I? Sometimes." Staring at her cup, she waited for him to digest what she was telling him.

"Is that your way of saying you're sorry, Jessie?"

"I don't have anything to be sorry for. I'm not sorry. I wanted to be with you. I needed you more then than I've ever needed you, Matt."

Fidgeting with his cup, rubbing his forehead, Matt chanced a glance back at Josh. He wasn't surprised to find Josh, apprehensive but trying to appear relaxed, looking his way. Licking his lips uncomfortably, Matt held his gaze for a few seconds before he sighed and looked back at Jessie.

Matt took the plunge. "This is what I can't deal with, Jessie."

Turning a bit sideways, she hugged her cup and met Matt's eyes, saddened to see how intensely they were studying her, as if Matt was telling her to listen closely as he bared his soul.

He continued. "I can't deal with references to a night and a day that I know I will never experience again. I can't deal with long, sad looks and I can't deal with being touched by you. To be honest, I can barely even look at you."

"Matt, we knew things would change. I thought I could accept that, I thought it would be worth it. But was it?"

"I don't know how to answer that."

"If Josh hadn't gotten hurt—"

Cutting her off by raising a hand, Matt jumped in. "Don't go there, Jessie. You're lost without each other. I'm wise enough to recognize that."

"And you're loving enough to allow me that grace, Matt. Thank you."

"Call it selfishness. I want you to be happy, Jessie. I want Josh to be happy. I want your kids to grow up in a family that's loving and connected. And I want the world to experience more Jessie Wheeler music that comes from a place of renewal and love."

"That's selflessness, Matt, not selfishness."

"It's how I feel."

"So what about us now? What happens now? This isn't new. People are always getting involved with others and having to walk away from those relationships, yet they still work together. Josh and Shanda are making it work, not that they've, well, you know. Except on camera—how twisted is that?"

"We're not other people, Jessie. We're us. You and me? We've been through hell and back. I don't know how to disconnect from you in a way that will enable us to get back where we were. Maybe you can turn it on and off, but I can't."

"Meaning what, exactly?"

"Meaning I know I need to walk away entirely. But I can't. Cutting you out entirely will feel like cutting a hole right through my heart."

Unable to help herself, Jessie grabbed Matt's hand. She pulled it away from where his coffee cup sat in its cupholder and clasped it tightly. The movement surprised Matt. The touch of her skin on his again was electric, but it was also calming. Brushing a thumb over her hand, he fixated on just feeling her, her physical essence, her presence. Closing his eyes, Matt blinked back the ache he'd been living with for months.

"I'm sorry," Jessie whispered, as Matt rested his forehead on his left hand, the arm of which was bent at the elbow on the seat's aisle armrest. "I know I'm not supposed to touch you, but I can't help myself."

He couldn't answer.

Behind him, Josh was half listening to Dan and Alin talk security, but his focus was on the bit of Matt he could see, and by the way Matt was resting his forehead on his thumb and fingers, Josh saw that the conversation was heating up. He tensed.

"Matt, don't leave us. It will get easier. You'll meet someone else, or maybe you and Catherine will continue to build a relationship, I don't know. We'll just keep things the way they are for now, with you coordinating things and stepping in once in a while when we really need you. We can do this. I can't lose my friend again. And you just said you can't walk away from me. From us."

"Us as in your family, Jessie?" Opening his eyes, Matt stared into the pale, hopeful eyes. "Or us as in you and me?"

"Oh, Matt. Please. Both of those. Look, it'll get easier. I swear."

"You have no idea, Jessie." He shook his head slowly from side to side. "You don't know what it's like, to miss you, to lie in bed and want you… I relive that night over and over in my head. It destroys me."

"You think I have no idea?" Her words were loud enough that Dan stopped talking and sent a nervous look across to Josh, who bowed his head and shuffled his feet. Jessie glanced back between the seats, and lowered her tone. "I have some idea, Matt. I'm the one who called you, remember? Who missed you, who needed you. What happened between us was not one of my little games, as you and Jacob like to call what I'm doing when I reach out for you. What happened was real. Real feelings, real desire. Real love, Matt. What you're feeling is not a one-sided thing, here."

Staring at her, Matt inhaled and jumped in further. "How can you sit there and tell me that, Jessie, when your husband is sitting a few feet behind you? How can you tell me that what we did meant something to you and that it hurts you in any way close to how it hurts me? You have a man in your life who we both know is the only man you will ever love to the point of desperation. Josh is a good man, I know that. Don't compare the way I feel about you with the way you feel about me. It's not the same."

"How dare you tell me how to feel, Matt! Don't you dare tell *me* how to feel! Maybe what you and I have is different, that's all. It's different, the same way Jacob and I were different because we have music. You are the same rock you wanted to be right from the start. Do you ever think that maybe one of the reasons I'm scared to let you go completely is because I'm scared…I'm scared that…"

Biting off her words, Jessie glanced again back at Josh, who, she discerned through the crack between her and Matt's seats, had heard what she said. "Oh, fuck," she moaned, sliding deeper into the leather.

She and Matt were still holding hands. He sighed, and gave her fingers a light squeeze. "You need me to be around to pick up the pieces if your husband goes off the rails again. So you're asking me to stay for my paycheck. Not because you love me."

"No! Matt, you're hearing this all wrong! I am asking you to stay because I do love you. I am asking you to stay because Charles and Dee love you, and my kids love you, and guess what, Josh loves you. I am asking you to stay because we have been through so much together that we are deeply ingrained in each other, all of us. And that means you, too, need watching over. Yes, I worry every day that Josh might lose it again, but I also know that even if he does I will never walk away from him again. I don't care how bad it gets. He and I said vows to each other that we've had a hell of a time keeping, and I intend to try a lot harder as time goes on. What I am trying to say to you is that I am worried about you too. According to Catherine, you weren't doing so good when she first met you. All of us have to look out for each other, and that includes the whole damn Keating-Sawyer camp watching over you too."

Humbled, and not just a little overcome, Matt lifted her fingers to his lips and kissed them, three times in slow succession, closing his eyes as he did so. "It would be nice for a change," he said softly, "to feel like I don't have to carry all of the weight, all of the time."

"You don't, Matt," Jessie breathed, leaning into him and wrapping her arms around his waist. "You don't. We're all here for each other. And if it means you and I share a moment every now and again, then I don't fucking care. You saved my life, you are and always will be my very best friend, and I love the crap out of you. I want and need you in my life, in my family's life."

"It won't be the same, Jessie. It can't be. I can't be hanging out at your home making pizza with you and the kids while Josh is off in Timbuktu working."

"Granted. Fair enough. And I can't be making drunken calls to you when I'm lonely. But Matt?"

"Mmm?" He smiled, relishing the cozy feel of her body against his.

"I need to be able to call you, to chat. Then I won't feel so lonely, okay? And you can call me too. Whenever you need to."

"I don't know if this is going to work, Jessie. I really don't know."

"We won't know until we try. Josh and I both recognize that we have people in our lives who mean a lot to us, who we need. As long as we establish and maintain certain boundaries, we will be okay."

"Ask Jacob how well that worked."

"Jacob and I did okay for a lot of years, Matt. We're doing great now. He's getting laid regularly, so that helps." A little giggle accompanied the remark. The sound lifted Matt's spirits more than they had ever been lifted since the moment he realized he had to walk away from Jessie in the first place. "I'll find someone for you. To, you know, ease the pressure." The giggle turned to a laugh.

Behind them, Josh relaxed and eased his attention back into Dan's far-fetched story, for Alin's benefit, of some security work he did for Metallica in Europe one summer. Soon there was raucous laughter coming from the couch and chairs in the back of the jet.

Closing his eyes again, Matt exhaled slowly and laid a hand over Jessie's on his stomach. He sank deeper into his seat, put the headrest back, and put his feet up on the footrest that extended from underneath. Leaning further into him, Jessie laid her head on his shoulder, but she stopped herself from laying her leg over his, the way she always did with Josh.

"Can we just stay here like this for a little while, Jessie?" he asked her. "Just let me have this for a bit, okay?"

"Yeah, Matt." Jessie's voice was suddenly thick with emotion. "You got it. I need this too." Raising her right arm higher so it wrapped more around his chest, she listened to his heart beating. At the same time, Jessie breathed in Matt's spirit, and the spicy, manly scent of him.

His eyes flitted open when he felt her fingers unbuttoning the top buttons on his shirt. "Jessie, what...?" he started, quickly laying a hand over hers to stop her.

Pulling back the shoulder of his shirt, Jessie ran her fingers over the scar that marked the ugly bullet that he took for her, that almost stole him from her forever. Laying her palm flat over it, she whispered to him, as Josh watched her hand move over his shoulder, "You and me, Matt. We've been together for a long time, and we're not meant to be separated. We don't know where life is going to take us. But see this?" Leaning forward, she kissed the scar.

Under her lips and the warmth of her hand, he trembled.

"This, Matt, is you and me. It's us. It makes us one. Do you see?"

A wetness formed in his eyes as Matt pressed her hand into his shoulder. Nodding, he managed a croaked, "Yes. I'm hearing you, Jessie." In his head, suddenly there was a new thought. He fixed his gentle hazel-grey eyes deeply into Jessie's soulful ice-blue eyes. *There is always hope.* Unbidden, a new thought flashed across his mind, unwanted and unasked for. It gave Matt a sudden chill, and he pulled Jessie closer as he fought it. *She needed me,* was the resounding message it left in its fierce, dark ache. *And she will need me again.*

Jessie felt the tremor in his body as the thought moved over Matt, and it frightened her, because she saw it too, the new sudden fear that passed through his eyes. "What?" she murmured, her body going rigid.

Afraid, but not sure why, Matt swallowed and shook his head. "I don't know."

"Oh, Christ, Matt," Jessie moaned. "No more bad stuff. Was that some kind of premonition?"

Pressing his lips to hers, Matt gave Jessie the last kiss he would give her for a while. "I'm here for you," was all he said. When he moved away, his breath still warm on hers, he added, "Always and forever."

Behind them, Josh watched the kiss happen, but the intimacy between his wife and her protector didn't unsettle him. In fact, it did just the opposite. For some inexplicable reason, it calmed him to the point of a blissful, spiritual peace.

I'm on the outside looking in, he thought. *It's like they don't even know I'm here.*

Leaning his head back against the couch, he raised his feet up on an ottoman, closed his eyes, and drifted off to sleep.

Chapter Twenty-nine

One thing Jessie and Josh agreed on when they settled back into Vancouver for a much needed rest after their hectic year was that the children needed to try school out again. Depending on Jessie's schedule the next spring, they were considering putting them in school in either Calgary or Canmore then as well, while Josh was shooting the second *Sacred Peace* season, instead of using a tutor as they did the year before.

"You need to see your friends," Jessie told a tearful Emily-Grace as they were getting ready to go out the door to head back to West Point Grey Academy for the first time in ages. "I'm sure they've all been missing you."

"It's almost Christmas," Emily-Grace fumed. "Everyone will already know the songs for the Christmas concert. The same for ballet. You want me to go back to class there too, but I won't know the dances!"

"Maybe I can help you—I'll talk to the teacher and see what we can do."

"But Momma, everyone will already have their places, and I can't fit in this late! This sucks!" Jessie raised her eyebrows when her usually docile daughter stomped her foot.

Nearby, Josh suppressed a grin. "She get that from you?" he asked his wife, who handed Emily-Grace her school bag and gave her a gentle push towards the door.

"Daddy!" Launching herself into her father's arms, Emily-Grace appealed to him. "Tell Momma I want to just keep taking ballet from Aunt Kayla."

"Aunt Kayla's starting her workshops again after Christmas, honey." Josh was sympathetic but realistic. "She won't have a lot of free time."

"Then Momma can teach me."

"Your mother never took ballet," Jessie reminded her. "I did a few crash courses. You need to learn the basics that I missed. Now come on, sweetheart, we don't want to be late for school your first day back."

Leaning in to Josh for a kiss as she passed, Jessie grabbed David's shoulder and urged him out the door as well. She bent to Dylan and hugged him tightly. "Be good for Daddy at Jack and Lydia's today. Soon you can go to school with the big kids."

"No!" Dylan copied his sister and stomped his foot, which at least got a smile from Emily-Grace. "I no like school."

"Lovely," Jessie muttered, frowning at Josh as she saluted him in fun and left the house.

Outside, the day was grey and foamy, a misty day in the cozy mountain-hugged city. By the time they got to Jessie's SUV and waved to Dan who was waiting in the driver's seat of his vehicle, which was parked behind Jessie's, they were already chilled.

"This is gonna turn messy." Studying the sky, Jessie pondered whether there were ice pellets in the forecast. Opening the back door of the Lexus, she waited while David hopped in. Buckling him up, she called over her shoulder to her daughter. "Hurry, honey. We don't have any extra time this morning."

"Momma, there's a paper on the car." Emily-Grace, who was just starting to circle the car to get in on the side where she usually sat, went back around, stood on her tippy toes, and grabbed a piece of paper that was stuck under the driver's side windshield wiper. Standing back on the pavement, she started to unfold it.

"What?" Finishing up with her son, Jessie stood upright and closed his door. "Emily-Grace, get in the car. Let me see that." In her haste to get the kids off to school, it took a minute for the importance of the presence of a piece of paper placed on her car in her personal driveway to sink in. When it did, a new panic hit Jessie like a rock.

Snatching the paper from her daughter's hands, Jessie stared at it before looking back up to Emily-Grace. The child was frozen; two slow tears were starting to trail down her cheeks as her luminous Jessie-eyes sent waves of terror across to her mother.

"I hate you, and I hate Daddy," were the words she fired heartlessly from her small pink lips to her mother's ears. "I don't want to go to school and I don't want to go to ballet. I just want to go back to bed."

"Oh, Jesus," Jessie groaned, her knees going weak. "Will this ever end?" Her face white, she glanced behind her at Dan, who quickly ascertained that something was amiss.

As Dan left his car and approached Jessie, she covered the last few steps towards him and handed him the note. "Change of plans, Dan," she said quietly, her tone infused with a somber fear that reached her eyes, turning them from light blue to a darker shade. "Follow me."

To her daughter she said softly, "Hop in the car, sweetheart. We'll talk while we drive." Scanning the street for signs of who may have left the note, she crumbled. To her surprise, Emily-Grace did as she was told. Jessie twisted a ringlet as she watched her, though, sickened at the way her daughter looked at her with judgment and alarm.

In the Lexus, as Jessie backed out and pointed its nose north, Emily-Grace's small voice filled the silence. "Sometimes I think a lot of people hate Daddy. And I don't know why. I wish we were still living with Jacob in New York. Or I wish you would have married Charlie, like Grammie Dee said."

Compressing her lips into a tight line, Jessie knuckled the steering wheel and peered through the rearview mirror at her daughter. "Honey, these people don't know your daddy. They don't see how good and sweet and kind he is. You are old enough now to know that you need to make up your own mind about him, and about me too. Don't listen to what others say. Don't let them affect how you feel about Daddy. You know he's a good person. Right?"

Fighting this new rising wave of panic, Jessie had to push back her own threatening tears. *How the hell do I make these children see that the world they are living in is warped and judgmental, but that they have the best daddy ever?*

David added his two cents. "What did that paper say, Momma?" Glancing back at him, all snug in his car seat, Jessie almost collapsed at the way he was looking at her now. David was a mini-Josh with his longish chestnut blonde hair falling over his cheek, and liquid chocolate eyes that, now, were wide with hurt without even really understanding what was going on.

Before Jessie could pad the reality and make it less awful, Emily-Grace piped up with her vicious interpretation, which she spat out loudly as if it were the absolute truth. "It says that Daddy pissed a lot of people off and that he better watch his back on season two. That he deserves to die. That's what it said."

"I'm gonna puke," Jessie mumbled, clenching the wheel and seriously considering pulling over. A new wave assaulted the first wave of dread, almost eclipsing it. Afraid to frighten her children further, Jessie pushed the thought aside in favor of what she hoped was good judgment, and she grabbed her cell phone and speed-dialed Charlie.

He answered on the second ring. "Hey, Jessie. Miss me already?" He had a mouthful of yogurt, which he was eating as he ushered Stella to their car.

"Charlie, you and your stupid TV show." Now that she had a familiar, friendly voice on the line, someone she trusted implicitly, Jessie felt raw emotion start to take over. It was fueled by something she knew well. Terror.

Charlie stopped in his tracks. "What?"

"Josh is not doing season two. There's no way."

"Get in the car, Stella." Charlie's voice was distant until his daughter was settled. "Jessie, what's going on? Talk to me."

"We got a note. Someone put it under my wiper, Emily-Grace found it." Crying openly now, Jessie had no choice but to pull over. In the back seat, the kids went still and silent. Behind her, Dan steered to a stop and started to get out of his sedan. "I thought this was over. I thought it was done."

"Jess, get the note to Matt and Charles. I'll meet you at La Casa."

"You can't come, Charlie. You are supposed to meet Josh at your dad's place. You need to go there and keep an eye on him for me. You know him, now that he's back in Van he's not interested in having security following him around."

"He knows he's being threatened again and he's refusing security?"

"No, we just got this note." Jessie put her window down so Dan could hear her conversation with Charlie. "He doesn't know about it yet. Charlie… I don't want him to know. I just want him to have…you know…some good days. A lot of good days. I need him to be happy."

And that, to Emily-Grace's young ears, taught her more about love than anything. Wiping away tears as her mother broke down in front of her, Emily-Grace stared vacantly out of the window.

Jessie reached up for Dan's hand and held it. It was a nervous habit, and the big man was there, protecting her and the children. His hand was there, gripping the window, and so she grabbed it. The big paw was warm despite the chill in the air. Jessie squeezed it and peered up at him from beneath wet lashes as she listened to Charlie.

"We all want Josh to be happy, Jessie," he was telling her. "More than anything. You know that. But I think this is something he needs to know."

"Jesus Christ, Charlie." Jessie leaned back and let her eyes close over. "A few fucking months of peace to see joy on that man's face. That's all I'm asking for."

"No more secrets, little girl." Charlie was adamant, despite his breaking heart. "Go to La Casa. I'll call Josh, okay? I'll get him to meet us there."

"Oh, for fuck's sake." Ending her call, Jessie didn't even realize she was holding Dan's hand until he gently tugged it away from her.

From the back, David whispered, "Swear jar, Momma."

"La Casa," Dan said. "I figured that's where you were headed. I already called Matt." He peeked into the back seat to see the two children he, and everyone else, had once thought they might never see again. Dan's big teddy bear heart melted. "It's okay, kids," he said quietly. "Look at it this way. There won't be any school today."

Emily-Grace turned her head back towards the front of the car and met her mother's stricken eyes in the rearview mirror. There was more than just sadness in the child's eyes. There was a whole new anger entrenched there; spiteful and furious, its intensity almost bent Jessie in two.

"Great," she intoned, and nodded at Dan as she put the SUV in gear. "I'll see you there, Dan."

Jessie landed at La Casa just after Matt, who was seated at the kitchen island talking to Charles over coffee and over one of Carlotta's raspberry scones that, Jessie noticed, he hadn't touched.

Trying to muster up some strength, she found it—along with a whole new sorrow—in his gentle eyes and tender touch, which came in the form of a long, solid hug.

Carlotta took the kids to the playroom while the grownups had their impromptu meeting, which soon included Ulysses and a concerned Deirdre, who came downstairs saying, "Did I just hear my grandchildren's voices?"

Spying the wan look on Jessie's face when she entered the kitchen, Deirdre paused. "What now?" she asked, deflating.

As they settled into a discussion over the note, which Jessie abhorred even seeing spread out on the island in front of them, Jessie stayed at Matt's side, soaking up his energy and warmth for the new fight ahead. To his credit, he draped an arm loosely over her shoulders and accepted that she needed him. Nobody questioned their closeness, even when Jessie leaned into him, wrapped both arms around his waist, and buried her face in his neck.

She didn't leave his side until the door opened and Dylan's small voice rang out. Then, Jessie met Matt's eyes one last time, inhaled deeply, and moved to the far side of the kitchen where she could lean against the countertop and start the process of memorizing Josh's features all over again.

Carlotta intercepted Dylan and swifted him away as Josh entered the kitchen, surprised and shocked to see the Keating-Sawyer security team present almost in entirety, and Charlie and Jessie there as well, huddled up next to each other in the far corner.

"I saw your cars," he managed to get out as he looked at Charlie and at Jessie who, Josh was dismayed to see, was almost on her knees, telegraphing worry and fear he had yet to understand. Afraid to move forward in the bitter silence, Josh remained at the entrance to the kitchen and let his hands drop to the pockets of his jeans. Something on the kitchen island caught his eye. A note—another threat, typed in the same fashion as the last note, unbeknownst to him—glaring at all of them as it lay in a benign warped beauty, the center of everyone's attention and trepidation.

Matt had his back to Josh initially, but now he turned and faced him, swallowing and straightening when he caught Josh's eye. *I'm here,* he seemed to be saying, as Jessie watched, afraid to breathe. *I'm here. I'll always be here.*

Josh acknowledged Matt's message with strength of his own, telegraphed across to him with a single nod and a frown.

Then his dazed eyes drifted back over to his wife.

Closing hers, letting a few final tears squeeze out, Jessie bent into Charlie's side until Josh crossed the kitchen and took her in his arms.

"Every minute with you," he whispered to her, "every second. It's all been worth it. No matter what happens, I'll always be with you."

She stilled in his arms, looked over his shoulder at Matt, and pushed the rogue hair behind Josh's ear. Taking his face in her palms, she brushed a thumb across his cheek, looked into the sad, lost eyes she loved, and said simply, "I know."

The meeting went on with Josh present, but neither he nor Jessie said a word. He took Jessie's place against the far counter and held her with her back pressed against his body. Both of them filtered out most of what Team Keating-Sawyer were discussing, and instead tuned in to the sounds of each other's hearts beating, their lungs filling and emptying, and the happy yowls of their two youngest children down the hall, which punctuated the meeting with odd, seemingly out-of-place bits of joy.

Emily-Grace's voice was not heard at all.

Occasionally, Matt couldn't help but look over at them. Capturing an image of the two of them together in some frozen imaginary frame, he placed it in the slideshow in his mind. What he saw was a couple often pulled apart by life, but desperate to be together nonetheless.

By then, Jessie had turned around to her husband, and was clinging to him in what appeared to be silent wonder as a finger played idly with the collar of his denim jacket. Josh was fingering her hair, her curls; his eyes were tender and moist, yet almost vacant as he stood there, humbled by the simple miracle of truly loving this woman, and of being loved by her in return.

Matt was lost in this almost spiritual, transcendent vision of Josh and Jessie until Charles called him back to the meeting by saying his name twice. Suspended in time and place, he floated back to the task at hand—which was mitigating any danger to Jessie Wheeler's true love, Josh Sawyer—and got to work.

The End.

Thank you!

Please remember to rate and review *Watch Over Me*—self-published authors rely on our readers to help spread the love!

Join the Drifters family by signing up at **www.susanrodgersauthor.com**.

As a welcome gift, I'll send you a free bonus/deleted chapter from Book One, *A Song For Josh*.

Happy reading!

Susan

www.susanrodgersauthor.com

Facebook: search **Susan Rodgers, Writer**

Twitter: **@srbluemountain**

Instagram: **SusanDrifters**

www.bublish.com

email: **fatcat@pei.sympatico.ca**

About the Author

Susan Rodgers' first novel *A Certain Kind of Freedom* was a Finalist in the Writers' Federation of Nova Scotia Atlantic Writing Awards for unpublished manuscripts. Her short story from the novel of the same name, published in two anthologies, has received rave reviews, as have the Drifters novels, Susan's all-time favourite books to write.

Owner/Operator of Bluemountain Entertainment, Susan is a 'Diploma With Honours' graduate of Vancouver Film School. She produces mostly documentary style client films and short dramas with plans to one day shoot a Feature Drama based on the novel Atlantic Blue.

Formerly a Museum Curator, in winter Susan lives with her partner Steve and her striped cat Oliver (Lucy Maud Montgomery once said the only good cat is a striped cat) in Summerside, Prince Edward Island, Canada. In summer, she hides in a small trailer in Darnley, P.E.I., where she writes novels, paddles kayaks, and crafts sandcastles on the beach. She makes frequent trips to Vancouver to visit her son Christopher, where she enjoys life in the hippie city while listening to great music and sipping on good espresso.

Books by Susan Rodgers

Drifters series:

A Song For Josh

Promises

No Greater Love

Riptide

Whispers of Home

And Then There Was Silence

Let the Music Cry

If I Could Sing You Home

After the Rain

Into the Blue

A Sacred Peace

Watch Over Me

Coming Soon:

A Certain Kind of Freedom

Seasmoke

Atlantic Blue

Feature Screenplays:

The Story of Jack & Emma

Atlantic Blue

Beautiful Jane

They Were Dreamers (adapted)

Short Stories:

S12

A Certain Kind of Freedom

A Gentle Peace

www.ingramcontent.com/pod-product-compliance
Lightning Source LLC
Chambersburg PA
CBHW060603030726
47498CB00005B/1519
* 9 7 8 1 9 8 7 9 6 6 1 4 5 *